Untamed: A Beautiful Nightmare Story

www.LCSonBooks.com

Print ISBN: 978-1-7336503-6-6

Untamed

A Beautiful Nightmare Story

By L.C. Son

To every woman who wondered whether she was worth it. You are. Don't let those who aren't willing to unearth your treasure make you discount the rare wonderfulness of you.

Dream Well,

L.C. Son

Dream Well,
L. C. Son

www.lcsonbooks.com

Contents

Prologue

For twenty years I waited. Hoped. Sometimes, I even prayed. To whom, I am not quite assured. Still, I remained hopeful someone would rescue us from this torment. This hell. Even at the tender age of seven, I knew the moment Dalcour Marchand rescued my family and I from fire and our impending doom, the tragedy that had become our life was yet to be determined.

I suppose I have always known the truth.

And that truth is simply knowing the joy which once held my family's state ended the day my father took his final breath. Nothing has truly been the same since that day.

Always a feeble and weak-minded woman, my mother slumped into such a depression at his passing of which she never truly recovered. Thankfully, we had my eldest sister Calida to serve as our matriarch.

But we have her no more.

Her zealous passions for the sciences and affections toward darkened skin men were her demise. With charges of witchcraft for alliances to both Decaux and studies of Galileo, her doom was assuredly absolute.

Watching my sister burn at the stake for a crime only alleged by fearful and impotent men, kindled a fire in me that will never extinguish.

Day by day that fire strengthens.

As my lingering hope for Dalcour's pledge to return to us lessened, the inferno, which was once my heart, grew ablaze. With my mother's sunken state, her only recourse led her to make a brothel our new home. Landing the eye of a local banker, my second eldest sister, Victoria, took off within months after we escaped here from the Great Fire in 1788.

Although young, I knew I had to do whatever I must to now be the caretaker of me and my youngest sister. And I have. Since my sixteenth birthday it became the expectation of my mother and her lover, Monroe, that I would oblige to the *house rules*. In fact, I have *obliged* the house rules with my eyes closed, and mouth gagged for more times than I can count. So as to ensure my little sister, Chalmette, never needed to serve up anything more than bourbon at the bar, I alone endured the nightly stench of sweaty, beastly, disgusting men if only to ensure she had a place to rest her head.

That is why I do what I do now.

I know with all confidence I will never allow my fate to become that of either Calida or my halfhearted mother. I also know I will never forsake my family like my wretched sister Victoria. It is clear I cannot rely on the salvation of men; supernatural or otherwise. Yet, I am required to still play their game. I must do more than match their parry. I will subdue them.

It is with such certainty I also know the allegiance I now form is one made from the pit from which all darkness is derived. But I see no other way. I refuse to be either captive or pawn. And it is with this surety I declare I will come on the other end of this darkness both unscathed and *untamed*.

Chapter One

"We've got forty bottles of madeira, twenty jugs of rum, and only twelve of port," I shout over my shoulder to Monroe.

"Only twelve?" Monroe yells back from the corner table. He barely looks at me as DeLuca and I work to steady the trough before it falls and spills the meager supply.

"Yes, I'm afraid this is all Ripley could spare without—Ow!" DeLuca squeals as I jar the heel of my boot into his foot.

"We'll get it to the middle closet, Monroe!" I force my words out before Monroe has a chance to make out DeLuca's garble. Sure, Monroe knows he owes Ripley more than he can afford to pay, but it will not help matters hearing it from DeLuca. Even if he is right.

Besides, Monroe hates being teased. He fancies himself a man of society, of which he is not. He is nothing but the keeper of a spirit tavern and brothel. While he hopes to hook the attentions of potentate gentlemen who are looking for a spirited drink and untethered coitus, nothing will come of his depraved ambitions. Between his day drinking and gambling, it is no wonder he is unable to remain afloat.

"Goodness, Red! You didn't have to stake my toe to the ground!" DeLuca whines, lifting his foot to his knee, posting himself to the doorframe. "I still have four other deliveries to make before nightfall or Ripley will have my hide!"

"Oh shut up, DeLuca!" I reply with a shove into his shoulder before pulling the bottles out of the trough to place on the shelves.

"Some friend you are, Red! Let's see how you'd fancy towing the wagon to Borden's and LaSalle's with your foot throbbing in a thistle!"

"Well, I'm certain I'd tough it out, unlike you my little Romani friend," I answer with a chuckle and a light peck on DeLuca's forehead. His big brown eyes stare back at me with a kindness I've only ever found in him since this life took me hostage. Still, I cannot resist squeezing his olive-skinned cheeks, puckering his rose-colored lips between my palms. "Now stop your bleating blabber or I'll have to ask Chalmette to tend to your wounds. At least she's no baby!"

"All right, all right. Enough!" DeLuca grumbles, snatching two jars of rum from me. He places the remaining bottles from the trough onto the shelves as I mark the inventory, hopeful I can give Monroe an account of our holdings before we open this evening.

"So, speaking of Chalmette," DeLuca quietly begins, leaning over my shoulder. A shooting ache pains through me as he says her name and for fear, I turn away from him, recounting the shelves. I have no desire for this conversation to go any further.

"Please, DeLuca, do not even speak your next words!" I wistfully snap, peering over his broad shoulders and into the barroom. Thankfully, I only see Monroe, still checking his receipts, frustratingly trying to make heads and tails of his earnings.

DeLuca steps in front of me, regaining my attention. "Look, Red, I know you don't want to discuss it, but you must, at least with me. I am now and have always been your friend. Have I not?" He adds with a soft smile that folds into his square jawline. The sincerity I see in his gaze, entreats me to soften the tension I feel in my throat as I exhale.

"Of course, you are my friend, DeLuca. But I am doing all I can to spare her my lot."

"I know you are. You are an adoring sister. Chalmette could ask for no better."

"She deserves much better."

"Well, you are certainly a fairer prize than Victoria. At least you did not run off and leave the girl to the dealings of Monroe, your mother or worse."

"Well, I fear worse has come for my dear sister. Her menses ended yesterday."

"Does Monroe or your mother know?" DeLuca asks, his eyes widened with the same fear I am certain reflects in my own.

"No, well—not yet."

"Not yet?"

"I've kept her in my room locked up. Monroe will normally grant seven full days and one for cleansing. Her days are far shorter, but they needn't know. I sincerely hoped Victoria would hold true to her promise and find Chalmette work in town. At least then she'd be assured room and board far from this dreadful place."

"And you've not heard from her?"

"No. I even went into town yesterday looking for her, but her husband said she was out."

"I am sorry, dear one. I know you do not wish for this to be her young life's end, but do you think, perhaps, you should prepare her? You know—for what is to come. To be with a man?"

"How could you even suggest such a thing?" I bite back, as a gnawing sting in my gut grows.

"Because you are her sister, and you love her more than anyone. If she should hear it from your mother—or worse—Monroe, who knows what her fate will be. At least from you—"

"From me, what? If I cannot keep her from the vehemence seeking to violate her virginity, what more can I do, DeLuca!" I contend, circling the trough in fear.

"Calm yourself," DeLuca begins, looking over my shoulder, placing his hands in mine. "You know more than anyone, the tricks of the trade. Do you not?" Squeezing my palms, DeLuca's sincere gaze seeps into mine and I know he's doing all he can to comfort me as he always has done.

Batting my eyes, I force my forming tears to the deep pockets of my eyelids and swallow the hard knot in my throat. I nod in understanding to DeLuca's questioning, and he smiles, loosening his grip. "Yes," I whisper in reply.

"Well, then you teach her all you can before your mother and her wretched beloved can get their vices on her. Teach her the things you told me in secret. The places you sent your mind. The songs you recanted. The lasting endearing memories of Calida and your father."

"But she has no such memories, DeLuca. She was only a baby when we took this place to be our home. What sweet songs does she have except the canter and strumming of barstools and prickling?"

"Then give her something! Anything! If anyone can teach her to turn her mind away from the slobbering drunkard atop her—you can and you must, my dear one," DeLuca answers, gently squeezes my wrist and strums my chin quickly, before pushing the empty cart out of the closet, leaving me alone.

The thought of any scallywag nightcrawler resting his palms upon my sister is repugnant to me. *Sickening.* But I know DeLuca is right. She is eighteen. Monroe will not keep his front foot from her for long.

I must do what I can to both prepare and protect her.

"Chartreuse!" I hear Corrine, one of the oldest house girls call to me from the hallway.

Pushing aside the tears that once again threaten their release, I rush out of the closet to see what is causing her angst.

"What is it, Corrine?" I shout back when I see her standing frozen at the bottom of the staircase.

Pointing up from her chin, she shakes her head and blows her blond tendrils from her face. "I'm sorry, darling. But you know you couldn't keep him from her for long. It's probably better this way. No need of giving her fantasies that will never come to be," Corinne says, tapping my shoulder softly before walking back toward the bar.

My heart beats like racing bulls in my chest as I race up the steps at her words. Glassy, tearful pools swathe my vision as I nearly knock several of the house girls to the ground as I storm down the hall to Chalmette's room.

Reaching her door, I am not surprised to find my mother blocking my entrance.

"Move out of my way!" I demand, staring up at the hardlines now squaring my mother's otherwise youthful face. Her sea blue eyes are always more pronounced in her anger and with the way her burnt ginger-laced curls frame her face, her glare is almost haunting.

But I am not afraid.

"Back away, Chartreuse! Haven't you done enough to worsen matters?"

"Me?" I say astounded, wondering what new blame she chooses to lay at my feet today. I try to push past her brooding frame, but she side steps me, placing her long arms across the threshold, preventing me further.

"Yes, you! It is always you, is it not? Not only did you choose to deceive us, knowing full well Chalmette's menses ended days ago, but now Monroe tells me your knicker-knocking with that Sincade DeLuca boy has given Ripley cause to cut the bar supply in half! How do you expect us to earn a living with you carrying around as you do?"

Once again, Monroe has lied on me to spare himself and once more has my mother believed his lies. From the first day he climbed upon me, holding me at my neck to claim my innocence, only to tell my mother that it was I who seduced him, has she believed his folly. Now, because of his gambling, day drinking, and other manner of frivolity does he seek to blame me for his shortcomings.

And now she stands idly knowing her lover's intent to maim yet another daughter's preciousness.

I will not let Chalmette's fate be that of my own. Not now or ever!

"Whatever new lies you choose to believe of your beloved are your transgressions, not mine Mother! If I can even call you that! You are no mother! You are nothing more than a—"

"How dare you girl!" Mother responds, striking a hard blow to my cheek. "You will not speak to me that way. Nor will I allow you to speak ill of Monroe in my presence. If it were not for Monroe, we'd be street peddlers. He is the one who took me in, when I was alone with you girls and pregnant. He's never asked for anything. Only that we all pull our fair share."

"Really, our *fair share*? Is that what we're calling it now? Father would never—"

"Your father is dead."

Those four words sting more than the ache of her hand to my face. While I may have been young at my father's passing, I shall never forget the kindness, generosity, and endearment of his manner. I doubt whether in this world or the next, there shall ever be his equal. Ever.

"Please, Monroe, no! You mustn't do this!" I hear Chalmette cry from the other side of the door.

Mother's nose twitches at the whimper of Chalmette's voice and her posture softens enough for me to push past her, busting the door open.

Chalmette is nestled against the bedframe, grasping her blanket at her chin. Her crestfallen face is flushed with red, and her eyes swollen with tears. Monroe is in nothing but a loose shirt with his trousers buckling at his knees.

Racing to Chalmette's side, I thrust her into my embrace, as she sobs inconsolably. "I've got you little sister. I am here."

"This is no place for you girl! Get out of here!" Monroe shouts as he works to pull his clothing back to his waist, staggering as he does. I see his day drinking knows no bounds. He is such a slobbering mess. Looking at him I still don't know what redeemable qualities Mother ever found in him. From his grease-laden, balding, coal black hair to his sunken eyes and rickety, missing teeth, he is revolting.

There may have been no one to fight for me when he "broke me in," as he called it, but there is someone to fight for Chalmette.

Me.

"Monroe is right, Chartreuse! This is not your place!" Mother contends as she tries to help Monroe with his fasteners, but he grumbles, refusing her aid.

"Oh I know my place, Mother and it is right here. Between my sister and that foul fool at your side!" I shout. Gasps erupt from the hallway and I am sure the other girls and attendants can hear our every word. Most wouldn't dare speak ill of Monroe. Somehow, he's cast the same spell over them as he has over my mother. A few of the housemates have contested he is better than most men of his stead. Whatever kind regard they have for him bears no weight to me. He is and forever will be a monster to me.

"Girl," Monroe yells back, "step aside. Little Mette must learn the way of things. It is time she contributes to the house. I'll not have freeloaders under my roof!" He falters, stumbling over the floor pillows as he tries to make his way to us.

"Look at you! You loathsome loaf! How pray tell did you expect to rise to the occasion? You're so full of Ripley's rum punch you can barely walk!" I sneer. He is almost laughable, but I rein in my need to taunt him further.

"Catherine, get your girl! I'll not have her mouthing to me!" Monroe yaps his words over his shoulder to my mother. If I didn't know better, I could have sworn I spied her posture shift, repulsed by his actions. But that would be all too motherly of her and she is not so.

"Chalmette does contribute to the house!" I quickly interject as my mother's mouth parts to speak. Raising her brow, Mother tips her head to the side, curious of my intent. "She sings," I say as though I were inspired. "Monroe, Mother, you both know she brought in much money singing last month. The bar was full every night during Mardi gras when she headlined the set. Why not let her continue singing? There are surely enough girls in the house. Chalmette needn't add to the number when she can attract many more with her melody."

"That was Mardi gras, Chartreuse. Merriment was plentiful. But these are hard times, girl. Tensions here in the once new world are at its peak. Shipments of port and mead from Britain have lessened and with talks of war brewing beneath the surface men look to places such as this for the small comforts we provide. Pillow and port."

"Please, Mother!" Chalmette pleads, lifting her head from under my tight grip. "I'll do whatever I must to earn my keep—but please, not Monroe! Please!" Chalmette's words churn within me, sickening me to my core. Although tears drench her face, I am surprised by her sudden change of disposition. Against even my own will, she's trying to take charge of her own fate. And while everything within me finds her posture impressive, I know she will yet regret her words.

"No, Chalmette!" I whisper, turning her reddened face to meet mine.

"It's okay, Chartreuse. You can't protect me forever," she whispers back.

"Catherine, I'll not let your wretched girls dictate the order of my house!" Monroe shouts in protest, staggering a few steps forward. "She will—"

"No, Monroe—you will not. Not this time," Mother's tone is strangely comforting. She looks over her shoulder at me and Chalmette and her eyes soften slightly. But it doesn't last for long. Narrowing her gaze once more, she scrunches her nose and turns back to Monroe. "You mustn't worry, dearest. Chalmette will agree to the house rules. She will work."

"Ha! That she will!" He grumbles, gritting his teeth and spitting on the ground. I push Chalmette behind me against the bedframe as I watch him take needful steps toward us.

Again, Mother places her hand at his chest, circling around him to get his focus off me and my sister. "Yes, beloved, she will work—but not with you. She has made a vow and she intends to keep it," she begins as she looks over her shoulder at us with an ominous glare filling her face. Worry grips me, fearing Mother's next words. Chalmette thrusts her sweaty palm into mine, and I know she too worries what follows. "It's been years since we had an auction and bidding. Men will pay handsomely to be with a virgin as lovely as Chalmette."

"Mother, no!" I gasp. While I know I shouldn't be shocked, I can't help it. How could she suggest such a thing?

"Yes," Monroe cackles with a malevolent grin as he scratches the stubble along his chin. "The lot of them paid generously for Marietta and she isn't even a looker not to mention wasn't a virgin. But they bought it. You are a genius, Catherine! I'll get Marius to make papers to post over town. They'll come from miles over for this sweet one."

"Please, no!" I protest once more, holding Chalmette deep in the cavity of my chest as tears soil my face.

"You should be happy girl. Now some wealthy pauper will have the honor. Unless you'd rather it be me? But if this doesn't work for any reason, girl—it will be me!" Monroe smirks, exiting my sister's suite.

Chalmette drenches my shoulder with her tears, screaming into my neck as she does. More water floods my face, but I keep my sights on my mother. Just when I thought I couldn't loathe her more, my disgust of her reaches a new low. She is no longer my mother. In fact, she hasn't been for some time. For years, I only saw her as victim to incidence gone awry, but no more. She is not a victim. A pawn, perhaps, but she is still well in control of her path and that of our own.

But no more.

Although I am unsure how, I will see to it that her control ends today.

Walking to the threshold of the door, she turns back to face us, this time her countenance is stoic. "Be sure she is cleaned up and presentable by the evening hour. And fix yourself up too. You are still required to work tonight as well. That is, if anyone will have you. Should you need anything, I—"

"We need nothing from you, Catherine! We never have." My words strike her heart just as I intended. Her eyes bulge at my sentiment and I know she is surprised. I have always done my best to hold her in some manner of esteem—even if it was minimal. Now, at this moment, it is all forfeit.

Rising from my side, Chalmette quickly paces to the door and slams it shut in her face. Screaming once more, she buckles at her knees and cries against the doorframe. Rushing to her aid before she topples to the ground, I take her in my arms and hold her tight.

"I've got you, dear sister. I promise now and always, I will never let you fall. Ever."

Chapter Two

Chalmette wept in my arms for almost an hour before drifting asleep. It pains my heart to see her in such despair that I almost hate to leave her, but I must. Once more, I must try to find my wretched sister, Victoria. While I know she wants nothing to do with our mother or this life, I have hope that perhaps an ounce of kindness toward our young sister remains.

Although Chalmette is not our father's child, but a product of our mother's carelessness when we first arrived in Natchitoches, I do not care any less for her than if she were indeed my father's seed. And yes, while Monroe did take us in while my mother carried Chalmette in her womb, it didn't stop his depraved intentions toward her while she was yet pregnant.

The thought of the two of them alone sickened Victoria. Of course Monroe had his sights on her from the beginning, but to my knowledge he never made any attempt to ruin her. I suppose he was waiting for her to come of age. But he was too late. Victoria was more shrewd than he calculated. One night a newly widowed banker came into the tavern named Cassius LaSalle. Beaming her infectious smile from ear-to-ear and adorning her newfound womanly curvaceousness, he was soon lost to her lure. Even though he was twenty years her senior, she did not care. Nor did he. After paying Mother and Monroe a handsome amount, the two were wed within weeks.

While my mother seemed almost happy to see her daughter not bound to our plight, Monroe grew more callous. I reckon that is why when he mounted me for the first time, he swore that he'd ensure no man would want me as a wife. *"You won't get away from me like your sister did,"* he breathed into my ear as he rutted through me.

Mournful tears scoured my face as the stench of his sweat curdled like sour milk in my nostrils. He was unforgiving as he took my innocence. If I am thankful for anything it is that he couldn't last more than ten minutes. But it was ten minutes too long. Every minute with him was like an hour.

For years I imagined I too would meet someone like Cassius, but my fantasy never came to be. A small part of me believes Monroe soured my reputation. From the looks men gave me days after he took me, I am sure of it. It didn't take long before he had men lined at my door to partake of me. I barely needed to come out of my room to fish for bait as Corrine calls it.

Some nights five men. Some nights ten. One of the worst was a private party for a bachelor. The sickening things they did to me and had me do to them had me in tears. The more I cried, the more lustful they became.

But that night something strange happened. I stopped crying. Somehow I willed myself to a deeper corner of my mind. Happier memories of my departed sister, Calida, reading to me. The stories she told me of fearless women warriors raided my mind. Joan of Arc and the goddess Isis were my favorite legends. Fond thoughts of Calida telling me a man's greatest enemy is a woman with her own mind, lingered in my soul. I knew then there was one thing I could control. My mind.

As the men took turns having their way with me, I began shifting how I saw myself. It was mother's weak mind and victim mentality that has brought us to such a state. *I would not be a victim.* I would control my fate.

That night was the last night I would be treated that way.

When I awoke the next day, I declared I'd take my womanhood into my own hands. I took the day bathing myself, primping, and preparing for the evening. I even sent Marius out with papers of my requirements. It turns out men of moderate means appreciated my proactiveness. They knew what they were getting for the evening. I even made provisions for things I'd not do—acts I found too vile to perform.

Seeing the need to protect myself further, I made a familiar out of one gentleman caller, named Scotty. For a fair price and consensual favors, Scotty agreed to be my doorman. Should anyone get too handsy with me or not adhere to the rules of my boudoir, Scotty will handle them for me. A butcher by day, his brawn, muscular frame is intimidating to most.

Scotty and I have a decent arrangement. He treats me civilly, which is more than I could ask of most men.

Then there is Sincade DeLuca. *My friend.* Sent by his boss Ripley to partake of me as payment for what Monroe owed him, it was clear on the first night we met, the thought of it all was almost an insult to him. Although most only see DeLuca as a lower-class gypsy, I see the potential of a potentate briming beneath his otherwise low profile and mild demeanor.

"*We are not doing this,*" were the first words DeLuca spoke when he came into my suite. He never gave me a chance to protest. Seating himself at my desk and tossing two dice on the Game of Snake board. We played the game for well over an hour until Monroe came pounding on the door. DeLuca told me to scream loud, feigning we were still busy as DeLuca playfully banged his hand on the wall near my bedframe.

I knew I gained a friend in him, but I was still strangely curious why he didn't want me. Simply, he told me, "If one is found in a tragic circumstance, it is a travesty if one in a similarly detrimental state should take advantage of their equal while in such a heartrending state."

DeLuca's words comforted my heart that day and nothing has changed since that day. Although my friend is quite a handsome catch, I've never seen him through romantic eyes, nor has he made an advance as so. He sees me as his equal as do I him.

Still, what I do desire is not an equal, but not necessarily someone better. I want the best.

I deserve it.

"What are you doing here, Treuse!" I hear Victoria shout over the fence as I wait outside her manor, breaking me from my reminiscent thoughts. With the sun nearing its departure, I know I am likely disturbing her supper, but I need her help now. "I couldn't believe it when my doorman told me you were outside. You know better than to come here!"

"Listen, Victoria, I know you do not care to see me, but our sister—"

"Half-sister."

Swallowing her disregard down my throat, I rush to continue. "Chalmette needs your help. If she could but be a serving girl or aid in some manner around your home, I know she would be helpful to you. Please do not allow such a life to be her fate! Please, I beg of you!"

Victoria stares at me, contemplative. I sense an inner battle brewing within her, but her defiant stance makes any bouts of empathy difficult. I'm surprised to see her wearing her auburn tendrils against her face. My staunch sister normally prefers her hair upswept into a lofty bun. Still, she keeps her face set opposite of me as though she hated to look me in the eye. I suppose my harlotry repulses her. I wish she knew how equally repulsed I am, and it is for that reason I do not wish for this to be our young sister's undoing.

"You needn't beg me anything, Chartreuse. I cannot help her," Victoria answers as her eyes gaze down the dusty red road, likely hopeful no one sees her with me. While my sister has always been stubborn, there is something more reining her in.

"Cannot or *will not*? Which is it, dear sister?" I counter. I am running out of time—and options. If she will not help me, I need to strategize something else to aid Chalmette.

"It does not matter which it is—the answer is most assuredly no!" Victoria snaps back.

"Victoria!" I hear her husband call to her from their stately covered porch. "Come inside! Supper will not make it to the table by itself."

"Coming dear," she hurriedly replies over her shoulder, forcing a bright smile. As she does, her reason for not helping me becomes evident. She needs just as much help as both me and Chalmette.

"Sister!" I gasp, grabbing her chin in my hand, pushing aside her long curls. Although she's tried to conceal it with powder, the bluish bruise encircling her right eye, tells me all I need to know. "What has he done to you?" I demand, bringing her face close to my own.

"It's nothing, Chartreuse!" Victoria grits through her teeth, pushing my hand away and out of my grip. "Now, please—go," she says in a quiet rebuke.

A free fall of tears race down her cheeks and she wipes them away, exhaling deeply, forcing herself to regain her posture. "And please, Chartreuse, do not return."

Turning sharp on her heel, she brushes her hair back to her face, squares her shoulders and walks down the long cobblestone pathway back to her home. I can only imagine the long walkway will give her time enough to gather herself before facing her brutish husband.

And while I never imagined it were possible, my heart breaks for her. All this time I only saw her as the sister who left us while she moved on to a better life. Now I see her life is not as enviable as I once imagined. She may not be captive to a brothel as am I, but she is certainly a prisoner of the brutality of humanity.

Perhaps the eligibility of salvation has evaded both Victoria and I, but there is still a chance for Chalmette.

Racing back to the tavern, tears cloak my sight as the strings of my heart pull for me and my sisters. Everything in me wants to rush into Victoria's home and teach a lesson to her brute of a mate, but I know I cannot delay getting back to Chalmette before her life is equal to my own.

Monroe will likely raise the price of the bar as he parades the house girls around with Chalmette center stage. With the stench of bourbon lacking their beards, they'll salivate at the sight of my lovely sister. If my mother gave anything of worth to her daughters, it is an enviable frame. Chalmette is well-endowed for such a petite stature. With rounded hips and a backside as taut as mine, Monroe is sure to have more than a few generous biddings to have the honor of being her first. Chalmette's angelic face, dusty rose lips and curvaceous figure could seal her fate for the worst if I don't make it to her in time.

"Red!" DeLuca screams my name from the steps of the Tavern as I round the corner. While I am surprised to see him here, I don't have time to talk to him. As much as I wish I could bury my head in his chest, sobbing in his arms as I've done countless times before, I haven't the time for it now.

"Not now, DeLuca! I have to get to her—Monroe is doing it—tonight!" I squeal through my waterlogged eyes.

"I know, Chartreuse. I know. Marius came by with the postings. That's why I am here. I came to help," he answers, gently grabbing my shoulders in his firm grip and preventing my entry. Stepping up to meet his assured gaze, the pacing of my heart slows, and I wonder what kind of help he hopes to give.

"Help?" I question, curious of his intent. "How so? I doubt Monroe will fall for the same ruse as he did on our first night together. He's grown quite callous since then."

"No ruse, Chartreuse. Something better."

"Better? Look, DeLuca, I really don't have time for this!" I say, pushing past DeLuca up the stairs.

Grabbing my wrist he turns me back to him, granting his normal cagey grin. "Claudius DeVeaux!" He grunts as if the name alone were an explanation.

"What? I don't understand. What does that little brat of a newsboy have to do with anything?"

"Claudius is the answer, Red. He fancies her!" His answer is almost resolute.

"How does that help her tonight, DeLuca?"

"Listen, he was with me when Marius brought the postings. The lad's face went pale when he read of Monroe's plans for her."

"Well, just because he's been sniffing her like fresh cut roses since they were both ten doesn't mean Monroe will have some change of heart."

"He will if there's money to be gained."

"Do you mean to tell me Claudius desires to be her first? Does he plan to bid? I mean even if he tried to enter the bidding, he'd need a considerable amount to even be with her tonight. Besides, even though I know the two have flirted, I don't suppose he's quite who she envisioned for her first time. I mean the boy is tad on the doughy side, not to mention he's a bit of a dullard."

"You don't understand, Treuse! This isn't about how cheery he is. He wants to marry her!"

"Marry her?" I gasp at his reveal.

"Yes, you heard me."

At his words, my thoughts wander back to Victoria. While almost anything seems better than life as a woman of night, seeing Victoria today reminds me marriage is not necessarily the answer either. And though my sister seems entertained at his flirtations, I'm not convinced she fancies the two of them a pair.

"I—I don't know, DeLuca. What if she doesn't want to marry him?"

"Would you rather her be subject to Monroe or this life a day longer?"

"I would rather it be her decision. But not like this! I can't bear to see another sister a hostage of matrimony." The latter words mutter through me as thoughts of Victoria's bruised eye flashes through my mind. DeLuca regards me with concern, but he makes a choice not to push me for an explanation and for that I am thankful.

"Well, I reckon the decision will be made soon enough."

"What do you mean?"

"While on the surface it appears Claudius is a mere newsboy, I discovered his father, Corbin, runs the printing press in town. His father, however, insists he learn the business from the ground—hence his errand boy reputation. He has told his father of his affection for Chalmette and asked his permission to propose."

"Propose?"

"Yes—propose, dear one. Of course, his proposal carries with it a rather sizeable dowry. I am sure both Monroe and your mother should be amenable."

Gasps are all I have to give as I heave pools of air at DeLuca's words. Everything in me says be happy for Chalmette, but I'll need to talk to her first and see if this is what she wants.

"I need to see her. Now!" I belt out my frustration, pushing past DeLuca to make my way inside.

With DeLuca following close behind, I race to the back of the galley kitchen where I find Monroe, Mother, and Chalmette on one side of the kitchen and Claudius and Corbin on the other. Chalmette's tearful face is reddened, and her sadness grips the core of my heart as soon as I see her when the doors swing open.

Just as I thought, *she doesn't want this.*

"Chalmette, it's quite all right. You don't have to marry Claudius or anyone if it is not your desire!"

"Quiet, girl!" Monroe's admonishment is sharp but if it weren't for DeLuca pulling my wrist from behind, I know I would've pounced him.

"I will not be quieted! Chalmette deserves someone to speak for her. I've been quiet long enough!" I contend.

"Oh, please, Chartreuse! You've done no such thing," Mother gripes. Her posture is tense, but I sense a hint of indecision in her eyes that makes me wonder what happened before I came into the kitchen.

"Miss, please know I only have the most honorable of intentions for your sister," Claudius begins, his round face blushing red as his glassy blue eyes plead his case to me. DeLuca's grip lessens at my wrist as I contemplate the obvious sincerity of his tone. I was young when Victoria left us and had no thought of discerning her betrothed's intent. This time is different. Watching him now, my gut tells me his intentions are pure.

Perhaps he does care for her.

"Your intentions mean nothing, I'm afraid," Monroe begins, clearing his raspy throat as he leans against the cool brick oven. Sucking his teeth and casting a glance of warning to both my mother and sister he assumes his bullying stance. Chalmette tearfully turns away, holding herself at the waist. "But the girl has a responsibility to her family first. After she fulfills her— um—duties of the house, she may be permitted to marry should you not find a more suitable dame."

"Oh just forget it! All of you!" Chalmette protests, storming out the back door of the kitchen and into the alleyway.

"Don't worry, poppet, I'll get her," DeLuca whispers in my ear from behind me and rushes through the main hall toward Chalmette.

"Then there shall be no such arrangement! Come now, Claudius! We will have no further dealings with these people!" Corbin seethes, as he shoves his son's shoulder, looping their arms together as they head toward me and out of the kitchen.

"Wait! Please, Mr. DeVeaux, don't go," I say, quickly stepping in front of him and Claudius, preventing their exit. I am not surprised when his eyes lock to the helm of my cleavage. A normal courtesy of men who come close to me—well, except DeLuca. Still, his glance remains brief as his eyes search mine. I can tell a man of his stature doesn't suit well around our kind for long, but I cannot let him leave just yet. At least not until I fully understand what is happening.

"I am sorry, Miss, but we must be going before someone sees us here. I am sure you can understand," Corbin adds with a strong but warm smile. Looking over his shoulder I see Claudius has an equally warm demeanor, but I also see his brokenness. He seems genuinely disappointed.

"I do understand, sir. But please answer me this, Claudius—do you love Chalmette?"

Claudius' eyes brighten and his youthful face almost glows as he wipes his copper coils from his brow. "Yes," he whispers in a shy smile. "I have always loved her and I'm most certain I shall always."

As his sheepish gaze locks with mine, I now understand my sister's tears. *She does care for him.*

"I'm afraid none of that matters, my boy. If these people insist she must go on with their business tonight, then I must forbid it. If the girl is sullied by port filled paupers, she is of no use to you! I am sorry, the hour draws late, and we must be on our way!" Corbin shouts as he loops his arm through his son's as they hurry through the galley doors.

"But—" I scream after them.

"Let them go!" Monroe yells, grabbing my shoulder with his hard calloused hands from behind me.

Turning to meet Monroe's scowl I peer over his shoulder surprised to see Mother with her face to the ceiling, batting her eyes as if she were trying to contain her tears.

"Look girl, I'll not have you hindering family business!"

"Family?" I sneer at Monroe's words. Thinking of him as family sickens me.

"Yes, and I suggest you not forget who keeps the roof over your head, girl," Monroe continues, perching his thick forearm over my head, resting himself against the doorframe. His putrid musty scent laced in rum makes me nauseous and it takes everything in me not to vomit in his face. "Now why don't you be a good girl, go out get little Mette and teach her a few tricks of the—um, trade, if you will. If I recall, she can learn a lot from you." Whispering his latter sentiment in my ear as he brushes past me as he walks through the double galley doors, it takes everything in me not to rip the pocketknife from my boot and plunge it in his neck.

At his departure, Mother and I are left alone in the galley. Gone is the hint of sorrow I saw as Claudius shared his affection for Chalmette. Once more, I'm left with the stoic, ice-veined woman I've come to know and loathe over the last two decades. While I am not sure how it is possible, I most assuredly detest her more than her lover.

Standing with her hands cupped at her waist, her narrowed eyes and stone-slicing glare assure me there is nothing parental left for her to give. And with Monroe's sickening advances against me, I believe she sees me as a rival. Oh how I wish she knew there was no contest. I want nothing from Monroe—or her!

"I will see to Chalmette," I begin, charging toward the back exit as it becomes evident there are no words left between us.

As I pass her, she cups my elbow, turning me to meet her icy stare. "You do that. Just make sure she is ready. We already had enough interest in her since the postings went out. Some are willing to take second rounds after the first. Teach her what you must because after tonight I doubt that doughy boy's father will let him within inches of her. So you be sure to tame her. I'll not have another uncouth and untamed daughter under this roof!" Mother snaps her closing words and every vile of venom she meant for me pierced my pores as she spoke.

"Have no worries, Catherine, dear. I will see to my sister. I always have!"

Chapter Three

Rushing out of the back exit, tears trail my face once more. Thoughts of running away with Chalmette fill my mind, but with talks of war brewing about and no place to go, I can think of no other options.

Chalmette must endure tonight.

But I will teach her. Not the tricks of the trade as Monroe's perversion suggested, but my tricks. The ways I guard my mind. The haunting melodies I hum to dissuade me from ending my own existence. The magical memories of old. Whatever it takes, I'll ensure she not succumb to the scythe seeking to separate her soul from her heart.

I do not wish for my fate to be her own.

"Chartreuse!" Bumping into Scotty's broad frame as I pace downstairs startles me and comforts me all at once. Wrapping his large muscular arms around me, I push my face into the cavity of his chest and cry. Thankfully, Scotty is no novice to my tears. On more nights than I care to recount, has Scotty held me while the rhythmic cadence of his heart serenaded me to slumber. "I'm here, I'm here," he says softly in my ear.

As much as I want to linger in the warmth of his gargantuan embrace, my sister is my only concern and I need to find her. Pulling away from him, I wipe my face and gaze up and down the back street.

"No worries, love," Scotty begins. "No one is out here. Just us." His tender gaze and caring smile warm my heart. Scotty knows I never let anyone see me cry since that night. Only him. Not even my dear DeLuca is privy to my tears. Just Scotty. Being a man of few words, I know I can trust him.

The night I met Scotty he was waiting outside my door when some welp got too handsy and started punching me because I refused fellatio. I think Scotty was actually waiting to be serviced by one of the other house girls when he heard the ruckus. Coming to my rescue, he knocked the drunkard out cold and tended my wounds.

Since then Scotty has become my big, burly bear of a protector.

A man of few words, struggling with his own issues, Scotty has endeavored to care for me over the years. Even in our arrangement, he never asks for more than I can give—although I am certain I give quite a bit. On rough nights, he often shakes his head, letting me know he will only hold me and nothing more is required. Often, he just sits in my parlor chair at the window quietly so that I can sleep.

With the power of his presence and the strength of his embrace, my dear Scotty has a way of quieting my storm.

"Thank you, Scotty. I am sorry I ran into you like this, but I was only looking for Chalmette and DeLuca," I say quietly.

"Yes, I know. That is why I am here," he mutters, still searching my face. His eyes fall slightly as one lone tear escapes to my cheekbone, and he trails his thumb along the surface of my skin, catching my tear. Holding my face in his large palm, everything in me wants to rest in the warmth of his hold, but I cannot.

"Do you know where they are?" I answer, pulling myself from his grasp.

"Yes, DeLuca took her upstairs when he heard Monroe looking for her. We should get you upstairs." At his words, Scotty wraps my arm through his hulking bicep, leading me back inside the tavern.

As we make our way through the tavern, I notice we have more patrons than normal. I am certain the bidding postings for the prize of Chalmette's virginity have made their way around town. The saloon hall is filled with both grisly natured and wealthy status men alike.

I snatch one of the postings from a drunkard on my way in and I see the bidding rate is higher than any other auction Monroe has solicited. It is clear he intends to wipe away most of his debts with the fares he'll receive tonight. And with all attentions turned to the growing conflicts with the British, Monroe needn't worry about vagrancy laws ensuing against his bawdy house.

Reaching Chalmette's suite, DeLuca is perched outside her door and I see Corine and Elena holding up an array of colorful fabrics to my despondent sister. Before I can rush inside, DeLuca steps in front of the door with his hands raised in caution.

"What is it, DeLuca? I need to get to Chalmette. We don't have much time."

"I know and I am sorry. I feel responsible for getting her hopes up. I had hoped knowing the young lad's intentions would be enough," DeLuca answers with regret.

"It is not your fault, DeLuca and I appreciate you for trying, but I must see to her now."

"I understand. But I wanted to offer at least one final gesture. That is if you and Scotty are comfortable with a change to your normal arrangement." DeLuca's words hang between the three of us and I see an unusual bit of tension shift in Scotty's posture.

"I—I didn't get to ask her yet," Scotty replies with his head buried to his chin.

"Ask me what?" I snap. I need to get to Chalmette. Looking over DeLuca's broad shoulder's I see Elena holstering cloth reminiscent of the sun and my frustration grows. I'll not have my sister adorning attire so loud on her first night.

"Well," DeLuca begins, stepping in front of my view of Chalmette and regaining my attention. "I have asked Scotty to serve at Chalmette's door tonight. I shall serve yours."

"What? Absolutely not!" My protest is so loud, Scotty cups his large hand around my mouth. Looking over the balcony inside the saloon I see onlookers glaring up at us and I realize I am bringing unnecessary attention upstairs. It is one thing to have Scotty outside my door but the thought of

DeLuca having a side seat to my night hour soils me with fear. I don't want him privy to that side of me. Although he knows who and what I am, I'd rather he not endure all it entails as my man-in-waiting.

"Listen, Red, I don't quite fancy it either, but what choice do you have. Scotty is far better equipped than I to handle some scallywag should his advances go beyond his reach. He can do more for your sister than I can."

"Sure, so then how do you expect to guard me if you can't even take watch of my sister?"

"Quite frankly, poppet, the difference is that unlike your sister you can certainly protect yourself. I'd serve as nothing but a mere watchman. Chalmette on the other hand—"

"Okay, I understand," I begin softly, pondering my dear friend's words. "Scotty, would you please take watch at Chalmette's door, please?"

"If that is what you want, lovely. You know I am at your service. Always and however you require me to serve," Scotty answers with his head bowed, resting his square jaw on my forehead.

"Good! Then we have an accord!" DeLuca blurts his words quickly, stalling my temptation to surrender to Scotty's hold once more.

"Not quite," I say looking over my shoulder and down the hall. "Marius!" I shout as I spy his lanky frame wander from the dark corner of the hall where he normally spends his evenings reading the post and sipping coffee. Dressed in his tan trousers, matching jacket, and ruffled collared blouse he makes his way to us in a few long strides.

"Yes, Madame Chartreuse," Marius replies with his typical demure and ready-to-serve tone.

"What are you doing, Treuse? I said I'd keep post for you tonight."

"No, you most certainly will not. I appreciate you, dear friend, but this world is not yours. It is mine. And for what it is worth it is also the world in which the three of us—Scotty, Marius, and I reside. I will not allow you to make the troubles and torment of my world your own. Now, please go. Marius will see to my door tonight."

DeLuca's usually olive-skin pales at my sentiment and his eyes stare back at me in awe. Although I hardly understand why I am turning him away myself, I know it is what I must do.

"Treuse, I must insist!" DeLuca's pleading words do nothing but cement my own further.

"No, DeLuca!" I yell back. I know I must be firm. If he senses even a hint of indecision, he will call me on my folly. "Now please go! Scotty, you know what to do—as do you Marius."

"Yes madame," both Marius and Scotty reply in unison.

DeLuca's eyes grow wide in both disbelief and anger. He is the last person I wish to hurt, but I know it is for the best.

At least I have to believe it to be so.

Placing my hand on his shoulder, I slide past him and enter Chalmette's room.

"Leave us." My announcement is more a demand than a mere statement and both Corine and Elena understand it as so. Dropping their fabrics in the chaise chair at the edge of Chalmette's bed, both women exit promptly with their heads lowered as I step aside allowing their departure. As they do, I turn to see DeLuca still standing on the other side of the door, his face still riddled with frustration. While it takes everything in me not to do so, I close the door with his pleading eyes glaring at me, but I know I must tend to my sister.

Neither his feelings nor my care for him matter in this moment.

"Well, sister, do tell me—what should I wear for my first night?" Chalmette has accepted her fate and the sight of her squared shoulders and raised chin should frighten me, but I am not afraid. Feelings of something that resembles pride swell within me. Still, it is too soon to be proud. I need to know she can go through with this.

All of it.

"Before we discuss attire, dear sister, we must discuss the particulars."

"Particulars?"

"Yes, my dear. *The Particulars.*"

"Ah, yes, Mother came by earlier stating something of me needing to be tamed to this life. I suppose I should. Especially since any thoughts I had of being with Claudius are now forfeit."

"Speaking of Claudius—why didn't you tell me of your affection for him? I could have been of help!"

"It matters not, Chartreuse. My affections, as it were, are rubbish. Besides, you cannot protect me from everything. Not even tonight. Now, please, help me select a garment."

Chalmette holds three garments from Corinne's wardrobe, and I shake my head. "No, we are not doing this!" I protest. "Scotty!" I shout his name knowing there's no way he's moved much farther from Chalmette's door.

Sheepishly peering his head in between the cracked door, he looks at me slightly confused. "Yes?" he answers hesitantly.

"Dear, can you please grab my French tulle and georgette gown?"

"The blue one or the newest one from Tabitha?"

Chalmette's mouth falls open as she realizes I am about to adorn her in my newest fabrics from France.

"No, Treuse! I couldn't!" She pleas to me.

"You shall," I answer definitively. "Yes, Scotty, the newest one. Thank you." Scotty acquiesces with his eyes only and makes his way down the hall. As he does, I quickly peer through the crack to see if DeLuca is still standing by, but I don't see him. I only see Marius, leaned against the wall reading his post. My heart aches knowing I have hurt my dear friend, but I hope in time he will come to understand.

Thankfully, Scotty doesn't give me long to ponder my pain as he makes his way back to Chalmette's suite with the fabrics in tow. Only waving them through the door, he quickly closes the door once I take them from his hand.

"Sister! You spent a fortune on these fabrics! There's no way I can take them from you!" Although pleading, my young sister's dancing eyes alone tell me she fancies the idea of wearing my pretty fittings. And with her lovely figure, I have no doubt she will be the envy of the evening.

"They are yours, my sister. As it always shall be between us—whatever I have is yours. Never forget that!"

"As with I, Chartreuse, all that I have—"

"Is yours, Chalmette," I answer, swiftly taking her chin in my hand. "I will never take from you, dear one, what is yours. Nor shall I let anyone else do so. That is why it is time to discuss the particulars of the night."

Chalmette's eyes glass with water, but she reins them in, permitting none to fall to her angelic face. Her crystal blue eyes stare into mine with both a haunting innocence and trepidation.

Escorting her to her washing bowl, she discards her clothing and up pins her hair as I sponge around her neck and back while she keeps her eyes fixed on her reflection in the mirror. Kneeling beside her as I dry her with a cotton cloth, I set my face to her mirrored image and see fear form in her face.

"As I have said, Chalmette, I will never let anyone take from you. That includes tonight."

"How is that possible, sister? Mother and Monroe would have those men take everything from me tonight. Everything!" She cries.

Taking her face in my palms, I squeeze her cheeks tight, preventing her cries and forcing her to set her eyes to mine. "No, Chalmette—no one takes anything. It is yours to give. Yours alone. Do not let them have such a power. Not on this night or ever. Even if you were to marry, I'd instruct you the same. As women, we alone hold the power to our most precious possession. Do you understand me?"

I wait as Chalmette nods with understanding and she slowly retracts from my hold. One lone tear drops from her eye, but she slaps her hand across her face, wiping her face free of her own tears.

"Yes, I understand, sister. Give them nothing."

"Yes, my dear. But take from them—everything! Make your body a temple. Make him surrender to your whim. Let him beg for more." Chalmette's eyes grow wide with understanding, but there's still more to share. "Your first night will hurt, but do not focus on the pain. Take yourself somewhere else."

"Somewhere else? How can I—"

"In your mind, sister. Make melody in your heart. You and I have the gift of song. Enchant yourself with such songs in your heart and mind. Hum if you must. He will think it is for his benefit, but you alone will know the truth."

Chalmette's eyes widen once more, and a small smile crosses her face. "Is that why I always hear you singing when they leave your chamber? I even heard one fellow say he had you so good, you sang."

"The song wasn't for him."

"No, it wasn't," she says with a sly smile. "I know the song you hum. The one of the mulberry and juniper trees? It is no mere lullaby." A wicked grin crinkles at the corner of my sister's sweet lips and while I am thankful, she understands me, it pains me to now see my own reflection in her eyes. I do not want her to become the monster I am, but I fear I have no choice.

"No it isn't, my sister and you know this well. But for them, they are never the wiser. As such, we must keep it that way," I whisper, watching her posture form dark and ominous before my eyes.

What am I doing?

"I understand, sister." Chalmette answers resolute. Her newly narrowed eyes and squared shoulders tell me she has fully accepted her fate.

Turning away from her, I allow her to care for her precious place and powder herself. Streams of tears race down my face, stinging me as they make their way to my chin. It pains me to see my sister immersing herself into this world. Even more, I am no better than the River Man ferrying her maiden voyage to the Underworld.

Looking out the window, I wonder if we perhaps have enough time to escape. It's been years since I've climbed down the brick sidings and I'm not certain Chalmette could keep up. But maybe we should at least try our luck. Monroe would surely look for us and Mother too.

How I wish I knew where Dalcour Marchand was?

For it was he who led us here from our impending doom in New Orleans. I was still a child when I last saw him, I doubt he would recognize me. Even if he would extend his courtesy, he does not know of Chalmette's existence. I was the youngest of the children when he led us to safety.

I still remember him holding me in his arms as he rescued us from the blazing fires caused by his brother, Decaux. He was so kind and gentle. Covering my eyes as we ran past scores of people running through the streets screaming in agony while burning alive.

"I've got you little one," he whispered in my ear. I can still hear his voice and the soothing fragrance of his scent as he held me in his grip. Even more, I

remember his promise that he would watch over us. *"Always."* He promised.

Yet and still, somehow, we have come to this.

Before I have another second to ponder rescuing my sister from her own impending doom, a loud knock on the door, turn both Chalmette's and my attention toward one another as I heave in a gulp of air.

"It's time," I hear Scotty call to us from the other side of the door. Chalmette stands from her vanity and takes a deep breath before gesturing her hand instructing me to open the door. She exhales and sighs hard as I open the door, but I realize I am still holding my breath.

In fact, I have no idea how I can breathe knowing what comes next.

Chapter Four

I opt to stand at the top of the balcony as Scotty escorts Chalmette into the saloon. I have a better view of the crowd from this vantage point, and I want to see the face of every man who crosses the threshold tonight.

Both Mother and Monroe look up at me, scrunching their noses with displeasure when they see Scotty with Chalmette. Even they know just his presence alone is enough to ward off any of the ill-intended. While Mother's scowl is more pronounced, Monroe's face isn't as annoyed as she. Perhaps, he knows as I do, only the wealthiest and well-intended of suitors will bid knowing Scotty will be seated at her door. A small smirk gathers over his face and I can almost sense the scent of greed pouring from his pores.

"She looks to be the belle of the ball tonight, Mon Cheri," Marius says over my shoulder as he leans on the railing behind me.

"Yes, she does look lovely," Elena sneers as she walks past me, rolling her eyes as she does. Tossing her long, brunette hair over her shoulder as she cascades down the stairs with a suitor already on her arm, her envy of Chalmette is hard to miss. She had grown quite accustomed to being the newest dish on the menu and now my sister has taken her place. Strangely, somehow Elena fancies herself my rival. I suppose having more suitors than me in one night is akin of a prize to her. It is a sad state really. On her best night she never fares more than me. Even if she did, neither of us would come out the victor.

"Chalmette is strong, she will be just fine," Corrine says sweetly, coming to my side. "She comes from good stock—like her big sister." I am thankful for Corinne's sentiment. Although her mood wavers often, I can trust— good or bad—she is being sincere. In my world sincerity is a rarity.

"Gentlemen, masters, and lords," Monroe begins from centerstage. I watch as he wobbles slightly as he paces the riser, feigning himself a man of statue. I am sure it is apparent to anyone with eyes that he is drunk. Even more, he looks ridiculous in a top hat and ill-fitted suit. His clothes are too tight and he's busting at the seams. If Mother had any care for him, she wouldn't let him embarrass himself as such. Then again, perhaps it is her own little mischievous fantasy—to see him carry himself about with such buffoonery. "You well know all the pretty and sweet treasures in our modest bawdy house, but tonight you'll be graced with our most precious gem—the Lovely Little Mette!"

Whistles and a series of hand claps echo through the saloon as the men cheer as some of the other house girls lead Chalmette up the stairs and onto the stage with Monroe. Grunting and a flurry of expletives explode in the atmosphere the moment my young sister's luminous frame takes centerstage. Monroe yanks her so hard to his side that she almost stumbles on the tulle layered at the sides of her gown. Still, she manages to keep her posture upright and her face firm. If this moment were a source of joy, my chest would swell with pride for my sister. She's doing remarkably well considering the situation.

"Now, let the bidding begin!" Monroe shouts as the room erupts in such a clamor it's difficult to tell to whom each bid belongs. Small strips of all manner of continental currency sift through the air, flying in front of the stage. Monroe's eyes grow wide in greed as he gives a knowing glance to Mother. The return smile she gives him, sickens me. How she could be happy knowing what is to come to her own child is unconscionable.

While the thought only crept in my mind once before, it is evident, my mother would've been best suited had she been sterile. She hasn't a maternal bone in her entire body. Of that I am certain.

The bidding floor bustles as burly, brooding men brawl with one another for the chance of crowning Chalmette's first night. *Bloody bastards.* Fists fly and tables turn as a few drunken men fight, challenging every contending bidder. Most, likely haven't a coin to their name to indulge in a pint of port, much less spend the night with Chalmette, but Monroe's perverted soul is aroused by the uproar itself. The more they fight, the more he loves it as if his own depravity feeds off it.

Sickening.

Marius' slender palm grips my shoulders, preventing me from making my way down the stairs. His strength strangely surprises me. While Scotty is who I look to for muscle, this new view of Marius is a pleasant revelation. Looking up and over my shoulder at him, I spy the softness of his almond-shaped hazel eyes and his crookedly perfect grin and I cannot help smiling at him in return, despite the chaos going on inside.

Why have I never noticed his handsomeness before? I suppose being Monroe's errand boy and cousin has earned him very few high marks in my regard. That is, until now.

Interesting.

"Stay here," Marius says as his cool breath prickles my pores. His tone is also more calming than I expected. Still I keep my sights set on my sister. From my view I can see how much the brawling around her is upsetting. Parting my lips to reply, Marius makes his way in front of me and snaps his fingers and two large men from both sides of the saloon make their way in front of the stage, keeping the bidders at bay.

Monroe looks up at Marius and gives him a cross glare. I am shocked when Marius tips his hat only in reply, keeping his shoulders squared in front of me almost protectively. Mother gazes up at us from Chalmette's side and a crooked smile glances across her face as if she were pleased.

"Catherine paid me to find two stooges to muscle the crowd if need be. I think she anticipated this response," Marius whispers over his shoulder.

"Evidently." I answer flatly. While the gesture may seem forward-thinking to Marius, it is despicable to me. The fact she has enough foresight to account for needed security, but no thought to put her youngest in such a position is reprehensible.

Monroe clears his throat, attempting to gain control of the crowd. He points to Crawley, his companion drunkard and resident pianist, to begin playing, hopeful to soften the atmosphere. As Crawley pulls himself from his stewed state, a slender well-dressed elderly man walks to the front of the stage and hands Monroe a small card.

The two flunkies Marius acquired close in around the man as he reaches out to give Monroe the card, but the man only gives a side-eye to both men, giving no thought to their otherwise intimidating posturing.

"Who is that?" I mutter to Marius as I step down to his side.

"I don't know. I have never seen him around here before," Marius answers, looking at me with the same mirrored face of confusion as me. Even Scotty looks up at us from the bottom of the stage and he too seems surprised.

"Well, well, well," Monroe begins as his eyes grow wide with wicked delight. Mother tries to peer over his shoulder, but he boxes her out, hindering her from seeing the note in full. Chalmette's posture shifts and she steps to the edge of the stage, but Scotty takes her arm, preventing her from falling. "Gentlemen, it appears we have our first full bid and well—it is quite generous, I must say."

"I've got twenty pesos!" One man shouts from the floor.

"Let me at her! I have thirty pounds!" Another screams.

Marius and I stare at one another, curious how far this bidding will go.

Monroe clears his throat once more above the clamoring snarls, "I am sorry, my most esteemed gentlemen, but unless any of you can make the good of six hundred pounds, I'll have to oblige this dear sir's request of the ever-beautiful Mette!"

Gasps ripple throughout the hall and Crawley abruptly halts his play. Marius' mouth parts with disbelief and I notice even my mother is taken aback.

Staring at this elderly gentleman dressed in a proper topcoat and trousers with a brim tucked beneath his arms, I can't fathom why such an unassuming yet wealthy man is interested in such a deal. A man of his stature doesn't belong here. His thick silver and black hair is impeccably groomed and even the shine of his shoes casts a reflection of his aged yet handsome face.

Pulling a few notes out of his breast pocket, his white gloved hand offers payment to Monroe as he steps near the staircase, gesturing his other free hand toward Chalmette.

Looking over her shoulder to Mother, Chalmette's face is fright with alarm. Typical of Mother, she allows no room for either empathy or pardon as she keeps her sights set on Monroe. I take note how Scotty's face tightens as Chalmette walks toward the front of the stage. A small but forced smile peers beneath Chalmette's sullied state as she takes steps closer to her first caller as he watches her warmly. However, her brief and tender exchange with the gentleman is cut short by Monroe as he quickly throws his arm around her waist and plants a kiss on her forehead.

Rage kindles through me as he does and I dash down the top stairs, sickened to see his hands on my sister. Marius pulls my arm back from behind and Monroe glares up at me with a devilish grin. He knows he's getting to me.

Sick bastard.

I am somewhat thankful to see Chalmette's caller throw his palm into Chalmette's tiny hand, tugging her from Monroe's grip. The two men close in around them, but the man maintains his place at Chalmette's side. Monroe's irritation with this new caller is obvious and I cannot help chuckle at his annoyance. Still, he doesn't stay annoyed for long as he stuffs the note wad in his pockets.

Scotty makes his way behind Chalmette and the gentleman, nodding at me as he does. I know he doesn't want me to worry but how can I not.

This is still Chalmette's first night with a man.

Although, I admit I am curious as to how her first night will go with someone so well advanced in years. In my experience the elderly either want me to fancy myself for their pleasure or spend the hour trying to restore a peak in their wintry forests. Either way, I am slightly thankful she won't have to endure the barbarity of the buffoons paraded here tonight. That will be, unfortunately, the task of me and the other house girls.

"You better make your way down," Marius suggests as Monroe snaps his finger once more to Crawley and he begins playing his usual Irish medley, beginning with *The Last Rose of Summer.* Most of the regulars know when that medley starts, the girls of the house will come out to partner up with someone for the evening.

Nonetheless, I can't help keeping my attention on Chalmette as she and her companions take the opposite staircase up to her suite. With nothing but a large candelabra hanging between us, Chalmette glares at me through the dancing flames of fire and I almost bolt to her side when I spy one lone tear fall to her cheek. Still, she lifts her chin up, smiles at me, and loops her arm with her new gentleman, whispering in his ear as she's seen me do countless times before.

While I admire the fight in her it pains me to see her in distress.

"Chartreuse!" Marius says once more, tugging my hand as he looks nervously over his shoulder catching Monroe's watchful gaze. "Don't worry, I have a bee line to Scotty. If anything untoward should happen, he will take care of her," he whispers.

"Thank you, Marius," I softly reply, gazing back at his sincere smile.

"Besides, I doubt the old prune will hardly be able to mount her much less cause a ruckus," Marius teases, pinching my shoulder. We both laugh as he does, and I do my best to shrug off thoughts of Chalmette alone with a man.

"Well, I suppose I better get to work. I hardly took time to attend to myself, so whatever my state will just have to do!" I say, unpinning my bun, letting my auburn ringlets drift down my back.

"Lovely." Marius' sentiment surprises me. Offering his hand to mine as I come down the stairs, I can't help seeing Marius as I've never seen him before. All these years I've only thought of him as the lanky and awkward errand boy of his wretched cousin, but tonight I see something more.

As odd as it may be, I almost wish I had allowed DeLuca to stay at my side instead of Marius. The thought of Marius having to endure my doorpost while I entertain another pains me. Even more as I now notice his sculpted chest peering through his top everything in me wishes he were the one to share my bed tonight. And from the desirous gaze set in his eyes and the shimmering sweat hovering atop his mustache, this feeling is mutual.

We share one final glance as his warm hand tightly clasps with mine before I begin shuffling my way through the tables. Marius perches against the wooden walls, swirling his chewing stick in the corner of his rose-colored lips and it is indeed the sexiest thing I have ever seen. His keen gaze latches onto my every step and the building magnetism between us as I mingle about is indescribable.

"Pace yourself, honey. Monroe's keeping his eye set on you," Corine mutters beneath a faux chortle, brushing past me as she walks about with two of her usual escorts on her arm. I appreciate her subtle warning and I work hard to turn my attention away from Marius and back to the men of the tavern.

"There's my sweet sugar," Preston, one of my regulars says, patting my backside. Looking at Marius I see he's talking with Crawley and I blow out a deep breath, thankful for the distraction. I need to focus and thinking of Marius isn't helping me. Besides we both know it's folly to think of ourselves otherwise.

Plopping into Preston's lap, I go along with our usual routine. He and his companions complain about their wives and gripe about the government, all while clinging their mugs of port and trading insults with one another. I laugh as though I were interested, remaining careful to side with Preston along the way. He is a generous tipper and while he normally pays for the entire evening, he never carries on longer than eight minutes and falls straight asleep. Once he was so eager, he never met my entrance, spilling himself all over my duvet and drifting to his dreams. Poor bugger. I often wonder if he really only comes here to rest. He surely does more sleeping here than anything else.

"Well, it looks as though I'm in the mood for something sweet," Preston announces as is normal for him. He says the same thing each time. "What do you say you and I make our way, my sweet girl?" He says with a sly smile, brushing my hair from my face and kissing my cheek.

"Lead the way," I reply in his ear while planting a light kiss just below his earlobe. As I do, I see Marius looking at me from across the room and the tense gaze in his eyes is hard to miss.

What is happening between us?

Preston cups his hand in mine, pulling me away from the table and I see

Marius making his way toward us and from his quick pace I wonder if he is coming to escort me or rip me from Preston entirely.

"My, my, aren't you a charmer?" Elena's slithering voice jolts my thoughts of Marius aside. Why she has planted herself in front of me and Preston is beyond me.

"Move out of the way, Elena. He's my tipper for the evening."

"Now ladies, I'd be more than obliged to have you both, if you're willing to split the tips," Preston coyly responds. If only Elena knew he barely lasts a few minutes she wouldn't bother with him.

Elena laughs as she runs her hands through his messy deep blonde mane. "Well, I suppose that's an option." Preston shares a laugh with her, and I look over my shoulder to see my mother now with Marius pointing him to the bar.

Even though Scotty is my usual runner, I am sure it is apparent to anyone that Marius is escorting me tonight, so I am sure Mother's interference is intentional. Marius looks back at me with disappointment as she pushes him toward the bar. Turning back to Elena and Preston my irritation with her grows.

"Enough, Elena! Go flaunt it elsewhere!" I snap.

"Oh, I'm sorry, Chartreuse but I'm just abiding house rules. And if I am not mistaken you already have a tipper—one of your usuals in your bedchamber already. At least that is what Monroe said when he told me to come pick up your slack." She answers pointing upstairs to my suite.

Looking up, I see my door is ajar with my stringed pearls and velvet rope on the doorknob. Seeing my normal signal on the door lets me know one of my other regulars has paid for the evening and is waiting for me. I am surprised because I have only noticed a few of my usual callers here tonight.

"Do you know who it is?" I question Elena as she playfully taunts Preston.

"How would I know that darling? I'm just the messenger, but I think I'll take on this tipper right here," Elena coos, twirling her tiny fingers through Preston's hair.

"Well, sweet one, until next time—or maybe later when you're done," Preston says while nipping at Elena's ear.

As if you'd be awake. I mutter to myself as I turn and proceed up the stairs to my suite.

Glancing around the hall once more, I see Marius bringing in barrels of port to the bar as my mother directs him and his two hired hands for the evening. A part of me is happy he is busy with other matters, I really don't fancy him on the other end of the door while I'm entertaining.

Reaching the top of the balcony, I see Scotty outside Chalmette's door and he gives me a nod, raising his thumb. I suppose it's a good sign.

Taking a deep breath, I sigh, blowing enough air through my puffed cheeks that my curls fly from my face. It is all I can do to shake off the disturbing images of my sister with her first caller.

Entering my suite, I see the flickering flames of the iron sconces on my wall, and I am surprised someone has lit the candles before I've had a chance to do so. Whoever it is must be accustomed to my routines.

"I see someone's ready for me," I call out as I cross the threshold, tossing my silk wrap on the stool at my vanity. Just then the door slams shut, and a large sweaty palm grips me from behind.

"Yes, I'm ready for you! And you will give me what I want!"

My muffled screams do little to penetrate my attacker's tight cuff, but I dig the heel of my boot into his instep and use the heel of my other foot to kick his knee. Groaning, his grip on me loosens and I wiggle enough to turn and see Monroe's grisly glare staring back into my own.

Chapter Five

"Monroe!" I scream as he grabs my shoulders, yanking me back to him. "Take your bloody hands off me!"

"Not until you give me what you owe me, girl!" He shouts back.

"I owe you nothing!"

"Oh you owe me everything and I am going to take it!" He slobbers his words, mashing his mouth along my neck, forcing himself to the helm of my cleavage. Pulling back from him once more, he slaps me hard and palms my face in his large hands, squeezing my lips toward his. "I know you don't like kisses, little girl but you will do that and more for me tonight. Did you think the little stunt you pulled earlier would go unpunished? And I've seen the way you've eyed my little cousin all night. You want that boy, don't you?" Trailing his slimy tongue along my neck as he holds my face, I work hard to breathe as my feet dangle beneath me.

He's trying to kill me.

"Well, you're not going to have him. And I'll never let him have you. *I'll never let anyone have you.* After what I'll do to you tonight, no one will want you, little girl. I'll plant myself so deep in you, you'll beg me for mercy. And I will not come out. I am putting all of my seed in you tonight; and you'll give me a son—maybe sons! You'll be tied to me forever and I'll never let you go!" He seethes his filth, and my mind goes dark with rage.

I will never be his! *Ever.*

Using what remains of my strength, I pull myself up and jut my knee into his groin. Hard. His eyes bulge as I do, and he releases me from his grip. Gagging, I try to regain my breath as I recover from his hold at my neck. Peering around the candlelit room, I look for anything to help me as Monroe writhes in agony.

Grabbing the poker near my fireplace I raise it to hit him, but he lunges forward, clasping my wrist.

"Did you think it would be this easy?" Monroe teases me, yanking the poker from my hand and tossing it aside. It crashes into my vaulted floor mirror and the clanging sound echoes throughout my suite. Forcing me down onto my bed, he opens his trousers and pushes my knee to spread my legs apart. "You walk around my house like you own it. But I own you, darling. *And I own this.* Now come on, I know you want this—but either way, you're going to take it like a good girl. And when the old man has finished with Little Mette, I'll make my rounds to her. I'll have both of you full of me by sunrise!" Monroe's ominous shrill, curdles like bowel in my mouth.

Thoughts of him with Chalmette send me into another fury and once more my mind goes dark with murderous intention. Slipping my hand under my pillow, I grab the pearl-hilted dagger that was once my father's and swipe it hard across Monroe's face, screaming as I do. Plunging the heel of my boot into his chest, I kick him away from me as he cries in anguish.

"You little b—"

Jumping up from the bed I jab him again across his chest before he can finish his swearing. Blood drips from both the cut along his brow to cheekbone and through the gash near his collarbone. His eyes glare at me with disbelief and fear.

"Are you mad?" He shouts as if I should regret my actions.

A loud bang at my door resounds and I hear Scotty shout my name through the muffling revelry of the tavern.

"You bloody bastard! You will never touch me again. Do not court me as some mere wench, you fool, or I shall become your darkest nightmare. I swear it!" Keeping my father's dagger raised high, my threats are met with a look of cowardice in Monroe's eyes. "Perhaps I am mad, Monroe. Shall we test the theory?"

"Keep away from me, girl!" He yells back. I hear Scotty bang on the door once more, shouting my name as he does. I peer over Monroe's shoulder wondering if I can get past him or if I should yell back to Scotty, but I don't want Monroe to believe he's bested me. Lifting my dagger higher, I watch Monroe's timidity dim as he reaches behind him and pulls a gun from his waist.

How could I forget he normally keeps a holster at night in case things become more disorderly than normal? While it is a miscalculation on my part, I will not afford him the satisfaction of my fear.

"Ah! So, now you are scared, little girl? Did you forget to whom the entirety of these four walls belong? Then let this be a reminder. Now drop your pretty little knife and your knickers and show me that pretty little—"

"Never! I'd die first!" I shout back.

"Have it as you wish, beloved. Either way, no one else will have you." Pointing the Flintlock pistol at my face, I embrace whatever end may come. Although I know my death would mean worse for Chalmette, I will not give in to his wretchedness. Who knows? Perhaps my death is the catalyst necessary for Catherine to finally be the mother she should have been and carry both herself and Chalmette from this horrid place.

Preparing for the next breath I take to be my last, I keep my eyes fixed on Monroe as he snarls and pulls the grip back, aiming to fire. The sound of the blast resounds through my suite and I hear my door crash open and a powerful gale force whips through the room.

My eyes can hardly capture the tornado-like motion funneling around me as I see Monroe's gun fall to the ground. A loud screeching scream along with a shuddering cry pierces my ears as I plug my eardrums to quiet the noise. I turn about and I see Scotty at the threshold of my door and his eyes are wide, laden in fright as he looks behind me.

Fear strikes me as I glare at him, wondering what could cause my gargantuan friend alarm. Staring at the gun on the ground, thoughts of the gun's blowback in Monroe's drunken state, fill my mind. Perhaps the fool shot himself?

As much as I wish that were the case, nothing prepares me for what I see when I turn around.

Dalcour Marchand.

For days—no for years, I had hoped this day would come to pass. I hoped. Prayed. Wondered—when would be the day of my salvation. When would he finally come to rescue me from—this hell? Surely, I never envisioned thoughts of him riding into the sunset on a white horse, but I hoped he could and would one day save me.

Even though I started to lose heart, a part of me still believed he had not forgotten his promise.

But the sight before me now is more than anything I could have imagined. I now understand the fear which glazed Scotty's sight as it now does my own.

Perched with impeccable balance at my armoire's edge, I see Dalcour Marchand with his hand gripped at Monroe's throat. Glowing embers of red illumine from his otherwise velvety pecan-textured skin as long, sharp fangs protrude like a dragon from his mouth. Monroe cowers, soiling himself in feverish fear at the haunting sight before him.

He should fear him. As do I.

Grim tales of he and his brother, Decaux's, otherworldly deeds fill my mind. While the word is faintly used beyond Celtic tales, I know what and who he is. *Vampire.* A creature of night. But as my dear sister Calida once told me, he isn't just any vampire. He is supernatural. A progenitor of all fallen to bloodlust and descent.

He is not human nor has he ever been.

And despite the darkened color of his skin, he is among few to have no cause to abide by ideals of slavery and segregation. He is ruled by neither human law nor faction. As Calida said, he is from the early people. Those who walked this decayed planet before humans ever came to be. He is an Altrinion. A supernatural of a power too great to be known among mortal men.

This is my rescuer. My only hope.

The pacing of my heart quickens as I watch venom from his pointy fangs graze the pulsing of Monroe's wilted jugular.

"Lord Marchand!" I scream and his fangs retract, quickly whipping his neck around and looking down at me. "Please, not here!" I plead, glancing over my shoulder to see Scotty's gaped open mouth at the door. But he is not alone. Mother now stands beside him.

Her face is pale as she stares at Monroe dangling in Dalcour's hold. She looks as if she'd seen a ghost.

"You—you are here," Mother mutters barely above a whisper as she stands frozen in shock.

Throwing Monroe to my bed like a ragdoll, Dalcour effortlessly floats back to the wooden floors and leans against my armoire, resting his hands in his pocket.

"Yes, I am here and by the looks of things, I've delayed my arrival for far too long," Dalcour replies, and the melodious tenor of his voice fills the room. Standing well above six feet, his broad, muscular frame seems to fill the entirety of my suite, making it appear too small for him. The glowing of his skin recedes as do both his fangs and his gangly features diminish, revealing the perfect handsomeness that is Dalcour Marchand.

"How—I—I-don't understand," Mother continues, stepping beyond the threshold with her eyes locked onto Dalcour.

"Well, I have been out of the country as of late on business. But after almost a decade without any word from you or letter, I only imagined the worst. Once I arrived back to my manor, I had intention to look for you and your little ones, but my brother's machinations stirred tensions in the parish once more, so I had to tend to other matters. And yet through all that time, no letters, or any word from you. Naturally, I grew concerned, especially since—"

"Wait!" I shout, standing between both Dalcour and Mother. "What letters? Mother, do you mean to tell me you have been in contact with him all these years? Why have I never heard of such?"

"Because it wasn't your place, little girl!" Monroe snips his words from the bed.

"I'll hear no more words from you tonight, you slobbering mass or I shall rip out your tongue and stuff it between the cheeks of your ass." Dalcour's flippant rebuke is followed by a swift kick to Monroe's chin, and he falls back to the bed, yelling in pain.

"Quiet, Monroe!" Mother shouts, looking over her shoulder and motioning Scotty to close the door. He does as she commands but remains inside my room.

"So out with it, Mother! Have you remained in contact with Lord Marchand all this time?" I question, closing the gap between us. Her face betrays her as her eyes roam back and forth between me and Dalcour.

"He promised he'd be back for us, but he never came! What was I supposed to do!" She snaps back, turning away from me, looking at herself in the mirror.

"I wrote you many letters, Catherine, showing my concern for your plight," Dalcour replies softly.

"Yes, letters but we needed more, Chartreuse. We couldn't exist off his mere promises alone!"

"Mere promises? What about my resources? I sent them to you quarterly. I paid for your keep at the Hamptons when I first brought you here. You later informed me that you found a nice gentleman to care for you and your children."

"What?" I say as the knowledge of Mother's dealings with Dalcour pain through me. My redemption was indeed nearer than I believed.

"Yes, and I told you I would yet provide for you and your daughters since you feared doing so would be a burden to this man. Months turned into years and I yet believed things had turned for the better." Dalcour's confession haunts me more than seeing him as he is.

"All this time you let us believe we were alone and in despair, but we were not! I thought there was no one who loved us. No one who cared. You lied to us! And what of this money, Mother?" Facing her squarely as I'd done earlier today is different. She is more an enemy to me than I first believed.

"What money? The little rations he sent us were barely enough to care for three girls much less for keeping a roof over your heads. If it weren't for Monroe—"

Dropping my father's dagger to the ground, my hand sears across her face with such a force she falls flat to the floor. Crying my name, she holds her chin in shock as a stream of tears flood her face.

Dalcour walks up behind me and I can feel him contemplating taking my shoulder in consolation, but he does not and steps back. I am sure my rage is too much even for him.

"Is Monroe the father figure you wanted for your girls, Mother? A man who, only moments ago, attempted to claw his way on top of me only to rape me as he's done so many times before on your watch! But what care you? Only hours ago he positioned himself to do so to your youngest daughter, Chalmette, and your only recourse is to give away her purity to some haggard, elderly man!"

"Chartreuse, please try to understand!" Mother's sobbing plea does nothing to assuage my rage. She's earned every measure of my ire and I intend for her to know it as so.

"Ahem—um, Chartreuse—" Dalcour begins, circling me and blocking my view of the sore sight of a mother at my feet. My eyes dart to him sharply and he tilts back as though he feared I'd strike him. A small smile crosses his perfect face and I grow slightly irritated that my anguish somehow amuses him. "If I may," he continues, "about young Chalmette—"

At the mention of Chalmette's name both my newly appointed irritation with Dalcour and anger toward my mother turns to trepidation. Looking to see Scotty now flanking my sides, I realize he's no longer guarding my young sister as he promised.

"Scotty, you idiot! Chalmette! You're supposed to be watching for her!" I shout, racing out of my suite. Faintly, I hear Dalcour call after me though my mother's screeching cries nearly muffle the would-be calming tenor of his tone. Still, I charge down the hall to Chalmette's suite, forging my way through the crowded hall of house girls and their mates. Pushing anyone aside and stepping over whomever in my path, I ram my elbow into Chalmette's large solid oak door.

Shutting my eyes as I do, fearful of what position I'll find my young sister in, I shout her name, hopeful at least her calling reply settles my growing angst.

"Treuse?" Chalmette whispers back to me in almost a chuckle, I fear what I'll see once I open my eyes. Opening one eye and squeezing the other shut, I am hardly prepared for what I see before me. "Are you well, sister?" Chalmette asks in her normal quiet and syrupy sweet tone.

I am surprised to find my sister and her tipper seated at her table with a deck of cards in their hands and copper tokens spread before them.

"Um, Chalmette, I—I was just coming in to check on you," I say, gazing around the room and taking note her bed is still well made and her hair kempt.

"By barging into my suite, Treuse? Surely you are not well," Chalmette replies with a warm smile.

The gentleman across from her keeps his sights steady at the table as if I never entered the room.

"We're playing Faro!" Chalmette says with a lilting chuckle. "Armando is teaching me!"

"Armando is losing," the gentleman answers gruffly, studying his cards.

"And you—you're okay?" I ask, staring back and forth between the two.

"Why, of course I am, Treuse!" Chalmette says, tossing three cards down to the table and moving the token. Armando mutters some curse in French, throwing his cards over his shoulder, obviously upset at his loss.

Jumping up from the table, Chalmette saunters toward me and rests her hands on my shoulders and smiles. Nervous energy rages through me as I search her face, trying to understand the cause at her now giddy state.

"Well, it's just as you've always said, sister. He really did come to rescue us! I am so happy, Chartreuse! Thank you for always taking care of me!" Pulling me in for a tight embrace, my thoughts scatter and I try to make sense of her words.

"Rescue us? Who? What?" I question as flickers of my encounter with both Mother and Monroe rage through my mind. Chalmette keeps her tight hold on me as she now peers over my shoulders, looking behind me.

Turning around I see him. *Dalcour*. For a moment everything with Monroe, mother, and thoughts of my sister giving herself away for the first time were the only thing holding my mind captive. Just that quickly, I forgot Dalcour was here.

Leaning on the doorframe with Scotty standing like a large shadow behind him, Dalcour smiles wide with his arms folded across his chest.

"I suppose had you let me finish back in your room you would've known that your sister is safe. I've had Armando keeping her company tonight," Dalcour says in a charming yet censuring tone.

"Armando lost all his money tonight," Armando seethes as he cleans the cards from the table and puts them in a small leather case.

"Oh stop your whining, old friend! You know you'll earn it all back and then some," Dalcour snips over my shoulder to Armando. Armando mutters something back in French, huffing as he does and Dalcour laughs.

"Wait—you two are friends?" I ask.

"Why, of course," Dalcour begins with a bright smile. Chalmette hugs me tight at the waist and her smile beams from ear to ear. Her eyes say it all, she's swooning. And rightfully so.

"I don't understand, Dalcour. Why are you here?" Although I've dreamt of this moment for what seems like my entire life, I need to hear him say it.

"You already know, Chartreuse. I am here to take you with me. Home."

Chapter Six

Home. My mind ponders the word. Not since my father's passing has any place truly felt like home. While my eldest sister Calida did all she could to maintain a sense of normalcy in our lives after father's death, even she couldn't bring back what we had lost.

"Yes, home, Chartreuse—for you and young Chalmette. Victoria is married, yes?"

I nod at his inquiry, but a part of me wants to tell him of her dire state. She needs rescuing just as much as Chalmette and me.

"Then gather any items of importance and we shall leave this horrid place at once!" The lightness of Dalcour's tone is botched when both Chalmette and I turn to find Mother standing at the door.

"I will not allow it!" She shouts. "You will not take my children from me!"

"We are not your children! And you have never been a mother!" Chalmette snaps back, charging toward Mother. I pull her back, stepping in front of her as I watch Monroe stumbling from behind.

"Neither of you is going anywhere with this demon nigger!" Monroe yells back.

No sooner than the words leave Monroe's mouth, Dalcour's hand is once more at his neck with his fangs protruding. His velvety skin shimmers in a reddened glow and I watch terror fill Chalmette's eyes and Armando is quickly at her side, turning her into his embrace. His protection of her seems almost parental and I wish I had time to consider how much they must have bonded in such a short time.

Plunging his way through the hallway with Monroe in his feverish grip, Dalcour hangs Monroe over the balcony. A few gasps echo through the hall but most are too enthralled with their own carnal dealings to notice Monroe dangling above them. Those who gathered in the hall scatter to their respective rooms and even those in the most drunken of state back away from Dalcour.

"I warned you!" Dalcour seethes, his tongue lashing against the sweaty skin at Monroe's neck.

"Take your hands off him!" Mother protests, but Scotty pulls her back as Dalcour's clawed fingers reach for her. A part of me is thankful for Scotty, although the look in his eyes tells me it is more for me than it is for her. Dalcour's black, soulless eyes gaze between both Mother and Monroe, snarling as his fangs extend beyond what I thought him capable, and I know he has every intention on ending them both.

And everything in me wishes he would.

Chalmette's cries behind me drown my desire to see them meet their demise. Gazing over my shoulder, Armando keeps her engulfed in the trenches of his hold, but her sobs puppeteer my heart strings.

"Please, no!" I plead to Dalcour and he growls, lashing his tongue once more at Monroe, holding him just shy above the chandelier. I know if he dropped him now all his entrails would spill onto the congregants below as soon as the sharp iron rods of the light fixture ripped through his ribcage. "Not like this!" I beg only for Chalmette not to witness such barbarity.

Stepping away from Chalmette and into the hallway, I look over to Scotty as he keeps a strong hold on my Mother. She gazes at me, and nothing but disdain mars her face as she pines for her foolish beloved. Why she constantly chooses him above her own flesh and blood is beyond me, but I will choose Chalmette before my own desire to see Dalcour end their lives.

"Please, my lord," I call once more to Dalcour. Slowly, his fangs retract, and he pulls Monroe back over the railing and holds him against the large wooden pillar at his left.

"Are you certain this is what you want, young one?" Dalcour questions over his shoulder without taking his eyes off either Monroe or Mother.

"Yes, I am certain," I say coming to his side, standing between both Monroe and my mother. "Their reckoning will come soon, my lord. And if fate should permit, I alone will see their reckoning at my hand." The vengeful sentiment of my heart meets my mother just as I intend. Mother's entire posture bucks at my words and sweat blazes her brow.

"So be it." Dalcour tosses Monroe into Mother's arms as Scotty pulls himself away from her. Even Scotty's lips curl in disgust at the sight of Monroe cradled in the arms of the one who birthed me.

Monroe's cries and curses remain muffled in the cavity of her hold, but she keeps her venomous sights set on me.

Looking at her, I have neither pity nor shame for her state. Her demise, as it were, is all of her own doing. Hers alone.

"Treuse!" Chalmette whines behind me as she races into my embrace. Armando allows a small smile to frame his otherwise stoic expression as he gives me a nod of what appears to be approval.

"It's okay, sister," I say, comforting Chalmette as she digs herself deeper into my hold. "Today is your last day in this place."

"Armando," Dalcour begins. "Quickly gather their belongings and meet us at the carriage. We'll need to make it to the other side of town before daylight breaks."

"Yes, my lord," Armando answers quickly, with a stifled bow.

"Only my father's dagger, please Scotty," I say to him as I see him scurrying to aid Armando.

"No, no Chartreuse! Don't forget these!" Chalmette whines, pulling out of my grip and runs to her vanity and grabs an emerald and black jewelry box. "Here are Calida's pearls!" she yelps as she races back to me, holding the long stringed set and tossing it around my neck.

"My word," Dalcour mutters under his breath as he stares at me like he'd seen a ghost.

"What?" I question, casting curious gazes between him and Chalmette.

"I knew you resembled her but seeing you now—in her pearls—you look just like Calida." Dalcour's muted words hang between us as he stares at me, his smile widening, and I see something at work behind his eyes I wish I could comprehend.

"And you'll end up just like her!" Mother yells from the hallway, slowly rising from the floor with Monroe in her arms. "Dead! You'll end up dead just like your sister! Better you be dead than my daughter! You're dead to me girl! Dead you hear?"

Like a Spanish bull, all I see is red. Racing toward her, everything in me wishes to toss her and her beloved over the railing. Consequences be damned.

"No, young one!" Dalcour's words halt my pacing as his swift motion carries him in front of my mother and Monroe in a flash. "Your time will come and when you are ready and should circumstances still necessitate it as so, you shall see their reckoning come. But not now. The hour grows late, and we must depart to safer ground," Dalcour says looking around the hall at the throws of white faces staring at him with murderous intent. Although I am sure he could best any who came his way, he knows too well the climate of the south and in his most subdued state, chooses not to tempt matters.

I could do anything I want, but it is he who would surely get the blame.

Looking up and down the hall, Dalcour stiffens his posture. His fangs release and eyes darken, but not quite as black as before.

"We are leaving now, and I implore each of you to return to your affairs of night. Know you have seen nothing, nor have you ever seen me. Should any of you seek to pursue me or my companions, know this: death will come on swift wings for you. And I shall most willingly usher you to death's door. Judging by your most immoral appetites I surely doubt there shall be any patron saints waiting to greet your arrival!"

At his words, the face of each man pales at the sight of Dalcour and every house girl watches me through both curious and fearful eyes.

Dalcour snaps his fingers and both Scotty and Armando follow quickly behind him as he trots down the staircase. Chalmette grips my hand in hers and we walk past our mother and Monroe and head down the steps. While most of the patronage seem somewhat unbothered by what occurred on the balcony floor, everyone seems to take note of Dalcour as he saunters through the saloon.

I am not sure how he made his way through without being seen before, but it is evident everyone sees him now. Crawley jumps up from the piano and races to the door, blocking Dalcour's exit. Looking over his shoulder, annoyance fills Dalcour's face, and I see the beginnings of his fangs lift beneath his incisors.

"Crawley!" I call in a cajoling tone, resting my hand on Dalcour's shoulder, hopeful to douse his rage and avoid a scene. "This is Lord Dalcour Marchand—from—London by way of New Orleans. Our families have long been acquainted," I say quickly.

Dalcour huffs, shaking my hand from his shoulder and exits abruptly with Scotty and Armando on his heels. Chalmette remains at my side and she looks around the saloon and her eyes grow wide as a lone tear drops to her cheek. It pains me knowing I must take my sister from the only home she has ever known, but I know it is for the best.

"Marchand-eh?" Crawley replies, raising a brow, swirling the chewing stick in his mouth. "And you're leaving? For good? On your own accord?"

"Yes, Crawley. For good and our own accord. Farewell, my friend," I say with a small peck on his cheek. He pats my head and holds the door open for me and Chalmette as we exit.

Just as the doors open, I hear my name from behind and the pace of my heart quickens. Releasing Chalmette's hand, I nod for her to continue as I turn to find Marius holding a small barrel of port behind me. He drops it and looks around the hall bewildered.

"Chartreuse?" He says my name with inquiry. "What—what's going on? Where are you going?" Peering over my shoulder, Marius looks between the cracked door Crawley holds open and his eyes spot Armando helping Chalmette into the carriage.

"I am sorry, Marius. This is goodbye," I say quickly, turning on my heel. I need to get away from him before the waterworks begin.

"Goodbye? I don't understand, Chartreuse. Tonight was our only hello."

I had hoped—well, tonight was the first time you'd ever seen me. I had hoped—that perhaps we could—"

"I am sorry, Marius. We cannot. *There is no we*," I stutter my words, rushing out the door. Pulling my arm from behind, Marius stops my movement and lifts my now waterlogged chin so I can meet his gaze.

"Who? Who, Chartreuse is taking you from me? And so soon," he asks, his eyes now forming glassy pools.

"Long lost family." I lie but I can think of no better way to explain. Crawley's brow raises at my pretense, but he turns his face away from us, still holding the door open. "I must go now. It's for Chalmette. I cannot allow this to become her fate," I continue, gesturing toward the saloon.

"I suppose I understand," Marius begins, his countenance downcast. "Will I ever see you again? I mean—will you at least return to visit your mother?"

At the mention of her and the thought of her disgusting deeds tonight, I work to swallow the hard knot in my throat. I can't tell him the truth because he deserves better.

"Chartreuse!" I hear Dalcour call my name from behind.

"I am sorry, Marius, but I must go," I say turning away from him. Once more he pulls my arm, but this time he pulls me into his hold and crushes his mouth to mine.

This is my first kiss.

My first real kiss, that is.

Twenty-seven years and countless tippers over the last decade and *this* is my first kiss. A farewell kiss. Salty tears mesh between our mouths and I can't distinguish his between my own. His sweet tongue wraps mine and the hint of rum punch and berry cobbler tickle my tastebuds. Holding my face between his palms, everything about his kiss is all encompassing.

All my fears, doubt, and the pain of both my tortured past and present state melt away in his grip.

As he kisses me, I recount the many days we passed one another or shared a laugh and I never saw him as I do now. How could I have missed him? He's always perched himself near my suite, even though his room was in the cellar. He made sure the cooks kept the best in the kitchen for me and ensured Scotty gave me my meals after my evening entertaining adjourned. Every morning he greeted me with a warm smile and shared the morning news.

He has always been there.

And now whatever we could have is gone already. I cannot stay in this place. I will not keep my sister here for Marius or any man.

I will not become my mother.

"I've always wanted to do that," he sweetly whispers, forcing a smile. His gaze is tender as he regards me, but it hurts more seeing the brokenness in his eyes.

"I wish you would have done that sooner," I whisper back, pressing my face into his palm.

"Madame Chartreuse," Armando calls behind me. "I am afraid we must hasten, lest we catch the sun."

Pulling my face from his hands, I take Marius' hand in mine as he escorts me down the steps.

"Promise me something, Marius," I say, looking up at him and trailing my hand over his face. "Don't let this place become your home. Build your own. You are better than Monroe. You always have been. Promise me you will leave this place," I demand in a tone stronger than I intend.

"I promise, Chartreuse. I will build something for us," Marius replies, planting a soft kiss on my wrist as he and Scotty help me in the carriage.

"No, Marius. Build it for you. *There is no us*," I answer resolutely. I hate the words coming from my mouth, but it is the only truth I can bare to him tonight. We can never be. Marius steps back at my sentiment and he turns away from Scotty, quickly wiping the tear from his face and makes his way back up the saloon stairs where he and Crawley enter.

Scotty looks up at me in the carriage and I marvel at the sight of the gentle giant who has ever been my companion and protector. "If only there was room for me," he says staring inside the cabin, his eyes tender as he shifts his gaze back to me.

"I know, my friend," I begin, patting his bulking shoulders. "Maybe I'll get you on my next trip," I answer in jest.

"Perhaps," he replies, with his head down. "But I didn't quite mean the carriage, poppet." Scotty's admission breaks me as he swats the back of the horse and backs away.

Tears flood my face as I witness yet another broken heart at my doing. This time, Chalmette holds me in her arms as thoughts of both Scotty and Marius rip my heart in two. Chalmette hums a familiar melody as she strums her hands through my hair as the carriage pulls away from the saloon. I faintly think I hear my name called in the distance, but I keep my face planted in her embrace.

For years, I've dreamt of nothing but leaving this place. Now the day has come, and I never thought leaving would hurt so much.

Chapter Seven

A loud knocking at the door jolts me awake in a panic. Bewildered, I stare around the room and try to gather my senses, but I cannot. My mind is still rummaging about with haunting nightmares too chilling to tell and too painful to recount.

Dark, looming thoughts riddle through me as I try to make sense of my bearings and note my surroundings. Gripping the cottony soft blue duvet at my chin, I look around the room and try to establish some familiarity, but I cannot. There is nothing faintly familiar about this place.

Instead of the stench of pipe cigars and port, the smell of freshly baked bread and the sizzling crackle of what I make to believe is salted pork, waft past my nostrils and my stomach grumbles in response. Although all signs point toward breakfast, the darkness surrounding me gives no quarter to the sun's light.

Thickly drawn curtains hang just inches from the crown molding, lengthening long enough to sweep the floor. The dark gray pattern is so thick, I am certain not even the sun's rays can permeate the suite. The pillowy soft bedding is comforting to the touch, but the frame of the bed is larger than one I've ever known, swallowing my petite frame in its center. I can't help imagining if one were to sleep on a cloud, this bedding should mirror its likeness.

Slowly, my eyes adjust to the darkness and even in such a dim view, I see this room is vastly different from my suite in the saloon. Flickering images of my tussle with Monroe and my raging with Mother flood my memory and then my mind forms a sharper image. Dalcour Marchand. Thoughts of him rescuing me from the makings of what sought to be my demise, settle my gnawing ire.

But there is one more memory. Marius. My heart warms with delight as I reminisce on the sweetness of our kiss and my eyes instantly glass knowing it was likely our last. Still, my heart rejoices that amid such despair the fates would grant me at least a modicum of happiness. And for that, I'll forever be thankful.

As my mind continues to replay the events of last night, I jump out the bed, planting my feet hard on the floor when my hand searches the bed, I notice my beloved sister is nowhere to be found. I land hard on the wood floor and the pacing of my heart quickens as the knock on the door ceases and I see the golden doorknob slowly turns.

The door opens and the bright light from outside my suite is almost blinding. Before I have a chance for my eyes to adjust to the new light invading my space, I hear a lilting chuckle and a hearty laugh break through, lessening my angst.

"You see, Armando, I told you she would be up. My sister never sleeps too late," I hear Chalmette giggle as I watch her shadowy form saunter into the suite.

"Well, she is certainly up, but why is she standing still in the dark? And why is she looking at us like she's about to strike," Armando quips, carrying a large metal serving tray.

"I agree, Armando. It is rather dark in here, sister," Chalmette laughs once more as she goes to the curtains and draws back one side.

Still trying to make sense of it all, I turn about and toss on a robe I see at the foot of the bed. Chalmette is all smiles as the sun reveals her lovely round face as she posts near the window. Her smile widens from ear to ear as Armando sets the tray of food at my bedside. He barely looks at me as he does but shuffles quickly to the threshold.

"I will leave you two now. I would say enjoy your breakfast, but its way past the hour. Help yourself to whatever you like in the wardrobe after you have eaten and washed. Lord Marchand will be up from his rest shortly. Madame Chartreuse, he will be expecting you in the parlor. I shall keep the company of young Chalmette in the study." Armando is out of the room before either my sister or I have an opportunity to respond.

"I guess Armando isn't much of a morning person," I mutter while examining the array of food on the tray.

"Morning? Please, it's well into the afternoon, missy! You slept the morning away. Besides, he's only huffy because I beat him again. He honestly thought he could win his money back from last night," Chalmette laughs, dipping a biscuit into the small saucer of jam and stuffing it into her mouth. "But trust me, he's actually quite friendly," she adds through full cheeks.

"I see, you two have made fast friends. Anyway, why did you let me sleep so long? After Dalcour said we'd rest the night in one of his itinerant estates, all I recall is falling fast asleep," I respond as I try to recount the details of the evening.

"We both did. But when I awoke, I just had to tour the grounds. This place is rather grand, Chartreuse! I've never seen anything like it!" Chalmette's eyes dance as she speaks, and I can tell she's quite impressed. While I know I should be equally ecstatic, I am not.

Memories of Dalcour's otherworldly face stir the core of me. I know what he is. Vampire. In all my rage toward both Monroe and Mother, I gave little thought that perhaps bringing Chalmette around Dalcour is simply trading one monster for another.

Sure, I have romanticized him rescuing us to her countless times over the years, a part of me never thought the day would come. Now that it is here, I fear I must still protect her from yet another threat. One even more dangerous.

Clearly, I did not think this through.

"Chalmette, sister, you should not have left this room without me! Much less traipsing through this estate as though it were our home. It is not!" I snap as thoughts of Dalcour's venomous fangs flicker through my mind.

"But I—I thought you said," she stutters in response, dropping her biscuit back onto the tray.

"Look, sister, I know what I said, but please understand, you cannot do that again!"

It's not safe! As much as I want to utter the words, I do not.

Chalmette gazes at me, her wide, doe-eyes filled with both shock and fear. I never meant to scare her, but I will not risk her safety by playing down the possibility of our peril in the hands of Dalcour Marchand. And for as much as I hate it to be true, there is some truth to Mother's words. We lost Calida as a result of her dealings with Dalcour's brother Decaux.

I do not wish to lose another sister.

"The ham is good," Chalmette says in a restrained tone as she nestles into a parlor chair adjacent to the window. She's mad at me. Thankfully, Chalmette is good at not sulking. No matter how difficult things get, she is strong-willed and refuses to let circumstances or people make her feel small. I love that about her. "Try some." Her tone is far more commanding than normal, but I know it's just her way of moving past this awkward place.

Slicing a crisp corner, I fork the meat in my mouth and smile. Despite all the foolery that had become our lives, my sister and I have always relished in a well-cooked meal. Over the years, we would imagine ourselves in fancy establishments, enjoying the most decadent of courses without regret. Mother, however, always chided our attempts of indulgence, fearful we'd fatten. I suppose doing so made us cherish mealtimes all the more.

"It is delicious," I mumble between chews, stuffing another portion into my already full cheeks.

"No need to force it, Treuse! There's more!" Chalmette teases, tossing a linen napkin at my face. "Wipe your dribble," she laughs.

"I'll do just that," I quickly reply, wiping my mouth and throwing the napkin back at her. She smiles as I do, and my heart is thankful knowing all is well between us once more.

Chapter Eight

After Chalmette and I freshen up and gather attire from the wardrobe as Armando suggested, we make our way downstairs. Although I am still bothered my sister toured the grounds without me, I do enjoy hearing her recount Armando's disclosure of the rare antiquities and paintings Dalcour has arrayed throughout the estate.

I am surprised to learn Dalcour has such an affinity for antiques and art. It's strange to think of vampires enjoying such human things.

I have always had an eye for fine art. Calida always did well to pique my interest in such things, but after her loss, Mother did all she could to deter me away from it.

A tall, crystal vase catches my attention as we walk down the long marble floor near the foyer. "Auriferous sand!" I gasp as the twinkling, gold iridescence shimmers through the vase.

"Au-what?" Chalmette questions, as she glances back and forth at me and the vase, confused.

"Rare gold deposits found in sand," I whisper back with my eyes still locked on the shimmering wonder before me.

"Ah, so you're much more like Calida than I thought," I hear Dalcour's lush tone call from behind us. His voice startles me, and I almost fall, turning on my heel to see his bright smile beaming back at us. "Continue, Chartreuse. What else do you know about these curious golden sands?"

Trying to recount my learnings from one of the books Marius dropped off at my room, I remember a few of the things I read about various minerals. "I don't know much, I'm afraid. But I do believe some of the gold we use today was collected from auriferous sand. Am I correct?" I ask.

"Yes, young one. You are quite astute it would appear. Very learned, much like Calida, indeed," Dalcour replies, rubbing his chin in apparent interest. His eyes dance once again like they did last night, and I wish I knew what musings were happening behind the crimson ring of his almond-shaped eyes.

"Not quite so much, my lord," I answer dutifully. I am nowhere as educated as Calida.

Dalcour laughs at my sentiment and the heartiness of it reverberates throughout the foyer. A giddy, girlish smile blushes across my sister's face and I inwardly groan knowing she's quite enamored by his charms.

"Well, my dear," Armando begins, now appearing suddenly at Dalcour's side. "It's time we let the adults converse. You and I shall retire to the study." Armando saunters slowly across the foyer, extending his hand to Chalmette and she smiles and places her petite palm in his.

"Now dear Armando, I hope you're not planning to regain your earnings." Chalmette gazes over her shoulder, winking at me as the two ambles down the hallway.

"No, my lady Armando does not wish to give anymore of his money to you. I haven't nor the heart or the means to do so," he replies with a witty chuckle. Chalmette rests her head on his shoulder and waves at me as they exit.

Smiling in return, I am somewhat comforted in the growing kinship between my sister and Dalcour's attendant. Even though he comes across stoic, his eyes tell of an almost fatherly tenderness my sister has never known. For as brief a time it was, at least I have fond memories of my father. Chalmette, on the other hand, never knew hers.

"Armando always wanted a daughter," Dalcour says, breaking my musing.

"I'm sorry, my lord?"

"A daughter. I think when he sees her, she reminds him of the daughter he always wanted."

"Oh," I say as I watch Armando lead Chalmette to the back open study. Pointing to a walnut bookcase, filled from top to bottom with books, Armando's arm waves about as Chalmette pulls books from the casing, her love for reading showing. "So, does he only have sons?"

"No, he doesn't have any children. In fact, he always said he never wanted boys. I think looking after me and Decaux all these years has been exhausting enough. After all the trouble we've given him, he believes girls would be an improvement," Dalcour replies with another hearty laugh.

"Did he marry? Is he a widower? Could they not have children?" My inquiry rushes out of my mouth as I keep my sights on my sister and Armando, my curiosity gnawing.

Dalcour circles me, regaining my attention and blocking my view of Chalmette and Armando. "No, Chartreuse," he begins, narrowing his eyes and searching my face. "Bulwarks do not marry, nor do they have children."

"Bul—what?" I mutter, gazing at Dalcour, once more confused. Dalcour stares back at me, frowning slightly as he rubs his jaw.

"Walk with me," he gently demands, opening his arm and allowing room for mine to loop in his. I do as he instructs, and he leads us down a narrow and dark hallway with a slender black door. Taking a large brass key from his side pocket, he unlocks the door and nods his head, gesturing for me to enter.

Lighting two oil lamps on the wall, I now see a small office with more books, a desk, and side chairs.

"Please sit," he says quietly, shutting the door behind him.

Looking around the quaint space, the pacing of my heart quickens, and I am unsure why being alone with him makes me fret. With Mother's hauntingly damning sentiment hanging over me, I can't help worrying I've made the wrong decision. Even more, I fear I've brought Chalmette along for the ride.

Dalcour is seated at his desk faster than my eyes can blink and I gulp a heap of air as thoughts of his otherworldliness teases the timidity building within me.

"Do you fear me?" Dalcour says pointedly, as he cups his hands together on a large leather-bound book on his desk.

"Yes." My answer escapes my mouth before I could form a lie.

"I'm glad you're being honest with me, Chartreuse. But let me assure you, I wish you no ill."

"And what of Chalmette?" I question. In this moment I care more for her safety than my own.

"Now, therein lies my conundrum," Dalcour answers with a crooked smile that worries me.

"How so, my lord?" I do my best and work hard to remain dutiful, but inwardly know if he says the wrong thing, I will use all of my might to end him.

Dalcour laughs at my words, leaning back into his chair and tosses his arms behind his head, holding steady at the back of his neck.

"Well, one of the last letters your mother wrote explained that Victoria had left to be married. Yet, not once had she mentioned your sister. It was not until I arrived last night I understood who she was."

Confusion grips me once more and what was once building in me is crushing my resolve to be the protective eldest sister. "I'm confused." My words are hardly above a whisper, but I know he hears me.

"As I began to tell you last night, I came for you."

"For me?"

"Why, yes, young one. Once I returned from my dealings in Washington and London to finally put an end to the ocean transport of Africans to the Americas—"

"What? Wait a minute—you had something to do with that?"

"Ha! Ha! Dear one, you'll find I've had my hand in all things civility as of late but that is beside the point," Dalcour wittingly replies with another sly smile that meets his eyes and I feel myself just as charmed by his vices as my sister. "As I was saying, I looked through the letters I'd missed during my departure and noticed I'd received none from Catherine. At first, I thought perhaps it was a good sign that the man she was with was doing his part. That is, until an old post of a gorgeous woman headlining a gentleman's saloon caught my eye."

"Oh my! I didn't know the postings of Chalmette reached New Orleans so fast," I ponder.

"It didn't," he answers in a flat tone. Looking up at him, his eyes narrowed eyes lock with mine and a deep thread of concern inverts his brow to his now scrunched nose.

"I'm sorry, my lord, I don't understand."

"Here is the posting that snatched my attention." Just then, Dalcour slams a black and white posting of me on the table. Taking the paper in my hand, quivering dread builds once again within me.

Jumping up from the table a thousand questions plague my mind.

Is he no different than Monroe?

Did I truly trade one monster for another?

Did he take me to himself so that he alone could have me?

My breathing quickens and I feel the small room closing in around me. Vertigo sets in and I can hardly judge the distance of the exit from my hand. I need to get out of here!

I can't believe all these years I thought of him to be my rescuer when he is no different than Monroe—just as Mother said!

"I am so sorry, Chartreuse." Dalcour's whispered words surprise me. My pacing heartbeat slows as I buckle at my knees, attempting to stop the room from spinning around me. Wrapping his large arms around my back, I am surprised to find him now at my side. "Please sit, young one. I did not mean to upset you," he says softly, now sitting at the seat at my side.

Taking a small leather sack at his hip, he taps my shoulder, smiling as I lift my face to his. "Here drink this," he demands. "It's not water but I was able to stow away a few vats of Monroe's rum punch last night. Hopefully, it will settle your nerves."

Laughing, I am surprised to learn he stole from the saloon. *Serves him right,* I think to myself.

"Serves him right, indeed!" Dalcour repeats my hidden thoughts, and I laugh again. I suppose we were both thinking the same thing. Taking my hand in his, Dalcour grips it tight and a warm smile crosses his face as he gazes at me. "When I saw your face on that posting, I felt responsible for allowing you to come to such a state."

"It's not your fault," I begin, but he loosens my hand, quickly rising up from his seat and paces back to his desk. Standing behind his chair, he grips the wood railing, squeezing it tight as he clinches his jaw.

"Had I not been on a campaign to aid in rectifying these atrocities here in the Americas perhaps I could have maintained my attention on matters that concerned you and your family. I promised you I would—and I have never gone back on my word. So when I saw your face—well at first, I almost thought it was Calida—I was flabbergasted! I didn't know whether Catherine had died, and you were doing all you could to preserve yourself or if someone had taken you captive. All I knew was I had to come for you!"

"As you said you would," I whisper back as a well of tears flood my face.

"Yes, young one, just as I said." Dalcour's tender smile is almost paternal as he looks at me and it slowly becomes certain, he is not Monroe. Breaking our eyes from locking further, he turns toward his bookcase and fumbles through it before turning back to me with his normal casual grin. Thrusting his hands in his pockets, he leans against the shelves and continues. "Like I said, I had every intention of coming to save you from ruin. I had no idea whether Catherine lived nor did I care at this point. The plan was clear from the beginning, Armando would escort you to your suite just as he did Chalmette, and then I'd appear, and we would take things from there. However, when I arrived, I found postings near the saloon of a young girl who bore your resemblance."

"That's when you learned of Chalmette?"

"Yes. And although I wasn't sure of everything, it wasn't until I saw how you looked after the girl that I knew she was more than your kin or friend. It was clear to me that any plan I had would be for naught if I didn't plan on including her."

"Well then, my lord your assumption was correct."

"Yes, my dear. What I hadn't planned for was just how low Catherine had sunken with her beloved buffoon. Her depravity was quite unexpected. Sure, I knew her to be in a state of despair—but to allow such a state to become of her own flesh and blood is beyond me. There is no way I could just stand by. Even if I had to drag you out kicking and screaming, my dear, I would have taken you far from that place."

Dalcour's words are resolute as he speaks, and I believe every word. In fact, I appreciate it. I know too well what it feels like to be taken against my will, but my heart leaps knowing his intent is, and has always been to rescue me from a place certain to be my undoing.

"I suppose I should be thanking you," I say quietly.

"There's no need, my dear. However, there is still the issue of young Chalmette."

"What issue, my lord?" Curiosity fills my heart again, but after knowing he only wants the best for us, the budding fear within me has resigned.

"My plans for you—well, for us really do not quite include your very young sister."

"Your plans for me? For us?" Heaving another gulp of air, I slowly wonder what he could mean. As attractive as he is, I know he could have any woman he wants. And for as ruined as I am, I doubt he wants me. Even more, I am not interested in him in that way. I've never thought of him as so.

Although, I can surely be persuaded—perhaps even with a little kicking and screaming. Abandoned thoughts cloud my mind as the intrigue of it all swarms inside me.

"I wanted to give you a job, Chartreuse," Dalcour announces, forcefully breaking through my burgeoning interest. His eyes narrow as he gazes at me and restrains a frown. Swallowing the thick air in my throat, I try not to reveal just how quickly my heart plummeted. Dalcour's face softens and he smiles wide before pulling his chair out from under his desk and plops into it.

"A job?" I question.

"Yes, as my curator!" He exclaims with an almost boyish excitement. "That's why I was so excited when you identified the auriferous sand. I must admit I was quite impressed."

"I don't understand. Do you own a gallery or something like that?"

"Or *something* is precisely correct!" Dalcour's eyes beam as he speaks, rubbing his hands together. As he does, everything in me knows the *something* he wants from me is more than I currently comprehend.

Chapter Nine

"**S**o it's an art gallery for vampires?" I would almost feel silly uttering such things if I were not looking into the face of the most renowned vampire this side of Louisiana.

Dalcour breaks out in his typical hearty laugh and shakes his head, knowing everything he's said for the past half hour is practically lost on me. "Well, not quite for vampires but to help vampires. As I have said, I'm on a campaign for civility, if you will, and that also includes those in the supernatural world. Much like you, there are humans who know of the existence of my kind and I want to capitalize on that knowledge. Creating a faction of humans of nobility—those who keep our secrets, help fund our needs and resources— we pledge to keep safe. The fine art we collect will serve as collateral and to also fund our activities over time. Like me, most supernaturals have access to rare findings like the auriferous sand—and most mortals are willing to pay handsomely for it. We'll also need to curate for things like blood banks and find donors where possible."

"Oh my," I say as he continues his rant. Now it becomes clear to me.

"This is why I don't think it's best to make your young sister privy to such things," Dalcour states.

"I couldn't agree more," I answer as Dalcour once more takes the words straight from my mouth.

"So are you up for the challenge?"

"Well, it all sounds exciting—at least I think so—but why me? I'm human. If this is for supernaturals, shouldn't you ask someone who is supernatural. Like Armando, for instance. I mean he is a Bul—whatever you called him before," I reply.

"He is a Bulwark."

"Precisely! And until now, I had no idea that was even a thing—or a person—or whatever he is!"

"I understand. I suppose I am not being clear. I want to do something I have never thought to do. I would like to sire you, young one."

My breath hitches at Dalcour's revelation. I can't believe what he is asking me. Even more, I cannot fathom why he is asking me. *I'm nothing special.*

Then again, that may be the reason altogether. Since I am already a ruined woman what difference would becoming a vampire make?

"I know this is quite unexpected—even for me, I must admit," Dalcour begins, breaking my puzzling thoughts. "Never did I think I would want to sire someone, but when I saw you last night it became clear."

"What did you see, my lord?"

"I saw you fight. For your sister. For yourself. I saw a woman who would no longer allow herself to be controlled."

"You saw all of that—*in me?*" Looking up at Dalcour, I shrink in his grand presence. While I have never considered myself weak, the fact someone of his grandeur would see strength in me is humbling.

"Yes, young one, I did. But I also saw myself in you. I saw how my actions led you to such a dire state that you had to fend for yourself. And I never want you to be in such a position again," Dalcour adds in an almost sulking tone.

"No, my lord, none of this is your fault. This is all Catherine. And Monroe. Not you," I counter, rising to my feet.

"Ah! There's the fire I saw last night. Still, I must confess my trespass. For if I had not forced my brother to come to New Orleans, he would not have fallen for your sister, Calida. At her passing, it was his broken heart that pronounced countless deaths in the Great Fire. Without Calida, your mother fell into disrepair, which led both you and your sisters into such a destitute state. And it is all those things, dear one, that burden my heart."

Tears flood my face once more at Dalcour's admission. Although I do not blame him for the tragedy that has become my life, the weight of it all shatters what remains of my heart.

Rounding the corner of his desk, Dalcour kneels beside me, taking my hand in his. Offering me his handkerchief, he smiles wide, and I am almost lost in the warming lure of his gaze. "This is why I make such an offer to you, young one. I know you are strong, but I wish to make you stronger. I know you can fight, but I want to make you impenetrable. Most of all, I make it my promise to you that Calida's fate shall never be your own. I will do for you what should have been done for her."

I am speechless as he speaks. While I suspected he had plans for me, I never imagined such a gesture.

"But it must be your choice," Dalcour begins, in a throaty tone darker than before as he stands back to his feet. "I will do for you what was never done for me." Looking up at him, I see a flash of hurt grimace his countenance. "I was born into my fate but you, my dear one, will have a choice. If you should decide this will not be your fate, then so be it. I will send you off, along with your sister, grant you an expense large enough that you will never have a need. But if you say yes, you will say farewell to your sister for a time—only until I teach you to tame your bloodlust. After that time, you will be stronger and more fierce than ever. And then, and only then will you have the power to do what you have always wanted."

"What is that my lord?"

"Protect your sister. And protect yourself."

My posture stiffens as he speaks, and it is though his words cling to my soul. He is right. I want that power. I never want to be at the whim of another ever again. Good people like my father and Calida perish. While those like Monroe and Mother are left to abuse and mistreat the weak.

I am not weak.

Nor shall I ever be again.

"Yes, my lord. I want that." The words spit like fire from my lips. A knowing smile grazes Dalcour's face as he folds his arms at his chest, and I see the ring of crimson dance once more behind his eyes. Rubbing the stubble along his jaw, a crumpled smile forms along his face and he laughs again, softening his posture.

"Well then, young one, I ask you once more. What shall we do with your sister?"

Nervous jitters run up and down my spine and I can't believe I've agreed to become a vampire so fast. But I know such an offer from Dalcour Marchand will not come around twice. Had I not been decisive, he would surely send me away with no other means to protect myself and my sister than money.

I desire more than money.

I want power.

Being a mere human, yet alone a woman, gives me no power in this world. Being a vampire, however, gives me the kind of power to assure me I shall never be at the whim of another ever again.

"Chartreuse?" Dalcour questions once more, breaking me from my musing.

"My lord?" I tepidly respond, trying to recall his earlier inquiry.

"Chalmette. What shall we do with her?"

"Oh, yes. I'm sorry, my mind wandered. Well, I'd like to talk with her first if you don't mind. There was a lad who had shown interest toward marriage for her. Of course Mother and Monroe saw to it that the two would never be—but perhaps he may still be interested. That is, of course, if my sister desires to be with him. If not, I should like to send her to school. She's never had a formal education."

"I see," he answers, now somewhat distracted as he pulls his pocket watch from his lapel. "Well, do check with her and see what she would like to do. But I do caution that you should not expose our plans of your transformation. At least not yet."

"Of course, my lord," I reply quickly, rising from my seat, hopeful to regain his attention.

"This young man," he begins, shuffling through the notebooks on his desk. He huffs loud as he looks around his office with a slight air of irritation. "Who is he? Is he of good breeding? What do you know of him?"

Staring around the room, I let my eyes follow his gaze, curious as to what is averting his attention.

"His name is Claudius DeVeaux. His father, Corbin, is the holder of the—"

"Corbin DeVeaux!" Dalcour says, flattening his palm on a stack of books as he stares up at me. Once more, his eyes dance and I sense something is calculating behind his otherwise entrancing gaze. "Yes, I know him well. He runs the leading Post. I dare say I am almost impressed. How did young Chalmette warrant the interest of such a worldly one as the son of Corbin DeVeaux? Surely, he has never stepped foot into the saloon as a tipper! DeVeaux is too haughty and thinks much more of himself than he should to ever allow such a thing."

"Honestly, that is why I want to speak with my sister. I was quite taken aback by his interest in her. I only knew Claudius to be nothing more than a paper boy. Apparently, he is much more."

"That he is!" Dalcour's voice resounds brightly and his face beams from ear to ear with interest. "Well then, I'll let you get on with your discussions with your sister. And do not worry about young Claudius. If your sister wishes to marry him, I shall see it as such."

"Thank you, my lord. But it may be quite a difficult task. At last we spoke, Corbin told us should Chalmette be ruined by a man, he would not allow the two to marry. Even though we both know nothing happened between her and Armando, I am sure that fool Monroe spread the news of her ruin to all who would listen. Surely, Claudius won't take her back."

My chin falls as I speak, and I realize my dark desires of being a vampire may be short lived. If Chalmette is denied by Claudius again, how can I just send her off to school in order to sate my own needs? I will not vacate her should her heart be broken. But if she doesn't want to marry him, then perhaps she will not be opposed to the idea of an education.

Either way, I know the decision will not be easy.

"Young one," Dalcour whispers, now at my side and lifting my chin to meet his tender gaze. "Do not worry about DeVeaux. If your sister wants Claudius, I shall see it done. My daughter, I make it my pledge to you it shall be done." Holding my face in his large palm, his eyes soften as he stares at me. It is the same look he gave on the day he promised to return to me twenty years ago. Even more, the sincerity of his eyes reminds me of the one my heart misses most. My father.

"Daughter?" I mumble almost incoherently as another stream of tears flood my face once more at his sentiment.

Not once in the last twenty years has such a word been uttered with such sincerity about me. And my, has my soul longed to hear it. Hearing it now, it's as though a repair is made to my once cast-aside and broken heart.

"Yes, young one. I've never wanted to sire anyone before because I knew the responsibility was akin to parentage. But now, here with you, I know it is why I had to come back. *You are only the beginning.* Now go, or Armando will have my head if I don't find his amethyst stone. Far be it from me that I be the reason he reverts to his otherwise gargoyle state," Dalcour mutters his final phrase as he shuffles around his office.

I want to linger and ask the meaning of his words, but I know I must speak with Chalmette.

Opening the door to leave, I look over my shoulder only to see Dalcour's hand shine with a bright blue iridescent glow as he whispers words in an unknown tongue. Shy and fearful, I rush out of his office, slamming the door behind me. Buckling slightly at my knees, I work to catch my breath. How I can be both intrigued and frightened at the sight of him is almost too tormenting to ponder.

Everything about Dalcour Marchand is hauntingly beautiful. And if I am now to be his daughter, I look forward to my new haunting form with great delight.

Chapter Ten

"Chalmette!" I shout her name as I race through the hall.

"Yes, sister," she calls back to me and I turn about, wondering where she is as her voice seems to echo through the large marble and oak hallway. I can't help inwardly wonder how my soon-to-be vampire senses would likely detect her better than my current frail mortal sensibilities.

Rushing to the back parlor, I see Chalmette and Armando seated at a small table drinking tea.

"Are you well, Treuse?" Chalmette questions, frowning as she sips her tea. "Why are you running through the estate like a derby?"

"Someone obviously has no care for civilities such as teatime, I see," Armando snips as he stirs a tiny silver spoon in his porcelain teacup, blowing it as he does.

Gazing up at the grandfather clock in the corner of the room, I am shocked to see how late in the afternoon it is. I obviously slept longer than I thought.

"I am sorry to interrupt but I need to speak with my sister," I say as Chalmette chuckles at Armando's reprimand. "Alone." I am not amused, and the annoyance of my tone sullies their shared moment.

"Armando knows when Armando is not wanted," he quips, quickly rising from his seat. He's still stirring his cup as he walks away but he turns and nods with a quaint smile to me. For a moment I thought he didn't like me as much as Chalmette, but even in the brief way his smile meets his eyes, I know this is not the case. I think he enjoys giving me a hard time.

"So what did you want, sister?" Chalmette asks, her apparent irritation with me showing.

"I suppose I should ask why my young sister fancies herself to be proper before old, brutish men."

"He is not brutish. He is debonair. Besides, it is nice to be with someone who'd rather teach me of the civility of the world. It's quite a turn of pages from any lessons either Monroe or Mother could ever give," Chalmette replies, while loudly slurping the remaining tea from her cup.

"Well, then he should have taught you that ladies of dignity do not slurp!" I feign my rebuke with a covered chuckle. Chalmette's shoulders relax and she smiles back at me and laughs.

"I reckon I have much to learn about being a lady, dear sister," Chalmette replies with another chuckle.

"No, my sister. You are quite the lady already. Never let anyone tell you different." Once more, my voice is stern, but only to ensure she hears me loud and clear. I'll not stand to hear Chalmette disparage herself. At least not in my presence.

Staring hard at me, Chalmette slowly places her teacup on the wooden tabletop yet still keeps her sights on me. "What's wrong, Chartreuse? What happened? Has Mother and Monroe come here to get us?"

"No, no, sister!" I snap back, trying hard to rein the frenzy I see building within her. "It is nothing of the sort. Quite the contrary, actually."

"Oh?" Chalmette questions, her face still a cloud of worry. "I—I just thought—"

"No, dear sister, there is absolutely nothing *for you* to worry about."

"*Nothing for me?* But what about *you?* Please tell me what is going on, Chartreuse!" Searching my face, she grabs my wrists as the weight of her sweaty palms tell me all I need to know of her growing angst.

"First, let me ask you a question. And, please, Chalmette, I need you to answer me honestly," I begin.

"Anything, sister. Now, let's hear it."

Pulling slowly out of her grip, I sit in the adjacent parlor chair. She smiles as I do, pushing her cup away from the edge of the table, allowing me space to rest my arms. "You're always so gracious, sister."

"What do you mean?" she replies, still smiling up at me.

"It's the little things. Gestures. It is how you move the teacup aside, to make space for me. Holding me in all my tearful mess as we left the saloon. You are always doing things like that, sister and I love you for it. And though I am the eldest of us two, so often you find ways to look after me."

"Why, of course, Chartreuse. We are sisters. That is what one does for her sister. Besides no one deserves it more than you."

"While that may be—and believe me when I say I appreciate it—this must stop." The words choke out of my mouth and I almost hate to utter such things. But I have no choice.

"What are you talking about, sister?"

"I am talking about Claudius DeVeaux, sister!" My tone is more brash than I intended, but as Chalmette jolts back in her seat, I know I've hit my point dead on.

"Claudius? What does any of this have to do with him? Why are you bringing him up?" Chalmette lashes back, her eyes pooling with tears.

"I do so, sister because you never did. Why did I never learn of your affection for him? Or him for you? Why did I see you in such a disconsolate state after Monroe denied his proposal?"

Quickly rising from her seat with enough force to push the seat back to the wall, Chalmette's face grows stark red and her eyes singe with fury. Her breathing heaves as she opens her mouth to speak. "Why? You dare ask, why! Now? Oh, sister, you have some nerve!"

"Yes, my nerve is diffident sister! That I know! Now tell me! Do you care for Claudius?"

"What does it matter? And what care you if I should have affection for him?"

"I care because you are my sister, Chalmette. Whatever is important to you is equally—if not more, important to me."

At my words, Chalmette's posture softens as she stares at me and a stream of tears trail her perfectly round face. "It doesn't matter," she shrugs, clasping her own wrists and looking up at the ceiling trying to force away her tears.

"It matters to me," I whisper back, turning her chin to meet my face.

"Yes, I do—or I did care for him, sister," she cries.

"Why didn't you tell me?"

"Because telling you meant you stirring another fight for me with Monroe and Mother. I knew had I told you, there would be no stopping you in getting me from under the house rules of Monroe. You would sacrifice yourself for me—once again. I couldn't let that happen."

"Is that what you think I would've done?"

"It is what you would do, Chartreuse. It is what you did when Monroe tried to take me."

She is right. Had I known, I would have worked to get her to Claudius sooner.

"When DeLuca heard what Monroe tried to do, he convinced Claudius to make an appeal. Of course, I never thought it would work. But for a moment, I had hope—then it was ripped away from me yet again."

"So DeLuca knew?"

Exhaling, Chalmette plops back down into her seat and blows out enough air to send her curls flying away from her face. "It wasn't on purpose, sister. He caught us together—not in that kind of way—but he saw Claudius bring me a flower. I asked him not to tell you. Please do not be upset with DeLuca. It was all me."

Drawing my face into a hard line, I force a smile knowing that if anyone other than me was looking after my sister's interests, I am thankful it was DeLuca. Although, I do feel slightly cast off, I understand her concern.

"Well, I suppose you were right about one thing. Yes, I will never stop fighting for you, my dear sister. Never forget that," I answer.

Chalmette smiles wide and wipes the remaining tears from her face. "That is good to know," she laughs.

"And now, dear sister, I must ask you this. How do you feel about Claudius?"

"I don't see what difference it matters now, sister. Surely, Monroe has brought my name to ruin. There is no way Corbin will allow his son to be with me."

"What if there is a way, sister? What if all were not lost? Would you want to be his wife?"

Chalmette frowns as she searches my face once more. I can't tell whether she's upset with me or if she thinks I'm teetering her emotions.

"Well, sister?" I question Chalmette again.

"Of course, I suppose but I don't see what difference—"

"Lord Marchand said he would see it done if it be your choice, that is," I force my reply before she has a chance to protest further.

"Why would he do that for me? What about you? Please don't tell me you'll return to Mother and Monroe. Or worse—do you fancy Lord Marchand?"

"Heavens no!" I shout back.

"Not that I would blame you, sister. He is quite fetching. But I am certain partnering with a negro, no matter his wealth or status would be quite difficult if—"

"There is no if, sister. Yes, Lord Marchand is indeed a catch. But he doesn't think of me that way. Actually, he wants me to—um work for him."

"Work for him? Doing what, might I ask?"

"Certainly, nothing in my former employ. Actually, he would like me to serve as an apprentice to aid in his art collections. Being a man of color, he figures it's far better to let me be the face of some of his dealings and work with his clients. That is, of course until people stop their plantation privilege."

It's a lie. But it is the best story I can come up with that she would understand. I doubt she is ready to hear the truth, nor can I bear to tell it.

"That sounds promising, sister!" Chalmette responds, her face full of hope.

"It involves a great deal of travel, so that's why I wanted to know where your desires lie. Whether it be schooling, marriage or both. I wanted to know what you would like to do. No pressure either way."

"Well, I don't understand how Lord Marchand can see to it that Corbin allows his son to see me."

"He knows him well. He has also agreed to tell him the truth. That you were not ruined, and your virtue is still intact. Lord Marchand can be very persuasive."

"Ah, I see," Chalmette says, exhaling hard once again as she runs her hands down the seam of her dress.

"Again, sister, there is no pressure from me. If this is not what you want—"

"But it is!" She immediately counters, her wide smile filling her face. "It's just I never thought this day would come to pass. Ever since I saw Victoria married, there was nothing I longed for more. I've only ever wanted to be married. And babies—lots of those!" Chalmette exclaims, her joy evident.

While I am happy for her, the mention of Victoria churns my stomach into knots. "Good, then I will let Dalcour know. He will send word to Corbin. I am sure Claudius will be glad to hear of it," I say with muted breath.

"What, sister? Your face is fallen. Do you not wish for me to marry? Do you want me to stay with you?"

"Of course I never want to be apart from you, dear one but there is something you must know."

"Tell me."

"Well, sister, it is difficult for me to say as I do not wish to sully your desires but—"

"Is this about Victoria?" Chalmette's flat tone slices through whatever colorful manner I intended to paint. Her eyes narrow as she looks at me and I slowly begin to understand my young sister is not as young hearted as I'd have myself believe.

Nodding in affirmation, she sighs and pushes the small curls hanging at her sides away from her face. "Yes, I know he hits her."

"How? When did you see this?"

"Her birthday. We missed it by a few days, and I had Marius pick up a basket of cookies that I could take her. You were out picking fabrics with

Corrine. Mother and Monroe were busy getting the roof patched after the storm. Anyway, Claudius went with me to take her the basket and when we arrived, we saw it. What was worse was when I protested, demanded that she return with me, she flew off at me, nearly throwing me from her porch."

"Why didn't you tell me about this then?"

"I didn't have an opportunity. Monroe had me working with Crawley on songs as soon as I returned, and you were actually in a happy mood with all your dressings. I didn't want to dampen the moment. Later, as I thought about how Victoria treated me, I decided she deserved her fate!"

"No, sister! She doesn't deserve that! No woman does! Do you understand me? She is *our sister*—no matter what. Do you understand!" Again, my words spit like a fire and I see a looming fear grow behind Chalmette's eyes. "I'm sorry, Chalmette," I say, pulling her into my embrace.

Her sobs send her tears pedaling down my neck as she repents of her wayward thoughts of Victoria in the cavity of my hold. Although our sister's actions toward us may be infuriating, she is still our sister.

"This is what I mean, dear sister. Marriage can be challenging but I want you to know no matter what, you always have me. Always and forever. Is that clear?"

"Yes, Chartreuse. I understand," Chalmette sniffles, wiping her tears once more. "I suppose you'll be happy to hear Claudius was quite repulsed by the barbarity of it all.

"As well he should be—and shall he always remain."

Chalmette's eyes lock with mine as the seriousness of my tone cements our shared understanding. Yet, without another word, she knows my sentiment is more than a mere threat. A small smile creeps from behind Chalmette's tense glare and she throws herself into my arms once more.

A loud clapping sound that seems to echo through the mansion breaks us from our embrace as we both turn to find Dalcour beaming behind us.

"Well, well," he begins, throwing his hands into a tight clasp as he stalks toward us. "I see Young Chalmette has agreed to marry Master DeVeaux! This is such a delight to my ears," he says with a broad grin, stretching from ear to ear.

Reaching for both Chalmette's hand and mine, Dalcour's warm palm firmly locks us in place. "Dear Chalmette, Armando is already making all the necessary arrangements to get your beloved here with haste. After which, your sister will accompany me ---and from there a whole new life begins!"

Dalcour's words hang between us and while I know there is more implied than he now cares to suggest, I am both excited and tepid to see what this new life means. And I have a feeling it shall be a new beginning for each of us.

Chapter Eleven

N ew beginnings take on a whole new meaning in the world of Dalcour Marchand.

Not only did we dine both sufficiently and decadently, Dalcour ensured we spent the better part of the next day pampered with beauty treatments fit for royalty. From our skin to our hair and even parts of our bodies requiring only the most delicate attention, both Chalmette and I were regally spoiled.

Although we were grateful for such a gesture, hearing Armando mumble something about getting the stench of the saloon off of us, makes me think this was all Dalcour's courteous way of making us appear as more presentable ladies of society. Reared as we had been, I am sure our missteps would be easily recognizable to persons of more esteemed pedigree.

And with the way Armando has crammed table etiquette down my sister's throat in the last twenty-four hours, I am certain Dalcour wants to ensure his deal with Corbin DeVeaux will stand.

Still, it is Chalmette's enthusiasm that has reined in my growing annoyance that my sister must make herself presentable for another man whether it be in society or a saloon.

I can't help wondering how Calida would have handled things.

Unfortunately, I will never know.

"What do you think of this one, sister?" Chalmette shouts, standing on the seamstress block. Swaying back and forth as she looks at herself in the mirror and back at me, the sea blue gown flows like a small tide against the oak floor.

"It's your third one in less than half an hour, sister. Please pick one. Both this one and the lavender gown make your eyes sparkle. I am sure Claudius will find you adoring in either."

"Oh you are no fun, Chartreuse!"

"And you are running out of time, dear Chalmette. Your betrothed will arrive any minute. Are you planning to see him in nothing save your knickers, dear?"

"Of course not!" She quips, looking over her shoulder one last time in the mirror before turning back to me. "I'll take both. This one for now and the other for later." Chalmette's girlish squeak would almost be annoying if I weren't just as excited as she. Although I would like nothing more than to share in her merriment, my mind is focused on what shall soon become of me.

Am I really about to become a vampire?

As eager as I am, I force myself not to linger on the thought. This moment belongs to Chalmette.

The bell on the porch rings, and I hear Armando grumble something about having to get the door and Chalmette leaps from the seamstress stool so fast she almost yanks the seamstress with her.

The seamstress shrieks a curse in French as she topples to the ground, ripping a hem of fabric as Chalmette rushes to the door to slam it shut.

"Oh no! He's early! Sister, you can't let him see me like this!"

"Calm down, Chalmette," I laugh, grabbing her shoulders, attempting to halt her growing fluster. "I'll go to see Claudius and check the temperature of things. I will keep him occupied while you freshen up and allow Marinette to finish your gown. That is, if you'll apologize and help her from the floor."

Chalmette's posture relaxes in my hold and she sighs as she glares over my shoulder, watching the seamstress attempt to gather herself.

"I am such a wrecking ball of sorts," Chalmette responds with a covered laugh. "Thank you, sister."

"Of course," I answer. "Now go, help Miss Marinette up from the floor and try not to stick yourself. Take your time as you prepare. If you must make him wait, at least make it worth it." Kissing her cheek softly, I rush out of the suite and head to the foyer.

Chalmette is right. He is early. I had hoped she would be with me when I saw Claudius again, but at least this gives me some time to discern his true intent with my sister. I'll not have her fall victim to Victoria's fate. Though, knowing Dalcour and Claudius' father Corbin are familiar lessens my angst, I'd like to weigh in on him all my own.

"Madame Chartreuse," Armando begins as he rounds the corner of the foyer. His tone and expression is surprisingly softer than usual as a tender smile grazes his otherwise stoic face. "Your visitor awaits you in the parlor," he adds quickly, before vanishing from my view.

He leaves me little time to ask whether Claudius came without his father. Or whether Corbin came without Claudius? Either outcome could prove disastrous for my sister, making me almost thankful she wasn't with me. If Corbin has once again refused my sister, it's probably for the best that I give her the news.

Hurriedly, I race to the parlor. If either Corbin or Claudius has come to turn her down, I must get them out of here before she has a chance to get her heart broken. Again.

Dashing into the parlor, I am shocked to find DeLuca standing beside the bookshelf, curiously thumbing through the display.

"DeLuca?" I shout his name, making him jump slightly at the questioning tone of my voice.

"Red!" He yelps back with a broad smile.

"What are you doing here?" I snap, looking around the room, hopeful Dalcour isn't nearby.

"Wow! That is surely no way to greet a friend!" He nicks back, plunging one hand in his pocket and leaning against the shelving.

"Get off of that!" I snip, yanking him from the bookshelf. "I'll only ask once more. What are you doing here?"

"Well, it's good to see you too, Red. Let me see, my trip was uneventful. Glad I made it here safe—"

"And how pray tell did you know where *here* is? Who told you where to find me?"

"Oh, I see. So you meant for me not to find you. I see. I guess that explains why you didn't answer me as I screamed your name at your departure. But now I understand, you have no interest in seeing your old pal DeLuca. I should have never come here!"

DeLuca's words hit me like the wrecking ball my sister recently spoke of. Hazy memories of my last night at the saloon and faintly hearing my name called as we left with Dalcour flicker through my mind.

"That was you?" I yell, racing beside him, stopping him from exiting the hall.

DeLuca looks up at me, his countenance downcast. "Yes, poppet. It was me. It's always me."

The brokenness I see within him, grips my heart, choking tears from me. Throwing my arms around his neck, I can't help the freefall of water erupting from my eyes.

"I am so sorry, DeLuca. I thought I'd never see you again. I'm so sorry. Please forgive me," I cry.

His posture remains stiff longer than I'd like, but I feel his tension ease as he wraps his arms around me, patting my back in consolation. "I know poppet, I know. Now stop crying and tell your old friend DeLuca what in the world is going on."

Sniffling, I wipe away my tears as I pull out of his hold. DeLuca's familiar, yet gentle smile warms my heart. I never thought I'd see him again. Wiping my hair from my eyes, he takes my chin in his hand and smiles once more, searching my face.

"So, Red, tell me. What is going on? What are you doing here?" DeLuca whispers his words as he looks around the mansion. His apprehension is apparent, and I wonder what he heard of my departure.

"Well, you first," I say, taking his hand, walking him to the sofa. "How did you find me?"

"I was with Claudius when the messenger came with news of Chalmette. I can't believe they are to be married! Scotty told me of how she was rescued before Monroe's plans had a chance to settle. I am thankful. But he also said your rescuer was Dalcour Marchand. Tell me, Red, is this true?"

"Wow! It sounds like you got all the high parts. I am sorry I didn't have a chance to bid you farewell. Everything just happened so fast."

"Yes, well, I can see that. Now here you are with butlers and adjutants." DeLuca's censuring tone is not lost on me. I know there is more behind his words and if I know my friend it will not be long before he belts it all out.

"Are Claudius and Corbin with you? Are they on their way?"

"I'm sure they'll be here soon enough. But please stop evading."

"I am not evading you, DeLuca. It's just that Chalmette thought Claudius had arrived."

"Oh and I suppose she will be saddened to only find me here instead," DeLuca responds, lowering his eyes.

"That is not what I meant. What has gotten into you? Why are you so glum all of a sudden?"

"Glum? All of a sudden?" DeLuca gazes back at me irritated again, but this time he shows no signs of running off. "I don't know where should I start? Oh, I know let's start with why you are here with Dalcour Marchand."

"Even more, let's start with why you are saying his name as though you two were familiar. Do you know him, DeLuca?"

"Do you?"

"What? I am here, aren't I? In his house no less."

"Yes, my friend that is the curious part. How exactly did you wind up here? And with the likes of a Marchand."

A Marchand? DeLuca's choice of words concerns me.

"You say that name as though it were not the first time. What do you know of it, DeLuca?"

Narrowing his eyes in a steely stare that locks with my own, I know my friend will not respond without some provocation from me. He wants to know what I know but I am afraid to tell. Dalcour's secrets are not mine to share. Even worse, I fear DeLuca has secrets to tell all his own.

"DeLuca!" The loud tenor of Dalcour's voice calls from the hallway, breaking us from our growing stand-off. Walking to the threshold of the parlor, Dalcour smiles wide with his hand outstretched in greeting. DeLuca quickly rises from his seat, nearly throwing his palm into Dalcour's grip. He forces a brief smile as the two lock hands. Dalcour casts a wary gaze back at me but brightens his expression as he looks over at DeLuca and continues smiling. "I thought that name sounded familiar. Would you be from Biloxi? I knew of a small coven—the DeLuca's. Are you of some relation?"

"Yes, my lord." DeLuca's pensive posture doesn't go unnoticed by Dalcour. With a firm grip at DeLuca's shoulder, Dalcour softens his stance as he gestures for DeLuca to return to his seat. As the two sit, DeLuca casts an awkward glance my way, but with Dalcour's eyes pinned on me, I remain unmoved.

"So, you are from Biloxi?" Dalcour asks.

"Not quite, my lord. I was raised there, but Biloxi isn't my birthplace," DeLuca quietly responds.

"Oh?" Crossing his left leg over his knee, Dalcour folds his arms across his chest and leans back, intrigue filling his face.

"Actually, I was orphaned. The DeLuca's took me in when I was a tot. I don't know much about my birth family and I left the DeLuca's and struck out on my own when I was nearly sixteen."

"I see," Dalcour says, rubbing his chin. "Well, it has been a while since I've ventured to Biloxi but from what I recall, the DeLuca's were a spirited bunch but a rather nomadic folk."

"Yes, sir. We were a very itinerant family, as it were," DeLuca laughs, forcing a sly smile. "I haven't seen everyone for quite some time."

"Interesting," Dalcour replies in a low tone. Pushing himself upright, he lowers his crossed leg to the floor and props against the arm of the chair. "So how do you two know one another? I don't think Chartreuse has ever ventured far from Louisiana."

"From the saloon, my lord," DeLuca mutters back, his gaze still wary.

"Oh?" Dalcour asks, raising his brow. I know he wonders whether DeLuca is a former customer and the thought of that frightens me.

"No, it's not what you think," I quickly interrupt. "He supplied the port and rum. We've known each other since we were young."

Looking back and forth between me and DeLuca, Dalcour searches our faces, likely looking to decipher anything more between us. A crooked smile dances at the corner of his mouth and he forces a light laugh and stands from his seat.

"Well, I guess it's a good thing the two of you are already acquainted," Dalcour says with a bright yet mysterious smile as a calculating dance churns behind his crimson eyes. "It will be good for Chartreuse to have someone she knows and trusts be with her to help her navigate what comes next. Besides, I am sure having another Altrinion around will come in handy when she's turned."

"What!" Both DeLuca and I shout back in unison, glaring back at one another and Dalcour with wide eyes and parted lips.

"You are an Altrinion?" I whisper in inquiry to DeLuca as the reveal of it all shakes me to my core.

"Vampire! Tell me you're not becoming a vampire, Red!" DeLuca snaps back.

"You first!" I shout.

"Well, I'm only part Altrinion. My birth mother was half. My father human. At least that's what I was told. But now, back to you—"

"Back to me? I can't believe you never told me all these years!" Folding my arms across my chest, I stare at DeLuca both in awe and anger. Knowing he kept this such a secret infuriates me.

"What's to tell, Red! I barely knew who I was, much less what I was. And I'm more human than anything so there's really nothing to tell. I have no powers, no source of magic. I am just me."

DeLuca's words hang between us as we both observe one another with new eyes.

Forcing a faux cough, Dalcour clears his throat and walks away from us toward the hallway, holding his hand raised. "I suppose I will leave you two to sort out matters. DeLuca, if you have no cause to return to your port and pub employ, you are welcome to accompany us. I could always use a few good folk on my team. That is, of course, if Chartreuse is amenable to the idea. At any rate, it was a pleasure to meet you."

We both keep our eyes fixed on Dalcour as he exits from our view, fearing what it means should we both turn to see the other in a whole new way.

Chapter Twelve

"Ah-hem," Armando coughs, interrupting our shared and silent staring into the now empty hallway. Turning my attention to Armando, I try to force a smile, but only a faint grimace etches my face. Still, Armando maintains his proper and unmoved posture. "Perhaps you two should take your discussion into the courtyard—away from the bride-to-be. It would be a pity to dampen her mood with such talk." Gesturing his hand toward the veranda and giving no room for our protest, both DeLuca and I take our leave outside."

"Well, then Red, I should suppose you'd better soak up this sun. Dare I say, such a sight will be a distant memory for you," DeLuca barks over his shoulder as he makes his way across the cobblestone path.

"You're mad at me? Really, Sincade?" I sneer, knowing how much he loathes his name. "How dare you? And all this time I never knew who or what you were!"

Spinning on his heel, DeLuca's daggered-eyed stare wrenches like a knife in my throat. "No, poppet, you've always known who I am. Just an orphaned kid trying to make something of his life. Yes, the DeLucas took me in and yes, I am one-fourth Altrinion. But what does that mean? Nothing good has ever come of such knowledge. As a matter of fact, I'd begun to think all the strange and eerie tales I had been told were nothing but mere bedtime stories. That is, until now."

"You mean until you heard Dalcour's name?" I quietly reply, sheepishly looking up at my friend.

"Well, hearing the name Marchand was quite a surprise. I had no idea you even knew the name, much less the man himself."

Walking toward DeLuca, I watch a small smile form in the corner of his mouth and his round eyes reflect the familiar admiration to which I've become accustomed. Smiling in return, I stretch out my hand and he places his warm palm in mine, and we sit at a small stone bench under a small pine tree.

"I'm sorry you had to find out this way, DeLuca. I've known Lord Marchand since my youth in New Orleans. Do you recall my mention of a family friend who helped my family and I escape danger?"

"Yes, I do. It had something to do with your sister who died, right?" DeLuca questions, his thick brow raised with intrigue.

"Calida was her name. She fell in love with Dalcour's brother, Decaux. And for their love, her proud femininity, and the darkened color of his skin, she was burned alive at the stake and accused of witchcraft."

"Red!" DeLuca gasps with both awe and empathy. "I didn't know."

"I know, my friend," I whisper back as he squeezes my hand firmly in his. A lone tear runs down my face and a tender smile graces DeLuca's face as he stares back at me. "And now Dalcour wants to ensure Calida's fate will never be mine nor Chalmette's."

"But are you sure this is what you want to do, Red? I grew up hearing the monstrous stories of both Marchand brothers. What makes you think your fate will be any better than Calida's should you become vampire?"

"Well, any fate is better than the road carved by either Mother or Monroe. And Calida's death was the direct result of the bigotry of both sex and skin tone. If they could have killed Decaux they would have but they could not because he is an Altrinion-Vampire. Like him, I need the strength to protect my family at all costs—"

"You mean at the cost of your very soul, Chartreuse! Do you even hear yourself?"

"What care I for my soul? It is already forfeit and ruined! There is no good left in me!" I cry.

Taking my face in his hands, DeLuca's narrowed gaze protests my outcry. "No, Red! That is not true. There is good in you. I have seen it myself."

"No, you haven't, DeLuca. Besides, if memory serves me correct, even you refused me on the first night we met. You wanted nothing to do with me."

"That is not true, and you know it. I have always wanted the best for you. What I refused was to treat you as a harlot. You are and have always been better than that."

Painful tears burn down my cheeks and DeLuca wipes my face clear and wraps his arms around me, forcing me into the cavity of his embrace. "Cry if you must, my sweet Red. Just know your DeLuca will always be here for you. Always."

"Always?" I tearfully repeat.

"Yes, my dear poppet. Have I not proven time and again there is no where you can run from me? Whether you are near or far, my heart shall forever be where you are. I need you to believe me," DeLuca sweetly says, brushing my hair from my face, trailing his thumb along my jaw.

Looking at Sincade DeLuca, I now see a fierce and resolute stance arise in him I've only glanced before. Perhaps this protectively staunch side of him has always been there, but I've been too blind to see it. At any rate, I am thankful for it.

"Even if I become a vampire?" I quietly question, casting my eyes to meet his tender gaze. The same crooked smile dances at the corners of his mouth once more and his eyes soften as I press my face deeper into his palm.

"Especially if you become vampire, poppet. I will not leave you to uncertain peril. I will be there for you no matter the outcome."

"How can you say that? What if I try to—to eat you or something?" I mutter, feeling both silly and curious as I utter the words.

DeLuca laughs, allowing his hands to fall to his lap, clasping them together. "Well, I suppose that is something to consider. How about this: if you bite me—I get to bite you in return."

"What?" I burst in laughter.

"No, actually, I am quite serious," he chuckles. "Listen," deepening his voice in a more serious tone. "Despite everything I said earlier, and while I meant it all, I do understand why *you* would want to become vampire. Truly, with the life you've lived—we both lived—I get it."

"Thank you, DeLuca," I say softly, searching his face and the concern I see brewing beneath his countenance troubles me. "Why do I feel a *but* coming?"

"That is because you know me well, Red. Like I said whether I think you should become vampire or not, I understand your reasoning. What worries me is why does Marchand want to turn you? What does he get out of it?"

Silence sits between us as DeLuca's assertion stokes a new fear in me that I quickly hope to squelch. As his eyes glide over my face, I work hard not to show any hint of how his words fill me with doubt. Even more, I know no matter Dalcour's reasoning, this is still what I want.

It is what I need.

Jumping up from the bench, I saunter near a thick rose bush and trail my fingers along the thickening buds.

"It's regret," I blurt my words, sharply turning on my heel to find DeLuca standing behind me. Frown lines invert at his brow as he twists his nose, turning his head slightly.

"Regret?" He questions back.

"Yes, regret!" I repeat with a lilt, brightening my tone. "I think it is his way of making amends for my sister's loss and our family's necessity to flee after Decaux lit New Orleans ablaze. Dalcour still blames himself for not only bringing Decaux to Louisiana, but also how his actions affected my family; leading us to ruin. All he wants is to right those wrongs and perhaps put me in a position where such an outcome would never happen again."

DeLuca remains silent after my rant, watching me intently as I twine my fingers through the rosebush, carefully avoiding the thorns.

Slowly walking toward me, DeLuca's restrained smile does little to hide his skepticism. "Everything you say makes sense on the surface, Red, that much is true. And if Lord Marchand's sentiment serves no other purpose than to give you power enough to protect yourself from succumbing Calida's fate or worse, then so be it. For if that be the case, it is a rare and beautiful gesture those of our status are not generally afforded. However, my dear poppet, it is my fear that you'll someday find no matter how lovely and blossoming such a proposition may seem, there may yet be a thorn capable of piercing that which matters most of all to me. You."

At his words, my forefinger catches on a thistle and a sharp prickle thrusts through my skin. I wince as it does and DeLuca gently pulls my hand out from under the bush, resting it softly on his lips as he kisses my throbbing finger. As he does, a stream of emotions overload and confuse me. Never have I thought of DeLuca's affection toward me beyond friendship, but today his ardent devotion rings aloud.

Cupping my entwined hand with his, he holds it beneath his chin and shoots his typical boyish grin at me and laughs softly. "All better now?" he asks, deepening his charming gaze.

"Yes, all better," I breathe back, still entranced by his regard for me.

"Excuse me, Madame Chartreuse and Sir DeLuca," Armando yells from the threshold of the terrace door. "The DeVeaux's have arrived."

"After you," DeLuca says softly with his hand extended toward the house.

My mind is a muddled mess as we make our way inside. Still, I do my best to push aside DeLuca's allegations. I have to believe Dalcour's intentions are genuine.

He only wants the best for me.

Thankfully, Chalmette's loud squealing shriek breaks me from pondering the worse.

"Sister! Sister!" Chalmette exclaims, running down the hall to me as soon as I round the corner. Claudius stands near his father wearing a caring smile as his doting eyes mirror my sister's movements across the floor. "Look what Claudius gave me!" she shouts, extending her tiny fingers as a sparkling emerald encased in a shimmering gold band meet my eyes almost blinding me.

"It is beautiful," I reply, nuzzling her chin and kissing her cheek.

"Isn't it?" Chalmette continues, still admiring the jewel. "It was his grandmother's."

"Yes and it has been in my family for more than three generations," Corbin adds with his chest filled with pride as he firmly grips his son's back.

"And it is my honor for my betrothed to now wear it. She is now family," Claudius says with a wide smile, stretching his arm toward Chalmette as she runs back into his hold.

"Well, it would appear that all things are settled," Dalcour declares as though he were an adjudicator.

"What about the wedding?" I curiously ask.

"After discussing it with Lord Marchand we all agreed it best to handle the nuptials here with a priest. A small and intimate wedding would be best."

"Oh and is that what you want, sister?" I question Chalmette.

"Yes, Treuse, it is quite all right with me. As Dalcour explained earlier it is more believable for everyone to believe it was Claudius and his father who helped us escape from the saloon."

"Ah, I see," DeLuca starts, sharing a knowing glance with me as he winks one eye. "So you are betting on folks thinking you two were so lovesick you married right away!" He says, rising to the balls of his feet as both Chalmette and Claudius nod in gleeful affirmation.

Dalcour casts a wary nod in my direction, likely hopeful I'll share in the merriment, but the idea doesn't seem realistic to me. "And you expect people to believe this? Really, my lord?"

Just as Dalcour parts his lips in response, DeLuca makes his way in front of me and takes my hand in his, lightly squeezing my thorn-pricked finger. "Well, now poppet, it may come across a bit Shakespearean, but convincing still. And with Monroe's high debts and sullied reputation, most will stand to believe the word of Corbin DeVeaux over that louse Monroe any day. Wouldn't you agree, my lord?" DeLuca says with a raised brow. A witty smile crosses Dalcour's face and I can tell his surprisingly impressed with DeLuca.

"Please, sister say you understand," Chalmette pleads, coming to my side and blocking my view of Dalcour.

"Of course, I understand, Chalmette. As long as it is what you want then I will be satisfied," I reply as she lifts her wide doe eyes up at me.

"Thank you! Thank you, sister! You shall be satisfied indeed, nor shall you regret it!" Chalmette merrily yelps.

"I will take care of her. I vow to be a good and faithful husband to her, Chartreuse," Claudius says now at Chalmette's side.

"You most certainly shall," I whisper, searching his face for one last look of impropriety. Thankfully, and to the benefit of both he and Chalmette, I find nothing but the one thing I too long for.

True love.

Chapter Thirteen

Chalmette's ceremony differed greatly from Victoria's. My second eldest sister's wedding was laced in lavish bouquets of pomp and pretty little details. The grandeur of her nuptials rivaled that of fairytales with the happiest of endings. Yet, when the last flower fell, it was my sister Victoria who withered like a plucked rose petal clinging to winter's chill.

Despite the stark simplicity of Chalmette and Claudius' vows, I have every hope that her flower will yet remain in bloom. Like a petunia, the love she and Claudius share will abound in every season. I have every cause to believe he will care for her and shower her with every goodness she deserves, and she will do likewise.

Now as I wave farewell to my sister as she and her new husband mount their carriage, taking leave to their honeymoon, the weight of agreeing to become vampire shrouds my being. Looking over my shoulder at DeLuca, he regards me warily and I wonder if he too senses my doubts.

"Sister!" Chalmette calls to me, pushing the door open. Racing to the carriage, my heart pounds. Perhaps she has decided not to leave? Maybe she is afraid? Is this too soon? Panicking thoughts mince my mind and I fear both my sister and I are acting impetuous.

Thrusting her hand outside the carriage, my eyes grow wide as I see my stringed pearls hanging from her hand. "These are yours!" She shouts with a sweet smile. "I only borrowed them for ceremony, but you keep them."

"No, sister it is fine. I want you to have them," I reply, looping my fingers between the pearls and her petite palm.

"I cannot," she answers stiffly. "These were Calida's. She was your sister. You are mine." A tearful grin covers her face as she speaks and my heart melts.

"Then what have I to give you?" I question, knowing I have nothing of worth to offer.

"You." Chalmette sweetly replies. "You are and have forever been my gift, sister. Promise not to keep yourself from me. Ever. Write me letters and visit often," she chides, swiping my hand aside as she pulls back to wipe her tear-worn face.

"And you, Chalmette, are mine. I do promise I will write to you," I pledge, watching Claudius wrap her in his embrace. "Now, go sister. Enjoy your marriage. Love your husband but do not lose yourself to him," I say barely above a whisper. Claudius nods in understanding as he pounds his hand on the outside of the carriage, departing the estate.

"Are you okay?" DeLuca asks as his large and wide eyes search my face.

"I am fine," I mutter in response. It's a lie. I am a mess inside. But I refuse to allow either him or Chalmette to witness my weakness.

"Well then," DeLuca begins, turning my head back to him as my eyes follow the carriage down the long dirt road. Looking back at him, I blink rapidly, hopeful to stop my impending tears their release. "It looks like someone is waiting for you." Turning his head slowly, DeLuca takes our attention to the double doors of the mansion where Dalcour remains posted.

Watching Dalcour as he stands guardedly away from the slither of sunlight, I marvel how that soon, such a fate will be my own. Looping my arm with DeLuca's we make our way back inside and my heart pounds like a racing bull in my chest.

Everything in me says I should run, but the truth is, I have nowhere to go. This is where I belong.

"Did you bid your sister farewell?" The dark and husky tenor of Dalcour's voice is unnerving as we make our way into the foyer. Now stationed mid-way of the staircase, Dalcour's looming stance darkens the hall and his glowing deep red eyes lock onto mine in a haunting glare. Tightening his hold on me, I hear DeLuca gulp down the thick air in his throat as his eyes grow wary of Dalcour's now more ominous form.

"Yes, my lord," my words quiver from between my teeth.

"Then it is time we began." The dissonance in Dalcour's tone is disturbing as he runs his hands together showcasing the same fiery embers as he did that night in the saloon.

"And what of DeLuca, my lord," I reply, fearful of Dalcour's intentions of my friend.

"I will remain at your side, Red," DeLuca quickly interjects, turning to me as panic fills his face.

"I am afraid that will not be possible," Dalcour answers, rushing his response. "The ceremony we shall perform is—um—intimate if you will. And where I am taking you, young one, is not permitted to bring mere mortals."

"But I am not a mere mortal!" DeLuca protests, releasing his arm from my hold as he steps a few inches away from me. "I am Altrinion," he declares, his once dark brown eyes now encased in a ring of gold.

Gasping, I am both impressed and taken aback to see such a revelation unfold before me.

"DeLuca!" I whisper his name. Only peering over his shoulder at me in response, he keeps his sights on Dalcour.

"Ha! Ha!" Dalcour's haughty and haunting laugh reverberates through the foyer and his stance softens as he leans against the staircase railing. "Well, well," he begins as he saunters down the steps. "That you are! That you are indeed!" He continues laughing, making his way to DeLuca's side, placing his hand on his shoulder.

DeLuca's posture relaxes and his eyes return to their normal hue and I smile at him, still impressed to see him take such a stand for himself.

My eyes trail to Dalcour's hand on DeLuca's shoulder and a shuddering chill pains through me as I watch long, pointy claws form and dig into DeLuca's flesh. Moving his hand from DeLuca's shoulder, he grips his neck and pushes him high against the wall.

"But you are more than Altrinion, my foolish friend," Dalcour snaps, lashing tongue forward against the nape of DeLuca's neck, clawing his other palm against his chest and pinning him flat.

"I am not!" DeLuca cries, struggling to breathe beneath Dalcour's weight.

"My lord, please don't!" I yell, rushing to Dalcour's backside, but Armando appears in a flash and pulls me away, keeping me locked in a sturdy hold.

"Oh but you are!" Dalcour continues as his fangs protrude and his once pecan textured skin glows red.

"No, I am not!" DeLuca protests.

"Please Dalcour!" I scream, unable to get from under Armando's strong grip.

Dropping DeLuca to the floor, Dalcour turns back to face me, and I watch his fangs recede as he returns to his typical form. Armando releases me from his hold, and I dash across the foyer to DeLuca, wrapping him in my arms as he works to regain his breath.

Panting, DeLuca pushes me aside and rises to his knees. "You're mad!" DeLuca shouts at Dalcour's back.

Turning quickly on his heel, Dalcour's lightning-like speed carries him back to DeLuca before I can blink, and he pulls DeLuca by his collar, lifting him to the tips of his toes. Once more, Dalcour's crimson eyes shine through the darkened hall and a wicked grin covers his face. "No, I am not mad. But you are young and foolish. Do you know what I am boy? I sire the sulking shadows of night. I grant both death and life with the single point of my bicuspid. I evoke fear and pain for no other reason than for my enjoyment. Whatever your kin told you of my kind, multiply it by a thousand and lock it in the darkest corners of the most depraved mind and you'll still not come close to the madness of what I am. Do you understand me?"

At his words he tosses DeLuca back to the ground, shivering in fear.

"Why, my lord? What has he done to offend you?" I cry, clinging to DeLuca.

"He has done nothing," Dalcour whispers back.

"Then why?" I repeat.

"He is mortal, Chartreuse." Looking down at me, I see Dalcour's expression has softened as a newly formed smile corners his face.

"I—I don't understand," I stay, stammering my words and searching his face for understanding. "But you—you said he is Altrinion."

"Yes, he is. But only a small amount of the Altrinion force flows through his veins. He cannot go where I take you unless he is ready to become your first meal." There is no pretense in Dalcour's tone. Staring in his eyes, I know his sentiment is sincere. My eyes fall at his words and I see the wisdom behind his threatening brutality. "If not your meal, then the meal of one of the others."

"I understand," I quietly say, sharing a gloom-ridden glance with DeLuca. "But I thought you said he could stay with us, my lord?"

"Only if he understands the risks," Dalcour replies sharply.

"I do understand," DeLuca adds, rising to his feet. Stretching his hand toward me, a warm smile crosses his face and I place my palm in his as he helps me from the floor.

"No, you don't." The resolution of Dalcour's tone is haunting but true. "Our world is different from any other. I know not what the gypsies of Biloxi taught you, fiercely foolish one, but Chartreuse's world is changing faster than you can comprehend."

"It is time, my lord," Armando calls to Dalcour, breaking our forming stand-off.

"Show Master DeLuca to his quarters," Dalcour responds as Armando quickly makes his way to DeLuca's side. "Young one," he says, now turning his attention to me, "take my hand."

"Chartreuse!" DeLuca screams as I place my hand in Dalcour's large palm. Dalcour offers a permitting nod and I look over my shoulder at DeLuca and smile. "No matter what happens poppet, I will be here when you return. No matter what."

A lone tear falls to my cheekbone, and I quickly brush it away as Dalcour leads us down a dark hallway adjacent to the parlor.

Chapter Fourteen

"What is this place?" I question Dalcour trying to see through the smoky corridor. Surrounded by large cinderblock and brick walls I turnabout, peering through the darkness, fearful of the hissing and growling sounds echoing around me.

"These are the taming wells," Dalcour answers softly, tightly gripping my hand in his.

"Taming wells?" I repeat, circling about and trying to get my bearings. The last thing I recall is being led down a dark staircase in the mansion and in a flash we were here. *Odd.*

"Yes, this is where we bring the newly bred for taming—to see if they can normalize among humans. Here they are tested and tried. They go through a series of events, each meant to ascertain their ability to walk among others without causing undue harm."

"So you domesticate them? Like a pet?"

Laughing as he looks down at me, Dalcour's eyes are tender as he watches me. "Not quite, Chartreuse, but you are close. The newly bred are far from pets and are still very lethal creatures. However, here we teach them how to um—use discretion. We teach them how to blend in society."

"And if they don't pass the tests?"

"They are destroyed." Dalcour's swift tone is brusque. Staring at me, he searches my face and I know his hard tone was intentional.

He wants to know if I'll break.

"I understand," I quickly reply, looking away, attempting once more to see through the dissonance of darkness all around me. "How did we get here so fast?" I ask, looking back up at Dalcour.

"There are taming cells beneath the mansion. As a matter of fact, I'm establishing cells like these throughout the America's. It's my way of trying to create some normalcy and civility among the supernatural community."

"The supernatural community? Aren't these taming centers only for vampires? Who else would need them?"

"That is a good question, dear friend." A dark and sultry voice calls behind us.

Straining my eyes to see through the murky corridor, the distinct scent of hyacinth petals past my nose, instantly calming my nerves.

"Titan!" Dalcour merrily announces as a tall bronze hued, herculean man stalks toward us. Slowly the haze of the corridor recedes, and I watch in awe at the deified man standing before us. His marble-gray eyes and long and thickly knotted sandy brown hair hangs to the middle of his muscular form. Wearing nothing but a cattle-hide sheath over his waist, his chest and stomach is meticulously etched, revealing his strapping handsomeness.

While Dalcour may be attractive, I have never thought of him as anything other than my protector. This man, on the other hand, evokes all manner of abandon within me. Had a man of his stature ever ventured to the saloon, I would have gladly shared all that I am with him and more.

"Chartreuse!" Dalcour snaps, tugging my hand hard and breaking me from my impious musing. Choking down the thick air in my throat and pushing my irreverent thoughts aside, I look up at him and smile. "I'd like to introduce you to Lord Titan. He governs these taming wells," Dalcour adds proudly as he and Titan share equally reverential glances.

"It is very nice to meet you, Lord Titan," I mutter in response.

"As it is to make your acquaintance. You are every bit of decadence as Lord Marchand described," Titan answers with a sly grin, looking me over.

His eyes trail from my face down to the tips of my toes. As he regards me, it's as though his gaze alone prickles my pores, causing goose bumps to erode through me. Glaring back up at me from the floor, his eyes slowly travel from my hips to my breasts. He lingers, gawking at my bunched cleavage, licking his lips, and narrowing his seductive gaze into my own.

"Titan!" Dalcour barks, quickly averting Titan's gaze back to him.

"Yes, my lord—yes, well she is quite fetching. I can understand your intrigue. As will your brother."

His brother? I hadn't given much thought to how Decaux might fit in. I can't help but be curious as to why Titan thinks Decaux will care anything about me. I haven't seen him since before Calida's death and he's made no attempt to see about my family after she died.

"Is he here?" Dalcour questions, his tone still coarse.

"He is where he always is this time of night. In the feeding room." The narrowed and evocative gaze of Titan locking eyes with me as he replies to Dalcour isn't lost on me. He is trying to scare me.

It will not work.

Dalcour looks down at me and back at Titan, sharing a wary gaze. "I'll only be a minute. Please stay here with Lord Titan. You'll be safe," Dalcour says with a hesitant smile.

"Perhaps," Titan adds with a lilting chuckle and his arms folded at his waist, looking me over once more. Dalcour gives him a rebuking glare, shaking his head in disapproval and squeezing my hand tight before he exits out of my view.

Prickling pores erupt again all over my body as Titan remains leaned against the cinderblock wall with sight set on me. Unprovoked, he lets out a loud and nefarious laugh as he saunters across the room and pulls out a small wooden chair. "Please, sit," he says with a broad smile, still laughing.

"I suppose it would be better if I knew the cause for your amusement," I say, curious.

Covering his mouth with his left hand and raising his right palm toward me, he continues giggling, but shakes his head, trying to contain his merriment.

"Lord Titan!" I snap, slightly annoyed.

"I am sorry, my lady, but you must admit the situation is quite amusing," he says, cupping his hands against his chin, restraining his laugh. As much as I want to take a moment to admire just how adorably handsome he looks when he laughs, I cannot. My concern is not understanding the cause of his glee.

"And the situation?" I question, wishing I could read his mind.

"Well," he begins, pushing himself upright, attempting to regain his composure. "It's surely not in jest that Lord Marchand wants to make you vampire. For any stiffer could see that a woman of such beauty would be highly revered arsenal in the community, but to try to offer you as such to Decaux, is well, absurd."

As Titan's bout of laughter takes over once more, my mind rattles about. "What?" I mutter, as panic and DeLuca's dreaded premonition lifts to the foreground of my memory.

"It is absurd, don't you agree?" Titan asks, extending his hand and awaiting my response.

"Well, I—"

"Of course it is! I mean sure, you are certainly a dead ringer for Calida, no pun intended; but *you are not your sister.* And despite Dalcour's need to play the broker of peace to his brother's newly found machinations, you shall never be a replacement. Further, Dalcour's time would be better spent trying to meet the tasks and obligations his brother has laid before him instead of this ridiculous notion of filling the void of Decaux's heart with you."

Silence sits between us as Titan glares at me awaiting a response. But I have none to give. I don't know what to make of this information. Thoughts of racing from here and back to the saloon swarm my mind, but the gnarling and hissing sounds echoing about, rein in my impulse.

Only one thought looms through my forlorn mind: DeLuca was right.

Dalcour does have other reasons for wanting to make me vampire. And somehow Decaux is his reason.

But his reasons are not my own.

As my mind replays Titan's words and thoughts of me being used and offered to yet another man torments me, a willful spirit of protest rises within me, erupting me from my seat to my feet. Titan's eyes widen as I spring forward and he raises his palm once more in caution, but the time for caution is gone.

I refuse to be bait or barter. Not even for Dalcour Marchand! And if my protest costs me my life, then so be it.

"Firstly, I—" Before I can finish my objection, I am stunned into silence when both Dalcour and Decaux come into the corridor, standing not only a breath apart from me.

"Brother," Dalcour begins with a broad smile spreading his face from ear to ear. "This is the lovely Chartreuse. Isn't she a beauty?" How it is even possible I do not know, but Dalcour's smile lengthens and his eyes dance just as I've seen before. However, this time I now understand the meaning behind it.

Decaux steps forward and his enticing yet bountifully aromatic scent nearly knocks me back into my seat as I stumble backward. And fallen I would have, if it weren't for the gentle wrapping of his arm along my back, preventing my blunder.

Unlike Dalcour, Decaux's face is not adorned by the soft creasing of a kind smile. Instead, his darkly crimson eyes deepen in my own with an air of both intrigue and displeasure. Despite his stately and handsome presence, warmth and compassion does not exude from him as it does his younger brother. Instead an ominous and foreboding glare fills his eyes.

Still, I cannot take my eyes off of him. Even though a brood of warning ripples through me, I can't withstand the entirety of his lure. From his supple, cranberry-stained lips to the bronzed sheen of his caramelized skin every part of him calls to every part of me. At the sight of him, darkened abandoned thoughts trigger my more seductive self as yearnings of employing every wanton desire permeate my being.

Lifting me into his hold, his eyes trail every part of me, and I work hard to stifle the willful grunt seeking its release. It is taking everything within me to withstand the full measure of his entreat.

A small, devious grin covers the corner of his face and his gaze slowly softens as I regain my footing and his arm gently slides from my back. As he does, I take special note of how his large biceps brush along my backside and the doting caress of his fingers as they glide along my waist.

Standing upright my eyes land square with his brawn pectorals and slender waist.

He is perfection!

Gone now are my thoughts of protest. Instead, and as much as I know I should object, I am strangely interested to see where this goes.

I know this is wrong—*or is it?*

For years, only slobbering drunks and cheating husbands were given to my bed. Never before has someone like Decaux Marchand been an option. If I must play harlot—perhaps--

"Beautiful she may be, but Calida reincarnate she is not." The sharpness of Decaux's tone cuts me in the gut. Circling me, Decaux looks me over once more, glaring down as though he were considering picking a pet. His swift movements are too fast for me and he is quickly perched atop the wooden chair, effortlessly balanced along its beam as he dangles one foot to the ground.

"What?" I mutter in response.

"Oh have I offended you?" Decaux snips back with a haughty laugh. "Truly it was not my intent. But you only have my brother to thank for making a fool of you!" He sneers.

"Come, Chartreuse, let us go," Dalcour says, annoyed, cupping my elbow in his strong palm.

"Look, Titan, I have offended both the marionette and her puppeteer!" He belts with a cringy chuckle. Titan laughs with him but looking at him I can spy his conforming pretense.

"I am no man's puppet!" I bite back, pulling myself from Dalcour's grip and charging toward Decaux.

I do not care who he is, I will not be treated like this. While I am well aware this man could take my life with the wave of his hand or by the snare of his fangs, if I must die because I refuse such manner then so be it.

Rushing toward Decaux, Dalcour is in front of me before I can blink. Placing his sturdy hands on my shoulders, he pushes me back, shaking his head in both warning and fear. "Chartreuse, be still," Dalcour says softly, and the coolness of his breath seems to quiet my gnawing errancy.

"Ah," Decaux begins, standing up and away from the wooden chair. "Perhaps I misjudged you, Little Calida," he adds, tilting his head and peering over Dalcour's broad shoulders.

"My name is Chartreuse!" I yell, breaking away from Dalcour's tight hold.

"Chartreuse!" Dalcour shouts my name in rebuke once more.

Cutting my eyes at Dalcour briefly, I keep my attention on Decaux. A part of me feels like I am trapped in the saloon all over again. This time, Mother is replaced with Dalcour while Decaux almost mimics that of Monroe. But unlike Monroe, Decaux has neither interest in me nor a display of Monroe's slavering stature.

Laughing as he saunters to Dalcour's side, Decaux rubs his chin, encircling me once more. Intrigue lifts his brow, and an arrogant smile frames his otherwise alluring face. "Well now brother, I see there is yet fire in this one after all. I suppose the spirit of Calida is not as dead as I once believed."

Dalcour's expression brightens like a child who just received a trinket as both the eyes of he and Decaux merrily dance about.

"Go now," Decaux begins, rubbing his hands together, illumining a bright golden light like a flame. "Begin your preparations. If this mortal has gall enough to stand in protest to me, I suppose she has the makings of a proper sireling after all."

"My lord?" I moan in displeasure but Dalcour keeps his sights fixed on Decaux.

Stepping to my side, I feel Decaux's towering presence loom over me, but I refuse to look him in the eye. "My, Young One, I wonder what shall become of you," he begins, turning my chin to meet his glowing crimson gaze. "Will your fire remain? Or will the taming of these halls douse the kindling I see behind your eyes? I should hope not. I'd much rather see what burns in the wake of your new form. Do not disappoint me, Little Calida." Despite my growing antipathy for him, Decaux's whispered words ride me hard, gripping me with a temptingly fearful passion.

Decaux exits before I have a moment to counter his sentiment leaving only the trail of his enticing scent and his haunting words behind.

Although I have no desire to play pawn, Decaux is right about one thing. If anyone has cause to light a fire it is me. But my plans far outweigh a mere flicker.

I intend to burn it all down.

Chapter Fifteen

Titan disappeared before I had a chance to notice, leaving only Dalcour and me in the darkened corridor.

Dalcour stares at me, searching my face, attempting to discern the fury fueling my thoughts. Anger holds me captive, and I feel like a fool. I cannot believe I am once again in this repose. I thought I could trust Dalcour. I thought he only wanted the best for me, but I was naïve.

"I see your confidence in me fading, young one," Dalcour says softly, making his way in front of me. As much as I want to, the appropriate response evades me. "Perhaps I should explain," Dalcour adds, pleading to me with his eyes.

"Perhaps," I force the words out.

"I deserve that," Dalcour continues in a slightly demure tone. "Please, sit," he says while extending his arm toward a small stone bench on the other side of the wall. Hesitant, I do as he asks as he takes a seat next to me. "Look, I know I should have mentioned my brother to you before now. I guess I had hoped things would turn out differently."

Although I can tell he is sincere, I refuse to allow the tenderness of his smile to lull me into a false sense of security once again. "And by different do you mean you thought we would've fallen madly in love at first sight?

Did you think Decaux would take one look at me and see his one and only true love—my sister? Or did you think I'd throw myself at him and play the harlot? I suppose that must be all you see when you look at me! Isn't it?" Spitting my words like fire, I work hard to hold back the tears that are so desperate for their release. I refuse to give him the satisfaction nor do I want or require his pity.

Dalcour's eyes bulge at my words and he swallows the thick air in his throat. Lifting his hand, he quickly pulls it back as he looks into my eyes, knowing I have no interest in any comfort he would seek to provide.

"Chartreuse, you must believe when I tell you that I do not regard you as a harlot. I never have."

"If that is true then why is your first recourse to pair me with your brother? I thought you said you wanted to give me the power to protect and care for myself. I did not think that meant coupling me with the likes of someone who'd rather see the world burn than to give regard to someone like me."

"While it may appear the contrary, I can assure you that was never my intent. Never." The resolution of Dalcour's intent is clear as he places his hand on my shoulder. Tears peddle down my face as he does, and I can no longer fight back my cries. Pulling me into his embrace, Dalcour runs his hands through my hair and kisses the crown of my head.

Releasing me from his grasp, he smiles at me as I use my wrists to wipe my face. "Please understand no matter how naïve it may seem; it was only my hope that maybe once Decaux saw you he would be reminded of his affection for Calida. But not only that, I hoped that seeing you would stir up whatever goodness remains of his stone-cold heart. Your sister had a power to bring the best out of him and when she died, she took that part with her."

"So I *was* but to be a mere replacement?"

"No, Chartreuse, not a replacement. Simply a reminder that good once reigned in his heart. I wanted him to see that all was not utterly lost at her passing. I had hoped because he loved her, he would—"

"Find it in his heart to love me too?" I mutter through my tears.

"I had no expectation for you two to become what Calida meant to him. But I wanted him to have a fresh start. Perhaps a chance to experience care for someone, but this time it would be different." Dalcour's finishing sentiment is soft as he stares distantly into the dark corridor.

"How?" I ask, leaning forward, hopeful to regain his attention.

"Because unlike Calida, Young One, you would never die."

"And that's why you want to make me a vampire? To bond me forever to your brother! And how does this benefit me, my lord? What good can I redeem from such a barter?"

"Life." Dalcour aptly responds, as he looks back at me, his expression more resolute than before. "I intend to give you a life that will be yours and yours alone. A life so full and free. No more dependences on tippers or saloon crooners. Power to protect yourself and those you care for. Not only that, young one, but the life I want to give you does not bond you to my brother in any way. Your sire bond is only between us two. You will be as a daughter to me and me a father. Being the monster I am, I could never hope for procreation, but through you I can finally apprehend such a notion. Last, even if nothing romantic were to become of you and Decaux, knowing he would regard you as family is equally important."

The weight of Dalcour's words tug my heart strings to the depths of my core, locking me in place. Knowing he simply desires to make me part of his family is both honoring and humbling. The life he wishes to provide is everything I've ever wanted. While I only spent a few short years under the love and influence of my natural father, it is a void I have long wanted to fill. No one will ever be able to replace my father in my eyes, but I am certain Dalcour's parentage would parry the likes of anything Monroe could ever offer.

Once more, tears escape my eyes, trailing my face and creating a glassy shield as I stare at Dalcour. This time I don't wait for his permission before throwing my face into his hollow chest, crying as he grips me in his hold.

"There is nothing to fret, young one. I've got you. Always," Dalcour says softly, holding me tight. Pulling a handkerchief from his pocket, he wipes my face and smiles broad as he lifts my chin. "Now tell me, is this what you want?"

Closing my eyes, I inhale as my mind replays the haunting highlights of my life thus far. I have few moments of merriment to ponder save my memories of my father, Calida, and Chalmette. Flickering thoughts of Scotty, DeLuca and even my recent encounter with Marius warm my heart as I reminisce on my relationships with them. Still, not even those fond memories are enough to ward off the stench of the saloon, Mother, Monroe, and the herd of scoundrels I had to endure.

Stirrings of anger rise within me and I know with all certainty what my response shall be.

"Yes, my lord." The words rush from my mouth and I know I have never been more sure of anything in my life.

Smiling back at me, Dalcour's charming grin stretches from ear to ear as he stands to his feet, extending his hand to mine. "Then it is time," he begins, as I place my palm in his.

"Time for what, my lord?" I ask, curiously afraid as to what will happen next.

"It is time for you to see what you shall become. If you still hold no reservations after what I shall show you then we shall proceed."

"And if my reservations should remain?" I question as Dalcour leads us to the edge of the corridor.

"Then you will be free to go at your own choosing. As I promised before, I will ensure you have enough resources that you shall never have need again. Either way, it is your choice. Do you understand?"

Nodding in affirmation, Dalcour loops his arm through mine and leads me down the long and dark corridor. Arriving at a large wooden door, Dalcour pounds it hard enough I think he's trying to break it down when it opens and a small woman with wide, coal-filled eyes and luminescent pale skin stands holding it ajar by a long iron rod.

"Lord Marchand," she says dutifully, dipping her head in a bow as we cross the threshold. He says nothing in reply as we stroll past her, but I hear a low hiss rumble through her as we continue forward. Dalcour snaps his head back in her direction and growls, expressing his fangs and she stumbles back, pushing the door shut.

"Don't mind her," he says in a softer tone than his scowl suggests. "She's been relegated to the taming wells for more than two weeks and still she can barely open a door without threatening the life of a human.

"Threatening?" I question, glaring back at her over my shoulder as she takes cautious steps along the wall, with her now deeply blackened eyes fixed on me.

"Yes, young one. And not long from now her desires will be your own," Dalcour answers in a dark tone that sends shivers up my spine.

Turning back around, I lock my arm tighter with his as more hissing and shrieking sounds echo around me. The screeching sounds are earsplitting, and I use my free hand to cover my ear while I press my other into Dalcour's bicep.

"Those are the sounds of the Scourge," Dalcour says as we stop in front of a stone and glass chamber.

"The Scourge?" I repeat, gazing around the hallway, trying to make sense of the harrowing sounds buzzing about.

"Yes. You call them vampire. But those in the community call them Scourge."

"What is the difference? Are they not one in the same?"

"No, my dear and it is important that you know there is a difference," Dalcour quickly responds, searching my face for understanding. "Vampires can be either Altrinion-Vampires like myself—you know those of supernatural lineage or humans like yourself who are tamed and can stand to be in society. Scourges are mindless, bloodthirsty creatures. With little memory of their humanity and no essence of supernaturality, they are trapped in a curse of blood, destined forever to be both a pariah and plague on this earth. For this reason, we call them Scourge."

"Is that what I shall become?" I inquire, pointing back at the pale-faced girl trailing us from behind. She pauses as I do, and her greasy auburn hair hangs to one side as she climbs the slick stone wall using only her pointy claws and feet as leverage.

"I suppose you could only hope," Dalcour begins, frowning as he keeps his sights set on the girl. "Although she certainly desires your blood, young Braelyn is faring better than expected."

"Really?"

"Yes," a loud and familiar voice calls to us from behind.

I am surprised to find Titan standing just beyond the threshold when we turn around. Walking toward us, I notice Titan has on more clothes than before. I work hard not to allow my earlier thoughts of him to invade my mind. Between the young Scourge on the wall and the sounds bellowing all around I know I must keep my wits about me.

"Is she one of yours, Titan?" Dalcour questions as the girl jumps down from the wall and perches near Titan's side.

"Yes, my lord. This is Braelyn. If you recall we retrieved her at our last raid north of Charleston. She is making progress, but I keep her close for more taming," Titan adds with a sly smile. With the way the girl is sniffing about him, I am sure her taming has become quite intimate.

"Will I be tamed in such a manner?" I quickly ask as fear looms within me once more.

Both Titan and Dalcour laugh and Dalcour pats my back and shakes his head in protest. "No, young one that is not my manner for taming. Titan has a style all his own but it's not quite my way of things. I prefer to do things the old way," he adds, pointing into a large glass room.

"What is happening here?" Walking closer, I press against the glass, trying to see inside.

"I wouldn't do that if I were you!" Titan teases from behind.

"Do what?" Not sooner than the phrase passes my lips, a large creature plunges into the glass wall, affixing its slimy body against the frame, screeching loud and baring two rows of razor fangs. A lizard like face stares back at me as a long reptilian-like tongue forks along the crease of the door. Banging on the door and shrieking loudly, the creature pulls at the door, begging for release.

"That." Both Titan and Dalcour answer in unison.

"What is that?" I squeal, ambling backward into Dalcour's arms.

"That, my dear, is a Scourge," Dalcour replies, speaking low into my ear. "This one is in rare form too!"

"I'm going to turn into that thing?" I snap, looking to both men and shooting a wary glance at the girl now hovering near Titan's waist.

"Not if you don't want to," Dalcour whispers back.

"What does that mean?"

"It means as long as you work hard at resisting blood and feeding on humans you can lead a relatively sage and normal life," Dalcour says.

"So if I don't feed on humans, what will I eat?"

Sharing a laugh, both men seem amused by my inquiry.

"Well, it appears she's not squeamish on the idea of where her food comes from," Titan laughs as the girl tugs at a leather flask strapped to his side. "Thirsty, are we?" he says as he puts the flask to her mouth allowing her to greedily sip the contents. Turning his attention back to me, he pats the top of her head as she drinks. "New vampires like Braelyn need to feed often. Like the ravenous beast behind you, both Scourge and vampires alike are constantly famished. Are you ready for that, my lady?"

Watching the girl at Titan's waist feverishly slurp the remaining contents causes me to ponder if this too will be my fate.

Even more, can I really do this?

"Chartreuse," Dalcour calls my name, making his way to my side, regaining my attention. "You are stronger than you know. I've witnessed your strength firsthand, and I have no doubt you will conquer this. Besides, resisting bloodlust is only a part of your taming trials."

"There's more?" I ask.

"Oh yes, young one, much more," Dalcour says, opening his arm so that I may loop mine with his. Waving over his shoulder at Titan, we continue down the hall, passing several Scourge on our way.

Some resemble the first lizard-like creature I encountered at my arrival, while others closely resemble more human features like that of the young vampire girl. "What's happening to this one?" I question, watching large fountains of blood fill the room as the vampire stands still in the center, quivering in fear.

"Ah, it is the last trial. Bloodletting. If this one can remain in this room without taking one drop of blood, the gates will open, and they can go free to live among society."

"And if not?"

"They die. For good this time."

"For just one drop? How is that fair?"

"Yes, they must resist even one drop. They must learn that when they are among humans even one drop can bring drastic consequences. To reach this stage a vampire must have passed earlier stages like bloodlust. Like Titan's newest feign, Braelyn, young Scourge have several attempts to master their control around mortals. But once they've reached this phase, they must endure it until the end."

"How long does this trial last?"

"It is different for each. Some only require an hour. Some a full day. It depends on how well they mastered their other tasks. Using the example of Braelyn, she keeps circling back to bloodlust, because she's fearful of the final test."

"And she's afraid she won't make it," I fearfully whisper.

"Do not worry, things will be different for you. I promise." While Dalcour's tone is sure, my doubts weigh heavy.

"How do you know that? What if I'm not as strong as you think?"

"Because unlike most of the vampires here, you will be sired. By me."

"I don't understand. Aren't all of these vampires sired by someone?"

"No, young one. They were all bitten, yes. And it was that bite which caused them to turn into vampires. Perhaps they were bitten by one like me an Altrinion-Vampire, or at the hand of a mortal-made vampire. But only Altrinion-Vampires can sire another vampire, creating a new strain, a familial bond. It is this sire bond that makes your transition different from all others. Your strength will be almost comparable to my own as you carry my blood within you. My strength will be yours. With exception to my supernaturality blessed by the Order of Altrinion, your power will rival that of any mere mortal-made vampire."

"So the sire bond makes me stronger—*much stronger*," I say on a gulp, as the totality of Dalcour's words ring aloud in my mind.

"Yes, young one," he laughs.

"But why me? I'm nothing special—as your brother has clearly stated," I whisper, uncertainty once again filling my mind.

"Oh you are more than special, Chartreuse. You are exceptional. Even Decaux could see that in you. Truthfully, though it doesn't matter whether he sees it or not—you must know it. And something tells me you do. Even if your thoughts sway a bit, you know you are made for more. Don't you?"

Dalcour's words stir something in me I had pushed aside as just a mere way to cope with my life. From the way I managed my business at the saloon, to the manner in which I dealt with both Mother and Monroe—I have always known I deserved and was meant to experience more in life. Perhaps it was the early seeds Calida sowed in my young life, or that I had to mature faster than most, I don't know. What I do know is that this is the life I want. It is the life I've always wanted.

Chapter Sixteen

Walking through the taming wells, Dalcour points out vampires at various points in their transition. Some are faring better than others, working hard to curb their bloodlust, while others succumb to temptation, sealing their fates.

One such vampire could not withstand the bloodletting phase and plunged himself under the small fountain of blood. No sooner than the first drop hit his ravenous mouth, a tall man, who slightly resembled Titan, decapitated the feign and lit the remaining part of his body aflame.

Cringing at the sight, I turned into Dalcour's arms, shielding myself from the horror of it all. As Dalcour tried to comfort me, I let myself peek at the sight of his ashing flesh. *This will not be your fate, Chartreuse.* I muttered the words like a mantra. Although I know such an outcome may be possible for me, I know I have the will to fight my carnality. I must.

A more curious vampire entering the last phase of her taming, intrigued me the most.

"What is happening here?" I ask Dalcour, surprised to find a man holding the hands of the vampire as the final test began.

"Ah, yes, this is an interesting one," Dalcour begins with a proud smile. "The woman, her name is Abigail. We found her on the same venture as we did the first one you met tonight—Braelyn. But this one is a fighter. She was too much for Titan. One of my halfling companions, Cedric, took exception to her and she to him. As time went by, she only took direction from him, so he took on the task of taming her alone. I dare say their taming became more intimate than most, but I digress. Cedric gave into the Altrinion curse of blood so that he would tame himself with her. Strange gesture of love, I know, but it is the lengths he went through to be one with her in every way. Now here he stands with her in the final hour. Whatever comes of this pair, I know one thing—they will be inseparable." I watch as Dalcour's latter words cling to him and the weight of his sentiment strikes my heart hard.

"I've never known such companionship," I quietly say, watching the man grip the woman's hands as blood fountains pour all around them.

"Nor have I," Dalcour whispers back, his eyes distant. Staring at him, a glimmer of his vulnerability is revealed to me and I am beginning to understand why having a family of his own is so important. Before I have a chance to pry further, he forces his throat clear and turns quickly on his heel, pulling us away from the glass chamber of the man and woman. "So, young one," he starts, squaring his shoulder and narrowing his gaze. "Are you still certain this is what you want?"

"Yes, my lord, I am certain. Family is all I've ever wanted and if it must be a family of the night then so be it," I answer, more sure than I have ever been.

"That is good to know. Then there is one final matter to discuss," he says with darkness filling his face. "While you will undoubtedly have a host of new family, you will also be departed from the world you once knew. No longer walking in the light of the sun, we are indeed of the order of night. Even after you master your impulses and completed your training, you will never be able to be a part of the world as you were accustomed. Until you get your feeding under control, your time with Chalmette and other humans may be limited—and even still after then. It takes more than a great deal of restraint to walk among mortals. It requires a willpower that too few have in their formative years. Do you understand?"

"What about DeLuca? He is the only companion I have." My sulking comes across more pitiful than I intend. At least Chalmette will be too busy being a wife to miss me. I am all DeLuca has.

"I understand, young one. That is why I pushed him so hard before we left the mansion. Being part Altrinion his blood may call to you stronger than most. I'd like to keep him around and introduce him to the others, but it may take some time before you can stand to be around him without his blood calling to you," Dalcour answers, still searching my face for understanding.

"And what of you, my lord? You are also Altrinion. Will your blood call to me also?" I question.

"Yes and no. There may be a faint desire, but the sire bond will override that impulse. Of that I am sure. And since you'll share a slight familial bond with Decaux, you should be fine around him as well."

I can't help rolling my eyes at the mention of Decaux's name. While I know his intentions are innocent, my gut tells me he still wishes Decaux and I to be a pair. I have no interest in being with someone who thinks the sight of me is laughable.

Dalcour frowns as I try to force my disdain of Decaux to the four corners of my mind, hopeful my expression doesn't mirror my thoughts.

"Now, Chartreuse—" Dalcour starts, his censuring tone, rings aloud in my ear.

Before he can begin his rebuke, a loud bell rings and echoes of screeching pierce my ears.

"Dalcour! What is happening?" I yell, cupping my ears beneath my palms. Although his hearing is impeccable, he can barely make out my words as he too looks around the corridor, dread filling his face.

In a blink Dalcour scoops me in his arms, flinging me over his shoulder and carries us with the speed of Mercury through the corridor. We are back to the main hall before I have a moment to process it all and he places me down, protectively at his side as he surveys the area.

"Lord Marchand!" Titan and another man shout Dalcour's name in unison, rushing up behind us.

"What is the meaning of this?" Dalcour growls back.

"Wolf attack!" Titan quickly responds.

"Wolves?" I mutter under my breath, surprised by this new revelation.

"By some means they've breached the halls, my lord. We also have a few open Scourge cages as well," the other man replies, keeping his eyes square on Dalcour. Titan gives a quick nod to me as I stammer behind Dalcour's hulking arms, holding tight to his forearm.

"This is totally unacceptable! What of my brother? Is he party to this?"

"No, my lord," Titan answers, turning about as the shrieking sounds grow louder. "He was equally surprised while feeding. He's taken a bunker. You should do the same."

"Absolutely not!" Dalcour snaps. "I'll not duck for cover in the confines of my own walls." As he speaks, he lifts me in his arms, once more taking flight across the hall and placing me inside an empty glass chamber. "Lock the door!" He shouts to Titan and I rush forward, banging my hand on the thick clear wall just as Titan pulls the large door shut. "I'm sorry, Chartreuse, but this is for your safety. You'll be fine in here until I return. Stay low to the ground so no one and nothing sees you. Do you understand?" He barks his orders to me, and I only nod my head in understanding. With his eyes falling briefly, I know while he is hesitant to leave me like this, he is only doing what he believes is best.

Dalcour and the others are out of my eyesight in a flash. Backing myself into a corner, I press against the concrete wall as the earsplitting screeching sound echoing through the halls rattles me to my core.

Is this really the world I want to enter?

Loud growling and bellowing roars shatter the hollow dissonance of the halls and I cave, pulling my knees to my chest. Memories of the word wolf rings through me and I shudder for fear there is more to this supernatural world than I first believed. I still do not know what Armando—a Bulwark— is nor has Dalcour explained it to me fully. And now there are wolves?

I cannot help the gnawing feeling in my gut there is more he has yet to share. Maybe he is just trying to protect me? Or perhaps it's all too much too soon? I don't know. In any case, it's only fair that if we are truly to be family, that I finally understand all I need to know about this new world.

The stirring noises around me continue to fill me with fear, but I do what I've always done when I'm afraid; close my eyes and take deep breaths. As has been my routine at the saloon, I hum, forcing my mind to the darkest parts of my depths. It is the place where I am not a victim, but the victor. It is where I replace the reality of allowing a drunkard into my preciousness with thoughts of me separating the fool's head from his body, discarding his worthless manhood into the same abyss I've sent countless others.

This is my dark place.

This is where I feel safe.

Once more, for fear, I have need to send my mind to my dark comfort. This time, instead as proxy for dreadful tippers from the saloon, I imagine that of vampires and wolves. Envisioning what I would do should their threat reach beyond my ears, minces the muddled places of my mind. I have never seen a supernatural wolf but if the thought of them caused such a panic in even Dalcour Marchand and Titan, I wonder if the same parlor trick I used to ease my fears is perhaps useful in such a case.

Clamoring shouts and clattering sounds still resound around me and I pull my knees to my chin, and tuck my feet under my bottom. The normal murkiness of the hall is replaced by a shroud of a thick dark veiling, ominous form that moves through the corridor and under my door.

Black smoke moves beneath the crack of the large glass encasement and fills through the metal piping along the wall. The stench of charcoal and burning ash stings my nostrils, filling my lungs and sucking the oxygen from me.

Pressing myself against the wall, I struggle to breathe and the formless thick and black cloud looms over me. Although I see no one in the room, I feel something pushing me to the ground as if a foot were lodged between my neck and chin. Working hard to push myself up from the floor, my strength is useless as I gag while the thick gaseousness flumes within me.

"This one is strong. She is not weak," a deep yet melodic voice calls from the shadowy darkness now filling this hollowed space.

"But is she worthy?" Another voice angrily whispers back, as my eyes bulge at the wraith-like creatures taking form before my eyes.

"Yes, she is. Sift her mind, sister," the first formless creature replies with a lighter tone.

"Dark as night. Mold as clay," the second answers and they both cackle, causing the thick smoke to gather about them, granting a slight outline of their phantom-like form. "She makes parry in her mind. She does not trust him. There is doubt in her heart. Filled with murderous folly."

"I am no murderer!" I shout back, wondering if this is all part of Dalcour's plan. Is this the beginning of my taming?

Both of the formless phantoms cackle once more in unison, their smoke thickens, and my breathing becomes more labored. Still I struggle beneath their ominous hold, hopeful to get up from whatever is holding me down.

"Provocation starts in the mind, my dear Chartreuse," the first voice whispers back. But this time something is different. If I did not know better, I would think somehow they have formed the shape of my dead sister, Calida's face in their shadowy haze. Blinking my eyes, I try to make sense of Calida's image before me and I try to reach out to take hold of her, but my hands graze through their ghastly mist.

"Calida!" I scream with tears rushing from behind my closed lids, marring my face.

"And what would Calida want you to do, dear?" The same one calls to me.

"Protect yourself," the other answers in an almost condemning tone.

As they speak, harrowing images of Calida being dragged in the streets and tied to a post form in their ghastly veil. I struggle to say Calida's name once more, but my own words fail me and I writhe on the floor watching, in horror, as my dear sister's body burns on the wooden post. Shouts, laughing, and cheers erupt as phrases like, *burn the witch*, rivet through the chorus of murderous pawns.

My sister's screams and pleas go deaf in their ears as the fire they lit grows and her flesh melts into the wooden beam.

"Stop this!" I cry, wanting such images to flee from my sight.

My memories of the day my sister was taken have always been too hazy to recall. All I remember is Mother rushing back to our home and for fear closing the curtains and commanding both Victoria and I to hide in the closet. Faint thoughts of men shouting outside our home have always haunted my mind. The only time she showed even an ounce of parental care, Mother nestled us in her arms and told us not to worry, even as the banging became incessant.

But then the clamor from outside our home ended. Silence hollowed the halls of our home and Mother feared the men were lulling us to a false sense of security. Thankfully, she was wrong. When she finally got courage to open the closet door it was Dalcour Marchand staring back at us.

He saved us.

"Saved you that time, yes. This time you must save yourself," the gruff one barks at me as the colorful memories of him carrying me in his arms score through my mind.

"Save myself?" I whisper back.

"Yes," the wraiths answer in unison.

Slowly, the weight once at my throat lessens and my breathing eases. I push myself up from the floor and back into the corner, keeping a wary watch of the shapeless creatures before me.

"Who—no—what are you?" I ask as the screeching and howling sounds around us grow and I no longer think any of this is a part of Dalcour's plan for me.

"We are never a part of the plan of tertiary creation!" I hear the more demure one answer my hidden thoughts. "Now tell us, young one, would you like the power to save yourself?"

"There is no power you can offer that Lord Marchand cannot give," I haughtily reply.

"Do you think he cares to save you, foolish child? He only cares to pervert your power for his own. If you benefit then so be it. But always know, he shall always be the benefactor of whatever comes from you. Protect you, he might. Save you, he will not!" The harsher-toned wraith whips its words, striking me in one hard blow.

"I don't believe you!" I protest.

"Then believe this," the softer one replies, revealing another shadowy image.

The face of a man I have never seen forms within her phantom form and my mind goes blank trying to make out who this man is.

"I don't know this man," I quietly reply.

"Ah, but you should, dear one. His name is Elias Peyroux."

Shrugging my shoulders, I laugh. "You must have me confused. I have never seen this man or heard of his name before."

"Lies. Deceit." They both squeal, once more in unison.

"There is no lie! I'm telling you I have never seen this man!" I shout back, swiping my hand through their shared ghastly veil. As I do, the image changes and I hear the man say my sister's name.

"They are just past that dirt road, deep beyond the tree line." I watch as the man points the way to two men in carriages as they head toward Decaux's private estate. Calida always said their place was such a secret, for fear of others she'd never take me or Victoria.

"Who is this man?" My tone lowers an octave as my throat falls to my gut as I watch him run away, stuffing a paper in his pocket, wearing a wide smile.

"Elias Peyroux. And he is the man responsible for your sister's apprehension and Decaux's imprisonment."

Tears fall to my cheeks as his image fades from my view and rage fuels my thoughts. I can't imagine anything my sister could ever do to set his ire against her—yet and still, he betrayed both she and Decaux. Mother said the murderous towns people looked for Calida and Decaux for days and never found them. Now I know how they discovered their whereabouts.

Heaving a gulp of air, I brush the back of my hand against my face, wiping my tears aside. "It doesn't matter," I begin, rising to my knees. "Decaux put a swift end to anyone who had a hand in Calida's murder. They are all dead," I answer firmly, swallowing down my doubts.

"But are they?" The two question me in unison as newer images of a now older Elias form before me.

"This one yet lives and Dalcour knows it so," the second wraith adds.

"Liar!" I snap back.

"No foolish child, only Dalcour lies to you. He desires to control you."

"Protect you, he may. Save you, he cannot. Will not. Only you can save yourself. With this," the first continues, now revealing a thick, black, slimy substance in the makings of its palm.

"What is that?" I question as puzzling thoughts of Dalcour and this new information about Elias Peyroux swarm my mind.

"Drink this and you alone will have the power to save yourself and protect who and what you will. It will bind to Marchand's sire bond with you but will give you so much more. He will not be able to control you as he wills, but your desires shall be your own. You will be more than a vampire—more decadent than a Scourge, and your own will beyond your maker. When you turn you will yet have one last day of sunlight. You will be able to control your form, but with the same melody of mulberry and juniper trees, you will consume those against you."

"I—I don't know if I should," I stutter my words. I am both fearful of letting the moment pass and accepting such an offer.

"Time is against you, child!" The second one lashes back.

Cupping its hand closer to my mouth, the inviting scent of berries and molasses fill my nostrils, making me salivate with delight.

"That's it child, take this and save yourself."

"How do I know it won't kill me?"

"It will." They answer in unison as my eyes fill with terror.

What? I think to myself. Looking up at their ominous form, small, yet wicked smiles frame their ghastly faces and the thickening smoke fills the glass and cement encased room.

"As you will also die to your mortality once Dalcour sucks the last drop from your body, so you will depart the life you once knew. But only when you take the life of the one who first breaks your heart will this blackness form within it. From that moment you will no longer be a mere puppet, but you will siren your own heart's song, dooming any who shall come against you."

"And what if I no longer want this?"

"*Only when you destroy the one who has truly harmed you, shall you be avenged, and the darkness leave you. The longer you wait, the more it shall cleave to,*" the wraith whispers back.

"Is it Elias Peyroux? Am I to take his life?"

"*Only you know when that day shall come, for in their eyes alone, you'll be undone,*" they speak, once more in unison. "*Now drink!*" they command, lifting the thick liquid to my lips.

Knowing that Dalcour's secrets may inevitably cause my demise, my heart sinks and I know this is now my only recourse. Even his desires to tame me, fill me with both doubt and fear.

This act may be my only assurance.

That is why I do what I do now.

I know with all confidence I will never allow my fate to become that of either Calida or my halfhearted mother. I also know I will never forsake my family like my wretched sister Victoria. It is clear I cannot rely on the salvation of men; supernatural or otherwise. Yet, I am required to still play their game. I must do more than match their parry. I will subdue them.

It is with such certainty I also know the allegiance I now form is one made from the pit from which all darkness is derived. But I see no other way. I refuse to be either captive or pawn. And it is with this surety I declare I will come on the other end of this darkness both unscathed and *untamed*.

Chapter Seventeen

Darkness envelops me as I take in the thick black substance. It coats my throat as I do, clinging to my jaw, tongue, and every inch of my mouth, locking it shut. Slithering down my airway, it sucks oxygen from my lungs, suffocating me as I grab my neck, fearful my death is eminent.

The two wraiths chant a haunting, yet lyrical limerick over me as I writhe against the cold concrete floor, gasping for air. The patois of their sonnet is wickedly beautiful, lulling my mind to a deep enchantment while my body thrashes and convulses beneath their shadowy form.

"Misty meadows and cold-wrought springs live within these hallowed beings. In the dark and buried deep, beneath the earth our secrets keep. Until fate and fear rise with time and horrid quandary fill your mind. Sing with sirens, snare, and break. Earthbound men their soul to take. Maiden kind you may subdue, yet only for measure of mortal feud. The bonding sires and sirens must groom but binding hearts will seal your doom. Return to dust those who sadden thy soul, end with surety, and take them whole. Remove what and who grieves you most and changeling no longer need you to host."

My head throbs as the two wraiths harmoniously chant over me. Their words confound and intrigue me. While a deeper part of me seems to comprehend its meaning, I wrestle with the dark magic taking over me and I am unable to speak. My mouth is sealed. Whether it be the black liquid I ingested or the power they now wield over me, I am unsure. All I know is whatever questions I had, will have to wait.

Stirring images of a golden white oak, lightning, and what appears to be earth splitting in two in a time since passed, fill my mind. Haunting flashes of a tribe of beings banished to a dark abyss while the golden white oak tree shimmers with such a brilliance the dark beings cower in terror, sting my heart. Feelings of pain, fear, and a sorrow too frightful to tell awake a melancholy within me I had not known.

"Now she sees. Now she knows. The dark inside her forever grows. With new eyes now you shall wake. The world before you, in blood and death you'll take."

With a closing ceremonious wail and cackling howl, the vise grip of the wraith's power frees its hold on me, and I am left once more on the cold floor, squirming in both pain and fear.

Before I have a chance to understand what just happened to me, the door swings open and the sight of Dalcour's thick leather boot lands in my eyesight.

"Chartreuse," Dalcour begins, now kneeling beside me. "Are you okay?" He questions, lifting me from the floor and propping me in the cavity of his hold. "What happened to you?"

"I—I'm okay," I stutter, looking around the encased room for any semblance of the malevolent beings. "Just a bit off kilter," I lie, pushing myself up from the floor.

"Are you certain?" He asks once more, searching my face with an intense glare.

"I'm fine." My answer is stiff as I pull myself from his grip as the haunting words of the phantoms plagues my thoughts. "What about you, my lord," I begin, feigning concern. "Is everything okay? I've never heard such sounds. And—the—the way you left in such a scamper—"

"Everything is under control," he replies curtly, cutting me off. He keeps his gaze set on me, lingering a bit as his brows brush with frustration. Squaring his shoulders, he walks to the threshold of the door with his arms behind his back and looks down the long narrow corridor. "No interruptions!" Dalcour shouts down the hall to someone beyond my sight and the lights go dim.

"Now, young one," he says, turning on his heel, his face now brightened. "Are you sure you still want to do this?"

At his words, my heart falls into the pit of my gut, with everything that just happened with the phantom creatures and what I learned of this Elias Peyroux, I had almost forgotten why we came here in the first place.

"If you're worried about the wolves, there's no need. We've taken care of them. I'll allow no harm to come to you." Dalcour's resolute stance is clear as he stands before me now. Although the thought of wolves is the last thing on my mind, a part of me is thankful to him.

"But will I be safe?" My words are mumbled as memories of Elias' betrayal of Decaux and Calida ring through me.

"Of course, young one," Dalcour says brightly, walking toward me with his arms outstretched. "I'll never let harm come to you. In all the ways that matter, you will become my family. Do you understand?" He adds, now resting his hands on my shoulders.

"But what about Elias Peyroux?" I blurt my words and a pang of fear pierces through me as I do.

"What?" Dalcour answers quietly, stepping away from me, his face is marred with both shock and concern. "Wait—where—what do you know of Elias?"

"Does it matter? You know of him. And you know what he did to my sister and yet he still lives!" I snap.

"Catherine must've told you," he mumbles under his breath, revealing my mother's knowledge of this fact. While I shouldn't be surprised, it still boils my blood to hear it. Rubbing his hand across his forehead, he sighs and turns away, pacing back and forth between me and the doorway. "Listen, Chartreuse, you must understand things are not as they seem."

"But aren't they? How could you keep such secrets? Why does this man yet live?" I demand.

"Contrary to what you may believe of my world—your soon-to-be new world, young one, not everything deserves the punishment of death. I know you may not understand that now, but you will."

"How can you say that? Because of him my sister is dead. And what about Decaux?"

"No! It is because of pathetic, bigoted, and worthless souls that your sister died. Not Elias. He was a mere rook—not even a pawn. Leveraging a man's freedom is not quite the payment you'd expect of betrayal. But alas, despite all your contrite experiences in this world you'll never know what it means to be treated poorly because of the hue of your skin."

"Perhaps but—"

"But nothing, Chartreuse! You need to see," Dalcour says, palming the sides of my head as he transfers flickers of his memories to me, jolting me into a trance-like state. "Unlike me or Decaux, wolves like Elias cannot roam the world free. A wolf's supernaturality only extends at the parting of the moon—unless he is an alpha. Otherwise he must live his life just as any man of color. In bondage. How can you comprehend such depravity? They gave him freedom papers for knowledge of my brother's whereabouts. But did Catherine tell you that Elias also told my brother in advance? Yes—he warned Decaux that they were coming, but my brother in his haughtiness thought himself untouchable. It was my brother's hubris that allowed both himself and Calida to be taken. Elias did right by both my brother as he also did right by his family in securing their freedoms. For that, he will never receive a punishment of death from me. Nor shall he or his kin ever receive such a punishment by your hand—swear it to me!" Dalcour's condemning and demanding words pierce me straight in my gut and my feet once more feel bolted beneath me.

"Yes, my lord," my words are contrite, and the thought of Elias' predicament stabs my heart.

"Listen to me," Dalcour begins in a now softer tone, strumming his fingers through my hair. "I do understand that your life was no easy stroll through a garden. I am well aware of how poverty held your state, taking you into unfathomable circumstances. Circumstances no one of your beauty and charms should ever experience. Now imagine, being denied the freedom to live as other mortals simply because others think you inferior."

"I understand, my lord. I just miss her so much!" I cry, plunging my face into his chest. While this overtaking of raw emotion may be new for me, it feels necessary. To date I only recall feeling like this two other times in my life—but this is different.

"It's quite all right, young one. Let it all go. Now the bonding can begin." Dalcour's dark and throaty tone reverberates through his hollowed chest. Laying my head against his muscular frame, I am surprised I hear no heartbeat.

Then I remember. Vampires don't have hearts.

"Begin?" I question, looking up through tear-laden lashes.

"Shall we begin?" He asks once more with darkened eyes as his fangs slowly protrude from his mouth before me.

Everything in me tells me I should be afraid—that this is wrong—that I should run. But I cannot. Will not. My soul feels anchored in this repose and I know this is what I want.

More than repaying vengeance, I must ensure my own safety. I must protect myself from perils known and unknown. I alone must look to my own interests. For truly not even Calida cared for what would be my fate when she entangled herself with Decaux. Father died and mother lost all parental sensibilities—if there were ever any. Victoria ran off and Chalmette is a new wife. I and I alone am left to secure my own protection.

"Yes," I whisper my words in response.

A low, guttural growl rumbles through Dalcour as he widens his mouth, showcasing rows of razor fangs. But something happens I did not expect, slowly, he raises his arm and tears into his own flesh. As he does, a stream of glistening dark crimson runs down his forearm.

Lifting his wrist to my mouth, he commands me, "Drink."

He doesn't wait for me to comply when he presses his arm to my mouth, allowing the sweet warmth of his blood to flow like a fountain into my mouth.

Not in my twenty-seven years have I ever tasted anything as sweet and succulent as this. It bears a liking to that of honey and wild berries. I have never tasted its likeness. The more I taste the more I want. My mouth clings to his wrist like a suckling child to his mother's breast.

I don't want to let go.

The sweet taste of Dalcour's blood implodes my tastebuds, bursting like tiny grains of sugar on my tongue. Unlike the dank flavor of the phantom's curd, Dalcour's blood flows through my mouth like a sweet water fountain and I do all I can to savor every drop!

As I continue to suck at his wrist, a warming sensation ripples through me and a golden hue emanates through Dalcour's aura. Throwing his head back, Dalcour moans and whispers an unknown tongue and the sound of a thousand voices echoes through the small room. A feeling of weightlessness overtakes me, and I notice we have lifted from the ground as Dalcour's strong arm now rests around my waist.

"That's enough, young one," he whispers, tugging his wrist away from my yearnful lips.

Cooing, I whine as he pulls himself from me and I reach out and try to pull his arm back to me. Everything in me wants just one more taste!

"No more, my dear Chartreuse. You're not quite ready for a second helping. At least not until your turning," Dalcour says softly, as we drift back to the concrete floor.

"My turning?" A waft of inebriation rolls through me and I feel like a tipsy saloon congregant. If I didn't know better, I would think there was more than one Dalcour in the room. The room spins and I topple to my knees, working hard to get my bearings. "Dalcour!" I shout, reaching out for him. Grabbing my wrists he laughs and says something back to me, but his speech is incoherent to me. "Dalcour! What is happening to me? I feel—I—"

Chapter Eighteen

Once more, darkness swathes my sight as both the sound of a thousand voices rings through my head as does the incessant and cackling cry of the phantom pair. Only the sweet taste of Dalcour's blood lingering on my tongue soothes the anxiety bubbling beneath my brim.

Horrid sights of death, murder and malice build in my forlorn mind, tormenting me as the duality of Dalcour's blood and the phantom's offering surge through my veins, like toxic venom. Writhing in agony, I want to scream but I cannot. I want to cry but I cannot. Some other force now holds my state, and it is stronger than anything I've ever felt before.

Reminiscent of the wraith-like boot, something or someone is holding me down, willing me into their submission. Still, I continue to fight. I will not be subdued.

"I told you she's a fighter," I hear a familiar and distant voice say.

"No surprise here. That's exactly why I chose her." A closer and deeper voice replies. "It's okay, young one. You are safe. You're among family. Now it's time to wake up."

"Dalcour?" I question, blinking my eyes hard, forcing them open. My view is blurry, but I can make out Dalcour's large frame seated next to me.

"Yes, it's me. Come now, open your eyes," he replies in a gentle yet slightly parental tone.

"Please, Red! You're starting to scare me!" I now make out DeLuca's crackling voice from afar.

"DeLuca?"

"Yes, poppet, it's me! Please tell me you're well," DeLuca responds, coming closer.

"And I told you she is fine, Sincade. She took in a bit more than a mortal should that's all," Dalcour lashes back.

"Perhaps it would be best if you two left her to Armando. She surely doesn't need to hear your grumblings back and forth." Although I've barely gotten my bearings, I'd know Armando's brash tone no matter my state.

"I just want to make sure she is okay before we depart," Dalcour answers, his voice is softer as he now cups my chin in his palm.

"Where are you going?" I whisper my words while continuing to force my eyes apart. The thought of Dalcour leaving me is upsetting.

"There, there, young one. Don't trouble yourself with worry. I'm not going anywhere until I see you are okay."

Finally, my eyes part wide, and I see Dalcour, Armando and DeLuca hovering over me. Looking around I notice I'm back in a large bed but it's not the same room Chalmette and I were once in. "Where are we?" I say, pushing up on my elbows, trying to take in my surroundings.

"Why beloved, we're in New Orleans," Dalcour answers, now standing up from my bedside.

"But how? When?"

"Tsk-tsk," Armando begins, taking heavy and hard steps toward me. "Now don't you trouble yourself with such things. All you need to know is that you are safe." Placing a cool towel on my forehead, Armando pushes a few pillows behind me, propping me up on the bed. "Take a sip," he says, offering me a glass of water.

"Can I drink this?" I ask, looking up at Dalcour. My eyes trail his forearm as I recount memories of the tantalizing taste of his blood. Nodding his head, Dalcour smiles as Armando lifts the glass to my mouth. Drinking the cool water, I feel the pacing of my heart quiet from the frenzy upon my awakening to a normal rhythm.

"Now doesn't that feel better," Armando says, taking his handkerchief to blot the corners of my mouth. I only nod in agreement and try to force a small smile while keeping my eyes on Dalcour's now shifty posture.

"Are you sure you feel well, Red?" DeLuca asks, concern marring between the inverted lines of his brow.

"I'm fine, DeLuca. I promise," I answer quietly, still keeping my gaze fixed on Dalcour as he saunters across the wooden floor. "And you, Lord Marchand?"

Turning to me, he smiles and waves his hand in the air, dismissively. "I am not the topic of discussion. Are you certain you feel well? You took quite a spell. Besides, I've never known anyone to take such a slumber after commencing the sire bond."

"How long was I sleep?"

"Two days, poppet! Two whole days! From the time Lord Marchand brought you back from the wells until we arrived here in New Orleans." While DeLuca's sentiment surprises me, I am still worried about the uneasy scowl now etched on Dalcour's face. "Did you hear me, Chartreuse? Two days!"

"No need to shout, DeLuca!" I quietly bite back. "My head is throbbing. But I am thankful to now be on the other end of things. At least we've gotten the hard part over."

Armando lets out a shrilling chortle, cupping his hands at his mouth. Dalcour quickly whips his head over his shoulder, giving Armando a rebuking glare, but Armando casually scrunches his shoulders as he exits the room.

"Perhaps you should leave too," Dalcour says, now turning to DeLuca. Huffing in reply, DeLuca looks over Dalcour's shoulders at me, waiting for consent.

"I'm fine, DeLuca. I promise. Thanks for bothering enough to care."

"I'll always bother you at least a little, Red," DeLuca answers with a caring smile. "I will be back to check on you." Before waiting for a reply, DeLuca darts a quick glance toward Dalcour, turning quickly on his heel and leaves.

"Now, young one, please tell me truthfully—are you well?" Dalcour asks once more, concern filling the void between his eyes.

"Yes, my lord. Truthfully. I mean, I am quite tired—and a little hungry, but I guess that is to be expected after being turned. Right?"

"That's just it, Chartreuse. I did not turn you. You are not yet vampire."

"What! But I—I thought—didn't we—didn't I—"

"Now, now, calm yourself, my dear Chartreuse," Dalcour gently adds, coming back to my bedside.

"I know this can't all be a dream! I drank blood! I heard shrieking! And wolves—I heard them too! And the young vampire girl—and the couple! And the phan—"

"Listen, please! Yes all those things happened, young one," Dalcour says, with his palm now at my mouth. While I'm still up in arms about it all, a part of me is thankful he stopped me short of sharing my encounter with the phantoms.

Slowly, I slide his hand away from my mouth and a jolting current blazes my finger at his touch. Looking down at me, a small smile curls at the corner of Dalcour's mouth and he squeezes our clasped hands together, resting it at my side.

"And that right there is a sign of our connection. My Altrinion blood now flows through your veins."

"But I thought you just said—"

"If you had let me finish, I would have told you that we began the siring, but I have not yet turned you."

"I don't understand."

"Well, to be perfectly honest, you are my first sireling. As such, I wanted to be sure I did it right. You took a little more from me than what is required which put you on quite a binge. I suppose you can liken it to a drunken stupor of sorts. Thankfully, your heart did not fail. So I knew you'd be fine in a matter of time."

"Okay, I suppose that makes sense. But why didn't you turn me while I was sleeping?"

"It doesn't quite work that way—at least not for the sire bonding to manifest. You must give consent to the bonding in every way. If not, you'd be no different than a scourge." Dalcour's intense and dark gaze sets into mine as he searches my face for understanding.

"Oh, I suppose that makes sense. So when do I turn?" My eyes fall as I ask, fearful Dalcour's intentions have changed and the desire I had to protect myself is now put on pause.

"That's what I wanted to talk to you about. Since you've now taken my blood, you'll have all the advantages of a supernatural and none of the disadvantages. No bloodlust. No rage. Just heightened senses, some speed, and enhanced strength."

Looking up at him through my unusually thickened lashes, my interest is piqued. "Really?" I can't help the lilt of excitement bubbling through me.

"Well, it's only temporary," he answers.

"Oh." My excitement falls to the pit of my gut.

"That is, until I return. Once I do, we shall complete your transition."

Again, my excitement builds inside me and a most unlady-like shout erupts through me and I toss my arms around his neck, pulling him into my embrace. While my behavior is surprising even for me, it feels the most appropriate response I can garner.

Working to free himself from my hold, Dalcour laughs heartily, and smiles as he holds my hands, resting them on his knee. "Well, I'm glad you are delighted!" He laughs once more.

"Wait—wait, what do you mean when you return?" I question, leaning back into the bouquet of pillows at my back, searching his face. "Where are you going, my lord?"

"No worries, young one, I will not be long at all," he replies, quickly rising up from my side. "I have some business to tend to in Lexington, but I'll return in a few weeks. I promise to be back before the power of the sire bond fades. Although I am not worried. I should return short of thirty days. When I do, we'll make our way straight to the wells and begin your transition to become supernatural."

"But wait, my lord, are you leaving me? Here? Alone? And with all this new power?" I reply, rising to my knees as swirling golden rays illumine through my fingertips.

"Ah, yes, your little illumination should fade in a few short days," Dalcour begins with a small chuckle. "Stay close to the mansion. Titan will keep an eye on you. He's building out another part of the taming wells as we speak. I have instructed him to look after you while I am away."

"Titan? You're leaving me here with him? I'd rather have Armando look after me, my lord," I say, sulking back into the bed, resting my bottom on my feet.

"Oh and here I thought you fancied Titan! Well, no worries, he's used to working with new supernaturals of all breeds." Dalcour smiles wide, stuffing his hands in his pockets and leans against a large wooden armoire. "Oh and I mustn't forget to mention I had Greta pick out a few things for you. You'll find quite an assortment in the armoire and chest of drawers. Of course, if you need to go into town to get more fabrics, Greta will be more than happy to accommodate you."

"Well, I'm not sure whoever Greta is, but usually DeLuca goes with me to fetch fabrics and such. Even still, I'm sure I can manage."

"Hmm—I see I still have quite a few holes to fill. My apologies. Greta is the governess for my estate here in New Orleans. She is an invaluable resource and even though she is human, knows the supernatural world very well. And well, since I'll be taking Master DeLuca with me on my travels, both Greta and Titan will keep watch over you. Not that they will need to do much since—"

"Wait! What! You're taking DeLuca where? Why?"

"My, my, do calm yourself, young one. No need to get huffy. I am still a man of color in the south and DeLuca will serve as my covering, if you will, should suspicions rise. Particularly in cases where tapping into my supernaturality would cause undue attention."

"But I'll be all alone," I mutter under my breath, falling deeper into the pillows at my back.

Before I can blink, Dalcour is beside me in an instant. Lifting my now lowered chin to meet his dancing crimson eyes, he smiles once more and says, "No, my lovely ward, you will never be alone again." His voice is gentle while his smile stretches from ear to ear as pools of water thicken in the corners of my eyes. "With the power of our bond and the stream of the Altrinion force now flowing through your veins, you'll feel my presence with you—always."

Pulling me into his embrace, tears rush from my eyes as I sob on his shoulder. In the few moments since my awakening I've gone from one high emotion to the next. Even now, I am overcome with a wrought and wild fervor I've never felt before.

And I love it!

"I suppose I understand, my lord," I whisper back.

"It's quite all right, young one. I promise you."

"But do you think it wise for me to be alone? So soon?"

"Yes, I know it's soon and for that I do apologize. I had hoped we'd have more time together. But as you witnessed last night, things in the supernatural community are tenuous. The Skull wolves attacking us were no accident. Since we don't have my brother's machinations to blame, I can only assume the Changeling witches are up to their normal predilections. Only they have been known to control the savagery of the Skull."

Looking up at Dalcour's now crestfallen face, a stone-like force drops to the pit of my stomach. "My lord? Skull? Changeling? I don't understand," I mutter, fearful of his response.

"I know you still have much to learn, and I promise I will teach you all I can when I return. But I'll not have you ignorant of the wretchedness that comes with this new world. The Skull are packless wolves—void of a leader or an alpha. They move in herds, attacking and killing all that come in their path. However, they do not hunt—at least not in a coordinated effort. If wolves are found devoid an alpha and eventually fall under a Skull curse, no longer can they shift into a mortal. They are trapped in their deformed wolf state, doomed to scavenge the earth. Only a Changeling of great power can control a Skull herd. Changelings, on the other hand, are the first non-earthbound supernatural entities of this world. Until their great fall, they had dominion over the animals of the earth. Since their descent, they practice only the darkest of power, possessing unsuspecting mortals and bending them to their will. For years, little has been heard of them until now."

"Until now?" I question, as memories of my encounter with the wraith-like creatures fill my mind.

"While I don't typically lay the desolation of humanity at the feet of the supernatural world, many believe it is the dark power of the Changelings fueling the dissent of men."

"How so?" Fear chokes the bile in my throat, and I am sick inside. Still, I work hard to stifle my feelings. Thankfully, Dalcour's preoccupied thoughts keep him from discerning my angst.

Biting his lip as he tosses his head up toward the ceiling and circling a wide woven rug at the edge of my bed, Dalcour heaves a sigh and continues, "As they consider themselves the first and true original beings of this world, they care not for Altrinions or humans. Since the beginning, they've been at the very core of every war and act of incivility of this broken world. Sure humanity has its own sins to answer for, but I have no doubt the witchcraft of the Changelings has long been at work."

Dalcour's eyes are distant as he speaks and the silence between us becomes deafening. His words trouble me. As much as I want to tell him of my encounter with the otherworldly creatures, I know I cannot. Not only will he be disappointed in me for falling to the wiles of the Changelings, but I know for certain he will not complete my turning.

And I will not let anything take that away from me.

Not even Dalcour Marchand or the witchery of the Changelings will stand in my way.

Sauntering across the wooden floor, Dalcour clears his throat, thrusting his hands in his pockets and forces a small smile. "Look, young one, I don't want you to worry about wretched Changelings or Skull wolves. For that reason, we shall not sully the mood by any further thought of the deplorable faction of the supernatural. Rather, this is to be a happy time for you!"

Dalcour's voice is lighter and more airy than I've ever heard, and I can tell he is forcing himself from the darker hold of his lingering thoughts.

"A happy time?" I repeat, watching his eyes dance again and I can't help wondering what musings dawdle behind his crimson irises.

"Why of course!" Dalcour says brightly with a wide smile that meets his eyes as he makes his way back to my side. "For the first time in your beautiful young life you'll only have yourself to worry about. Take this time to get to know yourself, apart from tragedy and shame. *Finally.* Enjoy the small indulgences of life that most take for granted. You'll have no fear of neither man nor woman. With the Altrinion force flowing through you, you'll have the strength and power to care for and protect yourself and none of the vices of the scourged curse of turning. So take this time, young Chartreuse and enjoy your beautiful life!"

My beautiful life? Dalcour's words intrigue me. To date, my life has been anything but beautiful. Nightmare yes. Beautiful absolutely not.

"Come see," Dalcour says in a darker tone with his hand outstretched. Placing my palm in his, he takes me from the bed, and we are quickly across the room standing in front of a large floor length mirror.

For the first time in what seems like forever, I see myself.

I am beautiful.

Not that I've ever thought of myself as unattractive but the word beautiful has never come to mind. Looking at myself, I see a woman that is almost foreign to me. With the Altrinion force flowing through me, my skin is flawless and my curves more pronounced. Eyes like jade stone stare back at me while the wavy, fire-burnt hair resting at my shoulders frames my face, revealing a hauntingly beautiful creature.

"Who is this woman?" I mutter as I fluff my hands through my hair, slowly trailing an outline of my hourglass form, staring in awe at my own mirror image.

With his chest puffed with pride, Dalcour stands at my side, careful not to block my view of myself. "I now introduce you to Miss Chartreuse Grenoble. The woman who will set this world ablaze."

Chapter Nineteen

For the first time in my memory, I am alone.

Not counting the moments I spent in my room before I was required to entertain the tipsy tippers of the saloon or the brief space of solace I spent putting ports of rum in the back closet, I am truly alone.

No friends. No family. Just me.

Watching both Dalcour and DeLuca take their leave from the estate, I now realize this is the first time in my life where I am not required to keep watch of a younger sibling, or thwart unwanted advances. A first in my recollection indeed.

Even knowing Armando is also gone with Dalcour and DeLuca is somewhat unsettling. For as brief a time as it has been, I'd grown accustomed to his snippy retort and uptight persona. Although, it was his farewell kiss and lingering embrace that assures me, I'll likely not see him again. Neither he nor Dalcour told me so, but for as many as I've had in my short life, I am no stranger to the finality accompanying a parting farewell.

Still, it is probably the way both DeLuca and I shared our goodbyes that grieves me most.

Walking in on Dalcour inquiring whether the two of us were romantically involved and hearing DeLuca declare a most emphatic denial, crushed my heart in two. While we never shared anything more than a congenial hug, DeLuca refuted any longing of his heart toward me as though he were asked to kiss a frog.

To salt the wound, the ghastly look on his face when he saw me at the threshold of the parlor sent a desolation through my soul I have known too well. In fact, it is a pain I should never hope to endure again.

It is quite beyond reason why Sincade DeLuca's negation of affection toward me pains me so, but it makes me actually thankful Dalcour has taken my little Romani friend with him.

I need this time for myself!

Sadly, our parting at their leave was sullen. There were no warm gestures, save my embrace with Armando and Dalcour's quick introductions of me to the house governess, Greta. Before I had a moment to process it all they were gone.

And here I stand, gazing out the large Palladian window at the top of the double staircase, looking out to a large and overgrown flower garden, I take in the grandeur that is New Orleans.

I was just a child the last time I was here, but the memories, both fond and frightening, still hold my heart.

A lone tear falls to my face as thoughts of my past and present state torment my soul. As haunting recollections of my childhood may be none can compare to whatever barter I made with the Changelings that is sure to be my doom.

As much as I know my reasons for taking their bait lead back to my loss of my precious sister Calida, here in New Orleans, there's a darker part of me which can't but acknowledge there is something far more sinister at work.

I can only hope I can disavow the bewitching mastery of the Changelings as ardently as DeLuca did at the thought of any romantic pairing with me.

"My lady," I hear Greta call to me from the foyer below.

Quickly wiping my eyes free of the waterworks building behind my lids, I turn to the other side of the railing and look down into the foyer. "Yes," I answer back.

Looking up at me, Greta's kind smile greets me as she stands with her hands folded at her waist. She is a petite woman, but her gaudy and stout spirit shows no sign of recoil. Not even in Dalcour's domineering presence did she shrink. It's as if she thinks nothing of her evenly five-foot frame. As a matter of fact, I was quite impressed to see she gave no deference to Armando, nor did she stand for his bullying manner.

"We need to discuss your schedule and plan your meals for the week, mon cheri," Greta says.

Making my way down the stairs, I take another look around this impressive and massive estate. I can't believe I'm in anything so grand! Smiling, I hold tight to the wooden rails as my new speed swiftly sends me square before Greta before I have an opportunity to comprehend the mechanics of it all.

"Whoa!" I shout, fumbling into her arms. "I'm sorry, Greta! This is going to take some time to get my bearings."

"It is quite fine, my lady," Greta softly replies. "Some of these effects will wear off as time goes on, so not to worry."

Staggering out of her hold, I work to get my footing as the dizzying spell of my swift motion settles. "How do you know how all of this works?"

"Well," she begins, grabbing my hand, helping to steady my movement as she leads us down the hall toward the parlor. "I've been around supernaturals most of my life. I've seen it all."

"Seen it all? But you can't be much older than me."

"Age is timeless in their world, I'm afraid. Lord Marchand took me from my former master and owner when I was still a girl. He bargained my freedom papers for my owner's life and that of his family. From that time until now I have been a part of this world," Greta replies, taking her hair out of its high bun, revealing long raven black hair that falls to the middle of her back. Her light brown eyes illumine the small freckles nestled across her cheekbone as her peach-colored smile frames her petite pear-shaped face.

"So, why didn't you become a vampire?" I ask, curious. "I mean wouldn't you finally have the means to avenge yourself? Your family?"

"I suppose that is one option," she answers with a small chuckle. "But in all truth, I wasn't interested."

"Really? Why not?"

"It's never been what I wanted. Quite frankly, I never knew such creatures existed until Lord Marchand saved me. But I like being who and what I am. *Human*. I never wanted to avenge myself of other humans. I just wanted to be treated with humanity."

Greta's sentiment sears the fabric of my heart like a hot iron. I wish I were like her.

"Now," she starts, clearing her throat, "to the matter at hand."

"Ah, yes, the meals and schedule," I add, flattening the back of my dress as I take a seat across from Greta while we sit at a large walnut table.

"Do you have any preferences or things to abstain?"

"I—um—I'll eat pretty much whatever you prepare. I have no sensitivities to which I am aware."

"Perfect!" Greta answers with delight. "Sometimes Lord Marchand's visitors can be rather choicy."

"Oh really," I say intrigued. I can't help wondering what type of visitors he's had over the years.

"And before you ask, yes they were all lovely," she adds, cupping her mouth. "Now about your schedule," she finishes. It is clear she isn't about to divulge any further information on Dalcour's guests.

"Well, I don't really have a schedule per se. I suppose I'll just see where the day takes me."

"Ah, I see. Thankfully for you Lord Marchand anticipated your response. As such he has taken the liberty of preparing a preliminary schedule for you. At least for the next few days."

While I'm not overly shocked to learn Dalcour has provided me with a schedule and likely a hefty to-do list, I'm not thrilled. I thought he wanted me to rediscover myself. How will I be able to do so, barreling down his laundry list.

"He has also left you a set of correspondence. Things he wanted to discuss with you that are of a private matter. He asks that you read them in the order transcribed within this leather folio he provided. Lord Marchand says you can use his folio as you conduct your business through town. Within it are monetary notes and papers for charging any necessary business items to his ledger. You'll find them all in here," Greta quietly mutters as she hands the brown leather folio to me, grunting a bit as she does. The folio looks heavy as if it carried a pound of bricks.

"Oh! It's lighter than I thought it would be."

"Maybe for you, my lady but I assure you for us humans, it is quite the weight to carry," Greta answers with a knowing stare. As she speaks, I am reminded of my newfound strength. I almost forgot about it.

"I am so sorry, Greta!"

"Please, don't make a fuss on my account. Now, we must get you on your way, Lord Marchand did schedule you a break away at the Refreshing Springs lounge just near Jackson Square. He figured you could use some pampering."

My heart melts. No one has ever done anything like this for me. Ever.

Squeezing my hand now resting in my lap, Greta smiles wide with her big brown eyes beaming and says, "Yes, yes, I see Lord Marchand was right. You need this."

"I—I suppose I do," I timidly reply as another tear brandishes my cheek.

"Well then, I shall prepare the carriage with haste!" She jauntily answers, jumping up from her seat. "I'll meet you in the foyer shortly."

Greta leaves no time for even the slightest response as she's up and out of my view in an instant. Running my hands over the smooth edges of Dalcour's leather folio, I unwrap the binding of the satchel and thumb through the contents.

Just as Greta said, Dalcour has placed everything in here with more meticulous care than I thought the male species possible. There is a small silver flask tucked deep on the inside. Pulling it out, I see my initials inscribed on both side in script.

A small paper is rolled along the top of the flask and I unroll and see a note that reads, *To sate your thirst in days to come. Acceptable for bourbon now.*

A wistful smile creeps along my face at Dalcour's thoughtfulness toward me. Since the day I met him, he's shown nothing but kindness toward me.

How I could allow the lure of the Changelings arise doubt in my heart is foolish on my part. All I can do now is hope I hold tight to how I feel in this moment, to ensure my heart sways no further.

Digging deeper in the satchel I now see three letters carefully placed in reading order. Each are sealed with his crest of an oak tree and his initials. Pulling the first one out, I see the front is labeled, "For Your First Night."

Fanning myself with the envelope, I gaze up and down the hall, wondering if I have time to read this now or if I should wait until I return. My first instinct leads me to stuff the letter back into the folio but no sooner than I put it inside, I yank it back out and rip it open.

"My Dearest Chartreuse,

If you are reading this before your trip to the Refreshing Springs, then my theories of your impatience are well founded. However, if you are reading this at your bedside after an evening spent of pampering and a proper meal, then my apologies, as I've thought you more impetuous than you may be.

Although, I am sure my first assertion holds true.

My only ask of you tonight is that you enjoy yourself. Truly.

You have spent far too much of your beautiful little life in the stench of a saloon. Tonight marks a new beginning. I have instructed the caretakers at the Springs to see to your every need. You'll be cared for in ways that should always accompany your likeness.

Dote on yourself and take with you whatever suits your fancy.

When you awake on the morrow, I'll expect you refreshed and ready to mark the entirety of New Orleans with the wonderfulness of you. And that wonderfulness will begin at the St. Louis museum.

There you'll meet a few of the human faction of nobility and Altrinions like myself. They will expect your arrival at nine o'clock. As I've mentioned before, I'll need your assistance in the museum hall. Those among your company tomorrow are assisting my endeavors in preparing for our Grand Ball all leading toward our greater purposes of civility. You'll understand more soon.

Upon your arrival ask for Kellan St. John. I have sent word for him to assist you. He is a proper, older Altrinion. Much like Armando, he'll do well to teach you the proper way of things.

Open the second letter next week and not a day before! Settle your little impetuous heart. What I have to tell you won't make sense tonight.

Until then...enjoy yourself.

With Favorable Regards,

Lord Dalcour Marchand"

A stream of tears race to my chin as I fold the letter and place it back in the folio. The entirety of this new life with Dalcour sweeps over me. A cascading array of emotions rummage my heart, and I am lost for words.

All I know is that I will do what Dalcour asks of me. I will try to enjoy myself. I owe myself that much.

And so much more.

It doesn't take me long to get ready and Greta has the carriage prepared as soon as I arrive at the front door. A handsome young man whom she calls Austin, assists me into the carriage.

"Austin will take the carriage to the Springs and have you back in time for supper. I'll make it a light fare tonight as I'm sure you'll be too relaxed to endure anything too heavy. Does that sound all right?"

"Sure, Greta—but aren't you coming with me? I'm not sure I should be alone. At least not for my first night in town."

"No worries, you'll be well cared for. Austin will see to it. Won't you, Austin dear?" Greta smiles wide at Austin and his eyes beam back at her with a bright golden glow, and he nods in agreement.

Gasping at the thought he is likely a supernatural, I slide deeper into the carriage cabin as I watch Austin climb back up into his seat. He takes off before I have a moment to wave farewell to Greta and I can barely make out her form in the distance.

We arrive at the Refreshing Springs in what seems like a flash and my stomach is a bubble of knots. Though I have little time to dally. Austin opens the doors and helps me out of the carriage where I see a pair of attendants awaiting us at the double door entrance of the Springs.

Austin leads me to the pair and offers my hand to a tall woman standing at the door. She looks down her long nose at me, scanning me over as she takes my hand. Her features are hard and striking. Everything about her screams intimidation. Yet, I am surprised when she smiles wide and squeezes my hand with an almost maternal assurance.

"It's lovely to meet you Ms. Grenoble," the woman says with a sweet and soft voice. "We have everything prepared just as Lord Marchand instructed," she adds in a dulcet tone.

Leading me inside, I am greeted by the sweet smells of jasmine and eucalyptus. The soothing scents instantly calm whatever remained of my angst and I exhale deeply, purposing my heart to finally do what I've never been free to do before. Enjoy myself.

Chapter Twenty

No nightmares. No dreams. Just the comfort of pillows and the scented oils of eucalyptus fill my suite.

Awakening to the harmonious revelry of chirping birds is like music to my ears. Taking in a deep breath, I am comforted by the clean smell of fresh linen instead of the rank odor of smoke and cigar-filled saloon. As I heave in copious amounts of air, a waft of breakfast tickles my nose, bringing joy to my grumbling tummy.

Although I was thankful for the split pea soup with minced ham that Greta prepared for me, it didn't quite sate my gnawing hunger.

I am not sure whether it was the toxin cleansing scrub and bath I was given at the Springs, but my body seemed expelled of more than toxins when they were through with me. I felt empty but refreshed all at once. At any rate, I'm most certain I'll gladly indulge in whatever delectable goodness Greta has for me.

As much as I want to drift deeper into the cottony softness of my bed, the large clock above my door tells me I have a little less than ninety minutes to make myself presentable, eat breakfast and arrive at St. Louis museum for my meeting.

Hurrying myself along, I opt just to freshen up my most important places. After all of the scrubbing, rinsing, and rescrubbing my body went through last night, I'm sure I don't require much in that department. Although I do take note at my new and swift pace.

I've never moved so fast in my life.

Most of it seems without much provocation from me. I'm not sure when I'll begin my training with Titan, but I hope I don't bring any undue attention to myself in the presence of humans.

Standing in the mirror after I put on clothes from the deep wardrobe Dalcour prepared for me, I flick my hands a few times in the air and wave them around. Thankfully, I see no trace of the glowing embers from my skin as I did yesterday. I know Dalcour said it would wear off and for that I am grateful. While I haven't been in my birth city in what seems like forever, I have no desire to exemplify anything short of the wonderfulness Dalcour described in his letter.

And wonderful I shall be.

Thinking over the lessons I heard Armando regale to my sister, I practice my curtsey and pace around my suite a few times. As I do, I stare at myself in the mirror, hopeful my posture is erect and fitting of what I know of societal women.

Still, I don't have much time to dawdle when I hear the crisp and clanging sound of a bell ringing from afar. I pick up a paper fan that matches my dress from the armoire and make my way downstairs.

"Perfect timing," Greta says, greeting me at the foyer as I make my way down. She wears a broad smile that stretches across her face as she watches me with her arms folded at her petite waist. "I hope you're hungry. I've prepared quite the spread. Since I'm still not sure what's your fancy, I made a sampler of sorts."

"Wow!" I say as Greta leads me to kitchen and I see the bountiful array before me. "There's enough here to feed an army!"

Greta laughs with her shoulders only, throwing her head back. A long strand of curly black hair bounces at her shoulders, falling out from under her upswept bun and I can't help imagining how lovely her hair must look when she wears it free. Unfortunately, she doesn't leave me time to ponder as she quickly tucks the piece back up to her bun and secures it with a pin from her pocket.

"Well, shall we eat?" I ask, pulling out a wooden chair from the table.

"That is kind of you, my lady. However, I have already had breakfast and I must move on to other matters that require my attention. You're not the only one to whom Lord Marchand provided detailed instructions," she replies with a nod and wink. "But, before I go, let me know if there is anything else you need? I've prepared coffee and tea as I didn't know your preference."

"Oh," I begin, my eyes scanning the large table of food before me. "I think this is more than enough."

"Very well then," she says and begins down an adjacent dark hallway. Stopping and turning quickly on her heel, she smiles once more. "I almost forgot. Austin will be outside with the carriage when you are ready to go to St. Louis'. And my lady, please do resist the temptation to clear the table. I'll have no way of knowing what you liked most if you do."

Once more, Greta leaves no room for gratitude as she exits promptly before I have a chance to respond. This time, however, I am thankful. And so is my grumbling stomach. Actually, she could have left faster.

In no time I devour a helping of cubed potatoes, poached eggs, and a helping of beignets which will most assuredly put my corset to the test today. Somehow, I even manage a handful of berries and a quarter of a grapefruit before I lean back in my seat, both satisfied and slightly ashamed at how I demolished almost everything in my view.

I take a few sips of tea but know I need something more. And thankfully it is in plain sight. I spy a small bottle of seltzer water on top of the ice chest, and I know it's exactly what I need. Thankfully, my years spent at the bar taught me how to twine elixirs of all sorts. Quickly, I take a few gulps of the seltzer and it does exactly what I need. Even though I'm alone, I can't help but look around the kitchen, hopeful no one heard the uncouth belch that erupted from my gut.

Not the most lady-like thing I know, but oh well.

Grabbing my satchel, I look at the wall clock and notice my time has been far spent and I know I need to make my way to the museum. After everything Dalcour has done for me, the last thing I want is to show up late.

Walking through the expansive estate, I'm still overwhelmed by the sheer grandeur of it all. Everything in me tells me, this can't be my life. This must be a dream. But I am well awake.

No dreams. No nightmares. I whisper to chant to myself reassuringly.

Even if it were a dream, I'd do whatever I had must to ensure no one wakes me.

The sun is bright as I make my way down the front stairs. Looking down at my yellow gown, it almost reflects the sun's rays and I wonder if the color is too much. Even if it were, it matters not. I have no time to change. I suppose spending a life cloaked in black, red, dark purples and blues, I wanted to wear something that was the polar opposite.

"Good morning, madame," Austin softly says, tipping his hat at the brim and offering his hand to help me inside the carriage. I offer the same in reply and a small smile curves the corner of his mouth and he closes the door behind me and climbs back to his seat.

As we ride through town, I am shocked to see how so much has changed since my departure. Still, for whatever changes may have come, I am pleased to see New Orleans has lost none of the charm I recall from my youth.

Bright colors of teal, lilac, and yellow adorn many of the buildings and the delectable smell of creole cuisine fills the air. I even notice a small corner bakery I remember to be my father's favorite. How he loved their pastries and croissants! I never had a croissant like the ones from his favorite bakery while living at the saloon; although our resident cook did make a decent dough—it wasn't the same.

I make a mental note of its location, hopeful to ask Austin to make a stop there upon our return.

While the smell of New Orleans is comforting, there is one thing I've missed even more. The sound of New Orleans.

The sound of trumpets and trombones blaring along with the fiddling jangle of violins fills my heart with a joy I had long forgotten.

Memories of Calida taking me and Victoria out to hear the music and dance in the Quarter during Mardi Gras send a flurry of emotions through me. I do my best to push aside thoughts of her demise and instead linger in the pleasantness recollections of my beloved sister bring me.

For the first time at the remembrance of Calida, tears don't flood my face. I actually feel happy. As odd as it even to admit it, a part of me hopes this feeling never goes away.

The carriage stops and Austin opens the carriage door as I take in the sight of the grandeur of St. Louis' museum before me. A tall red brick building with orange and green shutters stands out from the nearby buildings. I can't help gasping at the sight of it as it almost seems out of place along the array of taverns, small offices and bakery shops in its galley.

Stepping out of the carriage, Austin helps me down and tells me he will return in a few hours. Although I know little of the courteous young man who now holds my hand as I stand in front of the museum, I almost hate the thought of him leaving my side. He and Greta are all I know in this place I once called my home.

Pushing my angst aside, I pull the bell string at the thick black double door entrance of the museum, looking over my shoulder pensively as Austin prepares to leave.

"Can I help you?" A hoarse voice creaks out, making me a tad jumpy.

"Ah, yes, my name is Chartreuse Grenoble. I was sent by Lord Dalcour Marchand," I answer, my voice slightly cracking as I look down at the short rotund man before me. "I was told to ask for Kellan St. John."

"I see," he replies, rubbing the stubble hair on his chin. "And you must be his ward," he says with one brow raise and eyes fixed at my cleavage. Even though I've grown accustomed to men eyeing my bosom, it still bothers me. I step back, flicking my fan open to cover my chest and his gaze flits up to my eyes. A small smile hovers under the shadow of his pencil thin mustache, but the pipe at the corner of his mouth prevents his smile from stretching full. "Well, I am not him, but we were expecting you, my dear. Do come in," he says with a brighter tone than his first greeting as the door opens wide.

Looking back over my shoulder, Austin tips his hat to me, shooting a narrowed glare over my shoulder toward the man before smiling once more and swatting the horse with the whip to move forward. I smile in return and begin making my way inside.

My eyes stretch far and wide as I take in the array of art and antiques adorned in the marble floor hall of the museum. There is such a stately, yet decadent allure amid the golden sculptures, paintings, and treasures throughout the hall, it's hard to take it all in.

Simply breathtaking!

"The name is Oliver Burgin," the man says after forcing out a faux cough, breaking me from my apparent musing. "I am the curator to all you see here," he adds, pulling his suspenders and raising on the balls of his feet while proudly puffing his chest.

"It is very nice to meet you Mr. Burgin," I reply.

"No need for formalities here, Oliver will suffice. Mr. Burgin is my father, and that old coot kicked the bucket some twenty years prior." Laughing, his round belly shakes as he runs his hands up and down his suspenders. I only smile in return as he pulls the pipe from his mouth and extends his hand toward an adjacent hallway. "The meeting will start soon, my dear. Please follow me."

He leads me down a narrow hallway that smells of cigar pipes and coffee causing more reminiscent thoughts of my father reading at the kitchen table flash through my mind.

I had no idea being back in New Orleans would drive me to such an emotional state. Nonetheless, I force my thoughts aside as Oliver pushes a thick red curtain open, revealing a large hall. Four men and two women are seated along a long table opposite one another, each with either a cigar pipe or cup of coffee in their hand.

Pulling a tall wingback chair out from under the table, Oliver gestures for me to be seated as he walks to the head of the table and taps a man on the shoulder whose back is to the rest of the room. He whispers something in the man's ear and the man points to something on the other side of the room and Oliver almost races to pick up a large wooden chest and brings it back to the man. As the two continue talking with their backs to us, I look around the room and down the table, hopeful for a pleasant face.

"So, you must be Lord Marchand's ward," a petite woman says to me from across the table. Looking at her I smile, and she offers her hand, tipping it at her wrist as though she expected me to kiss it. Opting to wave at her instead, her eyes fall slightly, but she quickly forces a smile back to her face. "My name is Lucinda Warcraft," she adds with a light chuckle.

"My name is Chartreuse," I answer, purposely avoiding my last name. I am still unsure who knows the extent of my family's involvement in the Great Fire of 1788, nor do I have desire to bring attention to myself.

"Well, I hope you have something of worth to bring to the table. Something more than the delusions of grandeur Marchand is obviously selling," a tall man seated next to me huffs.

Turning my head to quickly meet his gaze, I see nothing that resembles strength behind his eyes. For years I've looked into the soulless eyes of men. Whether they be a cheap thrill of the night or pub congregant, the eyes of the weak are all the same. This man is weak. Even the words he speaks are those of fear, although he'd fashion his mind to think his retort revealed his strength; I know better.

There's no way this man would dare speak such things in the presence of Dalcour Marchand and live.

"Please, Thaddeus, you mustn't speak ill of the Lord Marchand in the presence of his young ward," Lucinda teases with laughter. "I am so sorry, Chartreuse. You must forgive Thaddeus; he is not the most refined of nobility. He is, after all, only human," she laughs once more.

"I need no pardon from the likes of you Lucinda. I may be what remains of the human faction represented, but do not forget my words hold the most weight," Thaddeus counters.

"Ha! Ha! Is that what we let you believe?" Another man barks two chairs down from us. "Once the wolves reclaim our rightful place, we'll have no need of you or any human!"

"Oh Cephas, not that again! For a wolf, you are such a bore!" Lucinda bites back. "I thought wolves were the fun ones." At Lucinda's lashing rebuke, the table breaks into an uproar and the sound of disharmony fills the hall.

"All right, that will be quite enough!" Oliver shouts, raising his short arms to his sides. "It is time we get started with the business of the day." The others quietly mumble among themselves, trading final trite remarks to one another as they slowly turn their attention to the front of the table.

I inwardly chuckle at how much life in the saloon prepared me for this mildly combative atmosphere. Although it is apparent the members here are quite apathetic about my presence, and even about Dalcour for that matter, I am neither bothered nor worried.

I suppose in this, Mother trained me well.

"We will now hear opening remarks from Master St. John." Oliver announces, extending his arm toward the tall man at his side.

As he turns around, my mouth slightly parts with a gasp, awe overtaking me at the reveal at such handsomeness.

His tall, stately presence stands just as tall as Dalcour's six-foot frame, dwarfing Oliver at his side. With curly brown hair framing his perfectly sheened, olive skin, his steel-gray eyes cut like glass as he stares down the table, instantly locking with my own. He offers a crooked smile that hides under the shadow of his perfectly sculpted mustache.

"Well, I see the young St. John is not quite grieving his father's passing as we may have thought," Thaddeus gruffly mumbles, narrowing his eyes over his shoulder toward me.

Thinking of my own father, my heart pains at learning of his father's death. While I don't know him, I know too well how tragic such a loss can be.

"Ah yes," Lucinda whispers back, swirling a long pipe in the corner of her mouth, "he seems quite distracted," she adds with a laugh.

"Anything of interest to report Lady Warcraft?" Master St. John sneers, pounding his hand flat on the long wooden table. Lucinda throws her head down shamefully and Thaddeus looks away from me. The sound reverberates through the hall and both Lucinda and Thaddeus straighten themselves in their seats.

Taking three paper rolls from Oliver, Master St. John lays them on the table along with a thick stack of paperwork before pulling out the large chair at the front of the room and taking his seat. "I see we have a new guest with us today," St. John begins as Oliver whispers in his ear.

"Yes sir," I begin, pushing myself up from the table to stand. "My name is Chartreuse. I am Lord Marchand's ward."

"Yes, ma'am and welcome, Ms. Grenoble. We are fortunate to have you here with us today," he says with a warm smile. As I take my seat, a few others grumble at the end of the table and both Lucinda and Thaddeus share knowing glances, and an eerie feeling swarms the pit of my gut.

As much as I should endeavor this a time to enjoy myself, as Dalcour instructed, much like my time under Monroe and Mother's rule, I see I'll have to protect my own interests.

And I shall do so by any means.

Chapter Twenty-One

The meeting ends just as combative as it began. It is a wonder why Dalcour wants to do anything with this group that bears no likeness of civility. As they are truly anything to the contrary.

Most of their angst seems to surround trivial matters such as the preparation of baskets of wine and cheese for distribution to notables and supernaturals during an upcoming grand ball. I suppose the thought of such a task seemed too trite for most in the room to perform. Since no one took an interest, I quickly volunteered my hand when Oliver read off the to-do list. No one seemed to bat an eye, likely thankful that I alone chose such a menial task.

Lucinda opted to work with a quiet woman on the other end of table in selecting the paintings to hang in the exhibit hall in preparation for a cotilion while Thaddeus agreed to secure financial backing for the event.

Master St. John was noticeably quiet during the remainder of the meeting after he made opening remarks about the cotilion and a bit of rambling about creating a formal census of the factions of supernaturals as well as notables in the City. The only time he had an affirming word to say, Thaddeus seemed to be the only other person who agreed a census was necessary, while the others balked at the idea.

Clamoring shouts and shared expletives echoed through the room for more than fifteen minutes before Oliver pounded a mallet against a small wooden board and the room went silent.

Without a word, everyone got up from their seats, taking their exits.

"Madame Chartreuse," Oliver says, now at my side, handing me a thin leather binder. "Here is the list of those requiring baskets of wine and cheese. You can return here at the same time tomorrow to begin the preparation."

"Thank you, Oliver," I reply, taking the binder and stuffing it in the folio Dalcour gave me.

"I trust you do know your wines. There'll be no time to educate you on the difference between a Bordeaux and a Chablis."

"Well, that depends on if you prefer a Larose over a Volnay, my dear Oliver. I tend to favor a Sparkling Hock or port of Madeira myself. What about you?"

"Ha! Ha! Very well Madame Chartreuse, bright and early then. Bright and early," Oliver says with a hearty laugh as he takes my satchel and helps me up from my seat and leads me down the hall.

As we near the main entrance, we come upon Thaddeus and another man who are talking with Master St. John.

"Listen St. John," the other man says, "I don't care what that superpowered negro wants to do, this will not work! We all know the mess the Marchand and Grenoble families inflicted on this City twenty years ago! I lost family! Friends! I tell you nothing good will come of this," the man exclaims.

Thaddeus catches my eye and taps the shoulder of his companion and the man glares at me with a tight scowl.

Horrific flashes of fires blazing through the city streets score through my mind. The sounds of shrilling cries echo in my memory as do thoughts of my family and I narrowly escaping those who wished we meet the same fate as Calida. My eyes glass with tears, but I bite my lip, refusing any droplets their escape.

I will not let them see me cry.

"That is quite enough Henrik!" Master St. John shouts back at the man. His eyes soften as he regards me, but he keeps a stern watch on both Thaddeus and Henrik.

Words fail to form in my mouth. Nothing but anger now fuels my thoughts as I push through the crowd of men and barrel out of the double doors.

I don't see Austin as I exit, looking up and down the street. Nonetheless, I begin walking east, recalling our path from this morning. A steady stream of tears floods my face, but I keep my march onward. I need to get as far from the museum as possible.

While I understand their pain, they fail to understand my pain is comparable to their own. For surely, they are not the only ones who lost something on that great and terrible day.

The sun is bright as I make my way down the street and its heat seems to dry my tears along the way. It's a comforting conundrum. The one thing that I shall one day see no more, is the only thing that now consoles me.

A small chuckle escapes me at the thought and a sweet and familiar smell feathers my nose. Stopping in place, I look up and notice I am at the bakery we passed by this morning. Smiling, I look up at the sun, thankful for yet another reassuring reprieve.

Going inside, memories of my father once more flood my mind and my once incensed thoughts dissipate.

"How can I help you, ma'am?" A young girl asks with a bright smile.

"Yes, I'd like two croissants and a small tow of biscuits," I answer, inhaling the savory aroma.

"Yes, ma'am," she answers as she gets a small woven tray. "I must say, that is a very pretty dress. The color suits your complexion perfectly."

"Thank you," I answer, thankful for the most sincere compliment I have received all day.

She smiles wide while putting the pastries on the tray, peering over my shoulder. "I bet you have all sorts of lovely fabrics that she'd look lovely in!"

"Yes ma'am, Miss Emily!" A lush voice calls from behind me. Turning around, I am surprised to see a face I had only seen in a shadowed memory.

"Oh yes, Mr. Elias has the prettiest fabrics this side of the Mississippi!"

The young woman exclaims, now placing the food in a small white box.

"Well, I am not sure about all of that, Miss Emily, but I sure do appreciate your kindness," he answers, tipping his feathered brim hat, smiling at us both as he exits.

My feet are tethered to the ground as I come face to face with my sister's betrayer for the first time. Heat rises from my skin and a kindling rage grows within me that feels almost sinister. Murderous musings score through my mind at the sight of him and it takes everything in me not to act upon the impulses urging me to strike him where he stands.

Keeping my gaze set on him as he walks out of the store and down the street carrying two loaves of bread, my heart beats like a mad drum in my chest. Feverish sweat thickens along my brow and above my lip and an almost sickeningly violent urge erupts through me. Still, I dig my feet deeper into the wooden floors beneath me, preventing the malice within from performing the vile acts flashing through my mind.

Closing my eyes, I am hopeful that lessening the sight of him will douse the errancy gnawing within me. Taking a deep breath, I work hard to force aside the enchanting words of the Changelings. But for as much as I try, haunting melodies of mulberry trees and juniper stir through me, igniting familiar homicidal thoughts of old.

Stay calm Chartreuse.

"Your order is ready, ma'am," the young woman says in a bright tone, obviously unaware of the melancholy brewing within me.

I take another deep breath and exhale. I can only hope the smell of the bakery and the fond thoughts that once captured my state, are enough to sate the sinister desires begging for their release.

"Ma'am," she calls once more, this time her tone reveals a shade of concern.

"I'll pay for it," a familiar masculine voice answers before I have an opportunity to open my eyes.

Blaring my eyes wide, I am surprised to find Master St. John standing just a few feet from me now. Paying the woman, he takes the small box from her and turns back to me with a luminous grin.

"I figured it was the least I could do—I mean after the foolery of Henrik and Thaddeus," he adds, still smiling wide. Staring at him, his face is more youthful than I originally thought. Even as he smiles, his perfectly peach-colored lips reveal a swoon-worthy perfection, I thought most men incapable.

"What are you doing here?" My tone is sharper than I intend as frazzled thoughts of Elias and the words of Henrik and Thaddeus replay in my mind.

"Well, it's good to see you too," he replies still smiling. His steely gray eyes search my face and I wait to see him do what most men do but he does not. Not once do his eyes fall to my cleavage and the thought alone puzzles me.

Maybe he doesn't find me attractive.

Just that thought alone worries me, and I feel like I'm back in front of Decaux Marchand all over again. I have no desire to be rejected again.

"Actually, my lady, I came to bring you this," he says handing me my leather folio. "Oliver was still holding it for you when you left. I met up with your driver and we found you here."

Looking out of the window, I am surprised to find Austin standing outside with the carriage. While I'm not sure how either of them found me so fast, I am more than pleased to see my way out of this more than uncomfortable situation.

"Oh, thank you!" I quickly reply, snatching the folio from his hand and tossing it over my shoulder. "Um, thanks—um—I—I should go."

No sooner than the words leave my lips, I race out of the bakery as the parting sounds of both Master St. John and the bakery attendant trail behind me. Almost knowing my mood, Austin flings the carriage door open and steps aside, giving me the space I so obviously require.

Moving with speed akin to Mercury, Austin has us back at the estate in what seems like mere minutes. I had little time to ponder the events of the day as both embarrassment and kindling rage held their sway over me.

My thoughts are still erratic as I rush back inside the mansion and even Greta allows the necessary space between us as I make my tearful way back to my suite.

Once I'm inside my room, I whirl around the room a few times, parading like a bull stampede. As if hearing how the locals still regard my family wasn't enough, my encounter with Elias troubles me on every level.

I try to recall Dalcour's reasoning for sparing his life, but my memory of his words is faint. I can think of no true reason such a trespass be made allowable.

Pulling the pins out of my bun, I shake my hair free to my shoulders as a loud scream churns through me. I don't feel like myself. I feel out of sorts.

Holding onto my chest of drawers, I look in the mirror, heaving a loud sigh as I bang my hands along the wooden frame of the chest. Looking at my reflection, I gaze into my eyes and work hard to stifle my ire.

Calm down Chartreuse. Repeating, I whisper the words to myself, shutting my eyes in hopes I can quiet the screaming of my heart's cry.

Opening my eyes once more, I am startled at the harrowing phantoms gazing back at me. Frightened, I step back, quickly closing my eyes and reopening them in one blink, hopeful the images before me are only in my mind.

But I am wrong.

"Had your chance, you did not take. Now with time your heart will break. Bound not sired, will seal your fate, if this form to new you do not make." Their haunting chant rattles my room with a ghastly wind that stirs around me, sending chilling tingles up my spine.

Confused, I shout back, "What is the meaning of all this? Speak plainly!" I furiously demand. This time I am not the same woman who cowered before them on the cold concrete floor some nights ago.

The wind blows around the room again, and I keep a tight hold on the wooden chest as I do my best to keep my sights fixed on the Changelings in the mirror before me.

"Plainly we will speak, but not so again. Listen well, or thy shall surely meet your end," the gangly creatures echo in unison.

One Changeling moves closer in the mirror. As it does, I see a face, reminiscent of a woman, break through its shadowy veil.

"What have you done to me? What do you want?" I yell.

A dark smile stretches her face, revealing black lips with only a hollowed inside to match. "All we have done, precious one, is given you the power you so desperately seek to protect yourself. Yet, when opportunity presents itself, you did not do what was in your power to perform."

"You mean kill Elias Peyroux? Is that what you want from me? Why? How does it benefit you?" I bite back, less fearful than I know I should be.

"We need nothing from you, nor does his death benefit us. It is what *you* wanted. It is what you always wanted!"

"Lies!" I shout back. "I knew nothing of Elias Peyroux until the day you first showed him to me. I could have gone my entire life without ever hearing that name. But you did this! You drove murder into my mind to kill that man!"

"Whatever murder lingers in your mind was there long before we ever laid sight to your cause," she answers in a surprisingly soft tone. "Still, it matters not," she continues, and her voice darkens. "You shall never take life from Elias as it was taken from you."

"If I wanted to kill him, I would." I state, the resolve in my response is certain.

"Not so, my precious one. Your Lord Marchand took that choice from you the day he bound his words to your steps."

As she speaks, the other Changeling waves her hand and images of me with Dalcour on the night of my siring form before me. *"Nor shall he or his kin ever receive such a punishment by your hand—swear it to me!"* I watch in both confusion and horror as I yield to Dalcour's decree.

"Ah! Now she sees. Now she knows. Altrinion compulsion, her heart now woes." The phantom cackles in glee.

"Yes, precious one, with his bond, your young lord sealed your doom. Now you are trapped. Bound to never take from he who took from you. Perhaps somehow you may still avenge yourself from your fate."

"How can I? I knew nothing of Altrinion compulsion. Dalcour tricked me!"

"Deceived? Perhaps. You should have asked." Laughing, both Changelings converge back to one being.

"And I should have asked you the same!" I snap. "What witchery have you also doomed my soul?"

The ghastly wind rips once more through my room and the mirrored view before me darkens. Shrilling sounds like a thousand voices echo in my ears and I look in the mirror only to see my own soulless, black eyes staring back at me.

Chapter Twenty-Two

What have I done?

My disconsolate heart lies dormant at my feet. Knowing I alone have brought such calamity upon myself is my own undoing. Whether it be due to my fear of powerlessness or revenge, I alone made dealings in the dark that cannot be undone.

Once more, the Changelings repeat the same enchanted words that have haunted my heart since that night. And for the first time the meaning of it all makes sense. Through the shrouded and murky view of the Changelings in my mirror, I discovered the depravations of my dealings with their kind.

Firstly, my doom. From the moment I ingested their filth, I have only thirty days to complete my turning. If I fail to complete my turning—if Dalcour does not return in time—I shall meet my end in death. "*Bound not sired, will seal your fate, if this form to new you do not make.*" The binding of the Changelings to human form, only lasts for a short while. Since I am mortal, their dark power would wholly consume me beyond the brink of death.

Second, I learned of Altrinion compulsion. "*The bonding sires and sirens must groom but binding hearts will seal your doom.*" As my sire, Dalcour can compel me to his submission. Whatever he wills, so it shall be. As such, he has commanded no harm shall come to a Peyroux by my hand. In this, I will never have my revenge against the one whose betrayal brought about my sister's demise. However, there is some consolation. Once I am turned and the power of the Changeling take rule, I will no longer be subject to his control. While it doesn't help in my quest against Elias Peyroux, it does assuage my angst a little.

Third, I am bound by Changeling rule never to harm women. *"Maiden kind you may subdue, yet only for measure of mortal feud."* Apparently, it's open season on men. The phantoms gave no room for questions, but from what I can gather, they find the male species deplorable. I suppose I can relate.

And finally, while their riddled musings still stir more questions in my mind than answers, I know one thing is certain. I shall be no mere Scourge or vampire. I will be something more.

And now I know the truth.

Or at least the truth as they describe it.

My truth, on the other hand, is that I have indeed dug a deeper hole for myself than I thought capable.

So yes, my heart is disconsolate.

Hollow and void.

Not even thoughts of my precious sister Chalmette stir the longings of my heart as it has before. Hanging my feet off my bed, I sit and stare at the darkness surrounding me, fearful of what more ominous outcomes await me. If Dalcour should delay his arrival by even a day, death shall be the victor. If he should complete my transition, I know not what vile thing I shall become by the Changeling's hand. And if there should be an in between of the matter, it has yet to be revealed to me. For I surely doubt there is yet a mediatory home for the dark quandary that is my soul.

A thin sliver of the sun's light beams beneath the dark curtains, making a straight line to the door. Lifting my head slowly, I realize I've sat on this corner of the bed for hours. After crying myself asleep, I only managed an hour or two of sleep once the tormenting cackle of the Changelings faded from my view.

Even then, slumber was no comfort. Frightful images of the phantoms, a dark nether world, and flickers of death and pain served me nothing but a cocktail of nightmares, forcing me out from under the covers, holding tight to wooden post at my bed's end.

As much as I hate to admit it, Mother was right. My dealings with Dalcour will likely lead to the same outcome as Calida; or worse.

A loud chime rings aloud in my room as the clock strikes noon, and for the first time I realize how much time has passed.

Looking around the room, tears flood my eyes once more, and I am surprised I have anything left to cry. I gaze over my shoulder to the large armoire and wonder if I could stuff a few clothes in a duffle and make my way out of the mansion without notice.

Greta hasn't come to my door to alert me for breakfast. Or she has, and in my misery, I didn't hear her. Either way, it stands to reason I may be able to escape. If I could but find somewhere to evade the evitability of facing Dalcour or encountering the Changelings once more, I would be happy. Perhaps, I could flee to behold my sister's perfect face one last time, before taking my repose away from the leading strings held by Dalcour and the Changelings.

I need to get out of here!

Pushing myself up and away from the bed, I circle about the room in one frantic motion, tossing whatever I can find into a small duffle. Racing into the adjacent bath, I clean myself, hopeful to excise my puffy eyes and tear-worn face. I scrub everything my eyes can see and brush my hair to one side. I don't even have energy to gather it in pins.

Staring in the mirror, I am thankful for the lingering effects of the siring. The supernatural sheen along my skin and flawlessness of my perfection help to douse the real sadness brewing within me. Anything that will keep anyone from spying the brokenness of my soul is helpful.

Tossing on a dark blue frock and light black cape, I trust this ensemble will help me remain elusive as I travel about. I have no desire to gain attention or suspicion.

Quietly, I crack open the door of my suite and listen. I am thankful I hear no one on my level nor do I detect the aroma of Greta making food in the kitchen.

Maybe she is off today, I think to myself, hopeful.

It doesn't matter. I need to leave this place.

I take light steps down the stairs, careful not to make a sound. Looking over my shoulder, I gaze back upstairs and down through the hallway and see no one. Taking a deep breath, I sigh, saddened this is now my only recourse. I smile as I stare around the mansion, thankful for even the brevity of relief I had away from the saloon.

Even more, my heart rejoices knowing my precious Chalmette found some semblance of happiness with her beloved. And while I don't wish to sully their honeymoon, I only need to put my eyes to her face once more. After that, I can fall into whatever dark slumber awaits me at the Changeling's behest.

Exhaling, I open the mansion door as quietly as I can, careful not to move the bell string, alerting the house to my departure. Before I have a moment to take in the early afternoon's air, I am surprised to find Master St. John standing with Greta on the lawn.

"Good day, Madame Chartreuse," Greta says with a sweet smile. Her dancing eyes flit over her shoulder toward Master St. John as he stands with a small bouquet of wildflowers in his hand. She nods gracefully, with her hands clasped at her waist and exits toward the south lawn.

"Thank you for your aid Greta," Master St. John calls to her as she rounds the corner of the mansion. Surprise fills me as I notice another carriage in front of the gate, and I see Austin and another attendant chatting next to their respective horses. "Well, Madame Chartreuse, you seem to have caught me a bit off guard. I hadn't finished setting up everything," he adds.

"Master St. John?" I question, uncertainty welling within me.

"Sebastian, please. Master St. John is so formal, and I am certainly a master to no man or woman for that matter," he says with a wide smile that expands the entirety of his face.

"Okay, Sebastian it is," I begin, still unsure what is happening. "But I suppose I don't understand—what's going on here?"

Extending his hand to lead me down the steps, he smiles and the sheen between his mustache and lips call to me in ways that are both unexpectant and entreating. "Well, I suppose that is what I meant when I said you caught me off guard. I had hoped to have everything ready for you out on the terrace before you arrived. But seeing you now, I'm thankful to have the chance to escort you myself. That is, if you are fine with the idea," he says, looping his arm with mine and pulling me close to his side.

Leading us down the marble stone path along the side of the mansion as he speaks, I am shocked to see a small table arranged on the terrace with an assortment of cheese, wine, pastry, and smoked meats.

"Sebastian, what is all of this?" I ask.

"First, these are for you," he smiles, handing me the small bouquet. "Greta helped me pick them from the garden."

"Thank you," I answer, taking a small whiff of the bouquet's floral scent. "But why?"

"Wow, not much for surprises, eh?" He asks with a raised brow as his smile shifts to the corner of his mouth in the sexiest way possible. Parting my lips to protest, he tugs my hand gently, leading us closer to the table. Pulling a small white metal chair from the table, he takes the bouquet from me and puts in a glass vase Greta places in front of my table setting.

"I'll take this from you madame," Greta quietly says in my ear, pulling the duffle from under my arm. She winks at me as she walks away, sauntering back into the kitchen.

Walking to the opposite side of me, Sebastian pulls out his chair and sits down. Taking a linen napkin from the table, he folds it over his lap and smiles back at me. "Yes, well, my apologies for catching you off guard, but when you didn't show at the museum this morning, I got worried. Especially after how everything ended yesterday."

"Oh," I mumble. The museum totally slipped my mind. And after everything I experienced last night, I haven't given much thought to what happened with Henrik and Thaddeus.

"Listen, I really want to apologize for both Henrik and Thaddeus. Their actions are more than regrettable."

"Please, Sebastian, believe me when I say, their actions are quite forgettable," I mutter, circling my fingers along the large stone white plate before me.

"I truly hope so." Sebastian's steely gray eyes lock with mine and everything in me freezes in place. A small wind blows and his curly hair waves to one side and he smiles, strumming his hand through his hair, taming it back in place. He looks almost boyish as he does and a small smile creeps through my otherwise gloomy state.

There is a lightness to his presence I have never known. Whether it be men from the saloon, or the ones I've known in this supernatural world, I have only ever been privy to the uptight, crude, or overly dutiful. He is an enigma to me. Something new entirely.

Still smiling, he reaches across the table and grabs a small basket of three bottles of wine. "Besides, I had hoped you and I could discuss wine selections and cheese pairings for the baskets. Oliver seemed to think you knew a great deal about wines."

"Oh, I am so sorry Master—I mean Sebastian, I forgot I was supposed to meet Oliver this morning. It's just been so—"

"You have nothing to apologize for, Chartreuse—I can call you Chartreuse, right?" He adds with a sexy smirk.

"Why—um—well—of course."

"Good, I'd rather there not be formalities between us, Chartreuse," he begins, his stare deepening into mine. "And to be fair, you were never going to be working on this with Oliver anyway. My family owns the wine press. So you were stuck with this old face at any rate. I hope that doesn't disappoint you, my lady," he states in a more controlled and lush tone, his gaze still set sharp.

"No, not at all," I reply, my tone husky.

"Perfect," he says, moving his hands across the table far enough that his fingertips touch my own, halting my circling pattern. "But first, I need to share two things with you." He pulls a small white box from behind the basket and puts it on the plate in front of me. "Open it," he directs me, pulling off the small yarn string holding the box closed.

I do as he instructs, and my eyes widen with surprise at the reveal of the contents. Two croissants and four biscuits. My order from the bakery yesterday. Looking up at him, I gasp. "Sebastian!"

Reaching across the table, he takes my hand in his and squeezes it as the familiar boyish grin covers his face. "Well, first my lady, an apology."

"An apology?" I tilt my head, curious. I've never known apologies to fare well for me.

"Yes, an apology. This is a new and fresh box. I ate the croissants and made quite a mess of the biscuits you got yesterday. So, I thought it only proper to bring you a fresh box. The apology and the amends of the fresh box are the first things."

"Oh, well thank you Sebastian, but you owe me no apologies. Given the way I left yesterday, I wouldn't be surprised if you never wanted to see me again—much less replace my pastries."

Squeezing my hand tighter, his gaze darkens as he keeps his eyes locked with mine. "That brings me to the second thing. I suppose I ate the croissants because I wanted to get to know you better. That is why I am here today. Sure, there is the matter of the wines, but truly if it weren't for the baskets— or the bakery—or that you left behind your folio, I'd find some way to get to know you better. I want to get to know you better. No, I *need* to get to know you better. And my lady, I have every intention of knowing you in every way that you will allow."

With his words, my lips part in a gasp and everything in me wishes he'd fill the void between my mouth with the entirety of him.

Staring at him, I hardly recall my earlier somber state. The horrid images that once filled my mind are now replaced with the gloriousness that is Sebastian St. John. Even the disconsolation from before seems assuaged with his presence alone.

However possible this may be, I know one thing: I want do not wish it to end.

Chapter Twenty-Three

"So which wine is your favorite?" Sebastian asks for the third time. His gaze has turned from curious to pensive as I teeter back and forth, tasting wine from the three small glasses in front of me. "Surely you must fancy one more than the other," he adds, blowing air from the corner of his mouth, moving his curly brown tendrils away from the side of his eye.

Laughing at his growing irritation, I take a bite of cheese, allowing it to reset my tastebuds. "Okay, I think I've narrowed it down to one."

"Well, for mercy, Chartreuse do not keep me guessing!" He whines, pushing himself closer to my side. Once we started the wine tasting he changed his seating and has been inching closer along the way.

"This one!" I exclaim.

Sighing with a curved smile at the corners of his lips, he takes the glass from me and sips. "Mmm," he moans with his eyes closed. My eyes linger on him as he licks his plump rose-hued lips, savoring the sweetness of the wine. "Good choice," he says softly.

"Like Oliver said, I do know my wines," I reply, forcing my eyes away from the enticing way his now wet mustache curls just so perfectly at the corner of his mouth.

"That's a first—for Oliver I mean. The old chum is never right about anything," he laughs. Taking my chin in his hand, he turns my face back to meet his darkened deep gray eyes. "But I am glad he was right about you, my lady. So tell me what you like about it most?"

Staring in his eyes I find myself lost. His gaze entrances me and I gasp lightly when I detect a small fiery glow resting behind his irises.

"Let me start," he begins, gently grazing his thumb along the curves of my lips. "I like this."

"What?" I whisper with my eyes still locked with his.

"The way you part your lips in an *O*. It's indeed more intoxicating than any proof found in these glasses." His palm firms against my face and he inches closer, taking in a deep breath near the nape of my neck. "And you smell delightful, like pomegranates nestling near an ocean's breeze."

"That's curious, my lord."

"How so?" He breathes in my ear.

"I've never seen the ocean," I say with a chuckle, pulling myself from his hold.

"I'm sorry, my lady am I moving too fast?" Sebastian questions, concern filling his brow.

"Well, no—and yes. We hardly know anything about one another. I mean you've told me how much you loathe working with the nobles and how you don't quite see the point of trying to impress the factions with imported cheese and wine, but you've told me little about yourself."

Pushing himself back into his seat, his posture stiffens, and he folds his arms across his chest. "So what do you want to know? I'm an open book," he replies, stretching his arms wide with an even wider smile to match.

"Okay, well, I heard your father passed recently. I am sorry to learn of it. What happened? How are you doing?"

"Ah, so you're starting with the big stuff first." Jumping up from his seat, he circles the table, craning his arms behind his neck and blowing out another heave of air, sending his hair away from his eyes once more. "My father, Kellan, died just a few weeks ago. He was killed in a Skull attack in Biloxi. I am not sure what business he had there, but he was here one day and gone the next. I had just arrived from Paris with a new shipment of port, wine, and cheese. The Guardians were able to put down the herd that attacked he and his company and that is my only comfort. While my father and I didn't see eye to eye on many issues, he was my father and I loved him. It was just me and him. My mother was killed by Scourge shortly after I was born so it's just been the two of us for some time."

My heart nearly breaks at his words. I know too well the hole left in my heart after my own father's death. His eyes glass, but he sucks the air in his throat down and forces a crooked smile.

"I'm sorry, Sebastian," I say, rising from my seat and walking to where he stands on the other side of the table. "I didn't mean to drudge up your pain—especially so soon after—I don't know what I was thinking!"

"It is quite all right, Chartreuse. To be frank, it's actually nice to finally have someone to share it with. Most Altrinions like myself don't do well with conversations surrounding death. I suppose the thought of our own mortality is a grim topic. And like many Altrinions, my father lived a long life. He saw more than four-hundred and eighty-nine years of life."

"Whoa, well how old are you?" I blurt, regretting my words just as soon as I utter them.

Sebastian laughs, taking my hand in his and walks us down the terrace steps leading to an overgrown flowerbed. "One-hundred and twenty." His tone is dry as he searches my face. "Does that bother you?"

"Well, no it doesn't bother me, but it is odd. I mean you don't look a day over thirty. Twenty-five even!"

"I suppose," he chuckles, swaying our hands as we walk along the graveled path. "Most Altrinions hit a spell of maturity and then we're frozen in time."

Looking out into the flowery meadow, my mind wanders. A man whose seen so much of the world, without much mortal limitation is likely out of my league. I've not seen a world much farther from the steps of the saloon until now and even this is in somewhat of a controlled state.

I am certain we have little in common.

"Chartreuse," Sebastian says, breaking me away from my downward thoughts. Cupping my face in his palm, he smiles, "Where did you go?"

Pulling from his grasp, I turn away and begin making my way back to the table. Using his Altrinion speed, he is in front of me in an instant. "Did I say something? Share too much too soon?" He questions, a puzzling frown marring his perfect face.

"No it's not that, Sebastian. It's just—just—nothing!"

"Please, Chartreuse, tell me. What can I do to keep you here with me?"

"Sebastian, please let me go. This just won't work!"

"Is it my age? Are you worried I'm too old? I assure you I'm—"

"It's just everything, Sebastian. You are supernatural. And I'm—" I want to say *doomed* but stop myself short of such an admission.

"You are beautiful. Lovely. Intelligent. Everything I have ever wanted in a woman," he replies, taking a tight hold at my wrist, preventing me from moving.

Everything. The word is as curious in my hearing as it is to pair it with any mention of myself.

"How can you say that, Sebastian? You hardly know me. As a matter of fact you don't know anything about me."

"Don't I?" He smirks, tilting his head to one side. "Well, let us see, by your wine selection, I now know your pallet enjoys the mixture of blackcurrant and cherries. And while you appreciated the wildflowers, I gave you earlier, you much prefer the scent of dried and crushed flowers as evident in this Bordeaux. But the fact the flavor of the cedar, smoked in a cigar box we used to ferment the wine was not as repugnant to you as it is to most women, you stand apart from them all and even so, squarely before any man without hesitation. Last, the fact you have purposed yourself in this very chaotic supernatural world, when someone as lovely as you could be anything else she wanted, I know you are a woman who chooses her own path, refusing to be tamed by the misogynistic ruling doctrine of the world. So yes, my everlovely Chartreuse, I do know you."

At his revelation, another gasp is all I have to offer in reply. How can someone I've known less than a day seem to discern more about me than those who should know me better.

Trailing his hands along my jawbone, his tender glance searches my face once more. "There goes that perfect parting again. May I kiss you, my lady? I must confess I've been longing to do so, since the moment you stepped out of the house."

"Yes," I rush my response, pushing myself into his embrace.

And kiss me he does.

Just when I thought Marius' farewell kiss was the first to make my heart patter, Sebastian's kiss is the first to send my will to all manner of surrender. Never have I wanted to yield myself in the hold of any man, but at this moment it is all I can think.

Sebastian's kiss is sweet and even without the tether of our tongues, the perfect placement of his lips between my own send my heart racing with electricity. His hold on me is gentle, yet deliberate. There is no escaping his grasp, nor do I desire to do so.

Pushing our mouths tighter, Sebastian holds me steady at the nape of my neck, running his hands through my hair. Every touch of his fingers is titillating.

I've never been held like this before. Ever.

Slowly, he pulls himself from our kiss and strums his hands through my hair, inhaling the scent of me wholly.

"Now I know something else about you," he begins with a sly smile.

"What?" I ask.

"Your lips taste as delectable as they look," he says. "But I do have a question for you, my lady. Is there a special someone in your life?"

Letting out a small giggle, I look up at him and shake my head. "Don't you think you should have asked me that before you kissed me?"

"Well, if he was really someone special you wouldn't be kissing me, would you?" He teases with another sexy smirk. "Besides, even if there was someone, I'd have to protest."

"You have no need of protesting, my lord, I can assure you."

"I just don't understand how such a treasure like you is on this earth unmated."

"I suppose the same could be said of you, my lord. In the same manner, I do ask, is there a Mrs. St. John?"

Laughing again, he runs his hands through his hair and smiles his boyish grin. "The only Mrs. St. John I've ever known was my mother. I have no wife if that is what you mean."

"How surprising!"

"Really? How so?"

"Someone as handsome and of class such as yourself should have very little trouble making pair."

"Oh, well, I suppose if it were up to my father, I would have been paired the moment I broke my leading strings. He's been trying to marry me off since I became of age. That is why I've kept my distance, cementing myself into the family business, hopeful to find other ways to make him proud. But he was an only son of an only son, so there's that—"

"Ah! So you mean to say you've just been out here sowing your royal oats in the interim."

"Not quite," he grumbles, feigning a frown. "But in all seriousness, I meant what I said earlier. I want and need to get to know you, Chartreuse. I want to know what you like, who you love and why. I want to understand your desires and your ambitions. But more than anything, for the first time, I can honestly say I want to stand in the sun with someone who isn't caught up in the musings of this world. Someone who wants to know my pain—and who actually asks how I feel. Not someone who merely sees me as a means to end or some status quota to fulfill. I simply want what everyone in this world wants. To be seen."

The sincerity of his sentiment cracks the usually hard casing of my heart. Never have I witnessed someone so succinctly reveal their vulnerability. Least of all divulge such privity to me.

Tugging me by the hand, so that our bodies are touching, he runs his hands down my shoulders, locking his eyes with me once more.

"So that it is clear, I want you to know I see you too. I don't know why you were running when I first saw you earlier. Yes, beloved, I saw your bags. Just know should you choose to run again; I promise to run along your side."

Chapter Twenty-Four

E^{*njoy yourself.*} Dalcour's parting words to me have never held more meaning than they do now. For the first time since I can remember, I am enjoying myself. And not just the mere enjoyment provided through the pampering of a wellness spa, living in a grand estate, and wearing pretty dresses. No, the enjoyment I now feel can all be traced to one singular name.

Sebastian St. John.

I never knew being with someone like this could be such a joy. Every moment with him is so sweet. Every touch of his hand, steely stare, or even the melodic tremor of his voice brings both merriment and delight to the inner-most parts of my soul.

It has been seven days since our first kiss. And I have spent every day since still kissing him. In fact, it has become my favorite pastime. That and holding his hand. I never thought I'd be that girl. To be perfectly honest, I hardly thought I was capable of swooning.

Yet, here I am, swooning. Panting even at the mere sight of him.

I can't help it. He is mouthwatering.

Sitting between two large wooden barrel crates, I watch in awe as his sweat-dripping, shirtless and sculpted body paces back, carrying large pallets of port through the wine press warehouse. Although I know it's an effortless feat for him being an Altrinion, my mouth still parts at the sight of his muscular form.

I don't know if it's the slender cut of his waist and brawny bronzed chest or if it's the sight of his strapping taut back that sends a gripping pulse to my preciousness, but it's taking everything in me to tame myself from enrapturing him wholly.

But he is more than pleasing to the eyes.

He connects with my heart and soul more than anyone ever has.

In the few days we've known one another I've shared more with him than anyone before. Not only does he know my favorite meal is ham, stewed apples, and biscuits, but he's discovered my fear of spiders and my zealous love for my sister Chalmette. Even more, I know he speaks three languages beyond English. He's fluently spoken French and Italian for most of his life and recently learned Muskogean while aiding negotiations during the French Indian War.

So yes, I am indeed enjoying this life Dalcour has laid at my feet and this is indeed the happiest I've ever been.

"Enjoying the view?" Sebastian asks over his shoulder while pushing a large crate of wine bottles on a metal rack.

"It's actually a pretty dull sight from where I sit," I tease, nestling myself deeper between the wooden barrels at my side.

"Is that so?" He laughs, turning quickly on his heel. Raking his hands through his hair and wiping the sweat along his brow, he smiles wide and races in front of me in a blink. I gasp as he pins himself between my legs with his arms spread to both sides of the barrels. "Well my lady, the view from where I stand is rather delightful," he says, donning his boyishly sexy grin.

Sweat from his forehead drips to my breastbone and I am still surprised that he manages to keep his eyes locked with mine.

In the last week that we've been together Sebastian has made no attempt to do anything more than kiss me. While a part of me admires his restraint, I can't help wondering whether there is something about me that he recoils.

Sure, the men in the saloon paid a pretty coin to enter my bedchamber, but I never had a problem with men noticing me. This is different.

So different that it puzzles me.

There is no mistaking our mutual attraction, but for the life of me I do not understand why he has made no advances toward me otherwise.

Nonetheless, I am more than thankful to have this beautiful man in my life, and I will gladly bide my time at his side.

I can only hope the time isn't far spent.

"Where'd you go, my lovely lady?" Sebastian asks, extending his hands to lift me up from between the barrels.

"I'm right here," I answer, forcing a dutiful smile.

"You do that a lot, you know?" He adds with a curious glare.

"What?" I reply, ringing out a cool iced towel and offering it to him.

"Thank you," he says taking the towel and wiping his face and neck. "Well, it's like you disappear but you're standing right in front of me. Your eyes grow distant, and you just stare off. I wish I knew what you were thinking about, but you are exceedingly difficult to read, I'm afraid."

"How do you mean? Read?" I ask.

Staring at me with a curious frown, he tosses the towel over his shoulder, opening his arm and allowing me to loop mine through his as we begin making our way through the warehouse. Turning off a few lights and checking the rutters of the large pressing unit he continues with his normal end of day routine.

Grabbing his shirt from a wooden stand he maintains his inquisitive gaze just as he parts his lips to speak. "I suppose I mean that since I am Altrinion, I should be able to read your mind, but I cannot."

"Are you serious? Altrinions can read minds?" I sputter my words, taken aback at this new information.

Crap! Does Dalcour know about my dealings with the Changelings? Has this been his plan the entire time?

My thoughts go awry at even the possibility my hidden desires are not as hidden as I had hoped.

"See, you're doing it again? I mean, for mercy Chartreuse! What is going on? Are you okay?"

"Am I okay?" I snap back. "You're the one invading my mental faculties! You can read my mind?" I shout, stepping away from him.

"Wait! Wait!" Sebastian protests with his hands raised in surrender. "Firstly, I've never read your mind. To be honest it's not a skill I've ever been more than mildly capable. It is a skill, Chartreuse. You have to work at it. In over a century I've never given much thought to the idea, because as I've told you, I'm not sold on the whole notion of our existence as it were. Quite honestly, I'm most happiest with humans and see little use of my supernaturality beyond normal means. So no, dearest, I've never read your mind."

"Never?" I quietly question.

"Never." He affirms with his shoulders squared and tone resolute. "However, it does make me wonder why you didn't know this. I mean you are Dalcour's ward. Has he not explained these things to you?"

First compulsion. Now mind reading. What else hasn't Dalcour told me?

Forcing myself from my self-brewing entrance, I exhale and don a quaint smile. "Well, to be honest I haven't been with him that long. Just as fast as we arrived in New Orleans, he was gone to tend to other matters. I suppose he didn't have the time. But he did say there was more he'd teach me upon his return." While it's not a complete lie, I have omitted quite a bit, but I am hopeful this helps to fill in the pieces.

"I see," Sebastian grumbles in a husky tone. "Tell me, would it be so bad if I did read your mind?" He asks with a deep narrow gaze.

"It depends," I reply, closing the space between us.

"On what?" He adds, taking my wrists in his hands, as his warm smile returns to his face.

"Well it depends on whether you really want to know what I was thinking as I watched you working earlier or not." Looking up at him through my thick lashes, I see his breath hitch and he sucks down the hard air in his throat while his steely stare holds me captive.

Good. He's not as immune to my wiles as I thought. And with his gaze now deepening into my own, I have no doubt Sebastian St. John is interested in more than mere kisses. Still, while I am surprised he's obviously chosen the more gentlemanly road, it does me good to know his interest in me is just as carnal as my own desires for him.

Releasing a low groan, Sebastian licks his lips and flings his head back and chuckles. "So I suppose that means you're keeping your secrets then," he continues laughing as he pulls me into his embrace and plants a light kiss on my forehead. "I reckon I must commit to memory the evocative little melody replaying like a hummingbird in your mind."

"What? *So you can hear something?*" I ask, puzzled.

"Yes—well—I mean—not really. It's just a low little churn of a ditty. Not really a song even. Reminds me of those old nursey rhymes of juniper and mulberry trees."

Sebastian keeps me tight in his hold as he softly rests his chin on the top of my head. In this moment I am thankful he can't see the dread of concern I know obviously mars my face. Although I am surprised to learn Altrinions can read minds, I now know the Changelings also have the power to keep my mind barred from such an intrusion.

I can't help wondering what other powers lay dormant within me. Between helping Sebastian prepare the wine and cheese baskets and throwing myself into all things Sebastian St. John, I've taken little time to understand the weight of my own decisions as of late.

"I hope you don't mind; I've asked Oliver to arrange dinner for us at Crème du Ponte just outside of the Quarter."

"Oh really?" I answer, surprised.

"And before you begin to worry, I've taken the liberty to tell Austin to relay the message to Greta. I'd hate for her to go through too much trouble."

"That is very thoughtful of you, Sebastian, but you didn't have to go through the trouble."

"I assure you it was no trouble at all. Although I contend, I'd gladly get into some good trouble for you, my little hummingbird," he answers sweetly, kissing the top of my head once more before looping our arms together again.

"Hummingbird, huh?" I teasingly repeat.

"Do you hate it?" He asks, worried.

"No actually, I love it," I smile, leaning my head into his shoulder as we walk toward the front door. "I've never had a real nickname or term of endearment before. That is if you don't count Chalmette calling me Treuse or my childhood friend calling me Red."

"Red? Really?" He scrunches his nose, irritated. "I don't much care for descriptive names and such. I mean, I'd hate to be called Curly or some oddity regarding my appearance."

"I guess I didn't think too much of it before, but now is different."

"How so?" He says standing in front of the large steel door, barring our exit.

"Before, those names only came from friends and family. This time—"

"It comes from your man," he completes my thoughts and steals a sweet kiss. "That's who I am Chartreuse. I am your man."

Once more, Sebastian kisses me. Soft yet deliberate. He leaves no room for retort or questions as he opens the door and leads us out.

Slowly, I'm beginning to understand there's a strong, domineering force lingering just beneath the veil of his alluring and boyish charms and I am more than eager to discover just how powerful such a force can be.

Chapter Twenty-Five

Dinner at Crème du Ponte is lovely. Not only has Sebastian secured a table for us in a private area of the restaurant, but he has given the chef a list of all of my favorites—even my croissants—to ensure I had a most pleasurable experience.

"Everything is perfect, Sebastian!" I exclaim before forking in one last bite of pork and seafood etouffee.

"I aim to please," he answers with a bright smile as he takes a linen cloth to wipe his chin.

"Well, I am most certainly pleased. And stuffed, I might add," I laugh.

"Good. That is, of course, the point of supper. However, I hope you're not too full. I had a few more surprises for you," he says with a sly grin.

"A few? Now I'm interested!" I smile back, resting my chin on my clasped hands.

Rising from his seat, Sebastian extends his palm to me and helps me up from my seat. "Come with me," he says in a low tone.

I do as he asks, and he leads us to a darkened room in the back of the restaurant hall. As we enter through two narrow double doors, a tall elderly gentleman with the clearest blue eyes I have ever seen, greets us with a dutiful smile.

"Master St. John, madame, please follow me," the man says with his shoulders hunched in submission. As we go deeper into the room, thick clouds of smoke and scents of hickory and cedar cigars fill my lungs. "We have Sir St. John's lettered box here as you required, my lord."

He offers a long, small, black and cedar trimmed wooden box to Sebastian, and he takes it after handing the man folded notes of money and the man smiles in return, nods at me and makes his exit quickly from my view.

"I thought you'd enjoy a smoke with me," Sebastian says in a tone lighter than the broody atmosphere surrounding us suggests. Looking through the dimly lit room, I spy several men chatting with cigars and pipes in hand. "That is, since you're not some conventional woman who'd rather dally with cross stich, I thought you'd appreciate the gesture."

"Well, my lord, you are quite learned. I'd love a smoke with you," I cheerfully reply.

Taking my hand, he helps me to a seat and his normal boyish grin stretches across his face. "My, my lady how perfect you are! I can't tell you how much I appreciate the wonderfulness of you! Most women I meet only care that I am of class or status within the supernatural community. They throw themselves into what others deem appropriate and lose sight of who they are. You are not that woman. I admire that about you. You like what you want because you want to! And even if you were to tell me that you had no desire to smoke, I'd be just as happy. I only want you to be happy with what you want in life, my little hummingbird."

"Sebastian, please don't make me cry. I'd hate to ruin the taut image you have of me," I mutter.

"That, my sweet lady, is impossible. Besides, if you were to cry, it would just give me an excuse to hold you once more," he says, squeezing my hand in his.

"There will be no tears!" I quietly exclaim, firming my grasp in his. "Just know you'll never need an excuse to hold me, my dear Sebastian. You are my man after all." I whisper back.

"Very well then," he adds with another wily grin, peering at me through his curly tendrils cascading his face. "I thought you'd like this curated box of

Fonseca and Sancho Panza. They both have the cherry and hickory flavors your pretty little pallet likes."

Smiling wide, he opens the small box and moves it to my side of the table. His eyes search mine and I can tell he's anxious to see which cigar I chose. Although I've only smoked a few times with Scotty, I never had the option of selecting a smoke. Scotty normally handed me whatever he had in his pocket. Some flavors were more robust while others were laced a thin layer of sweetness within the tobacco. Either way, I always relished our times smoking in the back of the saloon. As odd as it was, there were even times when Monroe would join us and for a moment, there was a semblance of peace between us.

But it never lasted long.

Without thinking too long, I pick up the cigar in the middle and Sebastian's wide Cheshire grin returns as he lifts a match to light it. "Good choice," he mumbles with a thick cigar now lodged at the corner of his mouth. "The Fonseca suits you. Sweet and bold. The grace in its smoke mirrors the manner of your stride. Hauntingly beautiful." Sebastian says while blowing out his first puff of air.

"Hauntingly beautiful? Another new endearment in one day, my lord. My head will swell with all of your accolades," I playfully counter, as I inhale the deep aroma of the Fonseca. Crossing my legs, I lean back into the wine-colored wingback leather seat and let the fragrant fumes fill my lungs.

Gazing at me through the cloud forming between us, Sebastian smiles as he too enjoys the coaxing relief of the Sancho stemming between his lips. "I must say, this is a different experience as an Altrinion. We feel everything deeper than humans. I can taste the leathery essence laced within the casing."

"Oh, for mercy, Sebastian, don't tease me. I was only just getting a bit of a lift," I laugh.

"Well by all means Miss Chartreuse, don't let me interrupt. For certainly, I of all people know just how ceremonious your lift can be," a familiar throaty deep voice says from behind me.

Sebastian's normal boyish grin grows into a menacing grimace and he quickly rises from his seat. "I beg your pardon," he growls back.

Turning around, I am shocked to find Preston, one of my saloon regulars now standing behind me. Everything in me freezes and I dig my feet into the carpeted ground beneath me. It's all I can do not to bolt from here. Dropping my cigar into the small ceramic bowl at our table, fear and embarrassment gnaw at my insides. Somehow, I fooled myself into believing I'd never have to lay eyes on anyone or anything from my past, save Chalmette.

And while both Sebastian and I have spent the last few days sharing our truths with one another, there is one part of my life I purposely omitted. I never told Sebastian of my life at the saloon, nor had I the intention of doing so. Now that I was in this supernatural world, I had hoped neither my past nor present would collide.

I was wrong.

"Pardon me sir, I meant no offense," Preston cowardly responds, ambling back from our table. The stench of bourbon reeks from his pores as it does the two men at his sides.

Still, Sebastian keeps his sight set tight at Preston. Extending his hand, he quickly lifts me from my seat, pulling me next to him and away from Preston and the two gangly looking men with him.

"It—it's just me and Miss Chartreuse know each other quite well. Don't we sugar?" Preston laughs. "In fact, we know each other so well, I'm actually one of her best tippers! Aren't I darling?" Reaching out to stroke my face, Preston stumbles over his associate's foot and his hand lands on my shoulder, narrowly missing my breast.

A deep growl echoes through Sebastian and he is instantly in front of me. I don't have a chance to shake Preston's grip from my shoulder before Sebastian grabs him at his wrist, squeezing it tight. "Listen to me well, you foolish drunkard, don't you ever put your hand on this woman ever again. I don't care if you two shared the same nursery and carriage! As a matter fact, I want you to forget she exists. All I want each of you to remember is that you are worthless, deplorable souls who don't deserve the air in your lungs, much less the companionship of such beautiful woman. Is that clear?"

Dumfounded, the men nod in acquiescence, entranced by Sebastian's compulsion. I don't know what is more frightening, having the grievances of my past made bare before Sebastian, or witnessing Altrinion compulsion firsthand.

Sebastian was right. He does such a great job blending into normal human issues, watching his display of supernaturality is hard to witness.

"Mr. Mitchell," Sebastian calls over his shoulder and the same elderly man who ushered us into the room quicky returns to Sebastian's side.

"Yes, my lord," Mr. Mitchell answers quietly.

"Please remove this man and his feigns from the presence of myself and Miss Grenoble. I think using the back door would be best." Sebastian barks his orders in a tone so gruff, I never thought him capable.

"If you would follow me, please," Mr. Mitchell says, snapping his fingers and the men allow him to lead them out of the restaurant.

Still frozen, my eyes trail Preston and his cronies as they follow Mr. Mitchell, hopeful the pains of my past are carried away with their footsteps.

Alas, I know better.

"Chartreuse, are you okay?" Sebastian searches my face as he holds my shoulders firm, concern filling the void between his brows.

My feet are still tethered to the ground and both the sight of Preston and memories of every horrid detail I've ever done with him sickens me to my core.

Why did he show up here?

Did Monroe send him? Did Mother?

"I need to go!" I bite back my response. I know Sebastian doesn't deserve my lashing, but unfortunately, he's here and Preston is gone.

"Please, wait!" Sebastian shouts as I pull from his hold and exit near the restaurant terrace. Lifting my dress at the hem, I race fast down the narrow galley and I see Austin standing near my carriage at the end of the galley way.

This time my movements are too swift for even Sebastian to parry. Pacing toward the carriage, I realize whatever remains of Dalcour's sire bond still flows through my veins, making me faster than I thought possible.

Still, I take little time to marvel at my speed. My only desire is to get out of here. I hear Sebastian screaming my name in the distance, but I cannot stop.

There is no way I can face him now.

Once more, Austin senses my need to flee as he flings the door wide at my clearing. Effortlessly, I'm inside the carriage almost as fast as Austin is back in his saddle commandeering the horses to our destination.

Our return ride is swift, but I barely can make out our path through my tear-filled eyes.

Arriving at the estate, Austin quickly flings the door open to aid me out of the carriage. I barely offer a hint of gratitude as I race toward the front door. Thankfully, the door opens as I arrive on the porch and Greta's warm smile greets me as I enter. Dutiful as ever, she bows her head slightly but curves it over her shoulder, sending her gaze to the threshold of the parlor.

Gasps and expletives rush from my mouth when I find Sebastian standing just a few steps from me. His gaze is tender as he stares back at me, but even that is too much to take.

"No, Sebastian!" I shout, refusing to surrender to his pull. As surprised as I should be that he beat us here, I am not. He is an Altrinion after all. With the same speed Dalcour used to rescue my family and me after the fire, I am certain, Sebastian's speed is just as surging.

Turning away, I make my way up the stairs as my embarrassment of seeing Preston tonight floods my being.

"Please wait, Chartreuse!" Sebastian yells after me, rushing up to me from behind.

I am mildly comforted by a lingering essence of the sire bond within me as I am able to make it to my suite before he beats me to the stair landing.

Still, Sebastian isn't far behind. Before I have an opportunity to close my door, Sebastian's hands hold the door steady, preventing me from closing it.

"Please, go!" I cry, pushing my back against the door. The thought of closing the door in his face is too painful.

"I need to tell you something. Just hear me out," he protests, forcing the door open wide enough that he enters through the crack.

"What, Sebastian? I don't know what you could possibly say," I begin, leaning against the door frame, exhausted. "I mean what do you want me to tell you. Do you want me to tell you how if it wasn't for Lord Marchand,

I'd still be a lady of the evening, sharing myself with any willing tipper of the night like Preston? Or would you rather I tell you how because my sister fell in love with a man of color, she was burned alive and that people like Thaddeus see me just as vile as the rumors spread about her? Perhaps you'd like to know how years later we fell on such hard luck; my mother reduced my sisters and I to harlotry and parlor tricks. Is that what you want to know?" Spitting my words like fire, Sebastian stares at me with a bleak yet empathetic expression. As much as I wish his gaze were enough to still the warring of my heart; I know better. "Please, Sebastian, just go," I sigh, opening the door wide and gesturing my hand for him to leave.

Walking toward me, Sebastian forces his boyish grin, but I still spy glassy pools of water behind his eyes. While it's not how I intended to tell him my life's story, I am thankful to have it off my chest. But I don't need his pity. I owe no apologies for my life thus far nor do I wish anyone to regard me as some wounded dog.

"No." Sebastian's clipped tone surprises me as he slams the door shut at my back. "No, I'm not leaving you Chartreuse Grenoble. I know that is what you want. You probably think I pity you. I do not. In fact, it's the complete opposite."

"How can that be, Sebastian? I see the way you are looking at me." I quietly counter as he palms the side of my face. His hold on me is steady as he keeps our gaze set one another.

"Because I see myself in you. More than you know," he whispers back and kisses my forehead.

"But—"

"But nothing, my sweet hummingbird. If you would just let me talk for a minute," he starts with his brows raised as he takes my hand in his and leads us to sit on the chaise in front of my bed.

"I—I don't understand. After everything I've already told you—how can you say you see anything in me that resembles you."

"Because I too, have a backstory, if you will. While our stories may differ, they have one main theme. We both were brought into a chaotic world not of our own making. For you it was your family's downfall and a life in a brothel. For me it is more than trying to not only avoid the Altrinion curse, or doomed state of the men of my family—being the only son of an only son—but my lineage is even more complicated because I am not quite what I appear." Sebastian's voice is husky as he speaks, and his more typical boyish features appear stoic and stiff.

A tinge of worry fills my heart as he stares distantly across the room.

"Are you a wolf? Hybrid?" I question, trying to recall my meager comprehension of the supernatural world.

A thick, coarse laugh erupts from him and he grips my hand in his and looks over his shoulder at me and smiles. "Well I suppose you're close when you say hybrid. But not quite."

Chapter Twenty-Six

Staring at him, I can almost see the apprehension building within him. Squeezing his hand and softly patting his shoulder, I smile in return, hopeful he knows he can trust me. "Please, Sebastian, you can tell me," I add.

"While it's not a cause for speculation or antipathy in the supernatural community, the lot befallen to me is one that separates this human world in two. North from South. Black from white." Pausing, Sebastian's gaze lingers as he searches my face for comprehension. Like a puzzle, I try to decipher his truth, but I cannot. Thoughts of my own past and seeing Preston tonight still weigh heavy on my heart. Keeping our eyes locked, I nod for him to continue. "I am colored, Chartreuse. Or as you humans would say, I am negro."

Shock and surprise stir through me as his truth is now plain before me. Gazing at him, my eyes trail his deliciously full lips, curly hair, and storm-cast eyes but still all I see is a man I've grown to care for in such a short time.

Before I have a chance to reply, Sebastian gets up from the chaise and walks toward the window. "It's not that I am ashamed of my lineage. In fact, I feel nothing but pride for who and what I am. My mother was black and my father white. Her father was also of mixed race, so she was fair. With times being as they are, my family decided that I'd live with the human privileges of passing myself as white, but never once have I denied who I am. It is known among those in the supernatural community, but we rarely share such a truth with humans. And well, with what happened to Decaux, supernaturals of every creed have unfortunately become more aware that our supernaturality is second to the color of our skin. Even still, I wanted to tell you, Chartreuse because I want you to know who I am. I want you to see all of me. That way, whatever you make of me, should you stay at my side or walk away completely, you'd do so knowing everything."

"Thank you, Sebastian," I whisper as the weight of his confession holds me in my seat.

"For what?" He questions, staring at me while leaning against the armoire.

"For trusting me with your truth. You have laid yourself bare before me and for that I will always be thankful. No one has ever—" my words trail to the corners of my mind and I realize that even his reveal does little to change the truth about who I am. "It doesn't matter, Sebastian. Whatever this is between us will never work!" I cry out, rising from my seat.

"Because I am negro?" he asks as his eyes glass once more with a look of hopelessness.

"Of course not! That doesn't matter to me!" I contend. "But I am no simpleton, Sebastian. My background is even more colorful than your own, if you will. Preston may have been the first to come through town, but he surely won't be the last. Just as word got out to Thaddeus of my sorted past, news of my life since that time will likely surface and in doing so, it will bring you undue shame.

"I don't care what deplorable situation you found yourself in, Chartreuse. That doesn't change how feel about you."

"And what can you possibly feel for me, Sebastian? I mean, for as much as I appreciate what you shared about your heritage, how can you compare that to me? The color of your skin was not a choice nor is it a crime!"

"That may be, but from what I understand, you had no choice either. As a matter of fact, from where I stand, that still makes you a virgin."

"What?" I question and the pacing of my heart concedes to the steely stare Sebastian is giving me.

"You heard me, Chartreuse. You're still a virgin."

"I'm far from that and you know it."

"Sure in the traditional sense, but the way I see it, you only did what you were obligated to do. I mean, truly my hummingbird, was there ever anyone to which you freely gave yourself?"

"Well—um—no."

"Like I said, *virgin.*"

"Okay, but that doesn't mean you can just forget my past and—"

"I'm more concerned with our future than your past, my lovely Chartreuse. Besides, I didn't know your past and I had the same intentions earlier today that I have in this very moment."

"What intention is that?" I question as I watch Sebastian take heavy steps toward me.

"At dinner I told you I had two surprises. The cigars were the first." With his hands in his pockets, he slowly paces the floor. His usual boyish grin is gone. Now a more seductive and calculating stare locks our eyes as one.

"And the second?" I swallow my words and my breathing quickens as he inches closer.

"To make love to you." He stops his pacing as he stands squarely before me. Taking my left hand in his, he strums his free hand along my jawline, biting his lip as he does. "I wanted tonight to be perfect. I wanted you relaxed and comfortable in my arms. But right now, I just want you."

"You want me?" I ask perplexed.

"Yes, beautiful. That is, if you have no objection to making love to a half-breed such as myself.

"Actually, I care not what breed you are, human, Altrinion, green, yellow or otherwise. I want you, Sebastian. I want you—*my man.*" Raking my hand through his curly mane, I pull him close as our lips lock tight.

Kissing him, I feel the weights that once held my state fall to the wayside. Knowing he wants me is all I needed to hear.

"And that you shall," he says as a fiery glow kindles behind his irises. Before I know it, Sebastian's mouth is once more crushing mine, this time his tongue intertwines my own and his hands work fast to untie my dress strings. The weight of my dark green gown shakes free from my body and to the floor in an instant. Lifting me up and out of the cavity of the dress, Sebastian carries me to my bed where he unlaces my corset, freeing my breasts.

"Beautiful," he says licking his lips. Removing his shirt, he wastes no time pulling down his trousers revealing the glory of his manhood. My eyes widen at the glistening sheen before me, and I realize never before have I wanted someone so much.

"Come now, my little hummingbird, I want to see all of you," he growls, leaning over me. At his words, my legs part and his eyes travel from my breasts to my preciousness. "Now that is indeed the best treasure my eyes have ever seen. You have no idea how much I've imagined looking at you like this."

Spreading my legs farther, his eyes grow wide with lust and his manhood stiffens, more sheen glistening the rounded top.

"Damn, I want you so much, hummingbird. Why are you tempting me so fast? I wanted a taste of you first."

"I'm here for you. Whatever you want my love, I'll give it to you." I moan, biting my lip, anticipation stirring the core of my sex.

"No, baby, I'm not a tipper. Between us, we please one another. It is not a one-way street. I want to meet your needs and you will meet mine. So you tell me what do *you* want?"

The needful glare in his eyes is just as telling as the glory of him before me now. Although I can tell it's taking every part of his will to muster restraint, knowing he's doing so makes me want him more.

"I want everything. All of you."

"I plan on giving it all to you. Just tell me what my sweet lady needs," he answers, guiding us back to the bed. Posturing me on the side of the bed he kisses the top of my head, slowly drifting to softly placing his lips on mine. Smiling, Sebastian hovers over me, awaiting my response.

I know what I need. As a matter of fact, I've always known. Yet, I've never wanted to share that part of myself with anyone.

Until this moment.

"No one has ever kissed me—*there.*" My hands strum through his curly hair and slowly push his face down through the center of my body.

"Then it will be my honor, beautiful. Just lay back and let me kiss you as you desire. Tonight, my hummingbird, I want to kiss every part of you."

"Please," I moan as Sebastian pulls me to edge of the bed, propping my feet on his broad shoulders.

My plea is heard as Sebastian's tongue finds my spot, mercilessly lashing my sex, making me squirm with abandoned delight. He shifts from kissing my preciousness to forking his tongue in such a swift motion, my legs quiver and I know I am on the verge of a long-awaited release.

I can count on one hand how many times I've had such a release. Each time it's been one of my own making.

This is the only time it matters.

Sebastian shows no mercy as he laps me like a starved and thirsty man and my knees buckle in response. My hips push up against his face and I feel his forefinger rubbing my sensitive spot as his tongue masterfully glides over me.

I do my best to hold my wits about me, but I am incapable and find my release in one final stroke.

Screaming, my body contorts and quivers beneath his hold and he growls into my sex.

"Oh no, my sweet hummingbird, you're not getting off that easy!" He says as he rises to his feet and lines himself up at my entrance. "You're gonna have to do that again. *On me.* Can you take all of this tonight?"

"Yes, Sebastian I can take everything you've got to give." I whine, squirming beneath his muscular frame.

"Ah, baby, that's all I needed to hear," Sebastian coos, leaning over me with his mouth at my ear. "For mercy, Chartreuse, everything about you is so beautiful. I could look at you like this all day. But I need to do more than look at you."

"*Please.* Whatever you need I'll gladly give it to you," I whimper, combing my hands through his curls.

"And I'll gladly take everything you have to give," he smirks, and I almost regret my words when I look at the thick, hard, monster awaiting at my entrance. Smiling once more he shoves his leading inside and he lets out a groan and curse. "Like I thought. You feel just as sweet as you taste. Just a little more, hummingbird."

He lied.

It is a lot more.

With my hands scoring his back, I yelp as he smoothly connects us as one. *Over and over again.* As soon as my body adjusts to his size, he pulls out, admiring the sight of me laying beneath him and continues his rhythm all over.

"Promise me," he grunts in my ear, grinding deeper into me.

"What?" I moan, taking everything he's giving me. It hurts but I've never felt anything so good.

"Promise you'll never take this—you—away from me. I can't bear not to have you," Sebastian continues, leaning up on his forearms to look at me. "Promise me!" he growls.

"I—I promise! Yes, Sebastian, I promise!" I shout as the wood posts of my bed rattle against the wall.

At my confession, he slows his pace and lowers his mouth to mine, kissing me once more. This time, his tongue gently laps my own as he holds me at the nape of my neck, keeping our lips locked together. His rhythm is so delicate as he circles his hips, grinding into me more gently than before, yet losing none of his fervency.

I whimper as he does and realize for the first time I am at complete surrender. *Missionary.* To date, I've never fancied this position. Never have I wanted a man to have such control. The only man before now to do so was Monroe and the cretins who raped me on my first night. Since then, as part of my rules, I ensure I am never left to the wiles of any man.

Until now.

This is different.

I feel no desire to buck Sebastian's whim, or flip him over to straddle his waist. Although I'd gladly get on my knees, allowing him the same intensity from behind, I am just as thankful to be on my back giving him all of me while joyously receiving all of him.

I've never made love like this before. Actually, I have never done anything like this before.

In this, Sebastian was right. I was a virgin.

But I am no longer.

Sebastian leaves no part of me untouched. Returning his mouth to my preciousness as well as exploring my breasts, he delights himself in every part of me. His kiss is as deliberate and his touch passionate as he lays hold to my waist and returns to his earlier intense motion, pounding me so hard nothing but a bouquet of pillows keeps my head from meeting the wall.

"I told you we would do this together. You give to me and I give to you," Sebastian moans, lowering himself back to my ear, his sweat dripping to my chin.

"Yes, Sebastian," I groan as he resumes his hold at my hips, circling and pounding in long hard strokes.

"Good," he growls, now slamming harder into me. "I'm about to give you everything in me, hummingbird and I want you to do the same!" He commands.

"Ah! Sebastian!" I scream, bucking my hips up to meet his thrusts.

"Come with me, my little hummingbird. *Together*." His husky breathing hitches as his tempo increases and his circling pounding motion drives me to another high of ecstasy. "Now Chartreuse!" He demands.

My body yields to his command and my heightened release explodes in tidal waves of passion as do his own.

And now I know how love making truly feels.

Chapter Twenty-Seven

"Your eyes are dancing again," Greta teases as she pours orange juice into a small glass. "As a matter of fact, I think your eyes have danced ever since Master St. John first stepped foot in this house a week ago." A warm knowing smile crosses her face as she walks back to the stove.

"And your cross little smile has teased me every day since the first day," I laugh as she places a small dish of biscuits and ham on the plate in front of me.

"Well, my apologies Madame Grenoble. You know I don't mean to poke fun," she adds with a light touch to my shoulder. "But truly I am happy for you. Besides dancing eyes are hardly a cause for alarm."

"Thank you, Greta," I quietly reply as she takes off her baking apron and puts on a clean one. Pinching the crusty edges of the biscuits, I take small nibbles, but notice I don't have much of an appetite.

"This is the third morning you've picked over your food ma'am. Are you not hungry?" Greta asks with her hands on her hips and her gaze narrowed with worry.

"Oh, I'm just a bit distracted is all," I mutter in response while watching my fingers pick through the baked bread.

"Is everything okay? The other mornings I didn't think much of it since Master St. John was here. I thought you were being prim for him. But he left before breakfast this morning and still you don't eat." Greta keeps her sights on me as she awaits my response, but I am not sure I want to utter my angst.

Forcibly clearing her throat, Greta plops down in the stool across from the kitchen table and crosses her legs and folds her arms at her waist, still glaring at me.

"I'm sure it's nothing," I mumble, now picking the hard edges of the ham.

Sighing, Greta raises her brow and leans back against the wall, unwilling to let this moment pass.

"I almost hate to say it, but here it goes. Have you ever had something so good happen in your life that you're afraid you'll either wake up from your dream, or fear it will soon be stolen from you?"

Sitting up, Greta takes a deep breath after palming the sides of her face.

"I'm sorry. Forget I said it. I know it sounds silly," I recant and quickly heave down a helping of orange juice.

"Every day of my life." With a pointed stare, Greta's tone is darker than normal and her eyes glaze with a fear I thought I alone understood.

"Greta?" I say her name, regaining her attention.

"Yes, ma'am I know the feeling," she begins in a slightly lighter tone. "I feel it every day. I felt it everyday on the plantation when nothing good in particular was going on. The only good was knowing I had a breath of life. But each day I feared someone would take that from me. I'd seen it done to my family and so many on the plantation. Most thought that because I was relegated to the master's house, life was easy. It wasn't. If it wasn't master making his way to my room or his wife beating me because he did, I yet lived in constant fear that soon the happiness that was the breath of life would be stolen from me."

"Oh, Greta, I am so sorry. I didn't mean to make you relive such a horrid time—"

"It's quite all right, Miss. Whether you say it or you don't I live it every day." Despite the darkness of her tone, Greta manages a small smile to curve and soften the corners of her face. Rising from her seat, she pats the front of her apron as if there were wrinkles and walks toward the window. Looking out into the patio she continues, "But the fear didn't end when I left the plantation. I still feel it here now. After Lord Marchand purchased the freedom of me and many of my kin, I feared one day someone would storm in this house and take me away. They would not care that I have a damn piece of paper to say I am no one's property. I fear they wouldn't give much leeway to a colored supernatural. I fear one day they'll still win."

While our situations are different, like Sebastian, I see our similarities. Even more—I see her. Here she is a woman who wants nothing more in life than to be free to live life as she wills and not at the whim of primitive men who fancy their skin superior. The depravity of it all sickens my core.

"They will not win, Greta!" I announce rising from my seat. "The very men who wish our demise will one day beg for mercy before our eyes. That I promise you!" While the cadence and intonation of my words mirrors that of the Changelings in my hearing, I mean every word.

In this, the Changelings and I agree.

Greta stares back at me as a frown dances between her brow and her eyes now search my face. I can only hope I didn't spook her too much.

"I'm sorry, Greta," I say in my more subdued tone.

Once more, she nervously pats her apron as she walks back to the stove and pulls another tray of biscuits from the oven. Looking over her shoulder curiously, she watches as I stuff a piece of ham into my mouth. I force myself to swallow it even though the thought of human food does little to appease me as of late.

Looking around the kitchen, I can't help wondering what Greta does with all the food she cooks. I'm certainly not eating the lot of it.

"It's quite all right, ma'am," Greta replies, interrupting my thoughts as my eyes trail the troughs of food and supplies in the corner of the kitchen. Blocking my view, she smiles wide and continues. "I suppose we both got carried away with our fears. That's just how it works. Fear is a powerful weapon. More powerful than a whip or a sword. It is the fear of what can happen that makes us a slave to the word itself. Sometimes the worst has yet to come nigh, but the fear of the worst can hold a person captive for a lifetime.

That is why you and I have to try to enjoy our moments of happiness. Sure, we may not know what tomorrow will bring, but we must hold to that which is good, ma'am. And we must hold on it with everything we've got!"

"*With everything we've got*," I repeat back. Greta nods in agreement and we both smile. She's right, I needn't give myself to fear. I guess when Dalcour stressed I should enjoy myself, he knew just how much of a challenge that would be.

"Oh I forgot to mention, Lord Titan popped in late last night to check on you. I told him you were—um—busy, so he said that he'd come back later today. I think he said he'd be here around three."

"Okay, Greta. Thanks for letting me know." I quietly reply. I haven't thought much about Titan since I'd last seen him.

"Yes, he said Dalcour left instructions for him to check on you," she says while grabbing a broom and begins sweeping the floor.

Crap! I forgot all about the letters Dalcour left for me. I've been so wrapped up in all things Sebastian St. John, not much else comes to mind.

As a matter of fact, until just a few moments ago, I haven't thought much about the Changelings either. It is as if being around Sebastian pushes all thoughts of the Changelings and their dark power away.

I suppose that is why I enjoy being around Sebastian.

Well, that's not the only reason.

Since our first night I have made love to Sebastian St. John every day for the last eight days. Often multiple times in one day.

We can't get enough of each other.

Had he not been called to urgent business by Oliver earlier, I have no question my morning would begin as it has over these marvelous eight days. Usually, Sebastian awakes me with a light spooning to my rear as he cradles me in his arms. Slowly making his way on top of me, he grinds us to our release only to lead us to the bathroom to freshen up and start all over again.

Lately, he's taken to having me on top at nighttime as though it were his very own lullaby. He says he enjoys the sight of me "having my way." Whatever his pleasure, I enjoy providing the gratification he needs.

Instead of being on top to control a tipper, it is a different feeling doing so because the mere sight of me delights someone I care for with all my heart.

Yes, my heart.

I've never led with it before but with Sebastian it's just natural. Just like breathing.

I am thankful neither Greta, Austin, nor Oliver have said anything untoward about us spending so much time together. In fact it's as though everyone is happy for us. Oliver seems pleased Sebastian has someone in his life. Meanwhile, Greta and Austin appear more into one another than they think I notice. Both have been dutiful since my first day and it makes my heart happy to know they may be a comfort to each other.

Making my way back upstairs I wash up and get dressed. Looking at the clock I notice it's almost one o'clock. Sebastian left early and since we didn't get to our normal activities, I took the opportunity to rest. I slept in as long as I could; that is, until Greta rang the bell at my door, willing me to awake.

Pulling the satchel out of my armoire, I see the second letter and begin reading.

Dearest Chartreuse,

By now you have made yourself of some reputation in town. No doubt your beauty, charm, and manner have taken many of the faction leaders to heart. Although I know some of their curt and cutthroat ways can be vexing, I trust you have found someone there to whom you can relate. At least a little.

I know there are still a great many things I have to share with you and promise to do so upon my return. Until then, I've arranged for Lord Titan to educate you on some crucial details in your soon-to-be new world. Hopefully, it will help you manage your expectations for your own transition. Think of it as the privilege of being my ward and sireling.

Know this, the privilege you will now carry extends far beyond your understanding. There will be those who seek to manipulate your privilege for their benefit, but you must best them. As I told you before, I did not choose you to obligate you, rather I chose you because for a purpose even greater than even I understand, you were meant for this.

Moreover, if I can play a small part in the becoming of your greatness, then perhaps, beyond an indelible mark on the world, I can yet find redemption. And even if my own salvation is unattainable, the thought of your happiness is more than any redemptive measure I could hope to find.

Until I return,

Dalcour

One last thing—ignore Lord Titan's broody manner; I think he fancies you.

Folding the letter into my chest, I smile. Not because Dalcour thinks Titan likes me—of which I'm sure he's wrong; but because I'm happy. Knowing that Dalcour only desires my happiness warms my heart with a joy I have never known until now. Even more so because I've found such a happiness with Sebastian.

When I left the saloon, I only thought of my sister's deliverance. Once her liberation was assured, I only sought to ensure no further threats would ever ensnare us again. But in this moment, I refuse to allow fear to grip me in bondage. I will not allow it to hold sway over me.

Instead, I choose to live freely.

Chapter Twenty-Eight

"So what questions do you have for me?" Titan says, leaning against the bookcase in the parlor.

Staring at him, I am surprised he's not as broody as Dalcour suggested. He seems more relaxed than when I first met him. I'm not sure if it's the doting wandering of his eyes every time Greta walks by or if he's just in a good mood, I am thankful to be privy to his more easygoing side.

"Well, I don't know if I have many questions, my lord, but perhaps you can share what you think I should know most. Like what is a Bulwark? And why is this grand ball tomorrow such a big deal?" I ask.

Titan's brows raise and a curious frown frames the corners of his mouth as he glares at me. "That's what you want to know? You don't want to know anything about becoming a vampire, how to control your thirst, or how not to get yourself killed in daylight?"

"Oh, well—um—"

"It's quite all right, my lady. I'll bite," he says with his hands raised in surrender. Walking from the bookcase he places his hands behind the oversized leather wingback chair opposite me and sighs. "Well firstly, I'll start with the easy part—the grand event. This ball is important because in order for civility to truly take root, all factions—supernaturals, humans, or otherwise must agree to come together and live peaceably in this world. Long ago, Lord Marchand did these functions separately. Vampires had their own as did wolves. But he believes showing a unified front helps ease human trepidation. The ball tomorrow will be the largest and first of its kind. So yes, it is a big deal, my lady. Bigger than you know."

Titan keeps his eyes locked on me, searching my face for understanding so I force a smile, thinking on Sebastian's annoyance with the idea of supernaturals posturing themselves for humans. "I suppose I can understand," I reply.

"Hmm…interesting," Titan adds, lifting his brow once more as he circles the chair and takes a seat.

"What is, my lord?"

"You." His tone is flat as he folds his long leg over his knee and leans back in the chair. "I can't read you. Why is that?"

"I'm sorry, I don't know what you mean, my lord," I nervously mutter.

"I don't have to read your mind to know you're lying. As a matter of fact, I think you know quite more than you're letting on. Lord Marchand asked me to come educate you, but you already have answers of your own. Don't you?"

"My lord Titan, I assure you I don't know what you mean." I lie, but keep a dutiful smile plastered to my face.

"Fine. Keep your secrets," he grumbles, clasping his hands together as his eyes flash with a fiery glow. "Perhaps it's nothing more than a result of your sire bond. I'm sure Lord Marchand would rather keep your musings left to him alone. But when he returns you best hope he can read you, my lady," he adds with an eerie tone, leaning toward me. "I doubt he'd have much use for you if he somehow managed to clip your marionette cord."

"I'm no one's puppet, my lord," I snap back.

"Indeed," he replies quickly with a sly smile. Laughing, he settles back in the chair and rubs his hands together. "I was waiting for the fiery woman I met weeks ago to appear. I was beginning to think the younger St. John had somehow squelched your fire. It's good to see the flame yet burns."

"I'm afraid I don't follow, my lord."

"No need to be coy, my dear. I am well aware of what you and that young Altrinion were up to when I came to see you last night. As a matter fact, word has spread in the Quarter about some lovely young maiden who has the very eligible bachelor's nose wide open."

Looking away, I grab the cup of tea Greta prepared and take a sip, hopeful to evade Titan's grimacing glare.

"But please know, you need not fear I'd divulge such delicate matters to your sire. Besides, I'm certain it is not quite the news he'd hoped to hear upon his return."

Titan's mouth twists into a wicked grin as he sits awaiting my response. Although I'd rather not dignify him with a reply, I suck down my pride. "Why would the thought of me and Sebastian bring my sire displeasure?" I ask.

"Ah, so it's *Sebastian*, is it?" he sneers with a shrieking laugh. "Well, I'm sure this will certainly put a dent in Dalcour's pursuits of aligning you with Decaux."

"Oh for mercy, Lord Titan!" I exclaim. I've grown quite tired of his flippant posturing. "Lord Marchand isn't trying to pair me with Decaux anymore than you have a chance at trading more than mere glances with Greta! Yes, I've seen the way you look at her. But I can promise you, she has a far better suitor!"

Although I spit my words like venom, Titan refuses to be mocked by the likes of me and with his Altrinion speed is now leaning over me. With his hands grasping the arms of my chair he snarls as his crimson eyes flash once more and his fangs protrude.

A twinge of fear settles in the back of my throat, but I press myself firmly in my seat and keep my eyes locked with his. I will not back down before him or any man.

"I don't know if it's pure gumption that holds your state or fool heartedness but know this. Whatever glance I share with the Lady Greta is not one born of lust. Now, understanding the makings of your past I can see how you'd mistake pure admiration for such carnality. But let me assure you, when I see her—a human—who with both moxie and sheer steadfastness, refuses to use her freedom for merely her own gain, but day after day makes it her mission to guide slaves to freedom in what should be her own free time, I can do nothing but admire her. She doesn't require the power of supernaturality to do powerful things and in that alone I find her worth more than a fleeting glance."

As he speaks, the weight of his words clings to me. Remembering my discussion with Greta earlier, I now have a whole new appreciation for her. At least now I understand where all the food she cooks goes. Unfortunately for me we are not alike as much as I'd hoped. She is certainly far better.

While everything in me wishes to break my stance against Titan, I refuse. No matter how moving Greta's story may be, I must hold fast to the makings of my own life story. And that story includes Sebastian.

Snarling once more, Titan glowers at me and is seemingly surprised by my unwillingness to relent. He takes in a deep breath and sighs, standing upright and back from me with his hands now stuffed in his pockets.

"You are quite an intrigue, my lady," Titan says in a more subdued tone as he walks to the threshold of the parlor. Turning back to me, his face softens but his brows still tighten with concern. "I needn't care what dark alliances you've made to make sanctuary the hidden things of your mind, save the incessant melody strumming an endless ominous cord. Even still, I'll tell you this—no I'll warn you. Whatever dealings you have brokered with the young St. John must come to an end. And soon. My reaction of the matter pales in comparison to the havoc your sire will ensue at learning such things."

While there is no love lost between Titan and me, I know his sentiment is sincere. Everything in me wishes to understand the true cause for his worry, but something tells me he wouldn't tell me if I asked.

Still, I cannot help my curiosity. "Lord Titan," I call as he turns to exit. Only turning at his waist, he looks over his shoulder and grants a small nod. "Is there something I should know about Sebastian? A real reason for concern?"

"Oh my lady there are plenty of reasons for concern but none that are my place to share," Titan softly replies with a kind smile that reaches his eyes. "But maybe the next time we meet we can discuss the redeemed remnant of the fallen fae, Bulwarks. Or perhaps then you'll be free to share with me what dark secrets you have locked in the far corners of your pretty little mind. Until then, I bid you farewell, that is, until we meet tomorrow. Oh, I almost forgot, be sure to be on your best behavior and dress yourself in whatever fine fabrics at your disposal. Your sire will arrive at the ball and I am certain he wants to see you arrayed in nothing but the best."

Turning quickly on his heel, Titan is out of my view in an instant. As he makes his way through the hallway, he exchanges a few pleasantries with Greta just before I hear his hard feet pounce the narrow wooden steps leading to the cellar.

My heart races as I think on Titan's warning. I don't know why Dalcour would object to me and Sebastian. Unless Titan is right. Has Dalcour truly relented of trying to pair me with Decaux? Even though I wouldn't have initially objected, the thought is somewhat repulsing. Not only was my sister Calida Decaux's one and only true love, but thought of being with me seemed more amusing than entreating.

Such is not the case with Sebastian.

With Sebastian I feel wanted, desired and adored.

Surely if it is Dalcour's intent that I enjoy this new life, he will be happy in knowing it is in Sebastian that I find such pleasure. Not Decaux.

While I am both surprised and nervous to hear Dalcour plans to return at the ball tomorrow, I will yet heed Titan's advice that Dalcour find me at my best. Since Sebastian and I already put all the baskets together in preparation of the ball, there is not much left for me to do other than prepare myself.

Not only do I need to be at my best for both Dalcour and Sebastian, I know it is Dalcour's intent to present me as his sireling to the supernatural community.

Quickly I ask Greta to inform Austin to take me to me the best dressmaker in hopes I can find something presentable in a short time.

As per all things Austin, he wastes no time bringing the carriage to the front of the mansion. Before long we pull up to the most quaint and adorable shop just a few doors down from the bakery with the delicious croissants.

A small bell chimes as I open the door and the savory scent of cinnamon and wild berries hits my nose like a wrecking ball as I enter. While I don't immediately see anyone, my eyes are instantly overwhelmed at the sight of the lovely array of gowns adorned throughout the shop.

Most eye catching is an emerald gown with gold ribbing. It looks like something made in France or worn by those of an esteemed elite class. If it were not for the money Dalcour left me, a gown such as this would be far from my reach.

Just one more reason to be thankful for my lot.

"I think the color would suit your hair and complexion perfectly," a gentle, elderly voice calls to me from behind.

Turning around, I am surprised to find Elias Peyroux smiling back at me. "Thank you," I nervously reply as I recall how the girl from the bakery mentioned his fine dressmaking skills. Searching, his large light brown eyes and kind face, I wonder if he remembers me from the bakery, but I look away and back at the gown.

"Would you like to try it on?" He asks as he turns a large floor mirror toward me, giving me an opportunity to see myself next to the gown. "It is no trouble at all. My wife is in the back and can set your pins and hem line. How soon do you need it?"

Sheepishly, I look back at him and with my new view of the world I can't believe how only weeks ago I wanted to exact vengeance on him. Now I feel nothing but shame for my thoughts alone.

"Well—I—um—would actually need it by tomorrow morning. I'm sorry, I know it's rather last minute," I answer.

"Ophelia," Elias shouts over his shoulder, never losing his warm smile.

"Yes dear," I hear her voice call from the back room.

"That lady who stiffed us on the check for the emerald gown—don't you think her measurements are about equal. Peek your head out for a minute!"

Gently turning me at my wrists, Elias points to a back room where a small round woman with thick curly hair pulled into a bun takes a look at me with two needles hanging at the corner of her mouth. She nods in agreement before gesturing for someone on seamstress block to turn so she can finish their hem.

"Good then, I don't think it would be a problem, miss. And since the gown seems to be meant for you, I won't even charge extra for the rush," he laughs.

"Oh, please do!" I exclaim, pushing a wad of money into his hands. "I am more than thankful, sir. Honestly, I didn't expect to find anything so soon. I deeply appreciate this."

Elias smiles back at me after shaking his head in disbelief several times. Pulling the gown from the casing, he looks up at me and smiles once more. "You know, there's something really familiar about you. I feel like I've seen you before," he says with a questioning glare.

I'd hoped he didn't recognize me, but a part of me feels thankful he does. It is nice to be seen, as Sebastian always says. "Yes, we met briefly at the bakery a few weeks back," I answer.

"That's it!" He exclaims with a wide smile. "I knew I'd seen you somewhere before. Well, at any rate, I'm glad you came here today."

"So am I," I add as he extends his hand.

"The name is Elias Peyroux," he says with a hearty handshake.

"Yes, I know you are of great reputation Mr. Peyroux," I reply. Tilting his head, he regards me curiously as he gently pulls his hand away. Pointing at the embroidered sign behind him, I smile and continue, "I figured since your name is on the sign, I should at least get it right. Not to mention being informed by the bakery attendant of your expert skill in gowns and fabrics." Although it's not a complete lie, I am hopeful my reply will suffice.

"Ah yes!" he answers merrily. "Well, we've got a lot to do to get this gown to you by the morning so let's get you to the back and measured."

Elias leads me to the back sitting room where I wait for Ophelia to wrap up with her client. As I do, I read the news of an outdated post sitting on the coffee table, humming as I thumb through the pages. My heart warms within me and I smile.

Never have I been so happy. Not only am I thankful no malice stirs my heart as I sit in the shop of Elias Peyroux, but even more, I feel something else stir inside me I'd never thought I'd know.

Peace.

Chapter Twenty-Nine

My merry melody continues in my carriage ride back to the mansion. Both the peace and joy residing in my heart overwhelm me with a state of security I've never known before now. Although it still pains me to know Elias had a small role to play in my sister's demise, a part of me empathizes with his predicament.

I may have never been a slave or kept in subjugation because of the color of my skin, but I too understand what it means to go to whatever end for the sake of family. For it was the thought of protecting Chalmette, myself, and even my wretched sister Victoria, that I forged such a dark alliance with both Dalcour and the Changelings. Just as Elias traded the whereabouts of my sister and Decaux for his family's freedom, will I also trade my soul just to protect those I love most.

And while I assumed the power of the Changelings would haunt me forever and will me to despicable deeds, I am yet fortunate to be in control of my own lot. For that, I am indeed thankful.

Arriving at the mansion, I notice the estate is darker than usual, save a few flickering flames evident in the window. As Austin helps me out of the carriage, my curiosity grows with each step we take toward the porch.

Before I have an opportunity to place a foot on the stairs, Greta immediately opens the door. She wears a dutiful, yet reserved smile as she nods at me as I enter while she quickly exits the mansion just as I make my way inside.

Strange.

Looking around, I see a few candles lighting the halls, but the mansion is eerily dark. Not only is Greta's departure sudden, but looking down the hall I notice the kitchen is also dark. While I wonder whether Sebastian has made plans for dinner, I am still surprised Greta left without apprising me of any details.

I hear the wheels of the carriage from outside, and I peer out the window and see Greta in the carriage as Austin rides her off. Smiling, I wonder if the two had a romantic evening planned. As my curiosity grows, I can only imagine what plans Sebastian must have in store for us to require everyone to vacate the mansion.

My heart quickens at the thought and my cheeks flush with red as I take off my wrap and lay it on the foyer stool. Shooting my eyes upstairs, imaginings of Sebastian preparing a bath for us as he did just the other night raid my mind.

"Sebastian," I call, leaning on the bannister as an ache of desire shoots straight to my preciousness.

"So it is true," I hear a lush deep voice call to me from the dark corner of the dining room.

The pounding of my heart drops to the pit of my gut when I turn around only to find Dalcour standing just beyond the slither of light creeping beneath the crack at the base of the door.

"My lord!" I gasp, surprised to see him.

Dalcour doesn't answer as I rush to make my way to him. Instead of his normal caring eyes and broad smile, his mouth is tight in a thin line and his crimson eyes narrowed as he watches each step I take.

"My lord?" I question, hoping to yield a response. With every move I make toward him, he steps back and away from me. While I'm certain he's in no rush to fuse with the lingering rays of light, something tells me it's not the light he recoils. "Lord Titan said you weren't due until tomorrow. He told me you'd be back in time for the ball. I'm glad you made it back early. I have so much to share with you!" I exclaim, optimistic my lighter mood will rub off on him.

It does not.

"So his is the first name you utter when you come into my house?" Dalcour bites back as though we were in the middle of an argument. "Answer me!" he demands, forcing his face through the sliver of light, allowing a thin layer of smoke to burn along his cheek as his eyes blare bright like a flame of fire.

"My lord?" I step back, frightened as I watch his fangs protrude and his skin glistens to a thick red sheen.

"Chartreuse!" He shouts back. "Have I not given you everything? Rescued you from your sordid state, aid you in helping your sister, given you free reign in my home, all while offering you a better, more powerful life—and this is how you repay me!"

"What, my lord did I do wrong? Please I meant no offense!" I plea, lifting my hands to cover my face, certain he'll take a hard blow to my cheek.

"What is this? Do you not know me? Did I not profess you as my family? And now you think I'll strike you? You truly insult me! Put your hands down, Chartreuse," he commands, and I quickly do so. Slowly, his fangs retract and the red sheen along his skin fades to his normal chestnut hue.

Tears stream down my face and I look up at him through my wet lashes, trembling for fear. "Please if you would but explain what I did to make you so cross with me, I promise I will lament of any trespass, my lord."

"Very well then," he answers in a gentler tone as he pushes a wooden stool across the floor and gestures for me to sit. "Tell me about your relationship with Sebastian St. John."

Recalling how Titan told me Dalcour wouldn't be happy to learn of my dealings with Sebastian, I take a deep breath and think carefully about my next words.

"Please, Chartreuse just tell me the truth," Dalcour adds with a lilt of exasperation as he pulls off his long black trench coat and brim and lay them over the bannister. Sighing heavy, he sits down on the fourth step, allowing his long legs room to plant his feet comfortably on the floor.

As my mind sorts through the last two weeks I've spent with Sebastian, I conclude all I can do is share the truth with him, confident he will be just as happy for me as I am.

But he is not.

Once I bring Dalcour up to date on the would-be fairytale of the story of Sebastian and me, I see nothing but contempt and irritation growing in his otherwise hauntingly entreating glare.

"But why him?" Dalcour's dark tone falls flat as he throws his head between his hands. "Surely, there were dozens—no hundreds of suitors you could have chosen—anyone but him!" He yelps, rising from the steps.

"Well—I—I—guess it's because I—love—"

"Don't you dare say it, Chartreuse! For mercy, Chartreuse, I promise if you say it, I'll kill him myself!"

It may not be the way I wanted to confess my love for Sebastian St. John, but in this moment, I know without a doubt, *I love him.* Jumping up from the stool, I use the remaining force within me and am square before Dalcour faster than I thought myself capable.

"You will not lay a hand on him!" I growl my words, tossing any remnant of trepidation aside. Staring into his fire-wrought glare, everything in me knows I should be afraid. I know with one stroke of his hand, Dalcour Marchand could end my very life.

But I don't care.

I'd gladly give my life for Sebastian St. John.

He is my life.

So this is what love feels like?

"Will I not?" Dalcour growls back, leaning into me.

"Then you'll have to kill me too." Although quietly spoken, I mean every word.

Stepping back, both horror and intrigue fills Dalcour's face. "So this is what it has come to? You'd rather die than know the truth."

"What truth?" I question, reining in my fury with concern.

"The truth that no matter how you feel for Sebastian St. John, he is to marry another. Tomorrow."

Grief, panic, and doubt swell within the core of me and it is as if all the oxygen in my lungs is sucked out. Ambling back against the wall, I buckle at my knees as the weight of Dalcour's words fill me with a brokenness I'd never known until now.

Refusing to let this new feeling overtake me, I leer up toward Dalcour as I sense his hand nearing my shoulder in consolation. "You lie!" I snap. Dalcour pulls away and the drift of concern that once etched his brow is now replaced with irritation.

"You think I'd lie to you, Chartreuse?" He softly asks, stunned. Almost vulnerable.

My heart tells me he is yet sincere, but I refuse to let this go. "It wouldn't be the first time," I flatly reply. Looking at me as though I'd punched him in the gut, he leans back, throwing his hands to his sides and circles around the wooden stool. "You didn't tell me the truth about Elias Peyroux. You didn't tell me you wanted to pair me with your brother, nor did you tell me you could read my mind or compel me."

Whatever remained of Dalcour's vulnerability toward me is stripped away with my last words. Once more his eyes glow bright red and a fiery sheen covers his face. "Then I shall tell you nothing but the truth now. Yes, I compelled you not to harm Elias because you bare no right of vengeance against him or his kin. And while I had every intention of informing you of both Altrinion compulsion and telepathy, I planned to do so on my terms, not yours! Lastly, beyond my initial inclinations of pairing you with Decaux I had left such thoughts behind me when I sired you that night—just as I promised. But for the first time, I will go against my own will and break that promise. Yes, Chartreuse I wanted you to find love. Be happy. Enjoy your life. I had even hoped that perhaps there was some remnant of affection between you and Sincade DeLuca as I wished to also welcome him to my family. Now all my plans of such a family are but an ill-fitted design! But if you want to challenge me, I shall show you what happens to those who dare do so and I promise it will not be to your liking!"

"Dalcour—I—I—" I stutter as the fury of his words are unleashed upon me and I watch with fear as the beast within him comes to surface.

"I'll hear nothing further from you, Chartreuse!" He shouts back. "Guardians!" He calls down the hallway.

"Please, my lord! I am sorry! I didn't mean to—I—I am just learning of this! I knew nothing of Sebastian being engaged or any of the sort. I promise!"

Dalcour's face softens as I make my plea and I see in his eyes this is not what he wanted for either of us. Parting his lips to speak, two men I've never seen before and the man and woman I once saw in the taming wells appear in the hall. The four of them look at Dalcour briefly and begin making their way toward me.

"Dalcour, please!" I cry, backing into a corner, hopeful I can prevent them from taking me to whatever punishment awaits me.

"Wait!" Dalcour says, lifting his hand and making his way in between the huddle now surrounding me.

"I didn't know," I plea once more, my voice hardly above a whisper as I look up at Dalcour through tear-wrought eyes.

"I know," Dalcour replies, almost regretful.

"Then why loose your venom on me, my lord?"

"Because seeing you now I know it doesn't matter the circumstance, you'll fight to the bitter end to be with St. John, beyond anything I could possibly explain."

"If you still see anything familial left in me, I beg that you try to help me understand! In the weeks I've spent with Sebastian he's never once mentioned a fiancé or lady in his life of any kind. Now you tell me he is to wed tomorrow. And I haven't seen him at all today. Perhaps if I could but talk to him—"

"Absolutely not!" Dalcour protests. The tremor of his voice shakes through the estate and even the Guardians tremble at his sides. Walking away from the huddle, Dalcour tosses his arms up and folds his hands behind his head and sighs as he paces back and forth. "Chartreuse, I know you did nothing to intentionally cause harm, but you must understand this is the way things must be."

"But why, my lord? And who is this woman? And why tomorrow?" I shout back, hopeful, he'll shed some light to this insanity.

Leaning beside a large iron sconce, Dalcour takes a deep breath and his more monstrous appearance fades again and his eyes fall as he regards me once more with care.

"Kellan St. John was my dear friend and ally. I was on my way toward other business when I learned of his death. Years ago, Kellan named me executor to his estate. At his will reading, an arrangement was made for Sebastian to marry. Unfortunately, Sebastian did not attend the will reading last week as Oliver stated he was busy with *other matters*." Looking under his eyes at me, he sighs hard once more and pushes himself away from the wall. "Now it all makes sense," he mutters under his breath.

Making my way through the crowd circling me toward Dalcour, relief hits me as I realize Sebastian did not deceive me. "He didn't know!" I exclaim, breathless.

"It matters not, Chartreuse! It is what he now understands that matters."

"What he understands?"

"Yes, dear one. No matter how he may have felt about you, the young St. John knows propriety above all things. He is the son of an only son and it is his duty to propagate his bloodline—with an Altrinion. And I regret to say, that is not you."

Once more, grief strikes a hard blow to my heart at Dalcour's words, pushing me back into my corner.

"I am sorry, Chartreuse. Truly I am. This is not what I wanted for you. But as you can see Sebastian has a duty to his bloodline. If he wants to claim not only his inheritance but maintain his place among the Order of Altrinion he must not forsake his obligation."

"But what about us?" I mumble, clasping my hands together at my waist. Thick droplets form at the corners of my eyes and I cringe knowing the one thing I feared has truly come upon me.

"The two of you can never be," Dalcour answers, with a twinge of remorse. Staring at him I see tears well behind his crimson eyes as he watches my own fall past my cheeks.

Turning his back, he snaps his fingers and two of the Guardians lift me up by my arms as the other two grab me at my legs, propping me on their shoulders.

"Dalcour!" I scream as they carry me down the hall. "Please, no!"

"You've given me no other choice, Chartreuse," he counters, as I peer over one of the Guardians' shoulders to see Dalcour's crestfallen face from behind. "Tomorrow both you and Sebastian will enter two quite different lives. You will be in transition as a newly sired vampire, hand chosen to walk at Decaux's side. You are my only hope in reining in his insidious rule. And though I thought to relent of making you such a pair, it must be done. Meanwhile, Sebastian St. John will enter into marriage with Jerrica Jeffers. She will give him at least one Altrinion pure-blood child. But you, my dear, will never see him again!"

"My lord! No!" I cry, squirming, hopeful to break free of the Guardian's tight hold.

"Where to?" One of the leading Guardians asks.

"To the taming wells, Cedric. I'm turning her. Tonight."

Chapter Thirty

S till squirming and screaming, Dalcour's Guardians cart me through the Civility Center on their shoulders. Their hold on me is steady despite my kicking and turning, making me almost tire of my efforts. But I refuse to go down without a fight.

I am not surprised to find Titan waiting at the end of the hall with the small vampire girl from before still clinging to his waist. He holds an iron bar door open as the Guardians carry me inside and lay me on a small bed near the wall.

Before they have a chance to exit, I spring to my feet and try to escape only to have the female guard snatch me by my throat. Holding me at the neck, my feet dangle as I struggle to breathe. Her eyes fade to black and two rows of razor-sharp teeth extend from her mouth as her long reptilian-like tongue lashes out, narrowly missing my jaw.

"Abigail!" One of the Guardians, named Cedric, shouts at the woman in warning. At his rebuke, she releases me from her slimy grip, tossing me back to the bed. Her face returns to a more normal state save the wide wicked grin now spreading from ear to ear.

As she turns to leave, Dalcour slides through the narrow space of the cracked door. Titan closes and locks the door shut only after casting a wary glance at me before he and the vampire girl make their way down the hallway.

Pushing myself into the corner wall, I pull my knees to my chest as new tears sting my face at their release. Gripping myself tight, I am in shock and awe at how suddenly things changed. This is not how I suspected my evening would go.

Rocking back and forth, a familiar melody of juniper and mulberry trees fills my mind. Humming between shallow breaths, I keep rocking, doing all I can to calm myself as I keep my sights fixed on the iron bars encasing me.

"Chartreuse," Dalcour begins, his voice strangely calm. "I know you may not understand this now, but I assure you it is for the best. Once you transition you will not be as you once were. You will not care for human pleasures as you do now."

Although I hear him, his words are faint in my ears.

Carefully, he sits down next to me and tries to catch my gaze, but he cannot as I continue my rocking motion. From the corner of my eye I can see a small smile frame his face as he begins to speak. "You'll be happy to know I've sent DeLuca to check on Chalmette. He should be back the time you've completed your trials."

*La-la-la...under a mulberry tree...*I sing to myself, still rocking.

Grunting, Dalcour stands up and walks over to the barred door and leans against it, folding his arms at his waist. "DeLuca is also inviting Corbin DeVeaux to the festivities tomorrow at my behest. I am making a place of nobility among the human faction for Chalmette and her family. She will always have a place of prominence along with you. And if your sister Victoria should also have children, I shall do the same for her," he says, now stooping down to meet my eyes and my rocking stops.

"No." I want to tell him that I'd rather not tie Victoria and her abusive husband to this supernatural world, but I refuse to share such a wound with him. "Only Chalmette's family," I whisper back, continuing my sway and humming.

"You should really give some thought to DeLuca. I think he cares for you more than you—"

"No DeLuca. *Sebastian*," I bite back and Dalcour quickly stands back and away from me.

"As much as I know you hate to hear it, but it is impossible, young one—unless—"

"Unless what?" I say jumping up from the small wooden bed, forcing myself out of my dark musing. "Tell me!" I demand.

"You would have to give up this life. Our sire bond would run its course and you'd be human again," Dalcour's whispered words are hardly audible, but with the strain now etched between his brow, I know he almost hates to utter them. "You would not be my family but his. Our sire bond, broken. Kellan truly only wanted him to procreate and continue Altrinion blood. I suppose an Altrinion-human mix would suffice. Since human-bred vampires cannot procreate, this is your only choice. That is, if that is what you want."

Hope swells within my heart at his words, but no sooner than it does, that same hope is snatched from me. Upon taking the Changeling's power I was warned my failure to complete my vampiric transition would result in my death.

Sure, just one more day in his arms is all I could ever ask for. But then what of Chalmette? Who then would be left to protect her and see to it that my own family's bloodline not be lost?

One lone tear drops to my chin as the looming reality of my dark barter rips my heart in two. No matter my decision, someone is bound to be hurt.

Such a fate is likely to fall to me.

Gripping his hand around an iron bar of the door, Dalcour catches my attention. "Chartreuse? What do you want? Shall we commence with your transition? Or will you walk away from it all for Sebastian St. John? Tell me now!"

Closing my eyes, I recount the sweet memories of being in Sebastian's arms, the gentleness of his caress, and the tenderness of his kiss. I know Dalcour said nothing would remain of my human inclinations, but I refuse to let anything take away what I once shared with Sebastian. Humming once more, I work hard to lock my intimate memories of Sebastian in the far reaches of my mind, hopeful they'll still be there when I open my eyes to my newly supernatural state.

"I will stay," I softly reply, allowing my tears their release.

No sooner than the words leave my lips, Dalcour pulls me in his embrace. Searching my face, Dalcour looks to me once more for permission and I nod, unsure what to expect next.

As I do, he tilts my head back and as I close my eyes, I see his fangs protrude just before they deepen into my flesh.

This is pain. This is pleasure.

Never before have I experienced such a duality. As Dalcour's fangs dig into my neck, my body pulses with both sensual delight and merciless agony. I am not sure what I expected, but this isn't it.

Not only does the sharpness of his teeth cause me to writhe beneath his tight hold, but the sting of his venom as it leeches itself into my veins, vexes me and tantalizes me all at once. While I am doubtful this should be an enjoyable experience, a part of me never wants him to let go. Despite the pleasure I feel, a remaining part of me knows such an act could surely be my demise.

Without the care of tenderness, Dalcour rips his fangs from my neck, breathing heavily as he does. Resting his hands on his knees as he bows at his waist, he works hard to catch his breath.

My vision blurs and the room spins around me. Wobbling, I stumble around, trying to find the bed, but my knees buckle beneath me. Dalcour reaches out to grab me firm to his side, keeping me from falling to the cold floor. Lifting me in his arms he lays me down on the bed and the sound of a thousand voices rings aloud in my head as a bright golden aura implodes the space between us. Hovering over me, I am unsure what happens next as Dalcour leans into me and the brashness of his wildflower scent permeates my pores, lulling me to a peaceful state.

Once more, Dalcour's fangs hang at his mouth and I fear he'll take whatever remains of my blood. Instead, he clamps his mouth to his own wrist. Just as he's done before he lifts his wrist to my mouth and instructs me to drink.

Recalling the sweet and savory taste of his blood, I eagerly part my lips and latch onto his wrist. Just as I remember his blood is the best thing I've ever tasted. But this time it tastes better than before.

I can't get enough.

A snarling, hissing sound purrs through me as I gulp down the final drops before Dalcour pulls himself from my grasp. He lets out a loud roar as he does and grumbles something in an unknown tongue. The chorale of voices slowly fades as Dalcour's light dims. Resting against the cement wall, Dalcour's shallow breathing is noticeable as he heaves air in and out of his lungs, laughing intermittently as he does.

Before I can ask him the cause for his laughter, my torso constricts, and my eyes fade to black. I grab the sides of the bed frame as my body shakes and contorts left to right, knocking the bed hard against the wall.

Screams, growls, and cries erupt from me, overloading every part of my senses. My body continues to squirm as spasms convulse me so hard I fear I'll shake to the floor.

"Lord Marchand, is everything okay?" I hear Titan call to Dalcour from the other side of the door.

"I think so, Titan," Dalcour answers with a lilt of worry.

"I've never seen anything like this before. Do you think it's the siring? You know I couldn't read her either."

"Perhaps, but I doubt it." Dalcour's voice is grim as he answers. "Keep an eye on her. Give this to her before you start her on her trials."

I want to open my eyes and see what Dalcour is giving Titan for me, but I am no longer in control of my body. Strangely, despite my writhing bouts of agony, I can still hear everything going on, but I cannot see.

"Yes, my lord," Titan replies.

"Be sure no one lets her out until her trials are complete. Is that understood? She must not be allowed to leave until after the wedding and not a minute sooner. It is important the human factions see Altrinions happy and in love. That is the goal when they arrive at the ball tomorrow. After Jerrica and Sebastian are wed, perhaps their misgivings of supernaturals will change. This has to work."

"I understand," Titan says. "And what of Sebastian? Is he truly willing to go along with this?"

"He now knows she is to become a Scourge. Sebastian has no love for their kind. There is no way he'll ever be able to see her as anything but a Scourge. This is for the best—for both of them." Dalcour's voice trails as I hear the iron bars close and the door locks. "Rest easy, young one. I'll be back to check on you soon."

My body still writhes in agony, but Dalcour's words hurt more.

One teardrop runs down my face and I know it's the last human tear I'll ever cry.

Chapter Thirty-One

It's been a little more than an hour and my contortions have finally subsided. Still I lay still on the bed, holding tight to the wood railing, fearful my bout of fits should return.

The darkness that once swathed my vision has dimmed to a murky gray and I can almost make out the outline of my feet at the end of the bed. My breathing is raspy, and my throat parched. There's a burning ache that seems to carry from my mouth down through my stomach.

I'm not sure if it's my blurred vision or not, but from here it looks as though my feet hover just inches above the bed. Slowly, I let go of the wood railing to feel around me and I can now tell my body is suspended in the air. Turning my head, I look around and I notice a new weightlessness in my movements I've never felt before.

As the moments pass, my vision clears and the images before me now aren't as muffled as I recall. Looking at the adjacent cement wall, I can now make out every divot outlined in the crevices. Things I know I could not see until now. Gazing over at the iron bars, I notice how every speck of rust is more pronounced.

My body convulses once more, but this time it only propels me higher above the bed, causing me to swivel about. Floating around the room, the weightless continues as if I were swimming—something I never learned to do. Looking at my hands, I see a new sheen along my skin and my nails seem to also lengthen before my eyes.

Reaching for the iron bars, I use them to escort me back to the floor. To my right, I look into a large metal frame and see a reflection of myself and I marvel at the sight of the new and hauntingly beautiful woman gazing back at me. My wavy ginger curls are thicker than I recall, and my already curvaceous frame is more voluptuous. Even my breasts busts through the ribbing at the top of my gown, nearly spilling out of my dress.

Inching closer to the metal, I can't help staring deep into my eyes, amazed at how my once dark green eyes shimmer like emeralds in the night sky. If I didn't know better, I'd be entranced by the sight of my own reflection.

Before I can look away, a familiar smokey gray mist covers my image in the metal frame. Murky images of the Changelings take shape and I step back, wary of their intent.

"Darkness grows, vengeance waits, your life your own, you must take. Sing with sirens, irons break, trials succeed and seal thy fate. Futile trite abandon all, lest thy heart induce thy fall. Give no quarter, consume them whole, we lie in wait to take their soul."

Cackling, the Changeling pair delight in their own musings as my mind rummages about, trying to decipher the meaning of it all. "Speak plainly!" I demand but they only laugh more in response.

"Plainly we speak. Plainly you hear. Avenge your heart, your path will clear." Their veiled faces and black stained lips are laced with wicked smiles as their images slowly fade from my view.

Avenge my heart? I think hard on their words but the burning ache in my throat worsens and my stomach churns, almost forcing me to convulse once more. Holding tight to the iron bars, I keep myself steady, hopeful I can maintain my posture. Closing my eyes, I breath deep as I try to tether my feet to the floor.

"You're up!" Titan exclaims as I look to see him now standing in front of my door. "I didn't expect you to be up so soon." He stares at me, noticeably taking in my new features as his eyes stay locked on my cleavage.

"See something you like?" I say, almost unaware of the new seductive manner of my speech as my eyes meet his at the crowning of my bustline. Reaching my arm between the bars, I trail my fingers across his bare chest, and I hear him heave air as I trace my hands along the outline of his muscles.

Moaning, his eyes drift back to mine and he cracks a crooked smile. While I always knew Titan was attractive, seeing him now I am unsure how I missed the gloriousness of his physique. His bronzed skin and dark gray eyes with a hint of crimson glow are only just the highlights of his perfection.

"You've grown," Titan breathes as his eyes fall once more to my breasts, down through my waistline and back up again.

"Perhaps you should come inside for a better look," I say, stepping back from the door.

"Tempting," he replies with a husky tone. Sitting back down on the bed, I lay back on my arms, with one leg bent, exposing my knee as it leans against the wall, creating a gap between my legs.

His eyes flash to my preciousness and back up to my face. Using his key, Titan enters and locks the door behind him. Reaching above him he pulls down a large metal door I hadn't noticed before.

Humming, my tone sounds more melodic than I recall, almost harmonious. Titan's eyes grow with lust as he stares at me.

"Still tempted?" I ask as he makes heavy steps toward me.

"Very," he answers darkly and climbs on top of me.

"Show me," I reply and pull him closer.

"I shouldn't," he replies, and I begin humming once more. His eyes flicker back to crimson as I do, and he plunges his face between my breasts. "I've wanted to do this since I first laid eyes on you," he growls.

His words surprise me. Titan always seemed more annoyed with me than interested. But he doesn't give me time to ponder his revelation as he rips my gown open from the ribbing. Titan's eyes glow bright red and he crushes his mouth to mine and I'm almost overwhelmed by the sensation of it all.

Lifting himself and locking eyes with mine, Titan's gaze softens, and a sweet smile glistens his supple lips. "Do you know why I got so upset with you the other day?" He asks between heavy breaths and kisses at my neck.

"Why?" I moan as he rotates between my neck and lips.

"You thought I wanted Greta, when I was just burning with agony because I wanted you!" He groans into my ear. "And now I will finally have what I want."

Feeling the growth of his manhood against my abdomen, he reaches between my legs and parts them wide as he plunges himself inside me, grunting hard as he does. Expletives fly from his mouth as he kisses my neck and down through my breasts. His lips trail down my stomach, but I stop him short of my preciousness as that is reserved for Sebastian alone.

What I do now is only a means to an end.

"I knew you'd feel this good. Why did you make me wait to have you? Can't you feel what you do to me?" Titan coos in my ear.

"I didn't know, Titan. I didn't know," I moan, enjoying the pleasure of every thrust.

"I would've enjoyed just seeing you bare, but this is so much better," he adds with another lap of my breast.

Holding his face, I gaze up at him and see the sincerity in his eyes. A part of me feels horrible for using him like this, but I still know how to use my body to get what I want. Altrinion or not—he is still just a man. A man who craves what every man does. So I shall give it to him to get what I want.

Raising my hips to meet his thrusts my only thoughts are of Sebastian.

"This has to be our little secret," I whisper in his ear.

"I'll never tell. I want this all to myself," he grunts, shoving himself deeper than I thought my body capable. "You feel so good," he screams and releases inside me.

Falling to my side, he strums his hands down through the center of me and clenches my preciousness. Unprepared for his finger, I squirm beneath his grip as his fingers explore the depth of me.

I know what he wants, but I will not give that to him. That alone is reserved for Sebastian.

Gripping his hand, I guide it back to my breasts, but he pulls his hand away and sucks his fingers before wrapping his arms around my waist. "Tastes like honey," he adds, licking his lips. "I know what you want," he continues, as the crimson glow of his eyes recede. "You want me to let you out of here."

Looking up at him I etch the side of his jawline and shoot him a gentle smile.

"And I know what you want," I slyly reply, strumming my hand to hold the strength of his manhood.

"Do you think that's all I want?" He grunts with his eyes closed, enjoying the grip of my hands. "What if I want you? All of you. Not just sex."

"That is not mine to give. It belongs to someone else," I answer, releasing him and sitting up on the side of the bed. I wasn't prepared for this. *Seduce him and leave—that was the plan.*

"There's more going on with you than even I and all my long years understand. But I know one thing, if you walk out of here intent on being with St. John, it will not end the way you want."

"Titan—I—"

"Look, I can't promise a romance like St. John might, but I doubt Dalcour would totally disapprove of us. And if Dalcour has his way, he is giving you to Decaux. I don't wish that for you. Let me be your intermediary, at least until you figure it all out." Titan seems sincere, but I must keep with my plan.

"You deserve better, Titan and I'm sorry for using you like this," I reply, sorrowful, I've stooped to such measures. Jumping up from the side of the bed, regret pours over me and I stare into the metal frame, unsure of this new woman I've become.

"I'm not." Titan says, pulling my arm as he sits up on the side of the bed. "Come here," he adds, bringing me in front of him. His eyes are flush with my breasts and I look down and see his manhood strengthen once again.

Pulling me close to him, he straddles my legs around him and sits me on his lap.

"Listen, Chartreuse, you are no longer human. You are something more. We are creatures of the night and we behave as such. Forget apologies. Disavow regret. You want what you want. You take what you must. You took me to get something you want just as I am taking you to get something I want.

"What could you possibly want from me?" I ask curious. I can't imagine anything of worth to barter.

"This!" He growls. At his words he pushes my hips down, forcing an alliance of my preciousness and his manhood.

This time, I am unprepared, but he doesn't care. He's taking what he wants. But unlike my days with a tipper, I am enjoying it. Although I love Sebastian, this unbridled abandon with Titan is just what I need.

Tossing my head and arching my back, he takes my breasts into his mouth as he pushes himself deeper into me. His movements are fervent and unrelenting. Titan is taking what he wants without mercy.

Tears stream down my face as I inwardly regret betraying Sebastian to seduction and lust, but this is necessary. Titan isn't letting me go without getting everything he wants, and I'll gladly give it to him. With my hands laid across his brawn back, I have to admit I didn't expect to enjoy him as I do now.

"You know what I want, Chartreuse!" Titan growls. "I'm not letting you go until you give it to me!"

"Titan!" I scream his name as his girth seems to expand inside me.

"I can do this all day! No one can hear you scream." He says, rocking the small bed hard against the wall.

Tenacious, he snarls, barring his fangs as his eyes glow bright once more. He knows what he's doing to me. He is intent on forcing my release. I know if I don't give in, my legs will remain a fixture at his waist.

"Give it to me!" He demands with a feverish roar that sends tremors through the entirety of me.

As much as I want to hold it all in for Sebastian, I cannot. Titan deserves this. Screaming his name once more, I rake my claws across his back and blood drips down the sides of his waist and my new fangs protrude. I explode in his feverish grip and he ruts deeper into me, taking everything I have to give.

Pulling me into his embrace, Titan holds me, keeping himself locked within me as I continue to pulse around him. More tears flood my face but not out of regret. This time is pure pleasure.

"That's it my little siren," he coos while running his fingers through my hair. "Now you'll never forget who took you first."

"First?" I question, sitting up on him as he firms his hold on my butt. I wiggle slightly, still surprised every part of him is still forged deep.

"That's right your first. You had your first as a human and now as a vampire. I bet this was different."

He is so arrogant. I laugh knowing this isn't the first time a man has said this to me.

Raising an eyebrow, he cocks his head to the side and smiles. "I'm not being haughty. I meant, it's different because you're more sensitive and feel everything differently now. Besides, I need no other proof than what just happened here and knowing I'm buried deep inside you to know I've made a lasting impression," he says, adding one more thrust. I whimper as he does, and my head falls to his shoulders. He grinds slowly, shifting my hips in his hands, forcing one last tremor at my preciousness and he groans in my ear, knowing he's hitting my spot.

Crap! Maybe I should take him up on his offer? *No—stick to your plan!* I scold myself.

Pulling myself out of his hold is no easy feat, but I slowly manage to bring my feet back to the floor.

"Like I said, Chartreuse, it's your choice. You can stay with me as long as you like—or until we tire of one another. Although, I doubt I'll tire of you completely. Nor you me."

"Tempting," I say, as I try to put my dress back on.

Laughing, he winks at me and grabs his trousers from around his ankles and pulls them up. "Either way just know you can always visit. I'm sure a woman of your—um—aptitude and skill will tire of St. John's monotonous bouts."

I try to ignore his dig at Sebastian as I tie my hair into a bun.

"What will you tell Dalcour of my trials?" I ask. I know he will have to give an account to Dalcour soon.

"As far as I'm concerned, you passed."

"How so? And don't tell me it was the sex!"

"Well, you endured the blood letting of an Altrinion. That, my dear, takes some skill. As I've said before, I know you're not quite what you appear to be. So I'll tell Dalcour whatever you wish only so that I may stay on your good side." Coming up to me from behind, Titan wraps his arms around my waist, kissing my neck and I am surprised his manhood maintains itself as he presses firm into my backside.

Turning to meet his face, he plants a soft kiss on my forehead, and I rest my head on his chest, thankful for whatever this is between us.

"I'm serious, Chartreuse, there will always be room in my bed for you."

"Thank you, Titan. For everything." Kissing my cheek once more, he kneels to lace my boots.

Smiling up at me, he finishes one boot and continues with the other. "Before you go, I'll need to get you something to drink. We can't have you roaming around thirsty. You'll attack the first human you see."

While I'm thankful for his suggestion, my mind wanders. "Titan, can I ask you something?"

"Anything," he says with a crooked smile, now leaning into me with his hand on the wall behind us.

"Do you do this with all those you tame? I mean, I saw the way the young vampire clung to you."

"Well, not all but I don't make a habit of turning down something I want either," he smirks and turns to lift the metal door.

Just as I thought, I am nothing special to him. He simply takes what he wants. That is the difference between him and Sebastian. Sebastian sees me. Titan sees what he wants. Although I enjoyed everything about this moment I know with all certainty, that is all this was. *A moment.*

Chapter Thirty-Two

"Let's see how you do with this," Titan says, handing me a glass of warm blood. "Drink it now before it chills," he instructs. Leaning against the wall, he folds his arms at his waist and keeps a tight watch on my face as I put the glass to my lips.

While it doesn't taste as good as Dalcour's blood, I gulp the entirety of the glass down like water. Licking my lips, I know my thirst isn't sated as my stomach gurgles as the savory liquid hits my core. "More," I say handing the glass back to Titan.

Quickly, he goes around the corner and grabs another glass and gives it to me. I do the same as the first. He scrunches his face, puzzled by my thirsts, but he makes three more trips before I've had my full.

"What are you?" He mumbles, looking me up and down. "I don't know if it's a good idea to let you out now—at least not with your thirst being so insatiable."

Pulling the iron bars open, Titan reaches in his pocket for his key, but I jump in front of him before he has a chance to lock me in.

Protectively, I begin humming and Titan drops the key to the ground and backs away from the door. Ambling backward, he bumps into the bed and plops down. His eyes are entranced in a bright crimson glow as he settles into the bed and stares at the wall.

Marveling at this newfound skill, I lap what remains in my glass as Titan stares into the distance. At the edge of the bed I see a folded letter that resembles the ones Dalcour left for me in my satchel. Recalling how he told Titan to give me something, I pick it up.

This is the third letter that Dalcour left for me to read.

Still humming, I notice Titan's gaze is still locked into the wall. Kissing Titan's forehead, I know it's time for me to leave. Kneeling down, I look into his eyes. *"This stolen moment, I now must steal. This time we've shared was never real. Fond memories of me you will keep, fantasy locked in shadowed sleep."*

As if it were second nature, I lull Titan to rest as he lays down on the bed. As much as I enjoyed our time together, I cannot risk him telling Dalcour, or worse, Sebastian. Without the Changelings confirming what I know to be true, I am beginning to understand what I am.

I am no mere vampiric being. I am something much more. But whatever I am, it will remain my own secret. Titan will not remember our time together, but he will forever have a fond place in my heart.

Closing the door behind me, I walk down the long corridor and resume my melody. Unfolding the letter from Dalcour, I read it as I walk down the hallway.

Dearest Chartreuse,

If you are reading this letter, you are in the taming wells making your final transition into the supernatural. The leap from human to vampire is not one to take lightly. If in the time to come we break all familial ties or even the very sire bond itself, it will always be my desire that you enjoy a long, happy existence.

To do so, here are a few reminders:

Bid farewell to the sun. As with both human-bred vampires and Altrinion vampires alike, the sun is our enemy. We are of the night and as such it's moonlit comfort shall remain our solace. However, Nature is not without kindness. You may linger in the sun's light for at least one full day, or until you've made your first kill. Whichever comes first. That said, most vampires do not make it out of the taming wells without having killed before they are released. Depending on your state, you may no longer be privy to the sun. At any rate, do your best to avoid it at all costs.

We are of the night. We remain in the shadows where no one sees. We are the dark secrets in the world of mortal men. Our secrets are our own to keep or to share. But we only share our secrets in blood and barter. For this, there is no exception.

You are no longer human. And with each passing moment you shall realize just how far from humanity you have become. We may live in civility with humans, but we can only uncover and share the darkest parts of ourselves with our own. As you transition, your new vampire instincts will come naturally. Your speed, strength, ability of flight, and the new burgeoning hunger you now have requires taming in order to exist in this world. You must conquer your carnality daily. Failure to do so could cost you your very life.

Even with all of this, I still want what I've always wanted for you. Enjoy this new life, my daughter. Always know, no matter what differences stand before us, I shall always stand with you.

Forever,

Your Father

Tears flood my face as I make my way through the end of the corridor. While I know Dalcour means well, I will not allow even his paternal overtures move me from pursuing the one thing in life I never thought I'd find. True love.

Pausing at the threshold of the door, I stop to wipe away my tears. Looking around, I notice everyone is sleep. Every vampire. Every Guardian. Everyone. It was surprising enough to see how my new talents worked on Titan, but I had not expected them to do so to everyone.

Interesting.

Continuing my haunting tune, I make my way out of the taming wells just outside the backside of Dalcour's estate.

Daylight greets me as bright sun rays beat upon me as I take my first step beyond the wooded lot surrounding the mansion. My eyes hurt more than anything and I lift my arms just above my forehead as a shield from the damning light. I know I have less than twenty-four hours of sunlight left, so I must make the best use of my time.

I stay close to the tree line as I pace myself to get as far away from the mansion as possible, hopeful no one sees me. Especially Dalcour.

Sebastian doesn't live far from here and I'm using the best of my newfound speed to make it to him without being conspicuous. It's early, so thankfully the streets aren't yet full.

All I can think about is seeing him. I love him and the thought of him marrying someone I know he does not love is driving me insane. My speed increases as I think of Sebastian in the arms of another and thick tears well the corners of my eyes, almost blinding my view.

The smell of fresh baked bread hits my nose as I collide with a young woman who I couldn't see past my teary-eyed view.

"I'm sorry," I say, offering my hand to the young woman I knocked into the ground.

"Oh, it's quite all right. It was just an accident," the young woman replies with a bright smile. She reaches around to pick up two loaves from the ground and tosses them back into her woven basket before extending her arm to place her palm in mine. As she does, the smell of fresh blood hits my throat and my stomach churns in response. My eyes dart to the sight of her injured palm as small droplets of blood seep from her wound.

"I've hurt you," I whisper, as I take her hand.

"It's nothing!" She answers more cheerfully than the dark urges within me suggest. "Besides, I can just—your—your face. What is wrong with your face? And your eyes!" She screams in horror.

Palming my face, the sharp tip of my fangs pokes my finger and I'm sure all my otherworldly features are on display. I don't know what the rest of me looks like, but it doesn't matter. She's seen my face.

Once more she screams but I quickly pull her into my arms and mute her screams with my hand. Resisting, she lifts her hands and tries to squirm from my grasp. I reach to grab her wrist, but it slips as her blood soaks my palm. A burning sensation rages my throat as I crouch, trying to calm the knocking in my gut, urging me to sink my teeth into her flesh.

Her eyes grow wide with fear and everything in me wishes I could save her this torment, but the invitation of her blood is too tempting, and I can no longer resist. My fangs lengthen as my mouth stretches wide to what feels like the corners of my face and I lean in to dive into her flesh.

Just as my teeth graze the surface of her neck a roaring sound startles me from behind and before I can make out its origin, I am knocked to the ground.

"Demon!" I hear a masculine voice shout as I jump up and perch atop a small tree. "I knew I recognized you! You are Calida Grenoble—returned! They were right—you are a witch! Or something much worse!"

Looking at him, a thick brown coating of fur outlines the sides of his jar and sharp canines peer from his mouth as sun-spun eyes glow back at me. Although he looks different than before, I know who he is.

Elias Peyroux.

And he is a wolf!

A low snarl bellows through me as he roars once more, squaring his shoulders, daring me to move.

"Ophelia!" he shouts over his shoulder to his wife who I didn't see behind him. She keeps her gaze set on me and her eyes glow bright gold, alerting me that she is also a wolf. "Get her out of here! Take her to Trieu first—she's the only Altrinion I trust to compel this evil from the poor girl!"

Dropping a long dress bag, his wife quickly picks the young woman up from the ground and the two run away from my view.

Slowly, I inch to the ground, keeping a firm hold on the tree at my back. "Please," I plea with a watchful gaze on Elias. "I am not who you think. Calida was my eldest sister. I am Chartreuse—"

"You are a demon! A witch!" He bites back.

"And you are a wolf!" I counter, taking a step away from the tree.

"What I am is a protector of that which is right. Just as I would not allow you to hurt that sweet young girl, I'll not let you hurt anyone on my watch," he snarls his words as the fur coating on his face recedes.

As he speaks, thoughts of his betrayal of Calida replay in my mind and fury rises within me. "A protector of what is right? How dare you even speak such words! For was it not your duplicity that caused my sister's death, my family's downfall? As a matter fact, the very vile thing that I've become can be laid at your feet! Had you not sold her location for your own freedoms, my sister would still be alive!"

A frenzied, feverish chill erupts over me as my rage reaches its peak and I lunge at Elias. My only thoughts are his death and demise. He took from me and now I will take from him.

His eyes bulge as I leap toward him with my arms outstretched while my fangs lengthen. I reach to grab him, but I cannot. Side stepping me, he avoids my reach and I turn once more to grab him, but I cannot.

Stretching my hands I try to take him in my hold, but he remains unattainable. If he were simply parrying my movements I'd be impressed, instead he now remains still, but impervious to my attempts. It's as though an unseen barrier shields him from me.

Until I remember…crap! The sire bond. *No harm of a Peyroux shall come by my hand.*

I forgot all about Dalcour's compulsion and sire bond. No matter how much I try I cannot harm Elias. Ever.

Once more Dalcour has screwed me over!

Elias belts out a haughty laugh as he stands back in obvious triumph.

"Ah, so you can't touch me I see. I suppose somebody up there still likes me," he laughs with his forefinger pointed into the sky.

A pang of fear rolls over me as I realize I've been bested.

Or have I?

Watching his careful steps toward me, I raise my hands in caution. He stops his pacing, frowning as he notices a sly grin form in the corners of my mouth.

"Just as I cannot touch you—nor can you touch me," I begin as we both circle one another's steps.

"What do you mean?" He asks, curiously tipping his head to one side.

"Well, I would think a man such as yourself who worked so hard to procure his freedom would not want to nullify it by—well—you know," I whisper, tracing my finger along my face.

"You think your white skin saves you?" He huffs back. "It didn't help your sister," Elias adds with a dark grin.

As much as I detest the thought of using the tone of my skin as a barter, I have no choice. The color of his skin doesn't matter to me. All I see is my enemy. He could be blue, and I'd feel the same.

The sounds of the morning and people venturing out to the street begin to permeate the wooded lot as both Elias and I remain in our standoff. Looking around, Elias softens his stance, and he steps back onto the street.

"I have no idea what you want or why you're here—but if you've returned for revenge—"

"As you can see, such retribution is not mine to take," I quickly interrupt him, as I tire of his posturing.

"You will keep away from me. You will keep away from my family!" Elias warns with his fist slightly raised. Slowly, he takes a few steps from me, expanding the distance between us. "I mean it! If I ever see you near me or my family ever again—"

"Elias, you and your kin shall be safe from me, that I swear!" I promise, placing one hand at my once beating heart. *Strange, I hadn't noticed it stopped.*

"Very well then," he grumbles as he makes his way back out onto the main road. "And you can keep the dress!" he adds before kicking the leather garment bag toward me and runs from my view.

Picking the bag up from the ground, I look around and am thankful no one seemed to notice anything happened between me and Elias.

As much as the thought of Elias infuriates me he is no longer my concern.

I need to get to Sebastian before he makes the biggest mistake of his life.

Chapter Thirty-Three

S tanding before Sebastian's door my stomach is in knots and a thick weight sits at the base of my throat. I have no idea what I'll say to him. Even more, I fear what he'll say in return.

What if his fiancé is here?

What if Dalcour is here?

I have no idea how I'll respond if Sebastian refuses me. But I know this, I will not give up easily.

Lifting my hand to knock, the door opens unexpectantly.

Frozen, I listen as the door creaks, stopping halfway while revealing nothing inside but darkness.

"Are you waiting for me to invite you in?" I hear Sebastian's voice distantly call to me.

"Sebastian?" I question, stepping over the threshold into his house. While his home is markedly smaller than Dalcour's estate, there is yet a grandeur to his modest Creole Cottage, centrally located in the lower Garden District.

His silence troubles me, but I close the door behind me and toss my garment bag on the side chair. I take note of the luggage assembled by the door, but I try not to linger on reasons for it.

"So I guess the rumors of Scourge needing permission to enter a home are only a myth," Sebastian grumbles as I turn to see him leaning against the French doors of his dining area.

"I suppose I deserve that," I mutter as I try to make out his face in the dark space between us.

"And you're still walking in the sun, so I take it to mean either you didn't go through with it or your final transition is not yet complete. Which is it, Chartreuse?" Sebastian's clipped tone pierces my heart as he ambles past a sliver of sunlight beaming in from the transom.

"If you but let me explain," I start, taking careful steps toward him.

"Yes, Chartreuse, please explain!" He shouts. "Explain to me how the woman I've shared the most remarkable moments of my life with, built all my hopes up, knowing full well she had every intent to regale herself a murderous leech!"

Gasping, Sebastian's sharp words cut me to my core, hurting me as only he can. I step back, clasping my hands together at my chin rummaging through my mind for the right words to say.

However, a lingering fury within me will not allow me to succumb to his jabs for long.

"The reasons for which I've chosen a life as murderous leech rather than a pawn of poor parentage or slick-talking sires is my own battle to contend, Sebastian St. John!" I snap and Sebastian steps back, shocked by my outburst. This is not what I had planned when I arrived but I will plea my case. "And what about you, Master St. John?"

"What about me?" He shrugs his shoulders and pushes his hands in his pockets.

"Don't think I haven't noticed your bags at your door, Sebastian. You mean to go through with it! You intend to marry her. Someone you don't love! And why? Because your dead daddy said so!"

Sebastian's eyes flash like fire before me and then back to their normal steel gray hue. His face softens and his boyish grin surprisingly forms in the corner of his mouth as he scratches his stubble.

"You know we've both got daddy issues, Chartreuse," he quietly replies. "I just never thought their issues would become ours."

"I'm sorry, Sebastian! I should not have said that—I didn't mean it—"

"It's all right, Chartreuse," Sebastian begins, slowly walking back towards me. "But I am the son of an only son. My father's only thought is that our bloodline continues."

"And it is your duty to fulfill that obligation," I add as tears pour from my eyes. Sebastian takes my chin in his hand and lifts my head to meet his eyes. "And that is not something you can do with a Scourge—with me."

"Chartreuse, you know the last thing I ever want to do is hurt you. I had no idea of my father's plan until Lord Marchand came and told me."

"Is that why Oliver called you away?"

"Yes. It was then that I learned you were sired to Dalcour." Sebastian's voice grows cold as he speaks, and he slowly withdraws his hand from my face. "How could you not tell me, Chartreuse? I meant for us to have a future together. If you thought that was your only option at one time I understand, but after we got together—I thought this meant something real to you!" He exclaims, turning away to go up the stairs.

"Sebastian wait!" I call after him.

The wood floors creak as I follow Sebastian into his room as he circles a small writing desk at the entrance of his room. Looking around, I smile thinking of more pleasant memories of the two of us in his home only days ago.

"Of course it was—it is real to me! When I made this choice, you weren't a part of the equation and by the time we fell in love, I was too far gone."

"So why didn't you tell me, Chartreuse? Did you think I wouldn't love you? I thought you understood the veracity of my affection for you. I thought you knew how much I loved you—how I love you still."

If I still had a heart, it would stop beating in this very moment.

"You love me?"

"Yes, Chartreuse!" Sebastian replies almost exasperated. "I've never stopped loving you," he says pulling me close to him.

"Sebastian," I moan as he takes my chin in between his fingers and draws me in with his kiss.

His kiss is so intentional and sweet as his tongue gently explores my mouth. Sebastian's breath grows heavy as he lifts me in his arms, swirling me around and pushing me against the wall.

"Oh my sweet hummingbird!" Sebastian says, kissing my neck and down through the helm of my cleavage. Ripping my gown open and freeing my breast, Sebastian grabs hold of me and carries his kiss from my mouth to my breasts and back again.

My dress is off me and on the floor in a matter of seconds as are Sebastian's clothes and somehow, he manages to keep me in his tight hold.

"Please, Sebastian," I whine as he lifts me in his arms and carries me to his bed, laying me in the center.

No sooner than his name leaves my mouth, the strength of Sebastian's manhood strikes my preciousness with such a hard blow I see stars. His grind into me is deep and willful as if he's intent on soaking up every part of me.

"It's good to see somethings haven't changed," Sebastian says with a crooked smile.

Keeping a firm hold at his back, I try to catch my breath, raising my eyebrow curiously. "Like what?" I breathe, gripping my hand along his back.

"I feared you wouldn't feel the same after you became a vampire," he adds, pushing himself harder as though he wanted to know just how far he could go.

"Do I feel the same?" I ask, with a light chuckle.

"Better," he groans, slamming himself into me as he holds the oak headboard with his right hand. "My little hummingbird feels so good."

"Oh Sebastian! Don't stop!" I moan.

"Not planning on it. I need more!" he growls back.

"Take it, Sebastian please!"

He does that and more.

The seconds float into minutes and minutes turn to hours. I don't know if missing a day caused Sebastian to store up everything he had for me, but I never thought he'd stop.

Laying in his arms now I feel as I've always felt since the first day he held me. Protected. Safe. *Loved*. It's not a feeling I'm accustomed to, but in the short days I've been with him it is the only feeling I know. It is to his protective, safe, and loving arms that caused me to run from the taming wells with my only hopes of being in his embrace again.

"That was," Sebastian begins, as his fingers softly etch the corners of my face through the length of me. His hands rests on my hip and he scoots me close, forcing me to drape my legs over his. "Wonderful." He adds with a soft kiss on my lips.

"Yes, Sebastian. Every time with you is wonderful," I reply, tracing my fingers along his chest. "Until now I never—"

"But it was our last time."

My mouth remains parted as Sebastian's harsh words strike a blow to my gut. Pushing up on my elbows, I look at him confused. His eyes are glassy as he stares back into mine and he tries to move from under me, but I keep my leg locked in his and bury the strength of my palm into his chest.

"What? Sebastian, what are you saying to me?" I snap.

"I'm sorry, Chartreuse, but as wonderful as this was—we can be no more."

Sebastian's mouth moves and I swear his lips don't match the cadence of the words resounding in my ears.

"How can you say that to me? After what we just did! You told me you'd never treat me like a tipper and now here you are! I thought you said you loved me?" I say pushing myself on top of him, straddling his waist, with my hands now gripped at his shoulders, holding him down.

He doesn't resist much, but he wiggles a bit and I can tell it's uncomfortable for him.

I am stronger than I thought.

"I meant what I said, Chartreuse! I do love you!"

"You love me so much, you just wanted one last trite and now you're off with your bags packed to marry someone you don't love? That doesn't sound like love to me at all!"

"I do love you, Chartreuse! But I must have an heir and you cannot give me one."

Once more Sebastian's words seem not to move in rhythm with his lips, but it is the words coming from his mouth that disturb me more.

Glassy pools of tears form in my eyes and his own eyes shimmer with thick droplets at the base of his eyelids.

Looking at him, all I see is the only man I've ever loved, but something has changed. Something about him seems off. But I know better. A person only says from their mouth what is already in their heart.

Perhaps...

Tears pour down my face and Sebastian reaches up and brushes my tears aside with his hand. His eyes plea with me to understand, but I cannot. He is breaking whatever remains of the hollow remnants of my heart.

Taking his hands by the wrist, I plant them on my breasts as I cry out. As I do I feel his manhood rise at my bottom and once more inspiration strikes. Although I never wanted to return to any part of me that resembled my life at the brothel and saloon, it's all I can do. I need to remind him of everything I have to offer.

Lifting my hips just a bit, I find his manhood and lower myself onto him and he grunts in willful delight as he squeezes my breast tight. With his hands finding my waist he grinds upward into me, growling as he does, tossing his head back into the pillows, clenching his jaws tight.

But I will not let him control this moment.

Pressing him back into the bed I swirl my hips, and he yelps, tugging me tight on my rear as he screams my name.

Dark musings stir my mind and I wonder if I'll have the same effects of him that I did on Titan. A low hum churns through me in rhythm with my grind and his eyes lock with mine as his eyes flash bright like a flame of fire. His eyes grow eerily distant as I continually hum my hypnotic musings, grinding deeper into him.

His hands warm along my hips and a bright golden light shines around him and a titillating sensation rivets through me as my serenade grows into a haunting melody while I feel my release churning within me.

"Chartreuse!" He screams bucking his hips upward as I feel him mounting to his own release. "Please, Chartreuse stop!" He shouts back as he grunts and moans, pleasure sweeping over us both.

"No!" I snap back and this time I notice my fangs have lengthened against my mouth.

"Chartreuse!" He moans while my pace increases as my release builds. "Ahh!" He growls as he explodes inside of me and the warmth of him fills the entirety of me.

As he does, I find my own release and I ride hard, waiting for my climax to subside. A loud, sultry, yet high note rises from me and I sing, holding out the note until I meet my release. My ears are muted as I sing out and a thick, grey mist encapsulates us. My body pulses all over at both the feeling of my orgasm and the shimmering misty dew now filling the room.

I buck and shout one last time as I ease down from my high and I blow out a deep breath, thankful for it all. Tipping my head back, another melodic note pours through me and I slowly look back down, hopeful Sebastian is as overcome as me.

Looking down at my hands, I notice Sebastian is no longer beneath me.

"Sebastian?" I shout, looking around the room, frightened.

Nothing but a gray misty film now outlines where I last saw Sebastian.

Calling his name once more, I turn about, peering into the bathroom and back into the hallway, but still I don't see him.

Stinging tears trail my face as I search above and beneath the bed, but still I don't see him.

"Where is he?" I scream to the thick, murky substance floating in the air. I've seen it enough times to know what it is. Changelings. Once more, I shout into the air, demanding to know of Sebastian's whereabouts.

Return to dust those who sadden thy soul, end with surety, and take them whole.

Looking into the mirror adjacent to the bed, the phantoms form before my view and I cry out, fearful of their words.

"What did you do to him?" I cry.

"We did nothing. Ashes to dust, broken hearts built from lust," the gruff Changeling adds with a cackling lilt.

"It was more than lust and you know it! Now tell me what you did to him!" I say, jumping from the bed and wrapping the bed linen to cover myself.

"Took him down and took him whole. Only Sheol now consumes his soul!" The phantom whispers back.

"No!" I belt out, breaking the mirror. The haunting sounds of their laughs taunt me as I hear as the cracked pieces of glass fall to the floor.

What have I done? I cry, buckling to my knees in tears.

"Madam," I hear Oliver say as I look up surprised to find him standing just outside the bedroom door. "Where is Master St. John?" he asks concerned, looking around. "Everything is arranged, and I've come to take—"

Fate will not even give me the decency to wallow in my own torment before it reminds me that Sebastian and I are not meant to be.

Looking up at Oliver, snarls erupt from me and I spring forward and pin him to the ground.

"Madam, no! I've come to—I'm only trying to he—"

I do not wait for him to finish before my fangs pierce through his flesh. I'll not hear another mention of Sebastian with another! Consuming him whole, his thick blood eases the pangs of hunger I've fought since I'd left the wells. Despite his age, his blood is surprisingly sweet, and I lap every drop until he stops squirming beneath my tight hold.

Titan warned me things may not go as I hope but hope is the one thing I no longer have.

Chapter Thirty-Four

I linger at the top of staircase landing for a few minutes after the last drop of Oliver's blood hit my tongue. Noticing the wad of folded papers in his hands, I have no doubt he likely had some business to review with Sebastian before he was to wed.

Seeing Sebastian's suitcases near the door is a troubling reminder that everything we intended was to end abruptly. Still, my mind rummages about with both pain and regret at thought of losing Sebastian no sooner than I thought he was mine. Instead of losing him to another woman or Altrinion obligation, I lost him to my own dark alliances.

I have no idea how Sebastian vanished during our bout of passion, all I know is the Changelings are behind it all. Just as I'd fought to steer clear of Dalcour's would-be puppeteering, I knew not to avoid such a similar fate brought on by my dealings with the Changelings.

The loud sound of the nearby church bells for six o'clock mass ring aloud in my ear. As the chimes ring, I carry Oliver's body down to the wine cellar beneath Sebastian's home and put him in the vault along with all his belongings. Returning to Sebastian's room, I clean up as much as possible, sliding the broken mirror under his bed, hopeful the shattered glass doesn't draw much attention.

With every touch of his things, outbursts of cries and curses erupt from me like a tidal wave. Thoughts of his demise sicken me and haunt me all at once.

But as much as I want to wallow in my own agony, I cannot. Not yet.

Although I may not yet know how to best the Changelings or alter their control over me, I need my sire to see me. The real me. Not the saddened soul he saved at the saloon, nor the tamed vampire vixen he'd hope to give as a prize to his wicked brother, but the real me.

The woman whose very song struck a chord in her own downfall. I want him to look me in the eyes, knowing I am not a woman he can control or master. Even if seeing him should mean my own doom, I'll not give him the satisfaction of the hunt and chase. I'm walking straight into the lion's den with neither care nor fear.

I laugh as I slip on the dress fashioned by Elias Peyroux. The irony of it all isn't lost on me, but I press on nonetheless. Since Sebastian ruined my gown I have nothing else to wear and everything Dalcour gave me is at his mansion and that is the last place I need to go.

Instead of pulling my hair into a bun, I leave it free to hang at my shoulders. I'm no longer interested in donning prim attire to cater to men's ideals of docile dames.

Looking into the floor-length mirror near the front door, I smile at the hauntingly beautiful woman staring back at me.

"I know you can hear me," I whisper to the mirror. "I may not know how I'll do it, but some day I will make you pay for what you did." Keeping my eyes locked to the mirror, I stand in wait, hopeful the Changelings will reveal themselves but they do not.

Lifting my eyes to the transom along the front door, I wait patiently as I see the sun slowly fade from my view. Not only has twenty-four hours passed since my making, but I've made my first kill. Awaiting sunset shall be my new daily recourse.

Opening the doors of the cottage, I tip my foot outside the door, thankful there is no sting or burn to force me back in the house. Good.

Using night as my cover, I make my way to the museum in a matter of minutes. I take note my speed seems faster than I recall from earlier. Interesting.

Looking around I am somewhat surprised to see so many gathered for the occasion. I knew both Dalcour and Sebastian insisted this would be a grand event, I think even they underestimated it.

Walking through the large herds of humans, Altrinions, wolves and vampires, I can distinctly make out the differences in variety. From the flaming embers of fire flashing beneath eyes of Altrinions, to the golden sun-spun glimmer of wolfen eyes, I am well aware of the company to whom I now keep.

Even humans smell different. Like dinner.

Their blood calls to me more than even Altrinions, whereas wolves smell almost repugnant. Not so much that I wouldn't take a bite, but I'd certainly think twice.

Dazzling glances are shared between me and other supernaturals as I near the entrance of the museum. Most smile in admiration while others stare on curiously.

My steps are long and sure as I make my way through the museum doors and I almost gasp at how splendid everything looks. Iridescent golden lights and scented candles flicker throughout the grand foyer, creating a shimmering sheen along the marble floors.

The sweet smell of lotus, lavender and gardenia flowers fill the hall with an aromatic scent that is both comforting and inviting. Attendants stroll through offering human guests petit fours, baklava, and fruit while supernatural guests mingle with humans discussing the art arrayed throughout the hall.

But it's when I see the baskets of wine and cheese being handed out to the guests along the long corridor that leads to the Great Room, that tight knots form in the pit of my gut and throat.

These are the baskets Sebastian and I prepared. This is something we were supposed to do together!

Sucking in the thick air in my throat, I blink my eyes hard, hopeful I'll force aside any tears seeking their release. I'll not allow it. I'll never let them see me cry. Not now. Not ever.

Continuing my stroll down the corridor, I spy some of the people I met, like Lucinda and Thaddeus. Their eyes follow my movements as I make my way down the aisle. Lowering my eyes to catch their gaze, my fangs drop just enough for me to reveal my new form and both Thaddeus and Lucinda stand frozen, shocked by my new form. Quickly, I retract my fangs, careful not make myself too conspicuous in front of the humans.

Looking to the end of the corridor I see Dalcour donned in a sharp tux. His broad smile stretches from ear to ear as he greets guests as each of them hover about to make their way to him. Even if I didn't know better, there is no doubt this is Dalcour Marchand's show.

He remains centerstage as he exchanges pleasantries with his guests but his eyes flit across the room as though he were looking for someone. A man I've never seen with Dalcour before comes to his side and whispers in his ear and points to the far side of the stage. My eyes follow his and I see a woman wearing a contemporary white dress standing in the corner.

She is beautiful.

Her youthful face is impeccably polished and painted and her raven black hair cascades to the middle of her back as one thick braid coils along the side as the rest of her hair hangs free. Holding a single white rose, a bright smile beams across her face as she looks out with Dalcour to the swarming guests, waving at each as though she were royalty.

Then it hits me.

This is Sebastian's fiancé.

Crap! No wonder he intended to leave me. Look at her! She is breathtakingly stunning! Watching the elegance of her manner and the grace of her steps, it's evident she is a woman of society. Unlike me.

More knots form in my throat as I gaze at her. It doesn't take a genius to see how taking this woman as a wife would be an improvement compared to a doomed life with a creature such as me. Although I know Sebastian initially abhorred the thought of such pomp and prim manner, even he knew the two of us were not cut from the same cloth.

Before I have a chance to continue comparing myself to Sebastian's fiancé, strong arms snatch me away. I don't have time to parry or fight, but I do catch a glimpse of Dalcour's eyes as I am pulled away. I cannot tell whether he saw me or not when my assailant tosses me into a corner. Sliding across the floor, I bump my head into a marble wall.

"I thought you'd be smart enough not to show your face here! Not after the stunt you pulled!" I hear Titan's voice bark as he comes from behind the shadows along the corridor's edge. "Really Chartreuse! You are truly a piece of work," he barks, lifting me from the ground and holding me by my throat. "I don't know what you did to get yourself out, but I'll find out!" He snarls as his eyes flicker with his normal red crimson glow.

Pushing myself against the wall, I kick him off me and quickly scale the wall, jumping down to the other side.

"You may be fast, Chartreuse, but you're not fast enough."

"I hope you don't think you're taking me back to the wells!" I protest, parrying his movements as he circles me.

"If I want to take you back there—I can and I will."

"Oh but, my lord have you not taken enough from me already?" I tease, swaying my hips and fluttering my eyes while I bite the nail on my forefinger.

"What?" He asks, curiosity filling between the hardlines of his brow. His eyes scan the entirety of me, lingering once more at my cleavage as he licks his lips. Even though I know he doesn't recall what happened, there's no doubt he'd like it to happen again. *And again.*

"What is she doing here?" Dalcour roars, startling both Titan and me. I hunch, backing up against the wall and look to Titan, wondering how he will reply. "Somebody answer me!" He demands.

"You told me not to let her out until she met the conditions of her trials."

"It's been just twenty-four hours, Lord Titan! You honestly want me to believe—"

"Well, I'm standing here am I not, my lord," I interject, quickly coming to Titan's side. "And well, there are humans crawling all over and I've not spilled a drop of blood. If that isn't meeting the conditions, my lord, I don't know what is."

Dalcour frowns as he searches my face, trading hard stares back and forth with Titan.

Grunting, Dalcour closes the gap between us and a loud rumble roars from his chest. "Then perhaps the two of you can explain why you both—"

"Lord Marchand!" A high pitched, feminine voice calls to Dalcour from a far corner. "No one can find him anywhere! The guests are getting antsy. If we don't wed soon—"

"Please, Jerrica don't worry your beautiful little head about anything. Besides, Sebastian understands how important tonight is. There's no way he'll miss it." Dalcour's manner and tone is gentle as he speaks to her. Cupping her hand in his, he places his free hand to her shoulder in solace. She reaches across her chest to take his hand in hers and her cheeks soften, comforted by Dalcour's hand.

While watching Dalcour dote on Jerrica is nauseating, it's how she's eating it all up that makes me want to claw that plastered smile from her perfect face.

"I know you're right, Lord Marchand! Talking with Sebastian last night I know he understands how important today is. Besides, it's a smart match if I don't say so myself," Jerrica adds, lifting her chin in assurance.

Her words infuriate me, and I take a step forward, but Titan steps in front of me and gives me a look of warning. Dalcour watches us from his periphery, yet keeps his attention fixed on Jerrica. But by the way his jaws clench, I know our actions frustrate him.

"Oh my," Jerrica begins, peering at me from beneath Dalcour's firm hold. "Where are my manners?" She exclaims as she saunters gracefully toward me. "You must be Lord Marchand's ward. Charlotte, right?"

"Chartreuse," I grit between my teeth as Titan holds me tight at my forearm. "Chartreuse Grenoble," I breathe out, forcing a faux smile.

"I am so sorry, love," she adds with a bright smile and her American-worn British accent ringing through. "I am horrid with names. Well thank you so much for coming tonight. I didn't think I'd meet you until after Sebastian and I returned from our honeymoon in Paris. He said it is his favorite city, so we both thought it would be a great spot. Now if only he would arrive and we could get started with the evening," she says, looking up and down the hall.

A sinister smile wanders on my face and for the first time since Sebastian's death, I find pleasure knowing her honeymoon shall never come.

"My lord," the same man I saw with Dalcour on the stage earlier pushes his way through us in the corridor.

"Yes, Lux, what is it?" Dalcour angrily barks back.

"It's Master St. John, my lord. No one can find him. We've sent the Guard to his home and there was no trace of him nor his attendant Oliver," Lux replies, flashing his golden eyes briefly as he looks around the group.

At his words, Jerrica bursts into tears and Dalcour instinctively wraps his arms around her. "He stood me up! *Me!* How could he?" she cries. "I mean I knew it was stupid getting my hopes up after our fathers arranged our union, but I would've thought after all these years Sebastian would've come around to the idea. Instead he'd rather run off than be with me!"

The sight of her tears brings me both joy and pain. Knowing I am the cause of Sebastian's absence crushes me from the inside but knowing this perfect woman before me is equally crushed gives me a hint of solace.

Jerrica remains in Dalcour's hold as she buries her head in his embrace, sobbing into his arms. While he does his best to comfort her, Dalcour keeps a menacing glare at both me and Titan.

"Lux, please take Lady Jerrica to one of my parlor rooms upstairs," Dalcour begins as he hands Jerrica to Lux. Wrapping his arm around her, Lux leads Jerrica from our sight and Dalcour turns quickly on his heel to face us.

"What did you do Chartreuse?" He shouts with a wickedly demanding gaze.

"Me?" I mock him, with my hands on my chest and batting my eyes. "Whatever do you mean, my lord?" I softly ask with a sly smile.

"Chartreuse, don't!" Titan warns, gritting his words out between his teeth. Dalcour's eyes flash to Titan as he comes closer, and his skin reddens while his sharp fangs hang between his mouth.

"What do you know of it? Titan speak!" Dalcour commands. Titan's posture stiffens at Dalcour's rebuking tone, but his shoulders remain square and his gaze narrows in defiance.

"I know nothing!" Titan growls back. I am slightly impressed he doesn't back down. The man obviously has a steel spine.

Dalcour doesn't buy Titan's words, but he shoots his glance back to me and before I can blink, his hand is at my throat. "But you do! Tell me Chartreuse or I'll end you in this instant!"

Squirming beneath his heavy hand, hissing, and snarling sounds erupt from me and Dalcour returns the gesture. Shouting my name again, his grip tightens, and I retract my fangs to reply. "Doesn't seem too fatherly of you, my lord," I sneer. It takes everything in me not to give in and falter. But I refuse to give him the satisfaction of being weak before him. His eyes slightly fall at my words and his hold lessens.

"Nor does it seem the way one would handle a gift meant for me." A lush voice calls from the shadows.

"Decaux?" Dalcour questions with surprise as he drops me to the cold floor.

Chapter Thirty-Five

"**I**s this how you treat my gifts, brother?" Decaux says with a wicked grin as he leans against the wall.

"What are you doing here, Decaux?" Dalcour snaps.

Decaux shoots a glance down at me and Titan walks in front of me, blocking Decaux's cagey stare.

"Well, I'm here to collect this lovely little morsel," Decaux answers as he walks past Dalcour and around Titan. Extending his hand to help me up, Decaux smiles and winks his eye with a quick nod as though we had an understanding.

Almost reluctantly, I put my hand in his as he lifts me from the ground.

"I mean truly brother; this is certainly no way to treat a lady. Surely our mother taught you better," Decaux continues as he wipes the floor dust from the sides of my gown. "I thought you had better manners."

"What are you doing here?" Titan says, pushing his way in between me and Decaux, keeping me protectively at his back.

"This doesn't concern you, Lord Titan," Decaux sharply replies as he looks over his shoulder at Titan. "Now, I have no grievance with you, but should you continue to place yourself between me and what is rightfully mine, then we shall be at an impasse."

"We'll be at more than an impasse if you think—"

"Titan!" Dalcour growls as he makes his way to our side. Once more, Dalcour's eyes shift back and forth between Titan and me, but he forces his wandering thoughts aside and returns his attention back to his brother.

"Whatever!" Titan huffs, backing away. His eyes lock with mine briefly and I recall his earlier plea for me to remain with him. Knowing what I do now, perhaps I should have stayed with Titan. Although it's clear Titan doesn't remember what happened between us, one thing is sure—*there is still something between us.*

But I don't have the heart or emotional fortitude to understand what that something is.

In a flash, Titan exits, leaving me alone with the Marchand brothers.

"As I was saying," Decaux begins with a tone more light than the scowl on Dalcour's face deems appropriate. "I am here to acquire the lady Chartreuse."

"I thought you said you weren't interested in me?" I shoot back, remembering his earlier disregard.

Circling both Dalcour and me, Decaux paces about with his hands stuffed in his pockets. His eyes scan the length of me and a cunning grin forms in the corner of his mouth. "Well, well, Little Calida, If memory serves me correct, I said I was waiting for a spark of fire. And unless I am presently misguided, it appears there is still yet a spark—or at least some semblance of it."

A brief smile frames Dalcour's face but it is too short lived. "Why now brother?"

"Firstly, you always make good on your promises. You promised me this maiden, as you did a world of civility. As it appears you're doing well to build that world. Seeing as though you'll likely have your hands full with that tearful one who just ran, sobbing past me into the parlor suite, it's probably for the best that I take this one off your hands."

"But you said—" Dalcour interjects, his face filled with doubt.

"And you said, you'd promise this Calida-reincarnate to me. Unlike her sister, the Lady Chartreuse is now built for this world. With her at my side, I have no doubt we'll take this world by storm. That is, at least, until you meet the terms of our barter." Clasping his hands together, Decaux's cagey grin grows from ear to ear.

Dalcour's eyes wander back and forth between me and Decaux, uncertainty filling his face. "Brother, I don't know——"

Although he's uncertain, I am not.

I must control my own fate.

"I will go with him," I force my words out, cutting through whatever sentiment lingered at Dalcour's lips.

Dalcour steps back in surprise with his eyes wide while Decaux's eyes narrow and his wicked smile shifts to the other side of his face.

As strange as it may seem, intuition tells me I'll be better at Decaux's side than at Dalcour's whim.

"But Chartreuse," Dalcour begins, his countenance fallen. "Why?" he asks.

"It is why you brought me here, is it not?" I quickly reply. "But it is clear we now want different things."

Dalcour's lips part to reply, but he closes them, swallowing his own words whole.

"Even more," I begin, taking small steps toward him. "You said you wanted me to enjoy myself. You promised that no matter what differences stand before us, you would always stand with me."

"You read my letter?" he whispers back, surprised.

"Yes, father," I quietly reply.

The frown lines in his brow recede but he continues searching my face. I am not sure what he's looking for or if he's trying to read me, but his expression tells me he does not see what he hopes to find in my eyes.

"We should go," Decaux says in an almost comforting tone. "Our young lord has guests to attend to and a jilted bride to console."

Dalcour's eyes glass, but there are no tears nearing release. In all his long years, he's mastered keeping his emotions at bay. Pulling me into his embrace, Dalcour holds me tight and kisses my forehead.

"Lady Grenoble," he says, lifting my chin to meet his eyes. His tone is more affirming than the condemning tone just moments before. Even more, it's the new notable, *Lady*, now attached to my name that warms the hollowed remains of my heart. "Wherever I am shall always be your home. The day of your making shall not be discounted in my memory. It shall be celebrated! For whatever you are—I am. Never forget that!" Dalcour exclaims and pulls me once more into the cavity of his hold.

Before I have an opportunity to reply, Dalcour disappears from my view in a flash, leaving me alone with Decaux. A lone tear falls to my cheek at his exit, and I look up surprised to find a warm smile glazing Decaux's face.

"Shall we?" he says, widening his arm, allowing me to loop my arm in his.

As I do, we begin walking down the corridor and I stop shy of our exit.

"Why?" I question, curious as to Decaux's intentions.

"For Calida," Decaux starts, he flits his eyes up to the ceiling and bites his lip. At the mention of her name, the typical mischievous and grim expression on his face softens.

He absolutely loved her. I think to myself as I observe the tenderness in his eyes as he speaks her name.

Forcing aside the memories of his beloved, Decaux turns to me, forcing a tight smile and continues, "Because I was unable to save Calida. I owed it to her to save her little sister from certain death. If my brother even caught an inkling of what you have done to Master St. John, I have no doubt you would meet your end. Although I am unsure how you've amassed such power in only a little time, I 'd rather have such a power at my side than destroyed."

"Then at your side I shall be," I reply with a smile matching the wickedly beautiful one looking back at me.

Locking our arms tight, Decaux takes us in flight through the museum and into the night.

The one man who I thought would be my reckoning has become my salvation.

Chapter Thirty-Six

Six Months Later

1809 Natchez, Mississippi

Being with Decaux is nothing as I expected. Knowing he was most callous of the Marchand brothers, I knew life with him would be different than the brief time I spent with Dalcour, but this is beyond anything I could imagine.

While Dalcour's intent was to make me a tamed vampire, worthy of thriving in civility with humans, Decaux's strategy is quite the opposite.

Not once has Decaux attempted to temper my growing appetite, nor does he balk when I bring food home. As a matter of fact he rather enjoys it.

Of late our routine has been to lure unsuspecting couples seeking a swinging good time of wine and song and feast upon their flesh until we've had our full. Decaux prefers masters of large plantations, but I've talked him into more inconspicuous patterns that don't place the enslaved in precarious predicaments.

Although the Changeling curse prevents me from killing women, it yet allows me to lavish in their blood. One such woman, Tabitha, a seamstress I've known for years, was the first person I made vampire from my bite.

Surprisingly, she took to her turning well and soon joined our ranks. That is, after DeLuca persuaded Decaux to sire him as well.

Once DeLuca learned of my place at Decaux's side, he left Dalcour and made his abode with us. Decaux wasn't too thrilled about it at first but seeing the advantages of some of DeLuca's skill as well as the fact that somehow, DeLuca can still abide in a slither of light, Decaux welcomed him into our family.

Also surprising, DeLuca and Tabitha have been inseparable. In every way imaginable. It would almost be nauseating if I didn't know just how much DeLuca deserved to finally find some happiness.

Even if it is not with me.

"We've got to slow it down, Red!" DeLuca snarls as he and Tabitha hold their latest victim down across Decaux's long oak table. "This has been the third night on the hunt!" he says slurping the wrist of the slain man beneath his grasp.

"Who's counting?" Tabitha groans, coming up from air, allowing her long tongue to wipe the blood from her lips.

"He's right, Chartreuse!" Decaux yells back from his corner where he holds two naked women at his sides. Looking at him, I'm thankful the long brunette hair of one woman covers his manhood. Much like me, Decaux prefers to seduce his victims before feeding. He says the rise in pheromones makes their blood more delicious.

Still the sight of him naked sends me into a frenzy. On my first night with him I attempted to be with him, but he refused citing that my being Calida's sister made it odd. But the thought of him was just too much to endure, so I tried everything.

I hummed but soon discovered that somehow, he is impervious to my lure. I think it has something to do with my sire bond with Dalcour, but I am not sure. Either way it didn't work. When that did not pan out, I pulled out all the stops.

I even started walking around his manor naked.

While I could tell more than his interest was piqued, he remained unattainable.

For some reason, the thought of not being desired doesn't sit well with me, so I needed to at least see if I could seduce him. I wanted to see how long he could resist me.

He was stronger than I thought.

It was only the first night we fed on a couple together that he took me. Drunk on blood, we soiled the couple's body, knocking them off their own bed and grinding mercilessly into one another.

Decaux was like no other lover I've ever known. He was more unrelenting than Titan. Taking me on all fours and sides, Decaux wears his beastly nature in full stride when we drink and pleasure together. There are no caring words, nor gentle and sweet caresses. Only the savagery of two monsters indulging in the highest form of depraved desire without regret or dismay. But once the moment ends, it's as if nothing happened.

After my ego learned to cope with the reality of what we are to one another, I've accepted both what is and what is never to come.

"Fine, this is my last one!" I shout back as I drain the last drop from the piano player I brought back with me from the pub. I really wanted to leave this one alive, but I couldn't help myself. My feeding frenzy has become quite problematic. Most tamed vampires are capable of feed and release, leaving their donors alive to wonder what happened to them in the morning. But not me. Once my teeth snare their flesh, I cannot stop. It's as if the wraith boot of the Changelings is on my neck, holding me hostage until I feel the last breath leave their body.

Both DeLuca and Tabitha can go days in between feeding. I can go a half day at best. The fact that I drain most of my prey also makes remaining inconspicuous difficult. Still, Decaux barely chides my predilections and seems rather revived by my otherwise monstrous campaign. DeLuca, on the other hand, grows noticeably irritated. Quite a monster himself, DeLuca would rather we live a bit more unassuming than what has been our recourse.

The beautiful blonde piano player's limp body falls to the ground just as I take the last drop and I wipe my hands together, licking my lips as I savor in the taste of his sweet blood at the corners of my mouth.

"He was a lovely lad," Tabitha says coming to my side, faux pouting while twirling her tiny fingers through her long brown tendrils. "I suppose it would be better if the ugly tasted better."

"Oh now darling," DeLuca begins, rolling the fallen to a corner now piled with other slain souls. "We both know Red here has no interest in the unattractive. I was the last pigeon nosed pauper she gave a lick of care about."

"But you are indeed the cutest pauper I've ever seen," Tabitha coos in his ear. "And now you're all mine!" The two laugh, nuzzling one another and I smile. It does me good to see my friend happy.

"We do need to do something about your feedings." Decaux is robed up and at my side before I have a chance to take my eyes off DeLuca and Tabitha. "If the Guard has to clean up anymore of your prowling, Dalcour will be forced to act. The last thing I need is to have him sniffing about. I have too many dealings in the works and I need him to stay focused on the task at hand. Not worrying about you! Balancing the supernatural order, reestablishing the Dunes Pack, and mending the factions."

Annoyed, my eyes roll to the side as I plop onto a side chair and sigh. Why Decaux is so fixated on Dalcour's work is beyond me. As much as he seems to revel in our lewd acts, there remains a part of him that yet roots for Dalcour's success. Even though I understand the bond of siblings, I'll never understand his interest.

"So to help you wane your cravings, I've had DeLuca working on a special project," Decaux says, snapping his fingers and waving DeLuca over to our side. Giggling, Tabitha keeps her hand intwined with DeLuca's as she paces at his heels.

Sitting up I look at the wide smiles etched on each of their faces and a shrill of trepidation flows up my spine. "What are you three up to?" I ask as DeLuca pulls a black velvety cloth from his rear.

Holding it in his palms toward me, DeLuca smiles as Tabitha throws her head on his shoulder, cupping her mouth to mute her excitement. Decaux folds his arms across his waist as a sly smile dances at the corner of his mouth. "Take it," he orders in a gently commanding tone.

Slowly, DeLuca opens the velvety cloth, revealing my father's pearl handled dagger. However, this time it looks different. "My father's dagger!" I exclaim as tears well in the corners of my eyes. Leaving all my belongings at Dalcour's estate, I never thought I'd see them again. Doing my best to stay far from Dalcour, I assumed whatever I left with him was forfeit. "How did you get it?" I ask, looking to both Decaux and DeLuca.

"Your friend here is rather resourceful," Decaux begins, patting DeLuca on the back.

"When I went back to New Orleans some time ago, I made it my business to collect your effects," DeLuca says while placing the dagger in my palm. "But we made a few adjustments."

"A ruby stone?" I question, tracing the crown of the hilt where the large red stone now sits.

"No, it's actually red jasper. A chakra stone used for healing, endurance, and protection. We believe it will help you with your cravings. Balance you a little," Decaux replies as he sits down next to me. "Being from Biloxi, DeLuca knew of a few healers and Shaman who were willing to help us with this."

"Yes, Red, and I hope you don't mind the changes we had to make to your heirloom. The stone had to be placed in something you held dear. Now we can only hope having the stone in your heirloom will help curb your cravings," DeLuca adds with the same caring eyes I've known since the day I met him.

Soft tears cascade down my face, as I hold the blade in my hands and smile. "Thank you! Thank you all!" I exclaim. This type of happiness is unexpected. Since my turning I've endured more heartache than I thought possible, but these last few months with my new family have brought me more joy than I deserve.

"Okay, can we see if it works now? Please?" Tabitha pleas with a bubbly laugh, clasping her hands tight and bouncing.

"Fine! Go get him!" Decaux gruffly answers, covering his mouth with his hands.

"What is going on?" I ask, looking up while wiping the remaining tears from my face.

Running to the back room, Tabitha is out of my sight in an instant. I look up at both Decaux and DeLuca, but they avert their eyes from me, keeping their smiles covered.

"Is anyone going to tell me what's going on?" I question, confused.

"Well, poppet, we want to be sure this thing works. Since you've indulged quite a bit tonight, by normal standards you shouldn't be hungry. Keeping the stone with you at all times, you should now be able to quiet your frenzy. So we were hoping to put it to test to see—if well—"

"To see if you can manage to keep me yet breathing," I hear a familiar voice call from the distance.

Tabitha's squirrely giggles ring aloud in my ears as she comes from the shadows of the back room with a tall and large form at her sides. A recognizable scent hits my nose, but it's not one I've smelled in months. The distinct aroma of Meade and Ripley's rum punch permeate the large room and I jump up from my chair as my eyes grow wide, watchful of the gargantuan figure amble out of the darkness at Tabitha's side.

"Scotty!" I exclaim as I see my oversized saloon mate now standing before me.

"In the flesh," he chuckles as DeLuca's eyes grow wide with an even brighter smile to match.

"The gang's all here!" DeLuca laughs as he stands on top of the slain piano player to wrap his arms around Scotty's neck.

"What are you doing here?" I squeal with both excitement and a tinge of fear.

"Oh, I'm just here to keep you safe, as usual," Scotty heaves with a faux sigh. DeLuca laughs merrily at Scotty's gripes as another freefall of tears hit my chin. Tabitha's smile is bright as she clings to both DeLuca and Scotty and a remnant of my would-be-heart is overjoyed to have my dearest friends with me once again.

"Ah-hem," Decaux adds, forcibly clearing his throat as he stands from his seat. "While this little reunion is indeed touching, it's best we get on with the matter at hand."

"The matter?" I questionably repeat.

"Yes, Little Calida—this matter." Before I have a chance to react, Decaux's sharp fangs are in Scotty's neck in an instant. Scotty moans deep in Decaux's tight hold but he keeps his eyes on me. Tabitha's eyes grow black with hunger as her sharp row of razor fangs protrude from her mouth. DeLuca's eyes also fill with bloodlust, but he works hard to maintain his composure, keeping his sights on me.

Thick warm blood runs down Scotty's neck and the invitation it brings calls to the pit of my core. But this time something is different. I feel no need to attack him. No urge or pull to dive into his flesh. Looking down at the blade in my hand, I watch in awe as the red jasper stone glows bright.

"It's working!" DeLuca exclaims, joyful. "I think we did it Red! I think we did it!"

For the first time since my turning, a new peace washes over me. Self-control.

Chapter Thirty-Seven

While I enjoyed indulging in troughs of blood night after night, knowing it was the power of the Changelings at work instead of my own, left me feeling powerless and lacking control. Now with the help of my friends and the new stoned hilt of my father's dagger, I alone control my fate.

Decaux promised Scotty that should he survive my test he would turn him vampire. Although he made it clear he would not sire Scotty as he'd done for DeLuca, Decaux held his end of the agreement. While Tabitha cleaned up the parlor and disposed of our carnage, Decaux took Scotty to the cellar to begin his transformation.

Unlike Dalcour, Decaux doesn't ascribe to the taming well method of transformation, but he does work with his new made vampires to ensure they can at least survive their first twenty-four hours. The hardest period for the newly made. Most either make damning mistakes such as walking in the sun, running into a Skull herd, fights with other Scourge or feeding in public which lead to their demise. Hopefully, Scotty will take everything to heart so that he too can join our growing family.

"Red," DeLuca says as he walks toward me after cleaning himself and changing out of his soiled clothes.

"Yes," I smile up at him while holding tight to my dagger.

"I'm glad you like it," he says sitting down next to me.

"I love it. Decaux gave me a holster so that I can keep it at my hip. I can't tell you how much better I feel knowing I can gain some control over my feeding. I was really starting to scare myself," I mutter, keeping my eyes on my blade.

"Yeah, I was starting to get worried too. I can't imagine all the pain the Changelings put you through."

"What?" I snap, startled by DeLuca's knowledge of the Changelings. Looking around the room I fear either Tabitha or Decaux heard him. Grabbing his knee, I narrow my gaze into his and see a small flickering resting deep behind his eyes. "What do you know of Changelings, DeLuca?"

Pushing my hand from his knee, DeLuca sits back and folds his arms behind his head. "I know more than you think," he says with a sly smile.

"Tell me!" I demand, shoving his shoulder hard.

"Did you really think you could fool me, Red? Me? Of all people! Vampire—Scourge or not I know my oldest and dearest friend. Even if you can't see the difference between love in your face from a meddling fly, I know you, Red!"

"I don't know what you mean," I sigh, pushing the blade in my holster. Despite his obvious affection for Tabitha, he never fails to find ways to suggest the affection both he and Scotty always had for me. Perhaps I was too blind to see it or chose to ignore it, I don't know. As I've told him time and again, that was a part of my human life and I am no longer human. To which, DeLuca replied by promptly mating with Tabitha. I suppose he was tired of waiting for me to see him in that manner. Still, whatever truth he's digging for now is beyond me.

"For once Chartreuse this is not about us. I've long let that ship sail. But I refuse to see your ship sink!" DeLuca shouts.

"Then speak plainly!" I bite back.

"I don't know how, when or why you did it, but I know a Changeling influence when I see it. Either Decaux is blind to it or doesn't care, or both, I knew right away something was different about you. You don't look like a Scourge when you turn and you're much stronger than most. At first, I wondered if it were your sire bond, but I knew better. Your feeding frenzy and ravenous hunger, all point to signs of Changeling control."

My eyes glass, but I refuse to allow their release, blinking rapidly, I peer at the ceiling and force my tears back behind my eyes. "They told me they could help me avenge Calida's betrayer. He yet lives," I quietly reply.

"And did you?" DeLuca's tone is somber and curious. Placing his hand on my knee he stares at me, breathing hard as he awaits my response.

"No." I answer flatly.

DeLuca heaves a sigh of relief and his shoulders relax at my admission.

"But I tried. I wanted to. He was within my reach." DeLuca's eyes sink and his posture stiffens as I reveal my intent.

"What happened, Red?" DeLuca curiously questions.

"Dalcour is what. He bonded me—compelled me from going after any Peyroux. When I tried to end him, I couldn't. I tried! I truly tried! But all my attempts were for nothing. So you see, whether it be the Changelings or Dalcour, there is always someone or something trying to control me!"

"But it doesn't have to be that way, Red! With your blade you are now free to roam without fear of overindulgence. If that be the case, Dalcour has no reason to control you—even if you can't do anything about this betrayer now, perhaps we can work up a plan to ensure his demise at another time."

"You'd help me do that?"

"Of course, my beautiful Red!" DeLuca's smile is sincere as he regards me.

"Thank you, DeLuca," I begin softly. "I know I've never been able to share more affection with you than friendship, but I suppose it's because I respect and care for you more than I have anyone."

"What about Sebastian?" DeLuca asks quietly.

"Yes, I loved Sebastian. Truly. But the Changelings even ruined that!" I reply as more glassy pools form behind my eyes.

"How so?"

"Well, I'll spare you all the sordid details, but I'll just say somehow they had me kill him while we were—um—together. I'm still not sure just how it all happened. It's still kind of a blur."

"Wait a minute! *A blur?* Please, Chartreuse tell me, did he say anything to you in the moment? Anything that seemed off—or out of character for him?" Frown lines cross DeLuca's brow and he leans into me with a deep and serious stare.

"Well, DeLuca he said a lot of things in the moment that don't bear repeating. Least of all to you—"

"I don't care about *those things*, Red! Anything of worth? Anything that threw you off?"

"Oh, I guess if you count the time, he told me it would be our last together or how he'd never be with me again. All I remember is how his words made me feel. I've never felt so hurt. So betrayed."

"Are you sure he said those words, beloved? Or did you simply hear those words?" DeLuca's pointed stare digs deep and my mind rummages with memories of my last time with Sebastian.

"It's odd. I do recall his mouth moving in a cadence different from his words. It was strange. My ears felt clogged, but I swore it was his voice."

"His voice perhaps, but I'm not sure it was him, poppet. I think it was the Changelings!"

"Impossible! I was there, DeLuca! There was no mistaking his words."

"But they were not *his words*, Chartreuse. That I can assure you!"

"How can you assure me, DeLuca? I was there, you were not!" I shout, rising up from beside him, but he pulls my arm, forcing me back down in the seat beside him.

"Because, my friend, I have never lied to you. Nor shall I ever do so. You know I told you I was an orphan. I was raised by gypsies. But they were no ordinary gypsies, they were a small trad of Changelings who've taken human form. They escaped their more wicked kin—much like the ones who are working their trickery against you. Since the beginning the dark ones have been at work to set an evil course against not only the race of men but other supernaturals. They want access to this world and will do whatever they can to make it so. Some say they've trapped the souls of pureblood Altrinions in Sheol, using their power as a source to gain more access to this world."

As DeLuca speaks, thoughts of Dalcour's recollection of the cursed deeds of the Changeling ring aloud in my memory.

"But why Sebastian?" I whisper.

"I don't know, poppet. I don't know. Perhaps because he was pureblood. Or perhaps just to get you to act in some manner—who knows?"

Shrugging my shoulders, I sigh and hug my knees to my chin. "I guess I'll never know, DeLuca. All I know is that I am the root and cause for Sebastian's death. He was the only son of an only son. His bloodline is now over and its all my fault!" I cry.

"No the only fault rests at the feet of the Changelings. But I can tell you this, whatever you believe Sebastian said to hurt you is not true."

"You don't know that DeLuca. Neither do I."

"Actually, I do." For the first time since he sat next to me, a broad smile covers DeLuca's face that beams from ear to ear. Handing me a wad of rolled and crumpled paper, DeLuca smile meets his eyes. "Take it."

"What is this?" I ask, unrolling the crumpled paper.

"When I went back to New Orleans to get your things, I decided to pay a visit to Sebastian's home. It's been quite vacant, so I thought I'd pry a bit. In all fairness, I wanted to get a sense about the pauper who'd stolen your heart in my absence," DeLuca says revealing an air of jealously. "Looking around, I found the surprisingly, yet mildly decayed body of an old chum in the cellar vault. I suppose the lack of oxygen in the cellar preserved him a bit longer than most. But what I found most interesting what the paper he gripped tight in his hand. Reading it, however, was more surprising. Take a look."

DeLuca nods at me to open the crumpled paper and I see two train and shipyard passes for both me and Sebastian.

"Tickets!" I gasp, surprised to see my name on the receipts. Even more shocking is that my name is listed as Chartreuse St. John not Grenoble. "He meant for me to leave with him?" I mumble to myself.

"Yes, beloved. Your Sebastian cared for—no *loved* you very much. He was willing to leave it all behind for you," DeLuca says gently. "Here, look at this," he continues, shifting the papers and pointing to a small note card.

Dear Lord Marchand,

If you are reading this letter, you are aware I have taken something from you. Chartreuse. Leaving in haste, we thought it best to tell you the news of our parting via letter. Should Chartreuse choose to write you, that will be her own affair. I only write this to you as a courtesy and not one of permission. I know what my father's plans are for me. I am also now aware of your plans for my soon-to-be wife. In the short time we have spent together, I've come to love her like no other, nor shall there ever be another. She loves me not for status or out of some fatalistic ritual but for who I am. Vampire or not she will be my wife. If it must be that no children are reared by name it is of no matter to me. I care not for my bloodline to continue if I'll not have her at my side. While I hope you can understand, I shall not wait for permission.

Please give Jerrica my best. I'm sure she'll find a love of her own. Perhaps right under her nose. Until the next time we meet, I bid you farewell. I promise I will take care of Chartreuse, with everything I've got.

Kind regards,

Sebastian St. John

Every bit of air is sucked from my lungs as Sebastian's letter falls from my hands into my lap. For months, I've agonized over the hand I had in killing Sebastian. Even more the thought that he did not love me as I did him pained my heart inconsolably as I alone shouldered the weight of my grief.

Now, I know my heartache was misplaced. While the Changelings did use me to kill the only man I have ever loved, they took more from me than I thought possible. Love. Not only did they want to pit me against Dalcour with the reveal of Elias Peyroux, but they managed to sully the care I alone shared with Sebastian.

Why they chose me to do their bidding I do not understand. But I will find a way to avenge the only love I have ever known if it's the last thing I do.

Chapter Thirty-Eight

"I'm ready to see my sister," I announce at the table as Tabitha pours second rounds of blood into our glasses as we sit around Decaux's pub table.

Everyone looks down the table at me as if they'd just seen a ghost, but I know better. They're still not fully convinced the jasper stone is keeping my frenzy at bay. Decaux raised concerns not long after Scotty's transformation was complete. He thinks because I held endearment for Scotty, I was able to rein in my impulse.

Perhaps he's right. Perhaps he's wrong.

At this point I don't care. It's been almost a year since I've seen Chalmette and the letters between us will no longer suffice. Especially since the last letter I received revealed she was expecting and nearing her third trimester, I can no longer wait to see her.

"Are you sure you're ready for that, Red?" DeLuca asks with his eyebrow raised. Tabitha keeps her hand at her waist, leaning on DeLuca's chair as she sips the remaining blood from the pitcher as she stares at me.

"You'll never forgive yourself if you do to her what you did to me," Tabitha quietly replies. While I know she doesn't wholly blame me for her transition into vampire, she'll never forget the day I bit her. Running into her in the City as she came to pick up new fabrics from the nearby port, I never thought the day would end with her transitioning before my eyes as my venom scorched her veins. Little did I know she was looking for an out while drowning in debt from her business. She's always said I helped her more than I know.

"And what about Scotty?" DeLuca questions once more as he leans back from the table. "Do you think it's a good idea to take him around so many so soon? He's still wet behind the ears."

"Chartreuse has been training me," Scotty mumbles as he stands up from the table to grab another pitcher.

"I've heard the training Chartreuse is giving you," Decaux says, casting his typical wickedly charming grin. "I don't think that training will help you master your bloodlust, my friend."

Scotty looks over his shoulder and gives me a smirking grin as he hunches his shoulders.

Decaux isn't entirely wrong. Scotty and I have returned to our typical musings except now he has no need of protecting me from tippers. While I care for him deeply, even he knows it's not what I shared with Sebastian. But I don't think he cares. Nor do I.

Scotty has changed since his turning. Gone are the awkward features that made him look more ogrish. Whatever flaws he had are gone, his teeth are pearly white, and his dark eyes are deep and dangerous; everything I love about a man. Already muscular, his large frame is more taut, and his body is now reminiscent of the fallen Greek deities of legend.

So yes, I take my pleasure in him regularly and him in me. I've even traded prowling partners, taking him over Decaux because at least I know he wants more than a depraved and sadistic screw. He wants me whether we're drunk on blood or not.

Having no other restraints than our own hunger, Scotty and I can go on with one another for hours at a time. Decaux has often suggested the jasper stone increases passion. I don't know whether it's true, but I'd never want it to change.

"Scotty will be just fine," I counter, winking at Scotty who now stands across the room.

"Have it your way!" Decaux exclaims, jumping up from the table. "But you'll have to do it without me. I have other matters to tend to and can't leave Natchez right now." Walking to the back room, Decaux leans against a tall wooden pillar and smiles. "I'm sure you'll be fine, Chartreuse but remember while your thoughts may glee about seeing your young sister, there are other worries to have beyond your own bloodlust. Be certain you are ready for whatever you may find when you return."

"Great! We can finally leave this little creepy town in Mississippi!" Tabitha exclaims, clapping and bouncing up and down. DeLuca laughs, obviously entranced by her luscious curves, he pulls her into his lap and crushes their mouths together.

I'm not the only one with a high sex drive, I chuckle, thinking to myself.

"Will you be okay all alone?" I ask Decaux as he glares at each of us from the doorpost.

A wide smile parts the corners of his mouth and he laughs while walking down the long dark hallway to his suite. "Oh my dear, I thought you knew. I am never alone," he laughs once more and exits into the darkness.

"Well then everyone," I shout, attempting to break up the exchange between Tabitha and DeLuca as I rise from my chair. "Prepare your things! We leave tomorrow at nightfall."

DeLuca and Tabitha only grunt in reply and Scotty and I take our cue and make our way to my suite.

"Are you sure?" Scotty asks, taking one last sip of his glass. "I'm not talking about seeing your sister. But your mother and Monroe. Will you revisit the saloon?"

The thought of Mother and Monroe never entered my mind when I first thought to see Chalmette, but I know both Scotty and Decaux are right. In the last few months, I've conquered quite a bit in my short time as a vampire. Everything—except this.

Despite not having a drop of supernaturality, I know the real monsters of my past too well. Whether I'm truly ready to face them remains to be seen, but I can stay away from my sister no longer.

Taking the glass from Scotty's hand, I rise to the balls of my feet and lick the outline of blood from his lips. While I know he means well, I'd rather not discuss Mother nor Monroe now.

Scotty's eyes darken with passion and I feel him instantly stiffen as I press myself against him. As is his custom, he rips my gown from my body, exposing my breasts first. Delighting himself at the helm of my cleavage, Scotty lifts me in his arms, and leans me against the wall while ripping the remnants of my gown from me.

Since Scotty and I have revived our time together, I am thankful to have a seamstress like Tabitha with us. I've gone through more garments in the last month than I can recall. If it wasn't a bloodstain, it was Scotty ripping my clothes from me.

"Is this what you want, love?" Scotty asks, lifting my left leg up on his hip as he teases my entrance with his fingers.

"It's what I need," I moan, leaning into his shoulder as his thick finger circles the depth of me. In all my years, Scotty has been the only one to spark my release just from the pad of his forefinger. Perhaps it's because his finger alone rivals the size of what most men tote between their thighs. Whatever the reason, I am thankful.

"Nice and ready for your Scotty as always," he groans, tapping my spot as I cry out in his arms. "Go ahead and let it out, love. Give your Scotty that sweetness." His forefinger and thumb war over my preciousness, sending me into a shrieking cry as I meet my climax. Pulling his hand from me, he licks his fingers, moaning as he does. "You're always so sweet for me."

"Ah, Scotty," I whine. "You deserve so much more." And he does. But right now I'm thankful for him taking my mind off what may await me.

"I deserve to be at your side. I was willing to face death itself just for the chance to be with you—and in you." Scotty pants, grabbing my precious place hard, tickling my entrance with his large fingers. I let out a gasp as he touches me, wishing he'd settle himself inside me. "You give me all I deserve and more," Scotty sweetly says, running his other hand through my hair. "Right now you know what your Scotty needs. Are you going to give it to me?" He asks as he lays me on the bed. Scotty's eyes darken with lust as his eyes stay fixed between my legs. Not waiting for my response, he lifts my legs his bulking shoulders and hovers over me as he and the strength of his manhood await my response.

Husky breaths are all I have to give as my femininity throbs with desire. "Yes, Scotty, it's already yours."

My lover doesn't waste much time plunging himself deep into the core of me, as my legs dawdle over his broad shoulders. Being such a big man, almost seven feet and wide as two doors, Scotty is surprisingly gentle with me. Even though he knows he can't break me, he refuses to lay on top me, and remains standing as he ruts himself into me.

Before we were vampires, he always insisted on taking me on all fours or that I straddle him, fearful he'd crush me. Receiving Scotty from behind is almost brutal; even more so now that he's a vampire. The way he punishes both my backside and preciousness is not for the faint of heart. With his hands at my hips, every time he slams himself into me, I fear will be my last. Growling as he rotates his hips until he reaches his peak, every unrelenting thrust penalizes my preciousness until my back is arched in willful submission, I thought I'd never know apart from Sebastian.

Maybe it's because we've been together before, or because he knows me for years, Scotty seems to anticipate my needs and wants more than anyone. Not much has changed. Once he's had his full of me on his feet, he lifts me once more to his waist as he lays on his back, allowing me full control.

I'm not sure if it's because he likes the bounce of my breast or the depth of my grind as I buck him hard like a Clydesdale until we meet our shared release, but one thing is sure Scotty enjoys every ounce. Knowing he simply wants me without a barter or request is more than freeing. Although I wish I could give him what he deserves, I am yet thankful he's willing to take what I have to give.

Chapter Thirty-Nine

N atchitoches. Never did I think I'd need to return here.
But my precious sister Chalmette is my only reason. Before leaving
Natchez, I ensured we all drank our full of both Decaux's supply and a band
of settlers we met on their way from out west. Through it all, I am surprised
at my restraint. With my enchanted dagger at my hip, I was able to feed and
release without much aggravation. Not only did I surprise myself, but both
DeLuca and Tabitha seemed pleased I was able to curb my appetite.

Scotty was a little hard to tame. I suppose DeLuca was right to be
concerned. Ravenous with thirst, he almost took down two grown men
at once. Thankfully, it didn't take much for us to help Scotty settle. Even
though DeLuca didn't sire him, he certainly curtails his bloodlust at DeLuca's
command. Something tells me there may yet be a hint of DeLuca's Altrinion
compulsion ringing through. Either way, I am happy Scotty is learning to
control his thirst.

He's still faring better than I did only weeks ago.

We arrived just before sunrise, taking refuge in Tabitha's place until the
sun set. Not a second after the final ray of light dimmed to the shadows, I
made my way out of the door. Barely taking a sip of the stash Decaux gave
us, all my thoughts were of Chalmette and my need to see her.

Images of her with a round belly and a smile brighter than the sun, stirs a happiness within me I haven't known in months. Although DeLuca, Scotty, Tabitha and Decaux have become my family, no one will ever replace or compare to the bond and love I have for my precious Chalmette. Knowing she and Claudius are bringing life into this world gives me a hope for the future I believed escaped me.

Checking the mirror often, I am hopeful my otherworldly face doesn't push forward. While I've made mention that I've discovered a new power in myself since we last saw each other, I've yet to tell her I am vampire—or whatever I am. I don't know if I'll reveal my truth tonight either. Right now, my only concern is seeing her lovely face.

Standing in front of the massive DeVeaux estate, it is the first time I realized the type of life my sister has become accustomed to in such a short while. Sitting on a plantation well over twenty acres, the grand ten thousand plus square foot home rivals any mansion I've ever seen. Despite the grandeur of Dalcour's estate, it dwarfs in comparison to Chalmette's new home.

"It's big!" Both Scotty and Tabitha say in unison as their mouths drape open.

"I think we can all agree it's not a good idea for us all to go inside. Corbin DeVeaux is a new human faction leader, taking the place of Oliver. While he's very familiar with our way of life, he will not take kindly to having all of us in his home at once. Besides, the last time I was here I discovered he had a Bulwark seal his home from otherworldly entry. Poppet, we'll need an invitation" DeLuca says, looking to me for agreement.

"Makes sense to me," Tabitha answers as her eyes remain fixed at the mansion.

"Me too," Scotty quietly agrees.

"Okay, well we have accord! Beloved, Scotty, you two remain here at the tree line. I'll accompany Chartreuse. If nothing else at least Corbin won't ask many questions of either of us," DeLuca adds as both Tabitha and Scotty nod in agreement. "Red, is that all right with you?" he asks.

Calling my name once more, DeLuca circles me, gaining my attention. I want to answer, but remain still, quietly listening to the sounds of the manor. A small shrilling shriek captures my attention before I have a chance to respond and I take flight.

"Chartreuse!" DeLuca screams after me and is at my side in an instant. "What's wrong, poppet?" he questions as we land on the porch.

"Shh—" I demand, lifting my hand in caution. "Do you hear that?" I ask as the sound of painful screams echo in my ears.

"I do," DeLuca replies as his eyes grow wide with dread.

Memories of seeing Victoria with a blackened eye score through my memory and I fear her fate shall now be my beloved sister. I may not have been able to save Victoria, but I refuse to allow Chalmette to come to such a pass.

Kicking the door open, I bellow a loud yelp, growling at the butler who stands with a white towel hung over his arm. "Invite us in!" I demand. His mouth quivers in fear, but he does as I command and DeLuca and are free to enter.

Tapping the temple of the butler's head as we enter, he faints, and DeLuca postures the man into a chair as we make our way toward the screaming sounds coming from upstairs.

"Red, please try to remain calm," DeLuca warns but I don't care to hear his admonishment. If someone is hurting my sister, they will face my wrath.

Once more the screaming sounds echo in our ears, but this time the sound is closer than before. Reaching the top of the staircase, Corbin DeVeaux and a small, elderly woman stands against the wall.

"Chartreuse!" He exclaims, surprised to see us. "What are you doing here?" he asks with a small smile. "How did you know so soon?"

"We heard screams," DeLuca snaps.

"Tell me where is my sister? Now or I'll tear this house down!" I shout.

"Just down the hall, first door on the right, but you should wait until—"

I don't wait for him to say more before I fling the door open and hear yet another cry, but this one sounds different. It's small. Tiny.

A round woman with a blood stained apron stares back at me, surprised by my entry. Even more surprising is the small baby now nestled in her lap.

"It's a boy!" The woman announces as Claudius runs nervously from near the corner window. His face is full of both joy and wonder. Tears well in in his big bright eyes as he cradles the baby in arm.

"Treuse?" I hear the raspy voice of Chalmette call to me.

Taking a deep breath, I work hard to force aside any blood lust and keep my eyes on my sister. As I keep my eyes on her face, it becomes easier to breath without feeling the pangs of hunger.

"You're here!" She exclaims with heavy breaths. "I—I'm so glad," she pants.

Nearing her large poster bed, nothing but joy wells inside me upon seeing her beautiful face. I didn't realize how much I'd truly missed her until now. With her wet auburn ringlets cascading her pillow, and the dewy mist of sweat at her brow she looks more like a woman to me now than the girl I recall learning table etiquette just months ago.

"Yes, I am here, my beautiful sister," I reply, running my hand along her forehead. She feels warm, hotter than she should, but I do my best to keep a smile on my face. There's also another smell in the air. A smell I've known too well in my recent months, but it isn't one I'd wished to encounter here.

"I—I'm so glad," she repeats, as her eyes roll to the side.

"Chalmette!" Claudius screams as he hands the baby to a small woman who was in the hall with Corbin and rushes to her side.

"My newsboy," she whispers, reaching her hand across her body to touch his chin.

"Sister!" I shout, shaking her free hand, but she slowly turns her head, weakly smiling back at me.

"What's going on in here?" DeLuca calls from behind, now standing at the threshold.

"I'm sorry, Mr. DeVeaux, but she's losing a lot of blood!" The woman in the apron yelps.

"Isn't there something you people can do?" Corbin barks, shooting hard glances at both DeLuca and me.

Shaking his head, DeLuca answers, "I'm sorry, sir. There's nothing we can do."

"Surely just a drop!" Corbin pleas. "Can you not? She's your sister!"

It takes everything in me not to detach his head from his body at his rebuke, but I know he means well. In her short time in this family, he too has come to love her. How could he not?

"Our venom doesn't heal. Only kill. That is, Red, unless you want to turn—"

"Don't you dare speak the words!" I lash back at DeLuca. "I'll never condemn her to our fate! My sister deserves the greeting of every patron saint awaiting her arrival. We deserve our hell." My words are cold and stoic as I utter them but DeLuca doesn't protest. He knows I speak the truth.

"But what about me?" Claudius cries at her side, running his hand along her forehead. "Our life was just beginning," he sobs.

"Claudius," I begin with a tone darker than I intend. "I see the light leaving her eyes. Bid your farewell."

Sobbing once more, Claudius cries into her chest and Chalmette forces a small smile. "It's okay, my newsboy. Sister will look after you. Won't you, Treuse?" A lone tear races down the side of Chalmette's face as Claudius holds her hand. "Where's Victor?" she whispers, looking around the room.

"Who is Victor?" DeLuca whispers over his shoulder to me.

"Victor is my father's name." I mutter back.

"She's going into the light," DeLuca replies, somberly placing his hand on my shoulder.

A small coo cries from behind us and the small woman brings the baby to Chalmette's arms.

"It's what we named our son," Claudius answers, looking at us briefly with a proud smile breaking through his otherwise solemn state.

At his admission, a waterfall of tears flood my face and DeLuca pulls me in close.

"Beautiful," Chalmette sweetly says as the small child nuzzles itself at the nape of her neck. Kissing the baby on his cheek, she smiles once more and takes her last breath.

Claudius screams in agony as her life leaves her body, holding tight to her hand as he cries almost inconsolably into his pillow.

The small woman takes the baby from Chalmette's arms as the baby cries, likely sensing the loss of his mother. "Would you like to hold him?" the woman asks, turning to me.

"Red, no!" DeLuca cautions as the woman places the child in my arms.

While DeLuca's warning is valid, I know I can do this. Looking at this small life in my arms, I know I can restrain myself for no other reason than I must. He is the last semblance of love I have. Watching the pain rippling through Claudius, Corbin, and the small woman I take to be some relative, it is clear my sister was greatly loved. Even this small child who will never know his mother, feels the sting of her loss.

She was a great light in this world. But her light was too short lived. Why a beautiful soul like hers is snuffed and a monstrous one like mine is allowed to remain is a mystery to me. She was too good, kind, and lovely for this world.

This world didn't deserve her. A world filled with monsters, wraiths, vampires, wolves, abusers, and those who take just to suit their fancy do not deserve the delicate and delightful manners of my father, Calida, Sebastian or now my precious sister. A world as cold and vicious as this one deserves the bitter cruelty monsters like me inflict.

"But do not worry, Victor," I begin, gently swabbing the side of the baby's rosy cheeks. "I shall ensure no monsters fill your dreams. I will guard you with all that I have. You my dear one will live a long and happy life. And after you, your children, and children's children. As long as your name remains in the earth, I shall see that happiness and peace be your fortune more than all."

Handing the baby to Claudius, we share a knowing smile and I plunge myself from the window, taking flight into the nearby forest.

The echoing pain of my cry expands the night sky. A shrieking yelp is all I have to give before I drop to my knees in grief. Although I can sense Scotty, DeLuca, and Tabitha near me, they keep their distance, allowing me the space I need to bear yet another loss.

Chalmette was the last tether of humanness I had in this world. I may not understand it yet, but I have no doubt her loss will have a lasting impact on me for years to come. While I've promised to protect and keep Victor and his family safe for as long as they remain, nothing will replace what father,

Calida, Sebastian and now Chalmette means to me.

If it be the fate of this world that I should endure without the only ones to which I cared for more than my own life, then so be it. Now this monstrous world to which I belong, will get exactly what it deserves.

Fangs, claws, songs, and all.

Epilogue

Patience. It is a virtue I never much cared for in my human existence nor do I care much for it now. However, for the sake of Chalmette's family and her precious son, Victor, I put my own cares aside to exercise this rare fruit.

It's been two weeks since Chalmette died. With Mardi Gras in high swing the priest thought it best to wait before commencing with her final rites. She was never baptized so there didn't seem to be much incentive for the priest to carry out her ceremonies. Thankfully, Dalcour can be rather convincing.

While I'm not surprised that he totes a strong reputation with both clerics and potentates alike, I was surprised with how quickly he acted when he heard of her passing. Despite everything that has happened between us, Dalcour yet makes good on his promises to treat me with familial care.

Still, seeing Jerrica Jeffers at his side at Chalmette's funeral revived my jealousies. I'd hoped she'd return to wherever she came from after being jilted at the altar. Instead, I find her aptly perched in his life. Not only is she now serving as curator, the job Dalcour once spoke of for me, but I've learned she's actively living in the mansion.

She has completely taken over a life meant for me. Although Dalcour contends they are nothing more than friends, my gut tells me she desires more.

Decaux sent a card, but contended he still had matters to tend in Natchez that prevented him from attending my sister's funeral. Although I'm sure this is true, a part of me knows he cares little for human affairs and refuses to insert himself in such matters.

I don't entirely fault him. The cares of this human world have become quite tedious over these past two weeks and acting as though I care for their rituals and conventions is rather vexing. Nonetheless, I do this all for Chalmette.

Now, however, my patience has waned.

After convincing Claudius to leave Louisiana with baby Victor for Boston soon, I have no further need to delay my vengeance.

Upon arriving back here, I had no desire or interest in returning to the saloon to exact my revenge, but now I have no other choice.

Catherine had one job in the entirety of her miserable existence—be a mother—and she's yet failed to do so, even to the bitter end. Claudius hand delivered notice of Chalmette's passing himself, and still she chose not to attend her own daughter's funeral.

She remains more a monster than I'll ever be.

Even my poor sister Victoria found a way to make it to the services, with her wretched husband at her side no less. Although, I have no intentions of leaving my sister to any further abuse of her spouse, at least he had a shred of decency to grieve with his wife; even if it were half-heartedly.

My Mother and Monroe couldn't even be bothered to attend.

I'll not allow them to treat Chalmette with such cruelty even in death!

"They're here," Scotty says, calling to me in the cellar of Tabitha's house. "Are you ready?" he asks as I take one final puff of the sancho cigar Corbin gave me as a gift for ensuring his family's new noble status among Dalcour's human faction.

"Indeed," I reply, through the cloudy smoke as I rub the tip of the cigar into the metal tray on the small wooden table.

Walking into Tabitha's dining room, I am surprised to find so many familiar faces looking back at me. Corrine, Gretchen, Yasmine, and Sasha are just a few of the house girls I've asked Scotty and DeLuca to round up on my behalf. A few more I don't recognize or names I forgot have also gathered around awaiting to see why they've been summoned.

"We've got this one too," Tabitha belts, as a squirrely shriek hits my ears when I see Elena held by Tabitha at the neck.

"Ah yes, Miss Elena," I begin, leaning into her, smelling the inviting scent of her fear-laden blood. "You are the most important," I say, running a long pointy nail down the side of her face.

"What do you want with us?" She cries.

"Soon, Miss Elena, soon," I whisper in her ear.

Turning away from her as Tabitha forces her down into a small wooden chair, I set my attention on the women gathered around. "Ladies of the evening, I am sure you are wondering why I brought you here tonight. Let me assure you, I am here to offer you an opportunity to control your own fate. For years, I served alongside many of you at the whim of a monster. Our job, lay on our backs and take whatever a man gave us. Well, ladies, that day is over. No longer shall we sit idly while men treat us as nothing but repositories for their impotent thoughts and weak manhood! The time of the woman has come! Not the doting women of society, embroidery, nursemaid and servitude—though if that be your choice—let it be your choice—not a requisite of men! What I offer you tonight is the chance to take back your power—through blood!"

Gasps and sighs erupt in the small space of Tabitha's dining room and the women look to one another, still curious of my intent.

"Chartreuse, tell us plainly, what are you selling?" Corrine bluntly asks. If there was anyone to force her way through the thistles, I knew Corrine wouldn't mince words.

"Ah, Corrine, darling, let me show you!" I answer, snapping my fingers in the air. DeLuca makes his way through the room holding Preston Savoy by the arms. Gagged with his hands tied behind his back, DeLuca forces Preston into a chair beside Elena. "What I have to offer you, means saying farewell to a world you once knew to take on a whole new life beyond anything you can imagine. All it takes is being willing to spill a little blood." At my words, my fangs protrude, and nails lengthen. Preston's eyes bulge as I pull his head to one side, digging my razor-sharp teeth deep into his flesh. Tabitha's eyes darken with bloodlust as I do and her fangs also drop in response.

DeLuca and Scotty growl low as I drink Preston like a fountain. Thanks to the dagger at my hip, I find the strength to release him still alive from my grip. The women groan and their eyes widen as they observe my new form while I lift slightly from the floor.

Using my speed, I zip through the huddle, baring more of my power and they marvel at my reveal with parted lips and clasped hands.

"Count me in!" Corrine shouts back first. "Do you know how many nights I had to endure the stench of mongrels like this one! I've lived through not only the diseases they brought to my bed, but their cruelty and disdain. Make me like you!"

No sooner than Corrine chimes in, more women lift their hand, ready for the gifts we offer.

"Are you all mad?" Elena gripes. "She's a monster! Something from the very pit! And you'd align yourself with her?" Making my way in front of Elena, I lift her chin to meet my blackened eyes and her eyes grow wide with fear. "Do whatever you want with them, but I don't want to be monster!"

"Oh sweet, Elena, did you think you were here to become one of us? Oh no, my sweet dear, I wouldn't dare think of doing such a thing." I answer.

"Good," she says, biting her bottom lip, puffing her chest with her typical arrogant stance.

"You're the first course," Tabitha whispers at her ear. Elena yells in response and Tabitha mutes her screams with her hands.

"Now ladies, this may hurt a little," DeLuca says from the back corner.

"But once your pain passes, you'll open with new eyes," I add. "And a snack," I continue with a wink to Elena.

Within minutes, Tabitha, Scotty, DeLuca and myself bare our fangs and venom into all the women except Elena, leaving she and Preston as their first meal. While most scream and writhe under our grip, none seem to relent of their choice.

Why would they?

Corrine has suffered countless venereal diseases and been beaten by some of Preston's companions. Yasmine was sold to Monroe to pay off a gambling debt of her brother. Gretchen, an orphan, was picked up off the street by my mother at fourteen and has spent the last two years used for Monroe's pillage rape parties. Sasha may be the only one who entered the house willingly, but with her hair and features reminiscent of Sebastian, intuition tells me she uses the saloon as cover to keep from enslavement.

Each of these women have reason to reclaim parts of themselves taken by the savagery of men. I intend on helping them take the reins of their own fates. While I know some may think we're simply stepping into more villainous acts, I'd beg to differ. The truth is a woman with her own mind is a villain to the patriarchy and victor to the feminine oppressed.

A few days pass before DeLuca agrees the women are ready. No doubt Monroe is up in a tizzy since so many of his main dames have been gone from the saloon this long. Most never spend much time away from the saloon, and if any, it's never this long.

Normally, we like to allow a little more time to train newly turned vampires, but my patience is far spent. Both Scotty and Tabitha have kept the girls sufficiently fed without allowing them out of the house, for fear they'd be too conspicuous.

Tonight is their first night on the prowl.

Watching them stroll down the street now, my chest swells with pride. With their more prominent and alluring features shining through, all heads turn in their direction as we near the saloon. There's a new stride in their step and the confidence exuding from them beams across their moonlit faces.

Looking at them makes me proud.

"Ready when you are, Red," DeLuca says as he and Scotty stand at the top of the staircase leading to the saloon.

Scotty looks at me and shoots me his dangerously sexy grin and winks as he holds his large palm on the large walnut doors. Looking behind me, I see the huddle of women at my back, each standing eagerly with an axe to grind all their own.

"Ladies, when these doors open, your life will never be the same. Tonight, you reclaim your power!" I shout as they echo in a chorus of hisses and snarls with blackened eyes.

Walking forward, DeLuca and Scotty part the doors wide for me and the women follow me inside. Tabitha and Corrine stay at my sides while both DeLuca and Scotty guard our rear.

Crawley is the first to see us and his hand clashes one singular note on the piano, halting his normal Irish melody. Looking around, I notice the saloon is not as filled as usual but there yet remains of barge of drunkards crowding the stage as Monroe stands with a new girl I've never seen at his sides. Some of the house girls I recall from before stop in awe, surprised to see me.

Only one house girl catches my eye I had not expected to see. Victoria. With a tear-stained face, standing at Mother's side, shock fills me as I see her adorned in one of my former fabrics. Staring at her, something tells me she was crying long before I entered. How she ended up here, is beyond me but whatever her cause will have to wait.

"That one is off limits," I whisper over my shoulder to the girls and they all nod in acknowledgement. DeLuca keeps his gaze set on Victoria as we both exchange glances, and he knows no harm is to come to her.

Mother's face tightens into a tight scowl as soon as our eyes connect. Batting her eyes quickly to Monroe, his gangly features seem more repulsive to me now than they did before. He shrugs, seemingly more drunk than usual.

"What are you doing here, girl?" Monroe shouts as I watch Crawley stand up from the piano, backing up against the wall.

"Well it's good to see you too, Monroe! You too Mother!" I snap, swiftly moving myself to the center of the room. Loud gasps and expletives pour through the barroom congregants as my girls parry my motion, positioning themselves throughout the saloon.

"Devil!" Monroe mutters as the loose cigarette from his mouth falls to the floor. The young girl at his side runs from him, barreling out the door, leaving him alone on the stage.

"Close, but not quite," I answer with a sly grin, holding up one of my hands, revealing my long claws. "I've noticed you needed more house girls, Monroe. Let me introduce you to my ladies of the night. I've brought them here to ensure everyone here gets the happy ending they deserve!" I continue with a broad, razor-tooth smile that stretches from ear to ear.

Looking to the door, Monroe looks to run, but Scotty's broad frame blocks it, leaving Monroe to run toward his back room.

"Ladies," I start, turning about to observe their dark, beautifully haunting faces staring back at me. "Give them nothing! But take from them, everything!" I shriek with a loud yelp.

The women do as I command, snatching tippers left and right, feasting upon their flesh. Some men scramble, trying to find exits but none do with Tabitha, Scotty and DeLuca marking their steps. Many of the house girls huddle together while Corrine quickly provides their options. However, I don't wait to learn of their fates. Their fates are not my concern.

Gazing around the saloon, I notice Mother has slipped away from my reach. I am thankful to find Victoria now at DeLuca's side and away from danger. I'll deal with her later, but now I must find the two who've to which my fury belongs.

Making my way to Monroe's back room, Crawley finds his way in front of me.

"I want in," he says as his eyes lock deep with mine. His words surprise me and for a moment I have interest. "The moment you left with Marchand I knew this day would come. I want in," he repeats his damning request. I don't take time to know if he truly understands the weight of his wish, but I snap my fingers and Tabitha is on his neck in an instant, releasing before she drains his last breath. Crawley doesn't buckle as her venom seeps into his veins, but he keeps his sights on me as I make my way to Monroe.

Entering Monroe's room, the stench of his musk and drunkenness hits my nose as soon as I cross the threshold. With a wooden chair in his hand, he hits his window, unsuccessfully trying to break it open. Only the chair breaks and he holds a broken piece of wood at me, shaking it in fear.

"Are you frightened, Monroe, darling?" I taunt him.

"Stay back!" He warns. "Well you're too late for Marius!" he shouts with a callous laugh. Pausing, it takes me a minute to recall the name. As I do, his menacing grin glares back at me. "Yeah, I bet you thought he would wait around for you. Why would he wait for a harlot? He's gone! Married too! Got a pretty little gal. Better than anything you could offer—"

"That's great news, Monroe. Now, Marius doesn't have to witness your end," I bite back. Whatever remains of my mortal mind finds solace knowing Marius won't have to witness my barbarity, but I truly could care less.

Inching closer, I bare my fangs and he drops the wooden leg to the ground. Reaching to his rear, he grabs his pistol and aims at me.

"I'll shoot! I swear it!" he says as the gun trembles in his hands.

"Oh I'm counting on it, darling," I begin with a low hum. "The only problem is you're aiming it in the wrong direction." Continuing my melody, I raise my voice an octave and Monroe's eyes glass with fear. His hands slowly ease as his trembling ceases and his hand turns toward his face. A part of him is fully aware of his actions, but with each note I sing, his will bends to my own. "I'll not touch you, Monroe, for your flesh has nothing to desire, nor does your blood entice the pang of my hunger. Your death be your own to take, your own deeds seal your fate," I sing as I watch his eyes grow as he puts the gun in his mouth and pulls the trigger.

Blood and brain matter splat to the wall behind Monroe as his limp body falls to the ground. A few girls crowd at the threshold of the door, salivating at the invitation of his still warm corpse.

"No!" I lash at them. "I'll not have another part of that man remain in the earth!" I shout. Turning to Scotty, now posted at the edge of the hall, I slam the door behind me and tell him not to let anyone inside and that no one is to feed on him.

Scotty nods in understanding and points upstairs to my suite. "She went up there," he says in a quiet tone. His eyes scan me for a moment, and I know he wants to ask if I'm okay, but with the girls looming about he only tightens his thin lips and resigns to ask for now.

Humming as I make my way upstairs, I do my best not only to lull the remaining victims into a calmer state, but also to douse the gnawing energy rising within me.

Opening the doors of my former suite, I find my mother perched in my window seat. The window is open halfway, and the cool air of the evening helps ease my nerves.

"I know you'd come back home," Mother begins, using my brush against her long, pillowy soft hair. "Its just what we do—it's in your blood," she adds with a piercing glare.

"You know nothing about what is in my blood, Mother!"

"Ha! I know more than you think. More than that devil's blood you've got coursing your veins now. You think because you let that monster do to you what they were going to do Calida that your fate would be different? You were always going to end up here! For it was a place like this where I first met your father."

"Lies!" I shout back and my eyes blacken.

"Truth! More truth than you know. When I met Victor, he was grieving the loss of his first and only true love, Elizabeth. She died giving birth to their one and only son. His name was also Victor. Unfortunately, the child was stillborn, and his wife died shortly after. Months later he found himself in a place like this and that is where we met."

"You're lying!"

"Oh how I wish I were, my beautiful girl, but I am afraid, I am not. My family were indentured and to cure our family's debts, my father sold us into a brothel much like this one. I was only a girl—twelve, I believe." A lone tear escapes her eyes as she recounts her memories and my mind warps at the truth of her words. "Anyway, your father arrived a few years later. I was only about sixteen. He took me for the first night in a room like this and the next day he paid my hand for marriage. Being older, I think he figured I'd be easy at breeding. He wasted no time ensuring I'd bare his first child. And so Calida was born."

"Why is this the first time I'm hearing of this?"

"Because you and your sisters romanticized him so much, I thought it better you not learn both of your parents to be monsters. However, seeing as though Victoria has met a similar fate, Chalmette has died in the same manner as Elizabeth, and that you've taken life as monster yourself, I suppose you can now learn the truth."

Tears fall to my chin at the thought my mother has lived her own torment. While it yet does little to douse my ire toward her, it does bring everything full circle.

"Why didn't you tell me? If I had only known—"

"Then what?" She snaps as more tears cover her face. "Do you think you would not still see a monster when you saw me? No, my dear Chartreuse. That changes nothing. Perhaps my monstrous behavior was just the provocation you needed to try to escape our fate, but I see that is not the case. Know this, beloved, no matter what we do, we'll always be a monster in someone's story. Better we control our own pen."

Deepening her gaze into mine, her eyes soften but for a moment, quickly darkening as she throws herself from the window, falling upward of three floors to her death.

A loud shrieking cry belts from my core as both sadness and an ominous peace swell within me. Although I had every intention to exact some measure of revenge upon Catherine, watching her demise before my eyes does nothing to heal my dormant heart.

"Poppet," I hear DeLuca call to me from behind. Turning to see his warm face, I smile, knowing that I am not alone.

For too long I've mourned the shadows of my human life. I am no longer human, nor shall I ever be. I am much more. I will not conform to dark curses nor the will of men. To my will alone will I avenge what now matters most—myself.

"They're ready for you," he says gently as he wipes a lone tear from my cheek.

Walking out to the balcony, I see the mass of newly made vampires, both women and men, staring up at me. Slain human carcasses lay scattered through the saloon and the scent of blood permeates the air. Snarls and hisses echo throughout and I issue a loud screeching yelp in response.

"I've only heard one thing that made sense to me tonight, only one thing that rings truer now than ever before and that is this: I have come home! And home I shall stay. Like a sweet wine press, we will crush what we must and make it into the sweetest Bordeaux. A Bordeaux of blood! And from its fountain we shall forever drink!"

Want more ● ● ●

If you want to learn more about the origins of the bloodthirsty quest of Deaux Marchand and his enduring love for Chartreuse's sister, Calida, read his short story,

With Hearts of Fire absolutely **FREE!** Click this link or visit https://dl.bookfunnel.com/3lsgdsqjcv.

About L.C. Son • • •

Known for her Amazon Best Selling Short Story, *With Hearts Like Fire* and the series starter and epic fantasy novel, *Beautiful Nightmare (Book One)*, L.C. Son is the happy wife of more than twenty years to her teenage sweetheart and the loving mom of three.

Growing up, she spent hours reading comic books she "borrowed" from her older brother which inspired her love for heroes and all things fantasy and paranormal. Much like the characters she adored, she lives a duplicitous life. By day she works tirelessly to champion the employment of persons with severe disabilities. By night, she puts on her wife-mom cape, sharing with her husband at their church and juggling their kid's highly active schedules.

Presently, she's working on the next installment in the Beautiful Nightmare series.

For the latest info and to join the member-only newsletter visit: www. lcsonbooks.com.

More from L.C. Son

Here are a few more books and short stories in the Beautiful Nightmare Universe:

Books

Beautiful Nightmare (Book One)

Hearts Eclipsed, A Beautiful Nightmare Novella

Awaken: Beautiful Nightmare (Book Two)

Beta Rising: A Beautiful Nightmare Novella- Coming Soon!

Untamed: A Beautiful Nightmare Novella- Coming Soon!

Breaking Curses: A Beautiful Nightmare Novella-Planned 2022

Beautifully Dark Things- Planned 2023

Dawn of Descent: Beautiful Nightmare (Book Three) TBA

Short Stories

I AM NO WITCH: A Beautiful Nightmare Short Story

With Clipped Wings of Butterflies: A Beautiful Nightmare Short Story

With Hearts Like Fire: A Beautiful Nightmare Short Story

One Winter's Kiss- Coming Soon!

For more info on my books, visit: My Books & Short Stories - L. C. Son Books (lcsonbooks.com)

Remember leaving reviews makes you a MVP!!

Thank you!

Acknowledgements

First, to my Creator, thank You for reminding me, even as I write, nothing can separate me from your love. Thank you!

As always, many thanks to my family! To my awesome husband and best friend, thanks for encouraging me to go for my dreams! Dark, twisted, and all! You are amazing! To my wonderful kids, thanks for your endearing and awesome support. I love you!

A special shout out to my A-MAZING L.C. Son Book team! Thanks for giving of your time, input, ideas, and suggestions. I could not have done this without you! Whether paid or just from the depths of your rare and kind human heart, I thank you!

L.C. Son ARC Team

Geeky Girl Author Services

Indie Sage Author Services

Roxana at Proofreadbooks.com

Leanne at TRN the Page

Sophie Hanks

RMGraphX

Every book blogger that posted, shared, and said any kind word about my book! Thank you!

L.S. Son – thank you for encouraging me to try new things! Mommy loves you!

…and last but not least…my beautiful Beta Team! Sydney, Terica and Jennifer—YOU Rock! Whether it was our late night emails, picking through dialogue or just rantings back and forth, your input inspired me more than you know! I truly appreciate you!

The END